W9-BUY-001

DARLINGTONIA

left bank books
seattle, wa

FIRST LEFT BANK BOOKS EDITION, 2017

Alba Roja is an anonymous collective of individuals strewn
along the West Coast of the United States.

Designed by Ben Cody

Left Bank Books is a not-for-profit project collectively owned
& operated by its workers, founded in 1973.

LEFT BANK BOOKS
92 Pike street
seattle, WA 98101
206//622//0195
leftbankbooks.com

Distributed by AK Press

Left Bank Books ISBN: 978-0939306138

Printed in Canada
10 9 8 7 6 5 4 3 2 1

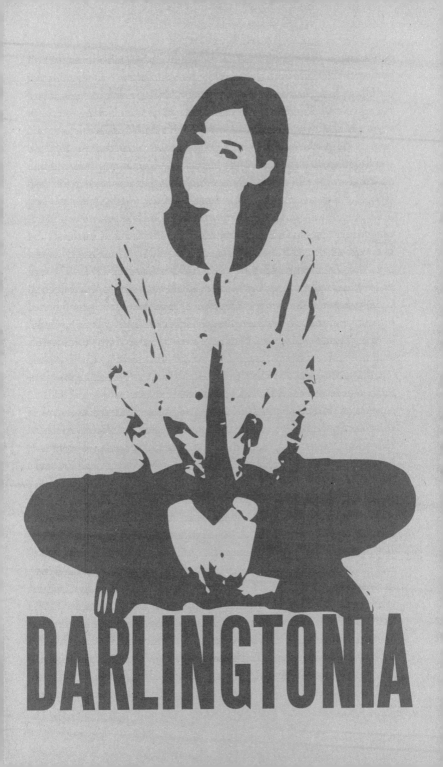

DARLINGTONIA

She walks these hills in a long, black veil.
She visits my grave when the night winds wail.
Nobody knows, nobody sees, nobody knows but me.

  -Danny Dill & Marijohn Wilkin, *Long Black Veil*

Very well then. I am going to try to do the
introduction. Since no one wants to do it for me.
Neither of the two who really made this book can
bring herself to do it.

        -Helene Cixous, *The Book of Promethea*

PROLOGUE

He hates doing this. Driving in darkness. Even without all the traffic, it makes him want to die. The other commuters are still waking up, their eyes barely open and still longing for sleep. Some drive Teslas and Porsches and Audis, others have an old Mazda or Hyundai or a busted up Toyota truck that can barely pass the California emissions test. A smartphone glows over nearly every dashboard, displaying a map of the freeway or transmitting music to the car speakers. The drivers chug coffee to stay awake, smoke cigarettes through slivered-open windows, and watch the morning dew burn away from their glass windshields. The unlucky ones are headed across the bay to San Francisco. Getting into the city is easy at this hour, but getting out is another matter, far more complicated and nothing anyone wants to think about. Not yet, at least.

He listens to the radio for the entire journey from the suburb of San Leandro to the Oakland waterfront. There is no gap between the cities, only a highway sign that announces the changeover. He takes the off-ramp for Chinatown and drives between the new luxury apartment buildings scattered around Jack London Square. He'll never live in one of these buildings, all made of metal and glass and polished, reclaimed wood. At the bottom are private gyms and yoga studios and expensive cafes and art galleries that he's never been to, places only meant for those in the new neighborhood.

His life is much different. He lives in a two bedroom apartment in San Leandro with his wife and their nine year-old daughter. The floors are linoleum, the cabinets are white, and the stove is electric. The nearest business is a gas station convenience store. He and his wife pay $1400 in rent every month, something they can barely afford, while these luxury apartments in Jack London Square cost around $4000 per month. Every morning, he sees well-dressed people emerge from these new buildings in fancy cars or riding expensive bikes or catching an Uber outside their front door. He despises how satisfied they look when they head off to work. It makes his heart pound in anger.

Jack London Square is named after a writer born in Oakland. He's never read any of Jack London's books or stories except one in high school that was about a wolf. There's a wooden cabin and an old saloon near the square that commemorates Jack London the writer, but he's never stopped to read the bronze plaques that explain their biographical significance. To him, Jack London Square is just a tourist trap with a cheap movie theater and a ferry stop, an old industrial strip slowly being converted into a replica of San Francisco. But he doesn't like to think about that.

He pulls his red Mazda into a parking lot near the train tracks, turns off the engine, and keeps the radio on. He smokes his morning bowl of weed from a glass pipe and holds the smoke deep in his lungs to get as high as possible. When it becomes too harsh, he blows it out through the open window. The car doesn't have a CD player or a USB port or even a tape-deck, only the radio. Month after month, he memorizes the lyrics of the latest pop songs and often sings them on the drive to work. But not even the weed can make this routine bearable, nor can the music. It can only trick him into thinking he's still asleep, that all of this might just be a bad dream.

Already dressed in his work uniform, he gets out of the car and walks across the tracks towards the hotel. The London Lodge is built on pilings directly over the water with a wooden boardwalk wrapping around its backside. It's a simple three-story building on the upper end of what the other hotels charge. He's been working at the Lodge for almost four years, just long enough to realize there might not be any escape. He started off as a parking valet but recently got placed behind the reception desk, something he should be happy about. Aside from the extra four dollars an hour, he hates his new job more than he thought possible. At least when he was a valet he could run back and forth from the parking lot to the hotel. Now he does nothing but stand behind a desk.

He lights a cigarette to mask the smell of weed on his body. He does this every morning, a trick he inherited from high school and every other job. Although marijuana is legal now, he's still locked in this habit of masking the scent with tobacco. Fortunately, he's never had to hide it from his wife. She smokes weed everyday and when they're at home they smoke together. She's still sleeping right now, enjoying a whole two hours worth of dreams. On his days off he loves to wake up beside her, smoke in bed, and make breakfast for their daughter. It reminds him he's still alive.

He stops at the edge of the wooden boardwalk and stares across the channel at the city of Alameda. Someone told him it used to be connected with Oakland but they dredged a fake canal between the two cities so poor people would stay away. He doesn't know if this is true but it always made some sense. Alameda was far safer, white-washed, and suburban than Oakland, a place to raise a family without the fear of bullets smashing through the windows.

He stares at this island every morning, so close to the hotel it might as well be the same city. He leans against the boardwalk railing and smokes slowly, letting the nicotine and THC dance in his veins like old friends who've seen hard times together. The waves below him are gentle and the eastern sky is beginning to glow a dark shade of purple. A few seagulls silently glide towards the Chinese freighters docked in the Port of Oakland. The tall, horse-shaped cranes unload the shipping containers with metal claws, their movements steady and predictable. It happens like clockwork. Everything is the same. Nothing about this morning would have been exceptional had he not seen the body.

It bobs up and down directly below him, the head knocking against the pilings. It doesn't make sense at first. He's far too tired to understand. But then he notices the black collared shirt, the nice black pants, and realizes this person used to be alive. Now they're floating in the water like the plot of a hundred movies. He takes out his smartphone and swipes his finger to unlock the screen. He pauses a moment, unsure of what to do next. The body moves with the waves and knocks lifelessly against the wooden boardwalk. A gust of wind blows in from the ocean.

CHAPTER 1

Dylan Kinsey wakes to the sound of her smartphone blasting the chorus of "Style" by Taylor Swift. She presses the red disable button and the music goes silent. It's 6:30 am. Dylan is out of the shower and dressed before 7:00 am. She stands in front of her bedroom mirror while her hair dries and puts on makeup. It takes only a few minutes to apply eye-shadow, eyeliner, and mascara. She picks a very light blue color for her lids, almost invisible, and it works very well with the black eyeliner and crow-black hair cut short at her neck. For the past year and a half, she's worn some shade of blue over her eyes. Her friends say this makes her seem severe, especially with her bangs, but Dylan doesn't think she's a severe person. Quite the opposite. Light, happy even. She flicks the mascara back into her case and then dresses: black pants, black blouse, and a pair of black leather boots.

While drinking a single cup of coffee from her single-cup French-press, Dylan eats a banana and scrolls through her iPhone 6. She checks her Facebook, her Twitter, her Instagram, and her Gmail. She doesn't open any of the links or read any of the emails. There's no real content there, at least nothing important to her. She sees a picture her mom posted of a crow. She sees pictures from high school friends and colleagues. She sees everything they like, everything they tweet, and everything they post. It floods her eyes with light and mobilizes her fingers into repetitive motions. She sees images of trees, rivers, hiking trails, fireplaces, glasses of red wine, the Virgin Mary, urban skylines, famous pieces of art, corporate advertisements, ruined cities, tiny houses, cracked smartphone screens, fancy dinners, new outfits, different lipsticks, and various cats. But none of it really registers. She's only concerned with the tech blogs, the stock performance of OingoBoingo, the gossip about the CFO, and the insensitive comments of the CEO. This endless cascade of information mesmerizes her. By the time she's finished her banana and coffee, Dylan is caught up with the latest news on OingoBoingo. She refers to it openly as *her* company even though she's only a graphic designer for the advertising department.

Dylan washes her coffee cup and the small French-press, puts on a silver Japanese designer leather moto-jacket, and checks the living room mirror to adjust her hair one last time. The red light on her flatscreen television blinks on and off, the refrigerator adjusts its own temperature, and her phone vibrates inside her bag from a dozen notifications. Dylan notices none of this. She gazes into the mirror and admires her perfect aesthetic of silver and black and a touch of blue. She looks like metal. She looks like no one can touch her.

It's 7:45 am when she leaves her apartment and walks down the central staircase. Above her head are abstract mobiles that dangle from the skylight, their monochrome colors lit up by the morning sun. This is a brand new building called the Vermillion, completed less than two years ago. It has polished, reclaimed wooden interiors, large glass windows, rustic copper handrails, and long light fixtures connected to the high ceilings. Every apartment has one concrete wall and an artisan steel door mounted on rollers. Each central hallway is painted vermillion. This brilliant red color makes Dylan feel warm and fulfilled.

She descends the central staircase alone, as usual. There's no one else leaving their apartments and the entire building seems empty. Her boot steps are the loudest sound. This is all normal to Dylan. She opens the steel security door in the lobby and steps out into the Mission District of San Francisco where the air is rich with engine exhaust, tobacco smoke, urine, spilled beer, and a tinge of salt blowing in from the ocean. A stream of Teslas, Porsches, BMWs, and white construction trucks speed down Mission Street in both directions. Several pigeons putter at Dylan's feet and look up at her expectantly with orange eyes. They think she's going to feed them.

Her bus stop is exactly twelve and half feet from her front door, a fact the marketers advertised in their pamphlets for the Vermillion. This convenient amenity is what ultimately encouraged Dylan to sign the lease on her apartment. Today offers exactly what was promised in that glossy promotional material: quick and simple access to cheap public transit. She takes out her phone, goes to the MuniMobile app, and learns that her bus is scheduled to arrive at 7:50 am. While she waits, Dylan scrolls through her various social media feeds at a rapid pace. She sees images of a fire, she sees images of a forest, and she reads someone complain about their cracked iPhone screen. None of this captures her interest. She looks through her Gmail to see if her coworker Ricky has written but finds nothing. His thread is gray. None of this is normal. Ricky's her closest collaborator and sends constant emails once he wakes up. He's her only real friend in this city, the one person she actually trusts.

The bus arrives a few minutes late at 7:52 am. Every seat is taken, every inch packed with passengers, and Dylan presses her body against the backdoor. Enough people eventually get off so she can reach the aisle and grip the metal rail. With her body crammed against two men, Dylan scrolls through her smartphone and looks for Ricky on his Facebook, his Twitter, his Instagram, his Reddit, his Tumblr, and his Snapchat. There's no new activity, not since yesterday afternoon. She keeps searching through his accounts in a loop, mostly to avoid the leering men beside her. One of them keeps staring, she feels his body inch closer, and when Dylan can no longer stand it she suddenly looks up and sees his eyes fill with fear. The man looks down at his iPhone. Dylan keeps searching for Ricky. She frantically swipes her finger across the screen but doesn't find a trace of activity anywhere. A coldness begins to spread through her stomach. The man doesn't look at her again.

Just before 8:00 am, she steps onto the curb in front of the red neon entrance to OingoBoingo corporate headquarters. The building is on Mission Street at the edge of the SOMA district and its illuminated lobby is lined with giant glass windows that stretch to the ceiling. Dylan walks into this transparent cavern and scans herself in at the security gate where two young black men are sitting behind a red desk. They both smile at her neutrally as she passes. The red plastic barriers hiss open and admit her to the hallway of elevators where different shades of electric red strobe on the walls. They change from dark to light and then back again. This is all quite familiar.

Dylan rides the elevator with seven other people. They wear Oxford shirts tucked into their jeans and spotless running shoes on their feet. Unlike herself, these people have identification badges clipped to their belt loops. All of them are men. These are actual techies, men who know how to program and write code and repair servers and design the OingoBoingo mind games. Dylan only knows how to use Adobe programs, how to download apps, and how to get music and movies from Pirate Bay. But she's not a techie, as she often tells people. She's an art student who works for a tech company.

"Nice jacket," one of them says to her. "Expensive?"

"I got it at a thrift store," she lies. "Ten bucks."

"Are you in advertising? I think I've seen you—"

"No, you haven't seen me. I'm not usually here."

"Are you a contractor or something?"

"Something like that," she says. "Are you enjoying college?"

"College?" one of them asks, almost laughing. "No, we're employ—"

"Oh, I'm sorry. I thought they were giving tours again."

"Tours?"

"For interns," she says. "Never mind, it's just that you look so *young*."

All of the men suddenly grow silent. Dylan does her best not to smile, making her appear even more severe than normal. The men get off on the fourth floor and leave her alone without another word. She hears them whispering to each other just before the doors close and the elevator begins to ascend.

Dylan gets off on the sixth floor and heads down the hall to her department. She sees her coworkers standing behind plates of glass and sitting at their red desks in the common room. Her friends Bernadette and Elizabeth are in front of their iMac monitors with headphones over their ears. They smile at her, mouth the words *hello*, and keep smiling as Dylan walks past. She waves to them but maintains a constant pace towards her work station. She avoids talking with any of her male coworkers until she's almost close enough to touch her desk. It's the manager, Chad, an energetic man with blonde hair and blue eyes. A pair of gold framed aviator sunglasses are in his shirt pocket. He appears in front of her like a computer glitch, possessed by his usual morning mania of testosterone and caffeine. She can hardly look him in the eyes.

"How you doing today, Dylan?" he almost yells.

"Great! What's new?"

"Nothing, just taking a vibe check, you know?"

"Is something wrong?"

"No, no." He taps on her desk and looks at something out the window. "Just checking in. Like I said. Any new ideas for the Childhood Memory Game?"

"Nope, the same ones as yesterday. I've got it all laid out, just tinkering now."

For the past two weeks, Dylan has been assembling a host of dream characters to populate a billboard for the new Childhood Memory Game. It's the second release from OingoBoingo and has already exceeded the success of its predecessor by reaching the unprecedented number of 400,000,000 daily active users. These daily active users are asked ninety-nine questions about their childhood memories, their childhood fears, the monsters they were afraid of, and the landscapes that terrified them. These questions then generate a complex game world individually crafted for each daily active user. No two worlds are ever alike and the novelty of this game experience made the Childhood Memory Game the number one downloaded game on the App Store.

"So you think you've got this billboard under control?" Chad asks.

"Yeah, I'll show it to you right now, just let me sign in to my—"

"No, it's okay, I need to—"

Chad wanders off to speak with her coworker Brett. They start to laugh loudly and Chad talks with him for longer than he did with Dylan. He even looks at Brett's monitor in approval. Dylan notices this discrepancy of attention, as she usually does, but in the end she doesn't want to talk with either of them. She sits down at her desk, puts on her headphones, signs into her computer, and opens up the designs for the Childhood Memory Game billboard. She puts on a chronological Taylor Swift mix and proceeds to check her Facebook, her Twitter, her Instagram, and her Gmail.

She finds no new messages from her friend Ricky. His black leather chair is empty. His iMac monitor is blank. Dylan sees the familiar Ester Hernández painting framed on his desk that depicts a woman with the Virgin Mary tattooed across her back. It's usually blocked from her view by Ricky's body. Now it only signals his absence. To distract herself, Dylan starts checking the tech blogs in a fixed and steady loop. She doesn't start actually working until 8:45 am when Chad shows up to look at her billboard designs. He glances at her monitor, gives her a thumbs up, and then starts talking to someone on his iPhone X. He wanders away after this. Dylan doesn't care.

Forty-five minutes later, her friend is still not at work. The latest Taylor Swift blasts into her earphones as Chad stands near Ricky's desk and anxiously texts away on his phone. There are ten desks in the common room and only one of them is empty. Dylan looks at Chad, his perfectly shaved chin, his brand new pants, his recently barbered undercut, and then turns to her coworkers. None of them seem concerned, not even Bernadette or Elizabeth. All of them are looking at their iMacs.

Dylan glances at Chad's empty office, one of three glass cubes that line the entrance to the common room. He's the only one with a private office in the advertising department. The other glass rooms are for concentrated work sessions and meetings with the different department heads. Mostly they are kept empty. Dylan doesn't like working in these glass rooms although Chad seems to like being on display. He usually retires to his own glass office once he's finished his morning check in. After that, Chad rarely emerges except for lunch.

For him to now stand silently in the center of the common room is very odd. He doesn't look up from his phone, nor does he stop texting. His face is flushed crimson with panic. Something is clearly wrong so Dylan takes off her headphones and hurries over to read his texts. When she gets close, Chad locks his screen and walks away. She grabs his arm forcefully, pulls him back, and asks, "Chad, what's going on?"

"Nothing, nothing," he mutters, not making eye contact, pulling her toward his office. "Ricky's probably sick. Just don't worry about it. Don't stress. We don't need stress."

At this point, Dylan can no longer stand his presence and lets go. He smells like department store cologne and the scent is far too heavy. It reminds her of the boys who tried to kiss her in high school. Chad heads into his office while Dylan stands alone in the center of the common room. All of her coworkers stare but none of them say anything. Her friends Elizabeth and Bernadette manage to emit vague smiles but they both keep their headphones on. The rest of her coworkers are men. None of them look Dylan in the eyes. She keeps standing there, waiting for someone to speak, but eventually her coworkers return to their screens and Dylan remains there long after they've looked away.

Dylan has no appetite at lunch. She sits with Bernadette and Elizabeth in the glowing red cafeteria and watches them eat their packaged salads. The three of them usually sit together, most of the time with Ricky, sometimes with a few of the other men if they aren't acting like pricks. Dylan doesn't eat today. Instead, she repeatedly texts Ricky the same simple message: *where r u?*

"Did Ricky say he was going to be gone?" she asks. "Do either of you remember?"

"I don't know," Bernadette says. "I don't think I talked to him."

"Has he ever missed work without calling?" Dylan asks.

"Yeah! *You* remember. He was sick a couple times," Elizabeth says. "But that wasn't a big deal."

"Maybe he has a hangover," Bernadette says, taking the pink band out of her blonde hair and letting it fall to her shoulders. "That's probably it."

"Chad looked nervous, though." Dylan tosses her phone onto the glass table. "I saw him. He was jumpy. He never stands in the common room like that. Something's happened."

"Why are you so upset? You never get like this," Elizabeth says. "You really don't."

"It's true, I don't."

Dylan says this flatly. She smooths down her hair and looks at her phone resting on the glass.

"Didn't you talk with him yesterday?" Elizabeth asks.

"Yeah, but mostly about the billboard. He was saying something about systemic crisis, how there was nothing anyone could do to stop it. And then we talked about Leonardo DaVinci, about what he would have thought of Silicon Valley."

"Sounds like Ricky," Bernadette says. "You two are always talking about something weird."

"Yeah, that sounds pretty normal," Elizabeth says. "Ricky's probably just sick."

"Anyway, did you see Chad and his stupid iPhone X?" Bernadette asks. "He keeps walking around with those fucking wireless ear buds. He's, like, the only one who still uses them."

"I hope that tool falls off a cliff," Elizabeth says. "And yeah, what the fuck? Why'd they remove the headphone jack from the iPhone in the first place? Only morons bought the new one."

Both of her friends keep talking about the iPhone X. Dylan says nothing to them. She keeps texting Ricky and searches for him on social media. She checks her Gmail every thirty seconds while her friends discuss how much they hate Chad. Dylan nods when she agrees. She waits for them to bring up Ricky but they never do. They keep talking about the iPhone X. They keep talking about Chad.

"There's *all* these posts on my feed today," Bernadette says. "Everyone keeps breaking their screens. I mean, not everyone, but like three people or something. I keep seeing the pictures they post when they get a new phone, pictures of their broken screens."

"It's because the iPhone is *so* slippery," Elizabeth says. "Intentionally slippery. I swear, its *made* to slip off every surface I put it on."

"They did it to create a secondary market," Dylan says.

"A what?" Bernadette asks.

"A secondary market. For plastics."

"Plastics?" Bernadette rolls her eyes and looks at Elizabeth. "Another conspiracy theory."

"It's not a conspiracy theory," Dylan says. "People buy those plastic coverings for their phones because they slip and the screens break and it costs money to repair. The average consumer just buys a new phone, which makes Apple happy. If their phones weren't slippery there wouldn't be a market for all that plastic or those repairs or those new iPhones. The fault is built into the product. Intentionally."

"I don't buy it," Elizabeth says. "Why would they do that?"

"Why wouldn't they?" Dylan asks.

All three stare at their iPhones sitting atop the glass table. The silver, chrome, and pink bottoms are smooth and sleek and offer no resistance to any surface they might encounter. To emphasize this, Dylan suddenly pushes hers across the glass. It slides into Bernadette's phone and causes both to spin towards the edge of the table. All of them laugh loudly, put their phones in their bags, and then Dylan notices the men across the room. Some of them are looking at Bernadette and Elizabeth. None of them look at her.

Dylan knows these men think the laughter was meant to capture their attention. She sees their smirks, hears their whispers, and feels the leering eyes cast on her table. Bernadette and Elizabeth grow silent and dig for their phones. Neither of them look at the men and stare intently their screens. Some of the men begin to laugh. Dylan shakes her head, takes her phone out of her bag, and resumes searching for her friend.

By mid-afternoon, there's still no news from Ricky, nor is there an announcement from Chad. He stays in his office for the entire day and only goes to the bathroom once. He doesn't appear to eat or drink. Dylan doesn't eat either. Whenever she looks through the glass walls of Chad's office, he's always on his smartphone frantically typing on the screen. He's still doing this at 3:01 pm when the entire department files past his office and leaves the common room.

OingoBoingo maintains a six hour work day for its employees with an hour provided for lunch. This fact is widely advertised by the PR department. Some critics in the media have written that this mimics the elementary school day and needlessly infantilizes its employees, although Dylan's always liked this arrangement. It allows her to be more productive and make the most of her time. Today is no different. She's happy to have the entire evening to herself. Tomorrow she'll wake up feeling rested.

Dylan and Bernadette are the last to leave the common room. They walk together past the glass walls of Chad's office. He doesn't acknowledge them, nor does he look up from his phone, not once. On his iMac screen is the image of a red and green flower that looks like a cobra. His jaw hangs open and his mouth is wide from either incomprehension or fear.

"Fucking imbecile," Bernadette hisses. "See his mouth?"

"Something happened. Look at him."

They each have one last glance at their manager's face before leaving the common room. They step out into the hallway just as the metal doors of the elevator close and lock. Dylan pushes the down button for the next descending car. It turns from black to an electric shade of red.

"Ricky *was* acting kind of strange recently," Bernadette says, straightening her blonde hair. "Remember how he started to disappear at lunch and never come back?"

"Yeah. I assumed he had a date at first," Dylan said. "But he said it was just work."

"You went on a date with him before, right?"

"*One* date. We're just friends, though. You know that."

The next elevator arrives crowded with well-dressed upper level employees and a few executives. Everyone is quiet. The air is thick with piney cologne and expensive dhalia perfume and the familiar scent of leather. Dylan manages to tilt her head and sees Bilton Smyth, the CEO of OingoBoingo. He has slick brown hair and wears a tailored black suit. He has a handsome face and sculpted chin and could be a Hollywood actor. He's whispering to a man in sunglasses that Dylan doesn't recognize. She can almost hear their words when the elevator car reaches the lobby and everyone rushes into the pulsing red light.

Bernadette and Dylan pass through the security gate with the outflow of employees and leave OingoBoingo headquarters through the giant glass doors on Mission Street. They're just south of Market, in walking distance of several other tech companies, a few gyms, and many new luxury apartment buildings. Neither of them live here.

"Want to get some food?" Dylan asks. "Sushi? I'm starving, all I've had is a banana."

"No, I need to workout." She motions in the direction of her gym. "What're you doing tonight? You want to go out later?"

"I'll probably just eat and go home. Ricky being gone scares me. I'm worried."

"Go eat then. Take care of yourself."

Dylan gives her friend a hug and a kiss before hurrying off to Yummy, the closest sushi restaurant. After being seated near the window, Dylan quickly orders before the waiter can leave: four unagi rolls and a bowl of miso. Then she checks her Facebook, her Twitter, her Instagram, and her Gmail. Chad has formally approved her billboard designs for the Childhood Memory Game. He's just waiting to hear back from upstairs. Multiple tech blogs carry stories about Bilton Smyth and his recent comment that wages should be universally depressed. The CEO of OingoBoingo believes that "wages should be kept low and thus equalized across the entire planet to ensure a final and definitive correction of the world economy." Since saying this at a recent conference, the internet has been aflame with memes, hit pieces, and feature articles on the unrestrained greed of the San Francisco tech elite, temporarily personified by Bilton Smyth.

The miso soup arrives at the table and Dylan chugs it down once the broth has cooled. She scrapes out the tofu and seaweed with her green plastic chopsticks and then returns to her smartphone screen. She keeps refreshing her Gmail but there's still no update about her billboard designs, nor is there any message from Ricky. She searches for him through all his social media accounts but there's no recent activity. He's never been this silent before.

She scrolls through her own social media accounts and sees numerous unflattering pictures of Bilton Smyth, mostly when he's in expensive clubs, with phrases like WORKS 4 HOURS A DAY, MAKES MILLIONS and ME = 50 MILLION, YOU = SUB-MINIMUM WAGE. Dylan stares at these pictures just long enough for the phrases to become legible and then disappear into her memory. The four unagi rolls arrive in the midst of this and when the waiter leaves, Dylan drops her iPhone and begins to eat. She's done in less than five minutes. Her hunger is gone, her mind is a bit clearer, and she doesn't pick up her smartphone, not even when it vibrates.

Back in her apartment, Dylan opens the freezer and starts eating ice cream out of a container. She removes her makeup with an apricot scented wipe while holding a plastic jar of organic pistachio gelato. Her smartphone continuously vibrates on her coffee table but none of the messages are from Ricky. She almost finishes the gelato but forces herself to put the jar back in the freezer. It's 4:27 pm and all Dylan wants to do is keep eating. But she resists this urge. She pees in the bathroom, wipes herself with toilet paper, and then decides to take a shower.

Dylan loses track of time while she's under the streams of hot water. She stares at the silver metal handles and the polished white tiles for so long that all her fingertips prune up before she's even washed her hair.

The water temperature doesn't change; it doesn't suddenly become cold, nor does it become scalding. It remains perfect.

It's 5:15 pm when Dylan finally leaves the bathroom and changes into some black sweatpants and a white Budweiser shirt. She returns to the living room and grabs her phone off the coffee table. In less than a minute, she's determined there's nothing important among all her recent notifications and sits down on the couch to watch something that will distract her from worry. This is when her land-line rings. Dylan reluctantly gets off the couch, goes to her bedroom, and picks up the plastic phone from her desk. The number is blocked.

"Hi, mom," she says. "What's up?"

"I haven't heard from you in *weeks*. Are you okay?"

"Everything's fine."

"I'm worried about you, Dylan. Are you—"

"Trust me, I'm fine. Seriously, I have to—"

Her mother hangs up before Dylan can finish. The sharp dial-tone rings through the speakers until she presses *OFF* and puts the phone back in its cradle. Dylan returns to the couch and picks up her smartphone. She switches on the digital flat-screen television with the remote control but concentrates on her Twitter feed. From the corner of her vision, she sees the flat-screen flicker and the menu appear, giving her a variety of options. She quickly goes to Netflix, waits for it to load, and looks back at her iPhone.

On Twitter, she reads about a progressive California Senator who's spoken out against Bilton Smyth and condemned him for his "anti-social behavior." Dylan sees the same thing on Facebook, even on Instagram. When she checks her Gmail, she finds nothing about her designs, nor is there anything from Ricky, although a few of the emails mention the Senator. After reading four of them, Dylan gets the sense that it's a big deal and everyone should be concerned, as it may affect the stock price. It takes too much energy to try and figure out why it's a big deal, so she throws her iPhone across the couch and starts browsing through the movies on Netflix. After about fifteen minutes, she settles on a film called *The Baader-Meinhof Complex*. She likes foreign films. This one is in German.

Although it's not what she's expecting, Dylan finds herself engrossed. She stops hearing the vibrations of her iPhone and intently watches a group of young German radicals go from student activists to urban guerrillas. There are a lot of guns, a lot of screaming, and a little bit of sex. All of the characters are attractive, especially the woman who plays Ulrike Meinhoff. Dylan can't stop looking at this actress. She finds her very beautiful, even her voice, very deep, very melodious. But this character dies in prison and the movie starts to become depressing, so she turns off the flat-screen television and grabs her phone. That is when she sees the email from Chad.

The heading in her Gmail reads "**On the recent tragedy**" and Dylan's already crying before it's open. There's no doubt in her mind, but she opens it just the same. *As some of you may already know, our friend and colleague Ricardo Florez was found in the bay near Oakland. The police have still not discovered the cause of his death, although suicide has not been ruled out.* Dylan doesn't read anything else Chad has written. She throws her iPhone 6 at the cement wall so fast it explodes, shatters, and bits of touchscreen pepper the hardwood floor like hail. Dylan screams so loud the neighbors call the police. When the officers arrive and begin to yell her name, Dylan is on the ground weeping. She's roused only by the sound of their batons pounding and pounding against the steel front door.

CHAPTER 2

DYLAN HASN'T REPLACED HER IPHONE 6. IN TOTAL SILENCE, SHE PUTS on black eyeliner in front of the living room mirror. She does this very slowly, carefully. The rest of her clothes are black; her dress, her shoes, her leggings, even her underwear. Dylan is the only person from OingoBoingo going to Ricky's funeral. Since his death, she's stopped talking to anyone at the office, even Elizabeth and Bernadette.

After destroying her iPhone, Dylan didn't buy another one. She started doing her online work at the office or in the bedroom using her desktop computer from college. The older machine was covered in dust but did everything it was supposed to. There was a significant amount of pictures and data on her iPhone but Dylan didn't care to transfer any of it to her desktop. She simply threw the phone into the parking garage dumpster.

At 8:01 am, Dylan finishes putting on her makeup and goes to the bedroom computer. She opens up the Chrome browser, types the words *watsonville cemetery* into the search engine, and waits for the Google Maps results to appear. She clicks on the small map and then types her address into the directions bar. Her route appears as a blue line running south from San Francisco to the small farming town of Watsonville. This route will take her into the redwoods above Silicon Valley, through Santa Cruz, and along the shoreline of the Pacific Ocean.

Dylan looks for a button that will allow her to print these directions. At first, she's convinced such a button no longer exists, that printing is no longer an option, but after a few uncertain moments she finally discovers it. She clicks the button and the color printer soon spits out the map. This is the first time she's ever printed directions for herself. Since her first year of college, she's always used her smartphone. Printing directions makes Dylan think of her parents. It's something they would do.

Beside the printer is a gold metal locket in the shape of a book that Ricky gave her as a birthday present. It contains an image of Dylan taken from her Instagram account where she's wearing black sunglasses and staring up at the sky. Ricky said she looked like a gangster in this picture. He never flirted with her, not even on their one date, not even when he gave her the locket. Ricky always liked Dylan. Ricky was her friend. And this gift is all she has left besides emails, texts, and instant messages. She stares at the locket a moment longer before grabbing the directions from the print tray.

At 8:06 am, Dylan puts her computer to sleep and goes to the living room. She grabs her black bag from the couch, stuffs the directions inside, and locks the steel door to her apartment. Down the hallway is an elevator she rarely uses that leads to the parking garage where her BMW has sat unused for over two weeks. Dylan scans her key fob against the sensor, presses the down button, and once the elevator arrives she descends into the giant concrete cavern.

The promotional literature on her building went into extensive detail about the construction of this subterranean parking lot. It was excavated using highly advanced tunneling techniques from Switzerland and its architecture could withstand a 9.0 earthquake. The vast parking garage served not only her building but also the neighboring one, the Empenada. Both buildings are owned by the same New York-based company, although the Empenada is slightly more expensive than the Vermillion.

Dylan's car sits inside a large steel rack that holds two other vehicles, one of them a red Tesla, the other a green Prius. This rack moves on a vertical axis and can sink until the uppermost slot is level with the pavement. Her car is in the center slot, the rack's default position, and Dylan never has to adjust it. This is a privilege for which she paid an extra $3,000. She gets inside her black BMW, throws her bag on the passenger seat, and then backs out of the slot. She drives up a gently curving cement ramp, clicks the fob to open the garage doors, and feels sunlight hit her face.

At 8:17 am, Dylan leaves the Vermillion in the car that was her high school graduation present. As she pulls out of the garage, a man and woman in dark clothing approach the BMW. The woman yells something at Dylan, spits on her windshield, and screams an unintelligible curse filled with venom. It happens very quickly. Both of them flip her off with big smiles on their faces. They look Dylan directly in the eye, unafraid, unperturbed, and calm. She hears them say the words *techie* and *scum*. They tell her to go home. They tell her she's disgusting. Her cheeks starts to burn, the couple walks off without looking back, and Dylan listens to their laughter fade away down the sidewalk. It's the third time something like this has happened.

Dylan is so angry she sees nothing but red break lights, yellow traffic lines, and the glare of sunlight for the next several minutes. She gets on the 101 freeway and starts driving over the speed limit without realizing it. Once she's past the Cow Palace, her heart begins to calm and it dawns on her that she's driving ninety miles an hour. Dylan lets off the gas and pulls into the slow lane. This is when images of what just occurred start to flood her mind.

She sees the woman who spat on her windshield. Her hair was dyed red. She didn't wear any makeup. She had nice teeth, a nice smile. She could have been from Mexico or Turkey. She imagines having a drink with her at a red lit bar. She imagines the woman is probably nice, humorous, a pleasure to be around, and this all just makes Dylan's heart beat faster. So she turns on the radio and presses scan, hoping for Taylor Swift but settling on Katy Perry. It helps her forget what just happened.

Dylan passes through the city of Millbrae and sees the billboard she designed hanging over the freeway. It's been up for the past three days and received favorable responses on social media. It displays the panorama of a cartoon city populated with a wide variety of fairy tale monsters, unicorns, dragons, and other fantastical beings. Several children of every race and gender stand among these monsters with expressions of confusion, despair, bliss, anger, happiness, fear, joy, and terror. All of them are looking at a central character, a dark shadow with red eyes and a toothy smile. Behind them are the towers of a multicolored city that nearly blots out the night sky. In the far right corner of the 48-foot long rectangle is the text CHILDHOOD MEMORY GAME written in red.

The freeway is not very congested so Dylan tries to slow down but only manages to admire her billboard for a short moment. She starts to smile and feels proud of her new work until she remembers the woman with red hair. Her heart begins to pound again. She forgets feeling happy or accomplished. She can only remember that woman's smile and how confident she was in her hatred.

Dylan eventually hears Taylor Swift on the radio although by then she's forgotten about the red haired woman. She passes through Menlo Park where Facebook has built its garden-roofed headquarters in the reedy marshlands of the bay. She sees another billboard for the Childhood Memory Game hanging over the freeway. She speeds through Mountain View and past the Google campus with its new domes and construction cranes rising above the water. She sees another billboard for the Childhood Memory Game as she drives through Cupertino where Apple has built a giant metal and glass ring to hold 12,000 employees. She travels through Los Gatos where Netflix has built its corporate headquarters along a creek lined with oak trees. And then she merges onto Highway 17, drives past two reservoirs that are very low on water, and suddenly finds herself in the redwoods. She can't look at the trees too closely, not while she's driving, but one thing that doesn't escape her is how tall they are, how they block the sunlight from the road.

It's difficult to drive and see the redwoods at the same time and she grips the steering wheel tightly for fear of losing control. It occurs to Dylan she could pull over, park on the side of the road, wander off into the forest, and smell the trees, although she never does this. The traffic is always too fast, there isn't enough room to pull over, or she simply decides it's not worth it and keeps driving. When she finally does find room to pull over there are no more redwoods along the freeway and she's on her way down the mountain pass.

Dylan reaches Santa Cruz, merges south onto Highway 1, and expects to see the Pacific on her right but finds her view obscured by hills and trees. In the absence of the ocean, Dylan begins to think about Ricky, his empty red desk, and the utter silence of her coworkers. After his death, Dylan went to the office day after day, just like normal. She worked on the new billboard designs, talked with her friends, and went to the group meetings, but not once did anyone bring up Ricky. She even made an announcement in the common room. She told her coworkers about the funeral, gave them the time and place, and announced she could drive four people if they wanted a ride. Bernadette and Elisabeth both nodded, a few others smiled meekly, but no one definitively told her they'd come. At home that night, not a single person emailed her in response. Dylan thinks about these events and keeps looking west in the hope of glimpsing the ocean. Eventually she sees it, and the brilliant glow makes her want to swim.

If she still had her iPhone 6, Dylan could ask Siri for the fastest route to the Pacific Ocean and receive precise directions from the familiar feminine robot. But this is no longer possible for her. The digital clock in the BMW says it's 10:07 am and the funeral doesn't start until 11:00 am, leaving her more than enough time to see the Pacific. Dylan knows the ocean is just to the west but it doesn't matter. She worries she'll get lost and arrive late to the funeral so she keeps driving south through long stretches of farmland until she finally enters the city of Watsonville. At the first stoplight, Dylan grabs the printed directions from her bag and reads the last steps to the cemetery. She'll never use these paper directions again but somehow they make her feel confident in herself. She doesn't know why.

Everyone is sweating, but no one tries to hide it. They're crying, nearly everyone, as far as Dylan can tell. Even she's crying. They all stand together in long rows of black, wiping their cheeks and their brows and the backs of their necks with handkerchiefs. The sun is hanging directly overhead and it pulls the moisture from their bodies. No one has an umbrella, although some of the older women have black fabric draped over their heads. There are over 200 people here, with dozens more standing in the back behind rows of folding chairs. Although she doesn't understand a single word, Dylan cannot stop her tears. The young people who address the crowd can barely complete their sentences without weeping. Only the elders are able to keep their composure and this just makes everyone cry harder. They know how much pain these old people must feel now that one of their youngest is gone.

Dylan is one of the few white skinned people to attend. Everyone else is dark like Ricky with smooth brown skin. She can't tell who's related to who. Shortly after noon, a group of young men and women in berets and sunglasses address the crowd one by one, taking their time but speaking loudly and firmly. None of them cry. The older people in the crowd seem uncomfortable when they talk, but many young people clap loudly. And then the funeral is over. The coffin is lowered into the ground, the priest says something in Spanish, and people begin to rise from their seats.

Dylan is about to leave when the crowd lines up in front of the coffin. She follows them towards giant bouquets of red roses arranged around the grave. Everyone is still sweating, but now they begin to speak in Spanish. Those too sad to notice Dylan before now look at her with curiosity. It makes her feel uncomfortable. No one speaks to her in any language, not even when they make eye contact. They just stare. When she finally reaches the grave and throws a red rose on the black coffin, a circle of silence has formed around her, a silence filled with tension. She hurries away from the grave with her head down but before she can escape someone grabs her by the shoulder.

"Hey, hey, excuse me?"

Dylan freezes and the person steps in front of her.

"You worked with Ricky?" she asks.

"I did. I'm Dylan."

The woman is dressed in black with her hair up in a pomp. She has a gaze that isn't suspicious but certainly not trusting. Her skin is dark and smooth just like Ricky's. She has the same brown eyes as her brother.

"Are you one of his sisters?" Dylan asks.

"He told you about me? So you knew him? Wait...you're the—"

And then she turns and beckons over a group of women. She speaks to them loudly in Spanish and the whole crowd seems to be listening. Dylan wants nothing more than to flee, to get in her car and speed back to her apartment. But she's surrounded now and has become the center of attention.

"These are my sisters," the woman says, motioning at the others.

"Did you understand any of that, any of the service?" one of them asks.

"No, nothing really," Dylan says.

"You didn't understand nothing?"

"No."

"You're the only one who came?" another sister asks. "From his work?"

"Yeah, I'm—"

"Good! Fuck 'em! You know he talked about you."

"Yeah, he told us about you."

There are seven sisters. Two of them yell in Spanish to the gawkers surrounding their huddle. Dylan notices the crowd begin to leave after this. They ignore her again, they pretend she doesn't exist, and this makes her feel less anxious even though the sisters keep asking questions.

"When was the last time you saw him?"

"How was he acting?"

"You know he didn't kill himself, right?"

All of the sisters nod in unison. Dylan nods with them.

"When did you see him last?"

"The day before he—"

"He died. Yeah."

"How was he acting?"

"Come on, come on, let her breathe."

Dylan's forehead is damp with sweat and she can only imagine what her cheeks look like. All of the sisters have dry rivers of black running from their eyes, just like Dylan. They stop interrogating her and explain they're going to lunch. They tell her she should come. When she starts to refuse they put their hands on her until she agrees. They tell her their parents are too crushed and want to be alone. It will only be the kids and extended family. They tell her it'll all be chill. They tell her she has to come, and she agrees again, even though she doesn't want to.

There are over forty people in the dark banquet hall. It's closed off from the rest of the dining area and a large buffet extends along an entire wall. Dylan sits at a circular table with Ricky's sisters while several men fix them plates of food. It makes Dylan think of knights and chivalry and princesses. The sisters have introduced themselves to her by name but Dylan's already forgotten them. The food at the buffet smells delicious. Dylan realizes she's starving. She can't wait for the men to return.

"How come you're the only one? That's what I want to know. Why does he know all these people in tech or whatever and none of them are here?"

"It's like they were saying earlier, this system stabbed him in the back."

"Those were his old friends, the ones in berets. They all used to be tight but Ricardo got into a brawl with one of them in high school. That was his childhood crew, you know, and they didn't talk after that fight. They was saying Ricardo tried to buy into the system, that he tried to play the game, tried to buy into the dream, and it killed him. That's why everyone was looking at you, cause they were asking where all his coworkers were. But here you are, so—"

"Ricky always liked you, though. He thought you were cool, down to earth. I guess that's why you're here with us right now. Only someone down to earth wouldn't have a heart attack or run away."

The sisters laugh loudly and one of them yells something in Spanish to the next table that makes them laugh as well. Dylan can feel her cheeks burning red and tries to smile but all she can think is how badly she wants to flee, how she isn't down to earth and is actually just afraid.

"We were always making fun of him for using those apps or whatever to meet people."

"What's it called again?"

"OkCupid," Dylan answers. "We used it for *one* date."

"Is it like Tinder?"

"Not really, it's a bit more complicated. More about dating than hooking up, I guess."

"And y'all worked together, in the same office?"

"Yeah, we did."

"What's up with that? Why use an app if you see each other every day?"

Dylan thinks for a moment before answering. She watches the men at the buffet heap spoonfuls of steaming soup into bowls and fill plates with strips of meat. Her stomach is a pit of dark acid filled with the remains of this morning's coffee. Her mouth begins to water.

"It's easier than a conversation," she tells the sisters. "You answer a bunch of questions about yourself, the app connects you with people that are similar, then you go on a date with them."

Dylan can't think of anything else to say and when she stops talking all of the sisters just stare blankly. But then the men arrive and hand them each a plate of food and a bowl of soup. Dylan mouths the word *gracias* to the man who brought it and immediately tries the soup. She burns the roof of her mouth but it's delicious nonetheless, filled with pork and hominy and spices she doesn't recognize.

After tasting the soup she starts to shovel rice and guacamole into her mouth. Dylan is so hungry she eats for a full minute. She quickly discards her fork and uses a corn tortilla to scoop up pieces of grilled steak and watery pinto beans and streaks of sour cream. When she looks up none of the sisters have eaten any of their food. They all stare at her, some in amusement, a few in disgust.

"You were hungry, huh?"

"Damn, girl, you ate half the plate already!"

"They don't feed you at OingoBoingo?"

"I was too nervous to eat this morning," Dylan says. "I'm sorry."

"No, no, no, don't apologize. We should be eating, too."

But none of them do, and now Dylan is too self conscious. She can no longer eat despite how hungry she is. One sister stirs rice into her beans but doesn't lift her fork from the plate. She just keeps stirring it. Another sister scoops beans onto a tortilla chip and looks at it for a moment. She eventually puts it in her mouth but doesn't eat another one. Not knowing what else to do, Dylan takes a bite of meat and rice and guacamole. It still tastes delicious but now it's hard to swallow.

"So you and Ricky got fixed up by a computer for that date?"

"An algorithm," she says.

"A what?"

"A computer program matched us together. We both liked art—"

"Yeah, no shit, he loved art like it was a goddess. Like it was the Virgin herself."

"He loved Ester Hernández, too! You know her art?"

"I do," Dylan says, wiping a piece of rice off her lip. "Ricky had one of her paintings on his desk, the one with the Virgin Mary tattooed on a woman's back and someone holding a rose up to the Virgin so it looks like—"

"Yeah, we know the one," one of the sisters says, wiping away a tear. "Esther's a friend of the family. My mom's known her forever.

That's how Ricky got into all this you know."

"Ricky never told me that," Dylan says. "We talked about her a lot, but I didn't know he'd met her. I guess...yeah, he never told me."

For a moment, all of the sisters appear to grin at her.

"He always loved Esther."

"Loved to sit in her lap."

"No, but art, that's what he really loved, it's true," one of the sisters says. "The business shit he just picked up from all the rich frat boys at Stanford. Fuck that place, you know, Ricky's old friends were right to say that shit about tech and capitalism and all that. Fuck that world, and I don't mean any disrespect to you, but it's fucked up what it did to him. I mean it killed him."

"He told you about our parents? You know they're farm workers, right?"

"There's no way Ricky killed himself. He's from *here*, he was hungry."

"You really don't know anything?"

"About what?" Dylan asks, her plate now empty.

"What he was doing before he died? Did he tell you anything?"

"Honestly, I've been trying to remember. He stopped eating lunch at the cafeteria, and I guess I assumed he'd met someone. I don't know, he didn't say. When we went out for drinks we just talked about whatever, you know, art and stuff. And at work he was really focused on feeding the data from our games back into advertisements, into the designs. We were always sending emails back and forth but I've been looking over it and he didn't say anything unusual, really, he just didn't."

"Look, I never understood half of the shit Ricky was saying to me, and what you just said kinda didn't make any sense. But whatever."

"We just want to know what happened to him."

One of the sisters begins to cry, and soon most of them have tears leaking from their eyes. They wipe their cheeks with napkins and when they've finished it's easier for them to eat. One by one they start into their steak and guacamole and rice. The table grows silent. Dylan stares at her empty plate, unsure of what to say, afraid to even look up. All she wants is to pull the covers over her head and go to sleep, but she's not at home, she's nowhere near her bed, and when she does look up none of the sisters are staring at her. They're far too hungry to care.

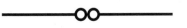

Once they've eaten, once their tears have stopped, the sisters talk to each other in Spanish and ignore Dylan. She takes this opportunity to grab her bag and mutter something about the bathroom. She leaves the banquet hall through the side exit, quickly gets into her BMW, pulls out of the parking lot, and drives towards the center of Watsonville. Much to her surprise, Dylan doesn't get lost. She finds the northbound entrance to Highway 1 without any problems.

Dylan takes this route all the way to Santa Cruz and realizes if she keeps heading northward she'll inevitably meet the Pacific Ocean. So she keeps driving past the off-ramp that leads over the redwoods to Silicon Valley and veers off onto a wide city street. She passes through the strip malls and tattoo parlors and cafes and apartment complexes of Santa Cruz, past the food co-ops and corporate grocery stores, and drives all the way to the end of town. The buildings give way to trees and barbed wire fences that contain nothing but hills and fields covered in dry grass. And then she sees it, just beyond a field of strawberries, the giant expanse of blue, white, and silver of the Pacific Ocean.

Further north, she pulls over at a park along the beach. She locks her car and wanders across a field of dunes towards the water where the waves crash against giant expanses of rock that look like pieces of a jigsaw puzzle left to disintegrate over time. Dylan climbs atop one of these rocks and discovers a large tide pool stretching off towards the water filled with anemones, barnacles, muscles, and clams. A wave suddenly hits the edge of the rock and the spray drenches her entire body. It makes her feel refreshed so she walks closer to the edge and waits for the next one. When the water hits her she washes her face and inhales the taste of salt. Dylan can smell the sun as it burns the moisture from her skin, leaving behind a ghostly white residue. It's real, the ocean is real, although she feels as if it hadn't been, not until this moment.

Dylan arrives at her building at 4:23 pm and opens the garage doors with her key fob. She drives her BMW down the ramp and parks it in the giant metal rack. Up above her is a red Tesla. Down below is a green Prius. She doesn't know who owns either car, nor does she know which units they live in. Dylan uses her key fob to access the elevator and takes it up to her apartment. When she gets inside, she removes her wet clothing and takes a long shower. It's 4:57 pm when she finally gets out, puts on a white robe, and goes to her bedroom where she wakes up her sleeping desktop.

Dylan checks her Facebook, her Twitter, her Instagram, and her Gmail. There are several stories about Bilton Smyth, CEO of OingoBoingo, and how he's gone silent to the media. No one has seen him in a week. Many articles insinuate he's back-tracking from his recent remarks about the global economy. In her Gmail, Dylan finds a message from Chad regarding the data set from the Childhood Memory Game. He explains there's a high correlation between new game users and the locations of the latest billboards. Dylan looks at a data visualization that depicts a glowing red, orange, and yellow blob stretching along Highway 101 from San Francisco to San Jose. Red indicates a high concentration of users, yellow indicates a lower concentration, all of it centered around the physical billboards. Chad congratulates the team on their work and reminds them of the visioning session scheduled for Monday. All of the department receives the same email. Chad doesn't congratulate Dylan specifically.

When she finishes this email, Dylan goes to Youtube and puts on the song "Look What You Made Me Do" by Taylor Swift. The electronic anthem blares through the speakers and causes her mind to wander towards the ocean. Just as the memories of the funeral begin to fill her mind, she grabs the locket Ricky gave her and opens up the golden book. Of all the things he could have given her as a birthday present, Ricky gave Dylan a picture of herself taken from Instagram where she's wearing black sunglasses and staring up at the sky. Dylan could be anyone in this picture and yet somehow she's only herself.

CHAPTER 3

Dylan decides to wear those same black sunglasses on Monday. She puts on a black dress and a pink version of the silver Japanese designer leather moto-jacket. Dylan likes the way she looks with the dark sunglasses and the pink jacket. It makes her feel impenetrable and confident. She hopes it will get her through the day.

At 7:16 am, she scrolls downs the feeds of her Twitter account, her Facebook account, and her Instagram account. Then she checks her Gmail. She sits at the kitchen counter with a single cup of coffee from her small French-press. She picks at a muffin and reads the news, emails, articles, and comments on her screen. On the counter is a banana she eventually plans to eat. At 7:47 am, Dylan's outside her building waiting for the Muni bus. She eats the banana very slowly and then tosses the peel into the street. A few people at the bus stop glare at her for littering but Dylan stares back silently with her black sunglasses until they return to their smartphones.

The bus arrives at 7:51 am and is so crowded that she's forced to lean into the woman beside her. Outside the window, Dylan sees homeless people camped underneath the freeway or passed out on cardboard mattresses. She watches a smiling man piss on a potted tree in front of an office building and sees a woman push a shopping cart filled with fabric and wooden sticks. The woman is dressed in black, she has brown skin, and for a moment she looks like a witch. There are less homeless people once they pass the freeway and when the bus reaches downtown the streets are cleaner, no one is sleeping on the sidewalk, and everything is made of glass and metal.

At 7:57 am, she gets off the bus in front of OingoBoingo headquarters, walks into the lobby with several other employees, and uses her employee badge to scan herself in through the security gate. The security guards don't look at her and keep their eyes on the front doors. It seems as if they're looking for someone.

Dylan rides the elevator and arrives in the common room to find Chad's office empty. Her coworkers are all at their desks with headphones on and she walks past them without taking off her sunglasses.

Elizabeth begins to speak but Dylan ignores her and goes directly to her desk. No one says anything else, no one looks at her, and the office fills with tension. Dylan powers up her iMac, puts her headphones on, plugs them into the monitor, and waits for everything to load. It's 8:06 am when she finally launches the Chrome browser, goes to Youtube, and puts on her Taylor Swift mix. The first track in the shuffle is "Shake It Off."

The horns, hoots, claps, and drums of this upbeat song fill her ears and make the sounds of the common room vanish. She checks her Facebook, her Twitter, her Instagram, and her Gmail. The tech blogs are still releasing articles about OingoBoingo CEO Bilton Smyth and his continued silence to the media. Some of her friends from college **like** or **love** or **wow** face the Childhood Memory Game designs she posted to Facebook. She sees an article on Twitter about the actual worth of OingoBoingo and whether the company is overvalued. On her Gmail, Dylan learns Chad will not be in for the day. He says all of them are doing a great job and is excited to see what they come up with. He says nothing specific to anyone, nor does he explain where he is. The email has a generally positive tone to it, just as it's generally meaningless, although it pleases Dylan to know she won't have to interact with him.

At 12:00 pm, the department goes on their lunch break. Dylan waits until everyone's out of the room, grabs her bag, and then goes over to Chad's office. There are no cabinets inside his private glass room, no drawers, no pens, and no paper besides a few business journals on the coffee table. There's only a single desktop computer, a 21.4 inch iMac identical to the one at her desk. The room contains nothing else. The glass walls reveal it perfectly.

Dylan walks out of the common room and heads straight to the elevator. Most of her coworkers are eating in the cafeteria but she doesn't look in their direction. When the elevator arrives, there are two men inside dressed identically in dark suits. She stands between them as the doors close and the car begins to descend. They smell like cologne and have leather bags in their hands. One of them is chewing gum.

Dylan looks at the man to her right and sees a standard WASP in his late thirties with blonde hair and blue eyes. He smiles but doesn't meet her eye for very long, just enough to be polite.

"You're in advertising?" he asks.

"Uh-huh," she says. "How about yourself?"

"How's that Childhood Memory Game working out?"

She looks down at his waist for a lanyard badge or identification card. He doesn't have one.

"Do you work here?" she asks.

And then the doors open and the two men rush out.

"Have a good lunch," he says.

She watches them leave the building quicker than anyone else but not fast enough to attract attention. For just a brief moment, Dylan worries they may have been journalists or hackers or spies from another company, but then she remembers her coworkers, she remembers Chad, and suddenly she is numb. She feels nothing. Those men could be anybody, they might even work for Bilton Smyth, but in the end she doesn't really care, even if they're actual spies, even if they just destroyed the company.

Dylan leaves OingoBoingo headquarters at 12:11 pm with her black sunglasses on and waits at the curb to cross Mission Street. All around her are glass towers and neon colors and luxury cars choking the pavement. The traffic signal changes, she crosses Mission, and all at once she becomes aware of someone following behind her, a woman with long dark hair. Dylan can see her figure at the edge of her vision but doesn't feel scared. The woman catches up, matches her pace, and stays just a few steps behind.

"Keep walking, Dylan," the woman says.

"Do I—"

"Just keep walking across Market and follow me. Don't turn around. It's about Ricky."

"How do—"

"Don't turn around!" she hisses. "Don't say anything. Just follow me after we cross Market."

Dylan continues onward and the woman stays behind her, even when she stops at the crosswalk. A few blocks down Market Street is the Twitter headquarters, the Uber headquarters, and the Square headquarters. Construction cranes lift metal and glass to fill the ribs and cross-sections of the new skyscrapers and luxury towers. The tallest of these buildings is the headquarters for BoonDoggle, the largest owner of commercial data in the world. The tower is curved and gray and shaped almost like a bullet with its massive glass windows reflecting the city.

The signal changes and the dark haired woman suddenly walks in front of Dylan. The woman is wearing tight black pants that shine under the sunlight and a dark green coat with its hood over her head. She has long nails painted bright red. Dylan follows, now enthralled and almost joyous at what's happening. The woman walks for two blocks, takes a left around the next corner, and then disappears behind a brick wall. Dylan hurries to catch up but doesn't run. She doesn't want to attract attention. When she looks behind no one is following, the sidewalk is empty, and once Dylan rounds the corner she finds the dark haired woman leaning against the red masonry wall of an old deli. Her eyes are lined with black pencil so she vaguely resembles a cat. Dylan doesn't know what to say. She just stands there with her hands inside her pockets.

And then there's a loud cough. An older man holding a beer can speaks to the brick wall. He tells the wall that it's not his fault, no one was there to press the button. The woman stares warmly at this old man, tightens her lips, takes some cigarettes out of her back pocket, and holds out an open pack of Newport's.

"You want one?" she asks him.

"Better get that helicopter," he says, instinctively pulling a cigarette out of the pack.

She flicks a purple Bic and lights it for him.

"Nothing but trouble in supermarkets, told him to get on," he says.

"Let's go," she says to Dylan, nodding down the street.

"That was nice of you."

"Nice?" She lights herself a cigarette and starts walking. "Yeah, I guess. Come on."

"So you knew Ricky?"

"I sure did."

They leave the man with his beer and walk down Turk Street into the Tenderloin. Dylan rarely goes this far past Market Street, although some of the men in the department often told stories in the common room about what they'd seen in the Tenderloin during their lunch breaks: people shitting on the pavement, shooting up on the street, selling themselves on the road, or offering to suck their cocks. It all sounded unpleasant to Dylan but it always made the men laugh when they talked about it.

"I like your jacket."

"Thanks," Dylan says, looking down at the pink leather.

"Do you have a phone?"

"No, I broke it. On accident. Why, do you need to use one?"

"No, no, it's just, you know—" She takes a drag and blows the smoke away. "A surveillance device. All smartphones are surveillance devices. For the government. And the corporations. Better not to have one."

"Yeah, well, I—"

"My name's Alexis."

"Nice to meet you," Dylan says. "How'd you know it was me?"

"Ricky showed me a picture of you once."

"Oh—"

"From your Instagram. He said if anything happened, I should find you. But to do it safe."

"If anything happened?"

"Look, listen." She takes another drag and then quickly blows it away. "I don't even know where to begin. You maybe want to get a drink or something? You hungry? It's lunch, right?"

"Sure, yeah, I could eat."

"Okay, there's this place up here." She points down the street and takes another frantic drag of her cigarette. "I'm sorry about springing this on you. I would've come sooner, but this is all kinda hard to believe. Plus, I had to be safe."

"From who?"

Alexis squints her eyes and takes another drag. The cigarette's almost gone.

"I'm not sure, really. It'll just sound insane. And it'll take a while. Come on, here it is."

They stop in front of a four-story building made of brown bricks. At the bottom level is a liquor store and beside it is Taqueria la Paz.

Alexis opens the door and stands with Dylan in front of steaming trays filled with beans and rice and meat. Behind them are four wooden tables pressed up against a tiled wall. Two of the tables are empty.

Dylan looks up at the menu and decides to get a wet super burrito with chicken and a large horchata. She asks Alexis what she wants and says she'll pay for everything. Alexis only wants three carne asada tacos, nothing else, not even a horchata. The woman at the cash register chews on a toothpick and smiles at Alexis as she takes their order. She has a gold canine tooth and a black tear drop tattooed at the corner of her eye. She talks with Alexis in Spanish for a moment and doesn't acknowledge Dylan, not even when she takes her money.

"She was flirting with me," Alexis says. "You couldn't tell?"

"I don't know."

They sit down at the table closest to the door and Alexis faces the street.

"Yeah, well, I bet she's looking at me right now."

"She is," Dylan tells her.

"Anyway." Alexis puts her elbows on the table and her cheeks in her palms. "Do you always wear those sunglasses?"

"No." Dylan takes them off and puts them on the table. "I forgot I had them on."

"You have nice eyes. Like my mom's."

"Thanks. So, I mean...can you—"

"Tell you what happened? To Ricky? No, I don't know what happened. All I know is he was scared when I saw him that night. The night he died."

"You saw him the night he died?"

"We met at this Airbnb I stay at sometimes, where I...it's complicated. Okay, so—"

"How did you know Ricky?"

"He was a client."

"Like a business client?" Dylan asks.

"No, come on, like...what? Me? No, he paid me to sleep with him. Sometimes he just needed a friend to talk with."

"This really isn't any of my—"

"It's fine, really. It doesn't matter. I've been doing it long enough to not care what you think. It's how I make $300 an hour. Four hundred.

Five hundred. Can you beat that? Nope. Anyway, *that's* how I know Ricky. He paid me, but I liked him."

"Is this where you work? In the Tenderloin?"

"Hell no!" Alexis squints and leans forward. "Are you crazy? The cops and nasty pimps control this place. No. I use Seeking Arrangement. That's how I met him a couple years ago. But me and Ricky only used the website once. I have an account on there, you know, to pick up older...it doesn't matter. But yeah, Ricky didn't want to use the website after the first time, he deactivated his account and I just charged him the usual."

"Three hundred dollars?"

"An hour. Yeah. But I always liked Ricky. I mean, I loved him, almost. It was never anything, though. A few times a month we'd meet at this Airbnb. That's where I saw him last, before he died. But we didn't sleep together that night. Like I said, he was scared. He kept talking about *if*, he kept saying *if*, like *if* anything happened to him I should find you. Then he told me what to do, where to wait for you, all the little details. But he wouldn't tell me what was going on. Then he gave me this—"

"*Cinquenta y ocho!*"

Alexis gets up quickly and walks over to the counter. She talks with the woman at the register in Spanish and leans close to the register. Both of them laugh loudly for a moment. Alexis returns with the food and Dylan feels embarrassed at having ordered so much. Next to her wet super burrito, Alexis' three tacos look modest or even humble.

"Damn, that thing's huge. You must be hungry."

"Yeah," Dylan mutters. "I'm hungry."

"Anyway." Alexis folds one of her tacos and eats half in a single bite. "I cried a lot, for like a whole day. But yeah, he gave me this thumb drive at the Airbnb that night. He said you'd know what to do with it. Does that make any sense?"

"I mean, no." Dylan looks at her burrito and picks up her fork. "No. I don't know about any thumb drive. I mean, I know how to open one on my computer."

Alexis looks at Dylan for a long moment. She holds her half eaten taco over the table and doesn't blink. It seems as if Alexis is waiting for something to flash through Dylan's eyes, some spark of recognition.

But whatever Alexis discovers is disappointing so she just finishes her taco while Dylan cuts herself a piece of the burrito and forces herself to eat. Once the food hits her mouth it tastes delicious and she cuts herself more with the plastic fork and knife.

"Well, I have the thumb drive hidden somewhere," Alexis says. "I didn't bring it."

"He didn't say what was on it?"

"No, just that you'd know what to do with it. I got scared so I stashed it. I don't know, maybe I should have gone and got it already. I'm scared to get it. Haven't been back there for over a week now. I left it in the Airbnb, I hid it somewhere safe. I was scared. I woke up there the next morning, you know, and then I just ended up lounging the whole day, and then I saw the news when I was changing channels so I hid the thumb drive and split."

Alexis shrugs her shoulders and eats another taco. Dylan is so overwhelmed with thoughts and questions that all she can do is concentrate on her burrito. Soon she's devoured half of the thick bundle smothered in red sauce and feels her stomach begin to tighten. Alexis quickly finishes her last tacos and leans back in her chair looking satisfied. There's a small streak of salsa stretching from the side of her mouth but Dylan doesn't say anything and Alexis doesn't notice, she just stares at the wet burrito.

"Gonna finish that?"

"No, want it?"

"Sure." Alexis pulls the plate in front of her and then smiles at Dylan. "I have to work in Santa Cruz all week, but maybe we could go to the Airbnb and get the thumb drive on Saturday. Would you want to come with me?"

"Yeah!" Dylan says, startling even herself. "Definitely I do."

"Cool. Thanks. I'm probably just being weird and paranoid, but it'd make me feel safer." Alexis cuts herself a piece of the burrito and starts eating it. "Was Ricky acting weird? At the office? During those last few days? Do you remember anything?"

"He was always leaving during lunch. As quickly as possible. And then he was gone a lot with no explanation. He was really busy, I remember that. He was taking the results from the mind games and trying to generate images for our advertisements."

"Ricky told me about that," Alexis says, finally wiping her mouth. "He said they brought in a few psychologists to help him or something."

"Psychologists?"

"That's what he said."

Alexis takes another large bite of the burrito and chews in silence with her eyes on Dylan. There's a long line out the door now and all of the tables in the taqueria are filled with customers. Dylan takes a long gulp of her horchata. Her back is covered in sweat.

"I never met any psychologists at the office," she says, putting down the styrofoam cup. "Ricky was good at coming up with ideas for the advertisements, and yeah, towards the end he did have a list of specific images—"

"That's it, yeah, the psychologists were helping him create images."

"I guess...yeah, he never told me about that. We were doing some complicated stuff, creating different advertisements for different regions based on what users in those regions fed into the mind games, stuff like that, but yeah, no psychologists, he never mentioned that."

"Ricky didn't like them, didn't trust them. He said your boss wasn't telling the truth about what they were doing with the data. I mean, the last dozen times I saw him, he was always bitter, talking about how racist everyone was, how we lived in a police state, like a dystopian science fiction story or something. He said everyone in the office was a zombie, but he liked you. He called you *güera*, you know, like saying good white lady, almost. It's one of those words that depends on the context. But, yeah, Ricky said you were the only one in the office who was down to earth."

"Down to earth," Dylan repeats, almost in a whisper.

"So I'm in town another day. You want to get a drink tonight?"

"Sure, yeah!" Dylan says, wrapping her fingers around the white cup.

Alexis smiles but doesn't say anything else. Taqueria la Paz is packed and the people waiting in line are loud and animated. The workers busily cook meat on the flat grill and warm tortillas and carry pots of rice from the burners to the steam trays. Every so often there's the old fashioned cling of the cash register and the sound of coins clattering against plastic. Alexis finishes the burrito and Dylan slowly sips on the pink straw of her large horchata. She doesn't know what time it is. There's no clock on the wall of Taqueria la Paz, none that she can see.

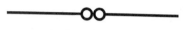

Dylan scans herself through the security gate at 1:07 pm. She's late for work and now an email will automatically alert Chad but Dylan doesn't care. All of her coworkers stare when she enters the common room but none of them speak. Dylan keeps her sunglasses on, sits down at her desk, and jolts her computer out of sleep. There's not even a whisper, nor the sound of a breath. She covers her ears with headphones, opens the browser, and starts her Taylor Swift mix on Youtube.

She checks her Facebook, her Twitter, her Instagram, and her Gmail. She discovers there's still much speculation on social media regarding the whereabouts of Bilton Smyth. A meme is circulating on Facebook that shows the CEO held captive inside a UFO with a cat in the stars asking *"the fuck you at bruh?"* On Twitter, a local author has publicly stated that she hopes Bilton Smyth jumps off the Golden Gate Bridge and that his body is eaten by sharks. On her Instagram, Dylan sees the image of a rose growing in the forest. In her Gmail, Dylan finds a new message from Chad explaining he'll be gone for the next several days. He says they can hold off on new ideas until the following Monday. He explains that he's really excited and wishes everyone a great week. He writes this to everyone and no one in particular.

At 1:34 pm, Dylan changes the photo on her Instagram account. She removes the image of herself wearing black sunglasses and replaces it with the image of a red rose. She positions the rose so its dark center dominates the frame. Dylan doesn't know why she does this. She only knows it pleases her. Once she's finished this simple task, Dylan stares blankly at her monitor and listens to Taylor Swift repeatedly ask, *"Are we out of the woods yet?"*

When the song ends, Dylan opens up Adobe and waits for her latest designs to load. It doesn't take very long and soon she's staring at the image of a digital teddy bear with an X in each eye. It's one of the 112 aggregate dream characters generated from the Childhood Memory

Game. Chad's last directive was to think big, just like last time, only to do it better. Dylan had taken his words literally. The last billboard contained ninety-seven game characters, so she increased the number to exactly 112. Any more characters would render the billboard visually unintelligible and repel the average viewer. She dreaded having to tell this to Chad, as he would most likely complain about her not thinking big enough, but now she didn't have to worry.

The teddy bear with an X in each eye is the latest character to be approved for use in the next billboard. Dylan stares at the teddy bear and feels nothing as it gazes back with expressionless eyes. She knows she must reduce the dimensions of the teddy bear, save the file, close it, open up the master billboard file, and then place the teddy bear image inside it. She knows this is what she must do, and yet she doesn't do it. She stares at the screen blankly and listens to Taylor Swift until 2:03 pm when she suddenly checks her Facebook, her Twitter, her Instagram, and her Gmail. Dylan idles away the next hour in this slow and circular manner, switching back and forth from Adobe to her Chrome browser without any clear reason or purpose.

When her coworkers begin to leave, Dylan doesn't look up from her monitor and keeps Taylor Swift playing at the maximum volume. At 3:10 pm, the common room is finally empty and Dylan shuts down her computer and packs up her headphones. On the way out, she looks at Chad's office and suddenly feels something pounding inside her chest. It's only when she's alone in the elevator that Dylan realizes what she actually feels: hatred towards Chad, her coworkers, OingoBoingo, and the stupid teddy bear with an X in each eye.

The elevator doors open and she walks out with determination, desperate to leave this glass building. In her haste, she bumps into a techie and nearly knocks him over into a potted plant. He says something indignant but she doesn't listen and keeps walking. At 3:17 pm, she leaves OingoBoingo headquarters and begins to run down the sidewalk of Mission Street in her pink designer leather moto-jacket and black sunglasses. She runs, frantic with rage, and stops only for red lights at the crosswalk. She sprints past dozens of homeless people lying on cardboard sheets or draped in sleeping bags or begging for change on the gray pavement. Their pants are dirty, their jackets are old, and their skin reveals every ravage of the streets.

And then she runs past pricey restaurants with packed tables and heat lamps and wine glasses and white table cloths. All of them have nice watches, expensive shoes, and perfect haircuts. None of the people at these restaurants think Dylan is crazy when she flies by, no matter how sweaty she becomes. Her clothes are far too tasteful, her bag is far too nice, her sunglasses far too fashionable. It's almost as if she isn't there.

Dylan enters the Vermillion at 3:56 pm. She's sweaty from having run all the way from SOMA and sheds her bag and clothing on the way to the bathroom. For the next thirty-two minutes, Dylan stands in the shower and takes long breaths of steamy air. Under the stream of water, she thinks about her coworkers and clenches her fists. This tension lasts until she remembers Alexis and feels excitement, happiness, even joy for a moment. But then she thinks of Ricky, how he's dead, how Chad isn't in the office, and how Bilton Smyth is missing. None of it makes any sense. She can hardly contemplate the nuances without wanting to vomit. Only the prospect of meeting Alexis for drinks calms her down. It reminds her to wash her hair, scrub her body, and turn off the water.

At 4:37 pm, she walks out of the bathroom in a towel and grabs her bag from the living room floor. She takes it into her bedroom, sits down at her computer desk, and searches inside for the receipt with Alexis' number. She tapes it to her computer monitor and then gazes at it for a few minutes. Her eyes dart back and forth from the phone number to the gold locket, from the digits to her image, from the paper to the metal.

Dylan and Alexis decided to get drinks in the Mission before they parted at Taqueria la Paz, although they didn't decide where. Alexis told her to call from a payphone whenever she was ready. She said not to worry, that her cellphone was a burner and not connected to her identity. She reminded Dylan not to use their real names, no matter what.

Dylan dresses in front of the mirror and puts on shiny black pants and a black long-sleeve turtleneck. He coworkers called her Steve Jobs whenever she wore this turtleneck to the office. It used to make her laugh, although now she can't stand the thought of looking them in the eye. She still looks good in the black turtleneck, especially when she wears the silver designer leather moto-jacket over it. Dylan takes another look in the mirror, smiles at herself, and returns to the bathroom to put on makeup. She stands barefoot on the white floor mat and puts on mascara, blue eye shadow, and eye liner. After thinking about it for a moment, Dylan puts on blue lipstick.

At 5:07 pm, she sits down on the side of her bed to put on a pair of thin black socks. She gazes at the gold metal locket, thinks of Ricky and his sisters, and slowly pulls the first sock up to her ankle. She sits there for an entire minute with one bare foot crossed over her knee, a limp sock in her hand, and her eyes fixed on the locket. It's 5:15 pm when she finally puts on the second sock, gets up from her bed, takes off her jacket, and turns on the computer. She checks her Facebook, her Twitter, her Instagram, and her Gmail. She finds nothing interesting in any of these mediums, nor does she find anything on the tech blogs. She sees images of the forest, hiking trails, waterfalls, and vacations on the beach. Nothing motivates her to read. All she can do is glance at the cascade of words and images, hoping something will spark her interest but ultimately nothing does.

At 5:31 pm, she sets her computer to sleep, takes her bag into the living room, and steps into a pair of black Adidas under the coat rack. She puts on her silver Japanese designer leather moto-jacket, slings her bag over her shoulder, and runs back to her bedroom for a final glance in the mirror. Dylan looks exactly as she desires to look, impervious and precise. She snatches Alexis' phone number off the monitor and then kisses it, leaving a solid blue lipstick mark. Dylan surprises herself so much with this sudden act that she needs to catch her breath and calm her heart before leaving the apartment.

Dylan calls Alexis from the payphone at the corner of 24th and Mission at 6:17 pm. They agree to meet inside the nearby McDonald's at 6:30 pm but will go somewhere else afterwards. Dylan walks into the fast food restaurant, orders a coffee, and sits in a booth by the window. She looks outside and sees a young man in black jean-shorts and a black t-shirt peddle up to the curb, lock his bike to the post, and walk into the McDonald's. He has a silver and black waterproof backpack over his shoulder. He doesn't take off his helmet when he gets in line. He stares at his smartphone until he reaches to the register and by the time he orders a young woman with an identical backpack is in line behind him. They're both bike couriers who deliver food from restaurants to luxury apartment dwellers like Dylan.

The couriers talk to each other after they order, share amusing images on their smartphones, and when his number is called the young man stuffs five Happy Meals into the waterproof bag. The two couriers laugh about the bizarre delivery, say something about techies, and hug each other before parting ways. While she's watching this interaction, Alexis slides into the opposite side of the booth wearing the same outfit from earlier.

"Hi!" Dylan nearly shouts.

"Sorry I'm late. So where you want to go?"

"There's a sports bar just down the street we can—"

"Yeah, I know it. We can go there. The Irish bar?"

"It's cheapish, not really a—"

"Hipster techie bar?" Alexis laughs and then steps on Dylan's toe. "Just kidding."

"I'm not a techie."

"I'm just kidding," she repeats. "I know. You went to art school, right?"

"Yeah, I went to Risdee?"

"What the fuck's that?" Alexis asks.

"The Rhode Island School of Design."

"Is that like an Ivy League or something?"

Dylan suddenly looks down at her thighs and begins to feel sad, disconnected.

"Not really," she says. "No, it's not. The founders of Airbnb went there, though."

The smell of french fries and oil and meat fill the air-conditioned room. A woman wheels a cart of clothing and blankets into the McDonald's before she gets in line. Very few people speak besides the ones ordering food. Most of the noise comes from behind the counter where the employees give orders to each other through the headsets underneath their red hats.

"So you wanna go?" Alexis asks.

"Sure, yeah." Dylan looks up and smiles. "I'm just exhausted."

"I know. I haven't been sleeping much either. This is creepy shit. It's heavy."

They get up from the plastic table and walk out of the McDonald's where the streets are crowded with commuters coming and going from the brick entrances of the BART station. Merchants cook hot dogs and chopped meat and onions atop little rolling grills set up on the edge of the sidewalk. Others sell pirated movies atop colorful rugs spread across the pavement or stand behind metal carts and wait for customers to buy plastic cups of freshly cut pineapple, mango, and watermelon. Dylan and Alexis walk away from this bustle down 24th into its endless cathedral of trees. Dylan finds this street to be the most pleasant in the entire neighborhood, so bright with murals and green leaves and market produce of every color.

"I hope I don't run into Bernadette," Dylan says.

"Who's Bernadette?"

"Nothing, just—" She rolls her eyes at herself and shakes her head. "A coworker."

"Oh, yeah? Those people kind of suck, huh?"

"She lives down the street. I just hope we don't run into her."

Dylan realizes Alexis has stopped walking and now there's something in her mouth. It isn't a cigarette, it looks more like a cigar, and when Alexis lights it there's the sharp and unmistakable odor of marijuana. Dylan follows her into a tree-lined parking lot where the walls are covered in murals that stand ten feet tall. Directly above her rises the Virgin of Guadalupe, radiant and beautiful, her hands clasped together in devotion. This image makes Dylan smile.

"You want some?" Alexis asks.

"I better not."

"I think you better. Trust me, this'll help you get clear in the head."

Dylan takes it, puts the blunt to her lips, and lightly drags on it. The smoke tastes like peaches and makes her nostrils tingle. She holds the smoke in her lungs, hands the blunt back, and begins to cough so fiercely she's unable to open her eyes as the world starts to spin. Alexis laughs at all this, takes a long drag, and blows the smoke towards the trees growing out of the sidewalk.

"You alright?" she asks.

"I forgot it's wrapped in tobacco," Dylan says, voice hoarse. "I'm fine."

"You don't smoke weed often, huh?"

"No, I just drink socially. I don't really do anything. I drink coffee, I guess."

"Everyone drinks coffee. Want some more?"

"Sure."

She tries again, taking a smaller drag and not holding it in for so long. It feels bitter and harsh, her nostrils tingle with peach, but when Dylan hands it back she begins to feel the effects. Now the Virgin is clearly the most beautiful figure on the wall, her colors so bright it feels as if the warm air of the early evening were emanating from her painted lips. Every green leaf begins to sing and hum, so loud she can no longer hear the traffic rushing down 24th Street.

"It's really fucked up about Ricky. Someone fucking killed him."

Dylan's heart begins to race, she can't stop it.

"It's not—"

"He didn't kill himself. No way, not a chance." Alexis takes a furious drag and blows a large cloud of smoke through the parking lot. "This is fucked."

Dylan stares at Alexis with a vacant expression, unsure if she can even speak. Her tongue feels like a deflated balloon stuck at the base of her mouth. There's now so much weed smoke in the air someone might mistake it for a fire. It spreads in long gray tendrils and swirls above the sidewalk and through the branches of the trees.

"Should we go inside?" Dylan asks.

"Don't get paranoid. Just enjoy it. Forget what I said. You come to this bar a lot?"

"I mean, sometimes—"

"Seriously, forget I said anything. Just try and relax. I mean, really, what are we supposed to do? Like, we're the only ones who know about this, aside from those psychologists and your boss or whoever. What are we supposed to do? Anyway, this is good weed, right?"

"It's strong."

"It keeps me going. I've been talking a mile a minute, I swear—"

Alexis takes an even deeper, more frantic drag off the blunt, burning it down almost half an inch. The cloud of smoke she releases is immense and while it disperses into the air Dylan notices a blue lowrider drift by on the street. Two bald-headed men in black sunglasses nod in their direction. Both of them smile like devils. Dylan doesn't know what to think.

Dylan and Alexis sit down at the U-shaped bar in a corner by the window where no one can bother them. When she sets her butt down on the stool, Dylan is still paranoid. She remains silent while Alexis makes a few jokes with the bartender, a young Irish woman with bags under her eyes who talks about her work visa, her lack of sleep, and her desire for the night to be over. Dylan hands the bartender her Chase credit card and opens a tab for them, barely able to verbalize the sentences necessary for the transaction. Alexis insists they order two pints of Guinness and when it arrives she clinks her glass against Dylan's, takes a large swig of the dark stout, and burps loudly.

All of this makes Dylan feel more at ease. No one seems to care that Alexis is being so loud, and it's unlikely they'd care about Dylan being stoned. The bar fills with baseball fans who line up at the bar before taking their drinks into the back room to play pool and watch the television screen. Alexis begins to ask basic, biographical questions and listens as Dylan quietly explains how she came to live in San Francisco. She tells Alexis about the Rhode Island School of Design, what her classmates were like, what the parties were like, how her grades were perfect, and how her dad's friend got her the job at OingoBoingo.

"You mean right out of grad school?" Alexis asks. "How old are you?"

"Twenty-five."

"You look older. Not in a bad way, though. Like, I look older too, don't I?"

"You look like, I don't know, you look—"

"You look stoned," Alexis says, laughing. "I'm just kidding, you don't look stoned."

"You look maybe thirty."

"Thirty! Hell no! I'm not thirty, I'm twenty-six! But seriously, no, I look older, huh?"

"I can't tell anymore."

They keep talking and Alexis asks for two more pints of Guinness. When the bartender returns, Dylan tries to ask for water but her voice is too soft and the woman doesn't hear so Alexis yells and soon enough they have two glasses of water filled with ice. Dylan drinks it as quickly as possible and begins chewing on the cubes while Alexis talks about her own past. She grew up in a desert town called Mojave, about two hours east of Los Angeles. Alexis was still in high school when she ran away to live with her cousin in Pasadena. She wanted to work in the movies but all she could find was porn, endless advertisements for porn, and doing that stuff for too long just made her depressed. It was easier to make money recording herself on a web cam. All she had to do was sit there naked on her bed and do what the men on the internet asked for on the little feed ticking away at the right side of the screen.

Alexis explains how she got into doing sex-work through the internet. It wasn't any worse than what her horrible boyfriends had done to her and most of the men were harmless and paid $300 an hour. Sometimes they'd pay just to have dinner. They bought her jewelry and computers and appliances and even books sometimes. She once received $10,000 to spend a weekend in a beach house with some old man. Alexis usually smoked so much weed with these clients that they fell asleep, none of them could keep up with her, and in the morning they paid happily, claiming it was the best time of their lives.

"What do you do with the money?" Dylan asks.

"What do *you* do with *your* money?"

"I don't know. Buy this jacket."

"I just stay happy. I pay the bills. I used to help out with some shit but, I don't—"

"What shit?"

"I'd help some of my friends, that's all. But I don't know where they are now."

"What do you mean?"

"They don't have Facebook. They don't have phones. They're probably in the woods or something. I don't know, I got into smack after they left, but I'm clean now. That's the worst right there, death spiral if there ever was one, combo from hell. That's when they got you by the ass, when you're strung out on *their* drugs and working *their* system."

"I'm glad you're clean."

Dylan grabs Alexis' hand and holds it. She feels at once protective and desirous, filled with both longing and admiration. Without any warning, Alexis kisses Dylan on the lips. Her body is sweaty and warm. Her mouth tastes like sugar. Dylan closes her eyes and lets it happen. She knows this is good. She isn't very drunk. She trusts her instincts. But then she hears men heckling them, making noises, saying things like *grab* and *pussy*, and Alexis suddenly stands up.

"Go talk to your mother like that, you fuck!"

Dylan focuses her eyes and sees the men. They're all dressed identically. They look like people from OingoBoingo, although she isn't sure. Only one of them has brown hair, the others are all blonde. They wear dark jeans and button down shirts and their smiles look repulsive. Something like possession then happens. Dylan has no control over it. She grabs her nearly full pint glass and hurls it across the barpit. The beer leaves the glass, travels in a perfect arc, and hits one of them in the chest, staining his shirt a dark brown color.

And then the entire bar erupts. Everyone is yelling. Dylan finds herself scrambling around the bar towards the men with Alexis at her side. They both scream insults and curses. They promise to kill the men. They try to run at them, to hit them with their fists, but they're held back and pulled towards the door. Before they're thrown outside, Dylan sees the men looking pathetic and scared, as if their lives had just been threatened.

"Alright! Get the fuck off!" Alexis screams at the bouncer. "Get the *fuck* off!"

"Let us go!"

"You two better get the fuck out of here quick," the bouncer says, pushing them both away. "Those techies called the cops."

"Come on!"

Alexis grabs Dylan's hand and they run towards Mission Street. When they get to the BART station, an SFPD cruiser speeds around the corner and fills the street with blue and red strobe lights. From the stairs, they hear the sound of an approaching train so they sprint down to the station, run through the emergency exit without paying, and make it onto the platform just as the doors for the eastbound Pittsburgh train close shut. They breathe heavily, laugh in exhaustion, and begin to kiss as the curious passengers stare at them. Dylan feels the weight of Alexis' breasts pressing against her own. She tastes her sweat, her tongue, and her saliva. It only makes her want more. They don't let go of each other until the train stops at the 16th Street station and Dylan pulls her onto the platform.

"Where we going?" Alexis asks.

"My place."

"You live around here?"

Dylan suddenly feels ashamed. She doesn't know how to answer, she only manages to nod and silently climb the stairs with Alexis' hand in her own. They run through the emergency exit without paying and bolt up the escalator. Dylan is surprised at how easy it is. She's never tried not to pay.

They leave the station and walk past a long row of men drinking in the shadows, listening to music, and smoking cigarettes. A few talk to themselves. Some of them sit on plastic milk crates. None of them say anything to Dylan and Alexis. A few of them smile.

"So you're inviting me in?" Alexis asks. "For a sleep over?"

"Uh-huh. You can borrow my toothbrush."

"You ever been with a girl before?"

"No. Have you?"

Alexis squeezes her hand and smiles.

"What do you think?"

Dylan notices a small patch of acne on Alexis' cheek and sees dried skin hanging on her lip. She stops walking and gently bites this piece of dry flesh. She holds Alexis and breathes her scent. She feels every inch of her back until Alexis pushes her away. Her green eyes are brilliant and outshine the darkness of the street. Dylan's in love. She knows it.

"So where do you live?" Alexis asks.

"Up there."

Dylan points at the glass and metal building. It looks monstrous to her now, especially when Alexis says nothing. They stare for a moment at the four stories of identical cubes that reflect the street light. Each story holds ten apartments, each apartment has four windows, and each window is framed with silver metal. The lights are on in each unit, a screen is glowing behind every window, and there's no evidence of children. From where she stands, the building appears empty, inhabited only by electricity and the flicker of flatscreens. It makes Dylan sad, truly sad, and she begins to cry.

"What's wrong?"

"I'm so lost," Dylan says. "I don't know what's happening."

"Me neither." Alexis holds her, tighter than before. "I don't know what the fuck's going on."

Dylan eventually stops crying and beeps them in with her key fob. They climb the stairs slowly and sway into each other with every step. They are quickly in bed, their clothes are on the floor, their skin breathes together, and Dylan experiences something she's never experienced in her adult life: she finally feels human.

CHAPTER 4

ALEXIS IS GONE WHEN DYLAN WAKES UP. SHE SEARCHES THE APART-
ment but it's completely empty. There's only a red lipstick mark on the
mirror with a note taped next to it that reads: *Call me on Friday from
a payphone. Remember to stay safe and be calm. Don't use real names.
Try to relax.* The word *love* is in all capital letters at the bottom of the
paper with a big letter *A* written next to it. There's also a heart with
two lines drawn in the upper corner to make it look shiny.

At 8:31 am, Dylan turns on her computer, waits for everything to
load, and then sends an email to Chad and the rest of the department.
Dylan explains she has the flu and will not be coming in to work until
she can walk again. She sends it to their Gmail accounts and waits
for a response. At 8:33 am, she receives an automated message from
Chad explaining he will be unavailable until the end of the week.
Dylan thinks about sending an email directly to HR, stares blankly at
the monitor for a moment, and then decides it isn't worth it. Chad is
the only one who's supposed to report her absence, and if he's absent
himself there will be no report to HR. She stays at the desk with her
hand on the mouse, unsure of what to do next. As the minutes go by,
her inbox fills with one new email after the other. Each of her coworkers sends her a message, they tell her to feel better, to get well, and to
feel better soon. Some of them even put <3 symbols at the end or an
XOXOXO. It makes Dylan feel ill, so she goes into the bathroom and
takes a shower.

At 9:04 am, when she's officially absent from work, Dylan emerges
from the bathroom in her towel and walks to the kitchen. She eats a
bowl of granola with yogurt, has a banana, and then makes coffee with
her small French-press. It wakes her up, quickens her heart, and she
returns to her computer desk at 9:22 am with the cup in her hand. She
goes through the tech blogs and her social media feed for any news
about OingoBoingo or its CEO but finds nothing, no matter how far
down she scrolls. Dylan is about to check her email when she sees a
headline posted on her Twitter feed that reads: *Tech Offices Filled
With Bros, Bathrooms Filled With Tears.* She clicks on the article and

reads about a new survey conducted in Silicon Valley. She discovers that a majority of women in tech never report sexual harassment. They view it as normal.

Dylan scrolls back up to find the author's name. The article is written by a woman named Natasha Malevich and was posted at 9:12 am. It's the main feature on the home page of Chumby, a local website that Dylan checks regularly. She clicks on the author's picture of Natasha Malevich and stares at it for a few minutes. Natasha is in her twenties. She has long dark hair, brown skin, and holds a cherry in front of her nose that makes her look cross-eyed.

At 9:41 am, while she's staring at this picture, Dylan suddenly closes her Chrome browser, shuts off the computer, and then gets into her clothes. She puts on a simple black dress, leather boots with flat heels, and throws on her silver Japanese designer leather moto-jacket. At 9:53 am, she leaves her building and waits for the Muni bus to arrive. Without her smartphone, Dylan has no idea when it will come. She stands there on the sidewalk, leans against a pole, and crosses her feet at her ankles. She thinks about Alexis, she thinks about Ricky, and once again she's possessed by rage. Dylan sees the OingoBoingo building consumed in flames, she sees the glass turn black, she watches it shatter, and then the bus arrives. It's far less crowded at this time of the morning.

There's no one on board that she recognizes so she walks to the back and sits down by the window. On the seat in front of her are the words *DIE TECHIE SCUM* written in black sharpie. Beside this is the phrase *BURN EVERYTHING DOWN* written in pink marker. Dylan reads these words over and over again. These words are real. They have always been real. Only now does she realize this.

She looks up at the other passengers and begins to smile. They're mostly students and people in their work uniforms, although a few have Twitter or BoonDoggle badges clipped to their belt loops. Most of these passengers wear uniforms for hotels, parking lots, restaurants, cafes, or are simply going to school in their normal clothes. Dylan never rides the bus this late, she never sees these people going to work. All she's ever seen are people like herself.

Dylan leans back in her seat and covers her mouth as the bus passes OingoBoingo headquarters. No one familiar gets on board and the bus barrels onward down Mission Street. She pulls the cord several blocks later and gets off in front of a five-story building made of metal and glass. Above the front entrance is a green electric neon sign that spells the word CHUMBY. It blinks on and off at irregular intervals, as if it were broken.

Dylan pushes open the glass doors and walks through the neon green lobby towards a woman behind a green desk. The woman has blonde hair, black-rimmed glasses, and wears a blue business suit. She scrolls through her smartphone and doesn't look up until Dylan is in front of her. Even then she's reluctant.

"Good morning," she mutters.

"I need to speak with Natasha Malevich," Dylan says. "Is she—"

"You said her last name right."

"How else would I say it?"

"Mal-a-vick. That's what everyone else calls her."

"Oh."

"Yeah, go ahead. She's on the third floor. The elevator's right there."

Dylan smiles and runs to catch the doors before they close. There are two men talking to each other in the elevator but they ignore her and start whispering. Dylan doesn't look at them, nor can she hear what they say, and she gets off the elevator before they do.

The third floor is a maze of transparent cubicles with two large offices in the rear. Through the plexi-glass, she can see that most of the employees are men. Each cubicle has a name written by the entrance and Dylan zig-zags through the office until she finds Natasha Malevich in front of her computer scrolling through a Twitter feed.

"Natasha?"

"Yeah?" she asks, not turning around.

Dylan sees a pen on the desk so she picks it up and starts writing on the nearest piece of paper. Natasha turns around, starts to say something, but then sees what Dylan is writing and leans closer. She squints her eyes at first but then her entire face lights up. Dylan takes her OingoBoingo badge from her jacket pocket, lets Natasha look at it for a moment, and then puts it away.

"Want to meet for lunch?" Natasha asks, taking the pen.

"Sure, yeah, definitely."

Natasha writes down the name of a bar in North Beach, waits for Dylan to nod, then crumples the paper and puts it in her pocket.

"Cool, well I'll see you at the Starbucks. At noon?"

"Sounds good. See you."

"Bye."

Natasha smiles as if she's just won the lottery and Dylan leaves the Chumby office feeling confident. She says goodbye to the woman at the front desk and then walks across the Financial District towards the Transamerica pyramid. The skyscrapers tower over her in every direction, thick wisps of steam rise out of the sewer system, and the streets are congested with Ubers, Lyfts, and yellow taxis. Bike couriers weave through the traffic, pigeons flutter above the passing cars, and the air is filled with the smell of engine exhaust. Dylan passes a clock outside of a Well Fargo bank that reads 11:03 am and when she reaches North Beach the air smells fresh again. There are trees growing out of the sidewalk, there's more space between the buildings, and Dylan can see the sky.

She walks into City Lights Bookstore, smiles at the man behind the cash register, and begins to pace through the fiction section. Dylan hasn't read a novel for nearly a year. She finished *Anna Karenina* when she went on vacation alone at a rented cabin in Point Reyes. Since then, she's only been reading her smartphone or a computer screen. Dylan liked *Anna Karenina* but it made her so depressed she ended her vacation early and went home without a refund.

After scanning through the shelves, she stops in the Italian section and grabs a copy of *The Unseen* by Nanni Ballestrini. It has a black and white image of masked protesters on the cover, the description says the book is about the Italian political struggles of the 1970s, and she holds onto it as she keeps pacing across the bookstore. In the end, she can find nothing else and takes the book up to the cash register. At 11:47 am, she uses her Chase credit card to purchase *The Unseen*.

"That's one of my favorite books ever," the cashier tells her.

"I've never heard of him."

"Did someone tell you about it?"

"No, I just found it. I guess I watched the Baader-Meinhof movie recently, so—"

"Right, yeah. It's similar to that, sort of. But he does interesting things with time. And there's no punctuation. The dialogue and descriptions are all mashed together in these block paragraphs. You'll see, I hope you like it. There's been a lot of interest in Italian stuff lately."

"Well, I'm happy to help."

The man smiles and stands at the register as if he's waiting for something. He's very nice. He's tall and skinny and wears all black. He clearly wants her number or email. But that isn't something Dylan wants so she takes the book from the counter, thanks him for his help, and walks across the street to the Vesuvio Cafe.

At 11:51 am, she uses her Chase credit card to order a Bloody Mary and then takes it upstairs. The upper level is shaped in a circle with a central well that looks down at the bar. All of the wall space is covered in framed photographs, paintings, and old advertisements. She sits at a table by the window and stares out at the corner of Broadway and Columbus. From here, Dylan can see people coming in and out of City Lights Books. Much to her surprise, many of them are leaving with paper bags filled with books.

"Hi there."

It's Natasha, still smiling like a millionaire.

"Thanks for coming," Dylan says.

"Sure. Little early for drinky, isn't it?"

"I just got it because there's vegetables in it."

"*Right*. I'm sure you're not hung over or anything like that." Natasha pulls out a chair and sits down across from her. "Who knows? Maybe we'll need it later, depending on what you've got to tell. I have to say, it's not every day an actual employee walks into Chumby."

"There's a lot to tell you."

Natasha takes off her black leather jacket, removes a notebook from her bag, and clicks a pen underneath her thumb. She smells like lavender, her wavy hair is pitch black, and she has to bite her lip to keep from smiling. Dylan likes her.

"So?"

"So." Dylan leans forward on the table and stirs her drink with a piece of celery. "I've worked at OingoBoingo for almost two years."

"What do you do?"

"I'm in the advertising department. I've been designing the billboards."

"Yeah. I've seen them, they're everywhere."

"Yeah, so that's what I do."

"And you want to tell me about sexual harassment at OingoBoingo?"

"Yes."

So she begins to tell Natasha about Chad and how he flirted with her coworker Elizabeth. At first he would just rub her back or grab her thigh in the middle of a conversation. Elizabeth would complain about it but when he invited her to a party at his house in the Marina she accepted. She later told Dylan that Chad probably raped her when she passed out that night. Elizabeth woke up naked in his bed, Chad was in the shower, and she left before he got out. The next week, Chad approved a raise she'd been waiting for. He stopped touching her after that. By then, he'd begun to push his affection on Bernadette.

"I mean—" Natasha put her pen down. "Just...being honest, this is all fucking depressingly normal. Not that it...whatever. You know what I mean?"

"I think so."

"Unless your friend—"

"Elizabeth."

"Unless Elizabeth is willing to come forward with this, it's just an allegation. You think she'd ever do that? No, of course not. Why am I even asking?"

"Yeah, I don't know."

"So what happened with Bernadette? The same thing?"

"At a different house though. Someone from Dropbox. He invited her over there, she passed out, and when she woke up everyone was having breakfast. That was the part that really disgusted me. She never understood why. She was so disoriented she just ate with them, drank coffee, then when she got home, that's when she realized what happened."

Natasha shakes her head. Down below, a group of loud tourists enter the cafe. Dylan watches four people with gray hair amble up to the bar and interrogate the bartender about the historical relevance of the Vesuvio. Natasha rapidly clicks the button on her pen and stares at Dylan with hollow eyes. The bartender spins stories for the tourists.

"Again, I'm not trying to be cruel, but this is all normal," Natasha says. "Unless they make an allegation, it's just the words of one employee. What about the other women in the office?"

"That's all of them, besides me."

Natasha blinks once. She puts her pen down on her notebook and takes a deep breath. She stares at Dylan until they seem to understand each other. Dylan thinks Natasha's brown eyes are very beautiful and her dark hair looks nice. She's glad she followed her instinct.

"How did you avoid all that?" Natasha asks her. "How did *you* avoid Chad's advances?"

"I stepped away whenever he touched me. And I never talked to him about anything other than work. He's never really liked me anyway, and he knew that I knew about what he did to them."

"Why'd they go with him?"

"I don't know. But they did."

"You three are the *only* women in the department?"

"That's right."

Natasha frowns and begins drawing a spiral in her notebook.

"I'll write it. I know how to write it. Like I said, it's all normal. This is all utterly normal. And it's good advice in general. Step away whenever they touch you. Don't speak to them. It's just so—"

"Depressing?"

"Listen, you need to tell me something. What's going on at OingoBoingo? I mean, I gotta be honest, that's where I was hoping this would lead. Where's Bilton Smyth? Where did he go? I mean, is this some Ayn Rand publicity stunt?"

"I have no idea. I saw him in the elevator last week, but since then, I haven't heard anything. But the thing is, Chad's gone. He's gone. I even sent him an email today, saying I was sick. It bounced back to me with an automatic message, saying he'll be gone until Monday."

"He didn't say why?"

"No. He left right after Ricky died."

"I'm sorry that happened. Did you know him?"

"He was my friend, yeah. But—"

Natasha leans forward, smiling again.

"Yes?"

"I don't think he killed himself. Listen, that...can we—"

"Yes, totally, let's go back to the original topic. Totally. So I think it's best we have no one's name in the story. I'll have to get someone to snoop around and make sure Dylan Kinsey really works at

OingoBoingo, but assuming that's all good, I'll have it ready for Friday. I trust you, it's just that I have to make sure you work there. It's for the boss, so he knows we won't get burned."

"They'll protect my identity?"

"He has before. It's in his interest. It *builds* his reputation to have *his* writers protect their sources." Natasha leans back in her chair and briefly looks down at the bar. "That's kind of like our life blood here, you know? It's all we have, really."

"No, I get it. But will your boss let you post it?"

"Definitely, yeah. Its direct from OingoBoingo. Listen, did you pay for that drink with a card?"

"Yeah, is that—"

"It's good I didn't buy anything then, eh? No, take out a bunch of cash, don't give them any more data, and *don't* use your card. And just so you know, I don't have my smartphone, but I do have this." Natasha takes a slim metal recording device out of her jacket pocket and turns it off. "It's for my notes only. It doesn't connect to the internet. I'll erase it all when my story's finished. Do you trust me?"

"I do. I knew it from your picture."

"How?"

"I don't know."

"Can we meet again, then?" Natasha asks. "How about Monday? After the fallout?"

"Just tell me where."

"You know, if everyone were like you we might have some idea what the fuck's going on in this place." Natasha tears some paper from her notebook and writes something on it. "Are you from here originally?"

"I'm from Connecticut."

"Ah, I see." Natasha hands her the piece of paper and smiles. "This is the place. Just make sure you aren't followed when you meet me. Okay? But, like, *actually* make sure you aren't followed."

"I will." Dylan puts the paper in her jacket pocket. "Are you from here?"

"Nope. I'm from Orlando."

"Are you Cuban?"

"Wow, look at Dylan. You know how many people ask me what race I am? *Everybody*. At some point, they might wait a week or a month, but eventually they ask, always in the same tone. Like, they pause before saying *race*, always. But yeah, I'm from Cuba. My dad's a white Russian, my mom's black Cuban. And here I am. By the way, that book right there is amazing, speaking of my dad. He gave it to me when I was in college. So good. Sad though."

"Really sad?"

"I'd say so. The only hope is in the fact you're even reading it."

"What do you mean?"

"It means someone survived to tell the story. That's all."

Dylan looks down at the bar and the people silently cradling their drinks. It reminds her of being alone in her apartment. The Bloody Mary drips condensation, the celery stands inert inside the glass, and Dylan cannot form another thought. So she picks up the glass and takes a long drink of the spiced tomato juice. The alcohol hits her stomach and makes her feel awake and alert. Without saying anything, Natasha takes the glass from her hand and then gulps down almost half of it. She takes the celery out of the glass, lets it drip for a moment, and takes a bite off the green stalk. Natasha chews loudly, crunches the celery with her teeth, and stares at Dylan the whole time. She doesn't stop grinning.

At 2:05 pm, Dylan goes to the Chase Bank on Grant Avenue and inserts her card into the ATM. For a few moments, Dylan looks directly into the surveillance camera mounted above the screen. She withdraws $2000 from her checking account and the machine dispenses twenty $100 bills. She puts them in her wallet, looks down the street in both directions, and notices how each skyscraper is covered in surveillance cameras. This realization makes her uncomfortable so she quickly walks away from the ATM and heads toward Market Street.

She catches a bus heading south and sits in the back seat beside a window. Dylan doesn't open her book, nor does she look at it, she just watches the metal and glass buildings stream by her vision. She sees the homeless pushing their belongings in shopping carts and men driving expensive sports cars down Mission Street. Every dark-haired woman she sees on the sidewalk instantly becomes Alexis. But these appearances always happen too fast for her to be certain. The bus rolls into the Mission, and she sees her lover on every street and down every alley.

At 2:39 pm, Dylan uses the key fob to enter her building and climbs the stairs to her apartment. She closes the steel door behind her, stands perfectly still, and listens to the ambient sounds: the air vents, the refrigerator, the hum of electricity, all of it's familiar. She goes into her bedroom, turns on the lights, turns on the desktop computer, and then tries to calm down. While everything is loading, Dylan sits on her bed and smiles at the mirror, the lipstick mark, and the note. She reads it again just to be sure it's real and that what happened last night actually took place.

Dylan spends the next three hours on the internet. She checks her Facebook, her Twitter, her Instagram, and her Gmail. There are several dozen emails from the department about the new ad campaign but she doesn't open them. None of these emails are from Chad. None of them are from HR. No one seems to notice she's gone. On her Facebook wall, she sees the department has sent their best wishes and hopes. None of them write more than a sentence. They've sent hearts and smiley faces and several other emojis at the bottom of their messages. One of them is a red devil head sticking out its tongue. Dylan doesn't know what it means.

On her feeds, she sees multiple articles about Bilton Smyth and OingoBoingo. One of them is from a writer at Chumby. She clicks on this article and sees the image of a tweet posted an hour earlier. It contains a picture taken from outside a fancy restaurant in Geneva, Switzerland and shows Bilton Smyth eating dinner with an unidentified blonde woman. It was taken earlier this evening.

Dylan reads every article on the absent CEO until she eventually exhausts them all. By then she's starving and goes to the kitchen and starts boiling quinoa. She chops up broccoli and garlic and onions, pulls a bag of potato chips from the cupboard, and stands in the middle of the kitchen eating chip after chip with her eyes fixed on the stove. She covers the pot when it starts to boil, puts the burner on low, and then stir-fries the vegetables. Once everything is done she piles it all into a bowl, sits down at the counter, and begins to eat. Only when the food is gone does Dylan realize how peaceful she feels, how content her body is.

She spends the rest of the night reading *The Unseen* on her living room couch. She leans back on the pillows and covers herself in a blanket. She gets up twice, once to get more potato chips, once to get a tub of ice cream. Over the course of the evening she reads seventy pages. The narrative goes back and forth in time, alternating between past and present, between prison and freedom. There's no punctuation and the sentences of each paragraph all run together. The story moves quickly, it keeps her engaged, but eventually she closes her eyes, the book falls to her lap, and Dylan is asleep.

CHAPTER 5

DYLAN WAKES UP AT 8:30 AM WITHOUT AN ALARM. SHE'S STILL ON THE couch with the book in her hands. She doesn't remember any of her dreams. The desktop computer has been on all night and she wakes it from sleep mode at 8:37 am. She sends another email to Chad and the rest of the department. She informs them she's still sick, still bedridden, and will not be coming in. She begins to type the word *facebook* into her browser but stops herself at *b*. Her browser has already pulled up the complete web address. It waits for her to push the enter key. But she doesn't do this. She erases the web address, goes to her Instagram account, and looks up her friend Melissa in the search bar, someone she hasn't seen in over six months. Dylan types the message: **want to hang out soon?**

While she waits for a response, Dylan scrolls through her friend's latest posts and pictures. Melissa lives across the bay in Berkeley and they've known each other since their undergrad at RISD. Her Instagram pictures are of trails in the Berkeley Hills and the various plant and animal life she encounters while hiking. One of them is of a brown deer standing in the grass. At 8:41 am, she receives a response from Melissa that says: **Real busy next few weeks. Maybe at the end of the month. Remind me soon. Love you.** Dylan responds back. She tells Melissa she loves her and hopes they'll meet soon. She presses *enter* and receives a <3 emoji in response. After this, she goes into the kitchen to make food.

Dylan cooks herself scrambled eggs and toast. She eats a banana and brews a cup of coffee. When she's done drinking it, Dylan takes a long shower and leaves the bathroom door open, allowing the steam to spread into her bedroom and fog up her mirror. She eventually emerges wrapped in a towel, discovers what's happened, and runs to the mirror with her heart racing. The steam hasn't erased the red lipstick, the mark is still there, and Dylan throws herself onto the bed in relief.

At 9:23 am, she checks her Gmail and finds the same response from her coworkers as yesterday. They all wish her well. There's no word from Chad, just another automatic response sent to her inbox, so she closes the web browser and starts to get dressed. She puts on black jeans, a black shirt, and goes to the mirror to put on eyeliner. She doesn't apply any eye shadow or mascara today. She combs her hair, rubs sunblock on her skin, and then puts her black sunglasses over her forehead. She doesn't wear any shoes. Dylan walks barefoot.

With the book in her hand, she leaves her apartment and climbs the stairs to the large communal patio on the roof. There are two dozen wooden deck chairs, a variety of potted trees, and a floor composed of large cement squares centered around a bubbling water fountain. All of it is lined by a glass railing. Dylan sits down on a chair near the edge where she can view the brown hills rising above the Mission. She sits directly in the sun, puts her feet on the railing, drops her sunglasses over her eyes, and continues reading *The Unseen*.

She dozes off a few times, but for the next four hours she does nothing but read. Dylan knows the main characters end up in jail but it doesn't discourage her from finishing the book. She enjoys reading of when they were free and formed rebel groups against the bosses. None of the characters have smartphones, there are no surveillance cameras, and computers still take up an entire room. There's only the police, the government, the phone tap, the prison, the television, and the remote control. There's no digital surveillance. The further she reads, the more she understands how thoroughly the government crushed this rebellion in Italy. Were it not for this book, Dylan would have never known it happened.

At 1:35 pm, with less than fifty pages left, Dylan returns to her apartment and takes the potato chips from the cupboard. She eats a couple handfuls, washes the grease off her fingers, and then eats a banana. Dylan stares at the small French-press for a moment but decides not to make coffee. Instead, she takes the book to the living room couch and finishes it within the hour. The last pages make her weep with a final, haunting passage about lights in the darkness. She reads these words over and over and starts the book from the beginning until her eyelids get heavy. She drops *The Unseen* to the floor, curls up on the couch, and sleeps for many hours. It's 7:24 pm when she finally wakes up.

Dylan rifles through one of her kitchen drawers and finds a flier for a pizza delivery service. At 7:35 pm, she uses her landline to call

Zingos and gives her order to a robotic female voice. It asks her what she would like, what size of pizza, if she would like a beverage, if she would like anything else, and then asks for her address and apartment number. At 8:07 pm, her landline rings and she buzzes in the delivery person. Dylan waits for the knock on her door, smiles at the young man holding her pizza, and gives him a $20 bill. When he hands over the neon box, the man peeks into her apartment with an expression resembling amazement. She quickly takes the pizza, tells him to keep the change, and then closes the steel door.

Dylan eats the entire medium sized combination pizza within fifteen minutes. When it's gone, she drinks two glasses of water and lies down on the couch. Her belly is distended now, a sensation Dylan is accustomed to. For her entire life, she's been able to consume large amounts of food without putting on weight. Her family doctor always assured her nothing was wrong and that she simply had an efficient metabolism.

Dylan picks up the remote control for the flatscreen television but ends up just staring at the buttons. She doesn't turn it on. She watches the red light blink on and off at a constant pulse. All the food in her stomach makes her feel tired, her eyes grow heavy, and she adjusts her head against the couch pillows until she's comfortable.

While she's reclining, on the verge of falling asleep, Dylan hears the sounds of tires squealing against the pavement. The living room window is suddenly lit up by police lights flashing red and blue. Dylan hurries to the window and sees an SFPD cruiser parked along the sidewalk opposite the Vermillion. A policeman stands in front of the idling car with something dark in his hands. It takes Dylan a moment to realize it's a gun pointed at a man across the street.

The man is wearing a blue sweatshirt and standing near a white wall, his body illuminated by the police floodlight. His hands are in the air and his eyes wide in fear as the officer approaches with the gun raised. The man shakes his head and almost trips on the pavement. He staggers while catching his balance but keeps his hands above his head. For a moment he appears to smile. This is the last thing that makes sense to Dylan.

There are five quick pops, each accompanied by a brief flash of light. The man is filled with bursts of red and his body vibrates and explodes in every direction. He collapses on the ground with his arms stretched out on the sidewalk and doesn't move once he's down. Blood streaks the pavement and is splattered across the white wall. The policeman talks into his shoulder radio with one hand, puts his gun away, and stands near the body as a crowd begins to form around the cruiser. All of them are angry, all of them point at the policeman.

Dylan yells something unintelligible and bites her fingers. Then she yells again. This is when it becomes real. More police arrive across the street. They push everyone away from the body, use their batons on the crowd, and bark orders like angry dogs while Dylan bangs her fists against the window. She hits and she yells and hits again but the glass doesn't break. She yells at the top of her lungs until she can no longer breathe. She wants to destroy the window, the police, and the entire building. This urge takes over her body. It numbs her to the pain and covers her face in tears. No one on the street hears her yelling, nor do they hear the sound of her banging on the glass. Dylan keeps hitting until her skin has split and blood is smeared across the window. She doesn't know why she does this. She holds her clenched fist in pain and howls like an animal. After that she only sees blackness.

Dylan wakes up on the carpet of her living room at 7:21 am. Her right hand is swollen and cut just below the pinky finger. She eventually turns onto her stomach and crawls over to the window. All the blood has been washed off the sidewalk, the traffic is flowing down Mission Street, and a few newscasters are standing around with their camera crews. Dylan spins onto her back and looks up at the red blood prints smeared on the glass like the tail of a comet. It makes her moan in pain.

Her temples are pounding as she forces herself up and goes to the sink where she drinks three glasses of water. This eventually makes her feel bloated and has no immediate effect on her migraine. She puts the glass down, opens a kitchen drawer, and takes three ibuprofen. After this she eats a banana, throws the peel in the trash, and then makes coffee. She drinks it with cream by the window and watches people leave flowers against the wall where the man was shot. They leave red roses and tulips and calla lilies and even orchids planted in small pots. When she's nearly done with her coffee, Dylan sees two old women place an image of the Virgin Mary in the center of the flowers. They take votive glass candles out of their bags, place them on either side of the image, and then say a prayer. By then, Dylan's head is no longer aching.

At 8:15 am, she goes into the bedroom and enters the closet. She takes out a blue shoe box, opens it on the bed, and removes the digital camera that was a Christmas present from her parents. She hasn't used it in years. When her computer wakes up, she plugs the camera into the tower and a window opens with all of her pictures from college. She begins to click through images of parties, forests, rivers, and lakes. She sees herself dancing at a night club, she sees herself standing below a tree, she sees herself in an art gallery, and she sees herself graduating from RISD.

At 8:24 am, Dylan opens up her web browser and checks her Facebook, her Twitter, her Instagram, and her Gmail. There are dozens of stories about the murder circulating on the internet. She learns the man was from Guatemala and an indigenous Mayan. There was no gun found at the scene, nor was there a knife. Every witness saw the man with his hands in the air and one of them even filmed the body to make sure the police didn't plant a weapon. While he recorded, the videographer barraged the police with a running commentary on their degeneracy, criminality, and fascism. He told them if they planted a weapon he would see it. This video has now gone viral.

On her Twitter feed, Dylan finds an article explaining how the 911 call most likely came from inside the Vermillion. Over a dozen commentators link this new murder to the gentrification of the Mission and the invasive luxury apartment buildings filled with high-paid tech workers. She reads an article that shows a picture of two SFPD officers entering the Vermillion. It's morning in the picture and was taken by a local journalist twenty minutes earlier.

Dylan unplugs her digital camera from the desktop, turns off the flash, and hustles to her front door. She rolls it open slowly, peeks down the hallway, and sees two cops leaning into the doorway of apartment number 23. They're speaking with her neighbors in hushed voices. With the door hardly open, Dylan zooms in on the officers and takes five pictures. No one notices her. She gently closes the door and locks it without making a sound. When she returns to her computer at 8:47 am, Dylan plugs her camera into the tower and uploads the pictures into a new file she names *V*. She goes to the Chumby website, clicks the *contact* button, and finds the address for news tips. She opens up her personal Gmail, clicks on the *compose* button, and titles her email **Shooting outside Vermillion – Urgent!!!**.

Dylan opens up a new tab in her browser and begins to compile a series of links. Dylan knows the last name of her neighbor and has talked with her a few times in the hallway. She knows what her neighbor looks like, what color her hair is, and her approximate age. With only this information, Dylan locates her LinkedIn account, her Facebook account, a business website she shares with her husband, and several news stories detailing her work. Her name is Anne Sterling, her husband is James Sterling. She works for Google. He works for BoonDoggle. Together, they offer web design and advertising expertise to restaurant owners. As she searches through the Google search results, Dylan discovers many of their client restaurants have been linked to gentrification. Dylan has eaten at all of them.

When the list of links is compiled in her email, Dylan briefly explains the context for the photos, describes the shooting she witnessed, and asks that her identity and residence be kept a secret. Dylan pauses before sending this email. She stares at her words until 9:04 am and then finally clicks the *send* button. She waits there impatiently, refreshing her inbox every few minutes. At 9:13 am, she receives an email from Jared Dejaque in the local news department. All it says is "**thanks.**" Below that is the link to a story on the Chumby website.

Dylan clicks on it and discovers that Dejaque has already posted an article that includes the pictures she sent him. It explains that a Google employee and a BoonDoggle employee were responsible for the 911 call that led to the shooting. It provides their pictures and also links to their social media pages. The article anonymously quotes Dylan's description of the shooting in its entirety and provides several other accounts, all with identical elements: the man had his hands in the air, he was standing by the wall, and then there was blood. Everyone remembered the blood.

At 9:21 am, she types the names of her neighbors into the Google search engine and clicks on the *news* button. There are already two articles from different news sites connecting the couple to the shooting. Before she can read them there is a sudden pounding at her door, hard and loud.

"Miss Kinsey! SFPD! We'd like to speak with you!"

"Miss Kinsey!" another ones yells.

Her heart clenches but she takes a breath and refreshes her Gmail inbox. The police keep banging on the door but she's already preoccupied with a new email from Chumby. Jared Dejaque wants to know if she actually heard the conversation between the Sterling couple and the police. Dylan listens to them pound on her door for another moment, waits until they leave, and then types the words **yes, I did, absolutely** into the email. After this, Dylan clicks *send*.

Dylan spends the rest of the day refreshing her browser tabs. She follows every Facebook post, every thread on Reddit, and every tweet with the corresponding hashtag. The story is covered extensively in SFGate, InsideBayArea, and all the local news stations, but during the afternoon there's a pause. People stop sharing the story. The same links keep circulating on Twitter. The words become repetitive. No new content is posted. Dylan uses this time to make herself a large sandwich, finish the rest of her potato chips, and eat the last of her ice cream. It makes her feel ill.

The wound on her hand is large but not very serious. Dylan starts to clean it with alcohol but quickly gives up and decides to just take a shower. She gets out of her clothes, pees, shits, and then realizes she didn't send an email to the department this morning. There's been no reprimand, no attention, and no notice of her absence. Dylan wipes herself, thinks nothing more of OingoBoingo, and then gets into the shower. She imagines Alexis' olive skin, her nicotine smile, her bright green eyes, and the invisible hairs on her neck. These visions last until the bathroom fills with steam and eventually Dylan becomes dizzy.

At 3:21 pm, she returns to her computer and types the names of her neighbors into the Google search engine. There are now over fifteen new articles that directly connect the Sterling couple to the shooting. The comments at the bottom of these articles indicate that a majority of readers believe the Sterlings called 911. In another article, Dylan learns the SFPD is refusing to confirm the identity of the 911 callers and has issued a statement condemning Chumby for publishing the photos. Dylan sees this statement heavily mocked and criticized on social media where thousands of people are expressing hatred and disgust at the SFPD on a new hashtag called #vengeanceformario.

At 5:30 pm, she comes across a tweet saying it will be no surprise when people start shooting cops. There are hundreds of tweets like this on the #vengeanceformario thread and Dylan reads them all. She's never seen anything like this, nor has she been at its center. It dazzles her senses, quickens her heart, and consumes her mind for hours as the number of tweets grows exponentially. Thousands of people express their anger, their hatred, and their desire for revenge. The story is covered internationally with Russia Today posting a new smartphone video of the shooting and *The Guardian* website describing San Francisco as a killing field for brown people. A famous local author says the situation has the texture of wet dynamite.

Dylan reads through every news source for an explanation. They each agree that the shooting happened, although no one seems to know why. Some articles cite lack of police de-escalation training, with one author explaining: *Officers are taught to always fear for their life, so that's exactly what they do. The only problem is they resort to their gun first and ask questions later.* One article suggests the white officer depicted in the smartphone video acted according to proscribed racial bias. This journalist explains: *The officer was taught to treat people of color as an inherent threat and trained to act with deadly force.* Another journalist writes: *The officer knew there would be no repercussions for his actions and came from a toxic culture of acceptance that provides nothing but positive reinforcement after a deadly shooting.* None of these articles satisfy Dylan. They don't explain why the police officer killed that man in front of her eyes.

Dylan eventually finds herself clicking on links to anarchist websites that are explicitly against the police. She finds these links by searching on Google for terms like *police brutality* and *police killings*. She finds multiple anarchist websites covering the story and offering their analysis. She reads their content and learns new narratives that describe the police as an occupying army of capitalism. One writer explains: *Without the arbitrary and imposed violence of the police, capitalism would not function. As long as capitalism exists, so will its police.* Dylan combs through this information but can't find what she's looking for. The anarchists explain why the police kill people in general, but they don't explain why it happened in front of Dylan's eyes.

At 9:45 pm, she finds an article posted on the r/anarchism sub-Reddit that begins to explain some of it. The author writes: *The police killed Mario to drive poor and homeless people away from the Vermillion. The SFPD and the capitalists want the message to be clear: if you look poor and linger in front of a luxury apartment for too long, the result will be death. This fear of arbitrary execution was meant to drive the poor and homeless into depopulated areas where they will no longer interfere with business or scare away prospective tenants. The SFPD are paid by the rich to enforce capitalist order and phase out the homeless population in San Francisco. They have full permission to do what is necessary so that the tech yuppies, the super rich, and the CEOs no longer have to see the poverty their system created.*

Dylan stares at her screen, reads the article three more times, but still doesn't feel satisfied, not completely. She doesn't know why her neighbors called the police, nor does she really know what they said. Two terrible possibilities arrange themselves in her imagination. One involves her neighbors and the building owner colluding with the police in a conscious strategy to drive away the poor. This thought terrifies her and makes her body numb. All she can do is breathe slowly until her heart calms down and she no longer wants to vomit. The other possibility is that her neighbors were simply afraid, thought the man had a gun, and called the police in ignorance of what would happen. She wants this to be the case. She doesn't want to imagine the other scenario.

Dylan stares directly into the camera on her desktop monitor at 10:27 pm. She blinks her eyelids several times and then shuts off the computer. The fan stops spinning, the monitor stops humming, but the camera remains as it is. It appears to stare at nothing.

CHAPTER 6

When she wakes up the next morning, Dylan doesn't turn on her desktop. She goes into her living room at 8:23 am and stares at the blood marks streaked across her window. The exposure to oxygen has turned them from bright red to a dark brown, almost the color of chocolate. After staring at this bloody imprint, Dylan goes to the kitchen and cooks herself scrambled eggs and toast. She eats them at the counter and then makes coffee in the French-press. When she's done eating, Dylan stares blankly at the flatscreen television in the living room and watches the red light at the corner blink on and off. She keeps her dirty dishes on the counter and remains seated for over ten minutes, her eyes fixed on the strobe of light.

At 9:12 am, Dylan goes into her bedroom and looks through the boxes in her closet. She finds a copy of her lease agreement and begins to read all the details and clauses. Her lease at the Vermillion is up in four months, at which point she'll have to renew it. The lease agreement has a glossy cover with a picture of the Vermillion printed in vibrant colors, its glass and metal glistening in the sun. The lease came inside a thick folder packed with information on all the various amenities and services. Dylan hasn't looked at these documents since she moved in. She sits on her closet carpet and reads them over and over until every clause of her lease is committed to memory.

She takes the folder to her computer desk, picks up her landline telephone, and dials the contact number listed on the lease agreement. It rings several times before connecting her to an automated answering service. After pressing a series of digits on her phone, including her personalized resident account number, Dylan is finally connected with a human representative.

"Resident accounts, may I help you?"

"Yes, hi, my name is—"

"I know your name, it's all on the screen here."

"Oh. Ok. Well, unfortunately I'm going to have to cancel my lease."

"You understand you'll have to pay the—"

"I understand." Dylan turns on her desktop and puts the phone against her other ear. "I just read it in the folder. So, yeah, I guess I'll—"

"Are you certain you want to cancel your lease? You'll have to pay an additional month's rent in order to cancel your lease and if the apartment remains vacant you'll have to pay each month until the vacancy is filled or the original term of the lease is expired."

Dylan nods to herself and opens up her web browser.

"Yep. I'm certain. But what now? What do I do?"

"First you'll have to sign into your resident account on our website. Have you done that yet?"

"You mean have I *ever* done that? No, I don't think—"

"Just go to the website and fill out the breach of lease form. You have to agree to every condition and then click submit. We'll approve it once you've done that."

Dylan hangs up the phone and goes to the Chase online banking website. She signs into her account and opens up the balance. In her checking account, she has $55,392.24. In her savings account, she has $253,321.73. This larger sum of money was a gift from her father when she got the job at OingoBoingo. The smaller amount is what she's saved from work.

At 9:31 am, she opens up her calendar on the desktop. OingoBoingo will direct deposit her next paycheck on Friday and another $11,934 will be in her checking account. At 9:33 am, she signs into her resident account on the Vermillion website and begins to fill out the online breach of lease form. She chooses the following Friday for her move-out day and then proceeds to read over and agree to a variety of conditions. She spends the next fifteen minutes on this form and at 9:49 am she clicks submit. A screen appears informing her she'll receive a confirmation email when the request has been approved. It tells her this will happen within 24 hours.

Dylan begins to search Craigslist for apartments in South San Francisco and Daly City. She finds a few that are less than two thousand dollars a month, both in nondescript housing complexes likely built in the '70s. At 10:03 am, she begins writing emails in response to the advertisements and keeps refreshing her inbox for the next half an hour. There's no response. She waits in front of the monitor for a bit longer, her eyes fixed on the static screen, and then goes into the bathroom to take a shit.

Dylan has a long shower and emerges from the bathroom at 11:12 am. With a white towel wrapped around her body, she refreshes her inbox to find there's still no response from any of the housing advertisers. For no clear reason, Dylan closes her browser, turns off the computer, and then starts to get dressed. She puts on a pair of black pants, a black short sleeved blouse, and then goes to the mirror to put on eyeliner and blue mascara. When she's done, Dylan stares at her reflection for a long time. She looks at the red lipstick mark on the mirror glass, reads the note Alexis left her, and then begins to cry for so long her eyeliner turns into a dozen black rivers wiggling down her cheeks.

Dylan forces herself to go outside at 12:03 pm. She wears her silver Japanese leather designer moto-jacket and has a roll of money in the side-pocket as she walks down Mission to her favorite taqueria on 16th Street next to the BART station. She orders three carne asada burritos to go, fills several plastic cups with green salsa, and once her food's ready she returns to the Vermillion. Before going back inside, Dylan looks around to see if anyone's watching her. There's a homeless woman leaning against the wall, a man waiting for the bus, a well-dressed gay couple walking their poodle, and several children following behind a school teacher. Dylan quickly opens the lobby door with her fob and then climbs the stairs to her floor. This is when she sees her neighbors standing in the red hallway.

"Did you send those pictures?" Anne Sterling asks.

"What pictures?"

The couple are both dressed in workout clothes, they both have blonde hair, and both of them are wearing the latest Apple Watch. Anne stands in front of her husband James. She breathes heavily and stares at Dylan with undisguised anger, although her husband keeps his eyes on the ground and his lips tightly shut. Unlike his wife, James Sterling looks frightened.

"You didn't send the pictures?" Anne asks.

"I have *no* idea what you're talking about," Dylan says. "I've been sick."

"See, I told—"

Anne waves away her husband's words and steps closer.

"You know there's people following us now?" Anne asks, aggressively. "Journalists! They've even put our pictures on the nightly news!"

"Really?" Dylan asks, pretending to sniffle. "Why?"

"Leave her alone," James Sterling says. "She's sick, screaming—"

"Then who took the pictures?" Anna asks the ceiling. "They came from right here!"

"I don't know, but I need to eat."

Dylan turns around and opens her door while Anne and James Sterling begin to argue. Once the door is closed, Dylan lets herself smile and listens to the couple yell words like trust, meekness, aggressiveness, and betrayal. It makes Dylan so happy her cheeks get sore from the effort. The couple eventually retreat into their apartment and the sound of their frenzied yelling vanishes behind the thick concrete wall.

Dylan turns on her bedroom computer at 12:57 pm and sits down at the desk to eat her first burrito. She peels the foil back, bites into the flour tortilla, and chews the rice, beans, meat, and salsa. She finishes it quickly and stops eating only to breathe. With a blob of sour cream on the side of her mouth, Dylan opens her web browser and goes to the *Chumby* website where she finds an article about the murder posted on the front page.

It details a similar shooting in Bernal Heights several years ago where someone called 911 and exaggerated the situation to the police. This is the sixth recent shooting of an unarmed Latino man by the SFPD and a demonstration has already been called tonight for 9:00 pm at the corner of 16th and Mission. The intention is to march directly on the Vermillion. Dylan clicks on the hyperlink for the protest announcement and is directed to an anarchist website where she reads a short manifesto against the police and capitalism. It says they'll show the police and the gentrifiers the consequences for valuing property over life. All of it makes her heart race.

Dylan remains at her computer for the next few hours. She checks her Facebook, her Twitter, her Instagram, and her Gmail. There are more well-wishes from her coworkers. Most of them include hearts and XOXO symbols. They say everything is going well, they say they are covering for her, they tell her not to worry about the new designs, they tell her they're on it. There's nothing from Chad, nothing from HR, nothing from OingoBoingo. This is the fourth day since she decided to be sick. No one seems to care very much.

And then Dylan sees an article from Chumby posted on her Twitter feed at 1:27 pm. It's titled *The Everyday Rape of Every Woman in the Office: an OingoBoingo story.* The article is written by Natasha Malevich. Dylan opens it up and scrolls to the bottom before reading. She sees a dozen pictures of every person in the advertising department, including Chad, including Ricky, including herself. The article is extremely long and takes Dylan thirty minutes to finish. The narrative is in the second person and provides no names or job titles as it tells the story of what happened to Elizabeth and Bernadette. Natasha writes: *You sit with your two friends in the lunch room on the fifth floor. A few of your male colleagues begin to mutter words like whore and anal. They think each of you slept with your manager to get ahead. They have no regard for your talent, none at all. You know this is true.* In between these details, Natasha explains the meteoric rise of OingoBoingo, the controversy behind its CEO, and the racial disparities in its workforce. The article ends with a reminder to step back from the men, tell them you're done talking, and then walk away. It makes Dylan cry.

By the time she finishes, her social media feeds are filled with reposts and retweets of this article. It spreads quickly at the end of the lunch hour when everyone is back at their work desks. At 2:12 pm, she types the word *rape oingoboingo* into the Google search engine and discovers two entire pages worth of links relating to the new Chumby article by Natasha Malevich. *The New York Times* tech blog says it's the first of its kind, more literary than journalistic, and it's only the tip of the iceberg. There's widespread praise for the bravery of both Natasha Malevich and the anonymous source inside the advertising department.

A famous Italian author meditates at length in *The Guardian* about the photos included in the article: *There are three women in the advertising department. Their faces can be seen in the article, but only one of them is the source. An air of mystery permeates every sentence, lending it urgency, gravity, and weight.* The famous author calls the article a masterpiece. She says it must be read.

At 2:31 pm, Dylan opens her Gmail and finds a dozen messages from her coworkers. She reads the fifteen emails from Elizabeth first. They say Dylan has betrayed her. She reads: **You've threatened my job and pretty much ruined my life you fucking bitch! How could you be so selfish!** The rest of the messages are more frantic. Elizabeth is desperate to get in contact, she tells Dylan to call her cell number and wants to know where she is. The final message reads simply: **WTF!** Dylan doesn't respond, instead she opens up the twelve emails from Bernadette and begins to read them. They're similar in tone, although Bernadette insists the rape never happened. Dylan reads: **It doesn't matter what you told the journalists. You made the entire thing up just to get leverage over Chad. If the press accuses me of writing the article I'll deny everything. He didn't rape me. I never said that.** Dylan doesn't read the rest of Bernadette's emails. It's too depressing.

Although Dylan's inbox is filled with emails from her other coworkers, there's no message from management, no email from HR, and no word from Chad. She doesn't bother to read any of it, instead she unwraps her second burrito, takes a large bite, and then pours green salsa into the fillings. Dylan eats ravenously. She peels the foil down in long slivers, wraps her lips around the tortilla, and chews loudly. She feels as if there's something inside her body, a spirit lodged inside her chest demanding to be fed. Grease and condensation dribble to the floor as Dylan pours the last of the salsa into the fractured burrito. When all of it's gone, she sighs in utter happiness.

At 3:17 pm, Dylan goes into the bathroom, uses the toilet, and then takes another shower. It makes her feel good even though she doesn't need it. She stays inside the steam for nearly half an hour and thinks about Alexis the whole time. After she gets out, Dylan changes back into her clothes, stares at the red lipstick mark on the mirror, and then puts on black eyeliner. She brushes her teeth, flosses her gums, swishes hot water in her mouth, and then spits out red, bloody liquid. It reminds Dylan that she needs to floss more.

It's 4:04 pm when she returns to her web browser and opens her Twitter feed. At the very top of her screen is a new story posted by TechCrunch. At first she doesn't believe it's real. The headline says *OingoBoingo to Be Acquired By BoonDoggle, 250 Laid Off.* Without hesitation, Dylan opens the link and begins to read the article. In a statement made at exactly 4:00 pm, Bilton Smyth explains that recent uncertainty with investors has left the company in financial limbo. Without external funding, the company cannot persist as an independent entity. In order to ensure a generous severance package for each employee, OingoBoingo will now be absorbed into BoonDoggle. All of the data owned by OingoBoingo has been sold to BoonDoggle for $12,500,000,000. Only a small fraction of the engineers and technical staff will remain employed by BoonDoggle to keep the games online and profitable. Everyone else will receive a $75,000 severance payment.

Dylan opens up her Gmail and finds a new message from HR. It's a long letter with several documents attached that explains the details of the compensation package. It lists what forms need to be signed, how they can be delivered, and reminds each employee to read the new confidentiality agreement. Before she can deal with any of this, Dylan closes her web browser, shuts off her computer, and then puts on her shoes. She goes into the living room, slips into her silver Japanese designer leather moto-jacket, and then stuffs the identical pink version into her bag. With cash in her pocket and keys in hand, Dylan leaves the apartment and locks the door. It's 4:23 pm.

She walks for over an hour in search of an old payphone. She takes random turns down one way streets, looks backward at every corner, and runs through alleys to make sure she's alone. This vigilance is all-consuming. Nothing escapes her vision.

Dylan eventually finds a graffiti covered pay phone near the Safeway below Bernal Hill. She takes out the receipt with Alexis' burner number and puts four quarters into the machine. The black plastic phone smells like years of sweat, beer, and cigarettes. She punches the number into the metal keypad, adjusts the phone to her ear, and then listens to it ring.

"Hello?"

"Hi," Dylan almost whispers. "How are you?"

"Fucking tired. Work was a bitch."

Dylan is silent and listens to the line crackle.

"You still want to meet up?" Alexis asks.

"Yeah. What're you doing?"

"Napping. I'll come up there, nothing to do down here."

"There's something you might want to go to."

"What is it?"

"You'll see."

"A surprise? Sounds great!" Alexis yawns loudly over the phone. "Want to meet at Cafe Boheme? You know that place?"

"I know it."

"Let's meet at 7:00, huh? I'll get my ass moving."

"I missed you."

There's short silence, followed by a humming sound. Alexis is purring.

"Yeah, I'm not gonna lie. I've been thinking about you a lot."

There are no more words. Both of them purr uncontrollably over the phone.

"See you tonight," Alexis whispers.

Dylan hangs up the phone and closes her eyes. Between the bus exhaust and cigarette smoke, she smells the sweet musk of Alexis, tastes her mouth, and feels her dark hair. When she opens her eyes, Dylan sees the grassy summit of Bernal Hill. Something tells her to climb to the top so she follows this instinct and walks up the long sloping streets away from the Mission. She ascends the cement staircases between old wooden houses where the scent of jasmine flowers and evaporating water fills the air. She sees people cooking through their kitchen windows and smells garlic and onions sizzling in oil. It makes her feel hungry again.

The neighborhood turns into a public park at the head of the staircase. It's here that Dylan sees a memorial in the grass surrounded by votive candles and red roses, all of it dedicated to the memory of a man killed by the SFPD at this exact location. While she's staring at the roses, a young woman in a running outfit stops beside Dylan and snaps a photo of the memorial with her smartphone. The woman says nothing to Dylan, nor does she acknowledge her. She straps her smartphone around her bicep, plugs her headphones into the jack, and keeps running down Bernal Hill.

Dylan reaches the summit and sits down in the shade of a cypress tree. She can see the Mission District spread out in a grid with the gray skyscrapers of downtown hanging above it. The new BoonDoggle tower stands over the city while a streak of shimmering sunlight ripples across the bay waters. Just to the west, an endless wall of thick fog perches behind the coastal hills. Only the eastern half of the city is bathed in sunlight. To the other half, it might as well be winter.

Dylan gets to the Cafe Boheme early. She waits at the corner of Osage and 24th and checks to see if anyone's following. Dozens of people walk past the cafe without going inside. It doesn't appear very crowded so she crosses 24th and walks through the front door. Only five of the wooden tables are occupied, some old jazz plays on the loudspeakers, and only two customers are speaking with each other. Dylan orders a small Americano with three shots of espresso. The woman who serves her at the counter looks upset and flatly states the price for the drink. She hardly notices when Dylan tips her three dollars.

Dylan sits at a table along the wall and gazes across the room at the blinking ATM machine. No one enters the cafe for the next several minutes. No one looks up from their computers, their smartphones, or their books aside from the two customers having a conversation. The jazz music plays while a Google bus drives past on 24th Street. The green lights of the ATM strobe on and off and a few flies buzz near the ceiling. Dylan takes a sip of her Americano and realizes she forgot cream. As she crosses the room towards the condiments, a man glances up from his laptop and nervously smiles at her. Dylan immediately looks away and pours the half-and-half. The cream spreads like a brown rose and swirls until the liquid resembles chocolate. It makes it taste much better.

"Hi."

Dylan puts the cup down next to the sugar. Alexis is in front of her wearing black jeans and a black sweatshirt. She has black Adidas on her feet and wears black eye liner. There are small green jewels in her ear lobes. Dylan steps forward and they hold each other for a moment in the middle of the cafe. Alexis kisses her on the neck, on the cheek, and on the lips. It makes Dylan feel wonderful.

"Let's go, huh?" Alexis says. "I want to be out in the world."

"You don't want coffee?"

"You want me up all night or something?" She grabs Dylan's hand and pulls her outside. "We can stay up all night, don't worry, but I want to be outside. Let's go to the park."

Dylan throws her Americano away and they leave the cafe in silence with their arms around each other. They stop at every block to kiss, to smell, to taste, to be certain they exist. Dylan can hardly look away from Alexis and the brilliant green of her eyes. She squeezes her hips and lets the world melt away until there's nothing but a low hum in the background. They eventually arrive at Dolores Park and climb the western slope where they sit down on the grass and face the skyscrapers, the blinking lights, the glittering windows, and the rotating cranes of San Francisco. Dylan leans her head on Alexis' shoulder and remains this way until the sounds of laughter intrude upon her reverie. She's surrounded by countless clusters of people drinking, smoking, and rolling around on the grass.

"So what the fuck's happening?" Alexis asks. "I saw there was the shooting. Are you—"

"It was so terrible, so—" Dylan doesn't want to cry so she looks away. "I've never seen anything like that, I never watched all those videos. I never wanted to see it."

"You never saw the Oscar Grant video? At Fruitvale BART? Or Eric Garner? 'I can't breathe'?"

"Never. I didn't want to watch. But then it happened right in front of me. I went...nuts. Look." She shows Alexis the long cut at the base of her pinky. "I kept hitting the window. I don't know how to explain it. I was yelling, crying. The feeling was like...I felt like an animal. I wanted to destroy them. The police, I mean. I just wanted to destroy them all. But then—"

Dylan finally looks at Alexis but receives only a blank stare.

"What's up?" Alexis rubs the tears on her cheek. "What happened?"

"You wouldn't even believe me. Honestly. I can't believe it. I really can't."

"Seriously. What happened? Did you lose your job, too? I saw that on the internet."

Dylan nods and explains the sale of OingoBoingo to BoonDoggle. She tells Alexis about the $75,000 severance payment, the new confidentiality agreement, and how she must relinquish the rights to her original designs. But then Dylan tells her about meeting with Natasha, she narrates their interview in Vesuvio Cafe, and explains what happened to Bernadette and Elizabeth. Alexis smokes one Newport menthol after the other, her face locked in a stern expression, and by the end of the telling she's lit herself a blunt.

"So *what* happened?" she asks. "The story comes out about Chad raping them and then, what, just a few hours ago they fire all of you? That seems really fucking weird, doesn't it? And where's this Chad fucker, huh? Did they kill him, too?"

Dylan raises her finger to her lips.

"I don't know," she whispers. "My job's over, though. I just sign the papers and then I'm free."

"*Free?* So you're happy about it? That was a good job, right? It paid for your condo."

"I canceled my lease yesterday. My last day's on Friday."

"Dylan!" Alexis hits the blunt and passes it to her. "Here, smoke this for a second. You need to calm down. You just keep telling me these things all quick and...it's a lot to take in. You've done enough this week. Go on, smoke a little, like you're sipping whiskey or something."

So she does. Dylan gently puffs on the tobacco and marijuana. She holds the smoke in her lungs until it starts to hurt and then blows it out. Dylan keeps talking while she smokes, she tells Alexis about the shooting, how the man had his hands in the air, how the wall became stained with blood. She explains how she took pictures of the Sterling couple, sent them to Chumby, and then watched the internet devour her neighbors.

"But why Chumby, though? I've seen them before, but what are they?"

"Like—" Dylan hands the last of the blunt back. "They're a San Francisco, half tech journalism, half city news beat kind of website. Something like that. I found an article Natasha wrote about sexism in the tech office, I read it, so...yeah, I just picked her because of that, I guess."

"So you've given Chumby *two* stories since I last saw you?"

"Uh-huh."

"Damn, girl." Alexis rubs Dylan's head and pulls her close. "I don't even know what to say. Everything's collapsing and you're out there like a ninja making things happen. I don't know, though, everyone at your company getting fired like that, so soon after Ricky got killed. It's like they're covering their tracks."

"I thought that, too, I did, when I first read it. And with Chad gone, it makes sense."

"Whatever's on that flash drive is probably important. We'll get it tomorrow."

"Why can't we go tonight?" Dylan asks.

"My friend's using the Airbnb until morning."

"So people *have* been there since I last saw you, right? It's okay to go?"

"Uh-huh. No police raid, no anything. It's weird, like they don't even see us."

"Let's hope they never see us," Dylan says, taking her hand. "We need to stay safe."

"So what's this surprise you were telling me about?"

"It's right here." Dylan grabs her bag, pulls out the pink designer Japanese leather moto-jacket, and hands it to Alexis. "I want you to have this."

"No way!" Alexis holds it in the air. "This thing cost like ten thousand dollars, didn't it?"

"No, more like two thousand."

"Oh my god, thank you!" she says, rubbing her cheek. "I'll wear it right now."

Alexis takes off her sweatshirt, slips her hands through the leather sleeves, and stretches her arms to make sure it fits. She hugs Dylan tightly and they writhe in the grass like beached water mammals. There's no affect to their longing, no self-consciousness to their movements. They do this for so long the crowd around them grows silent.

"I can't believe you *did* all this," Alexis whispers, her cheek on the grass. "In one week, you sunk this power couple, sunk your boss, exposed those fuckers and how they do. And then you watched your company implode. It's incredible."

"Are they going to come after us?" Dylan asks.

"I don't know, but we need to be careful. It's good you're moving out of your place."

DARLINGTONIA

"I have a lot of money, you know? Enough to live on for...for a long time."

"How much? A hundred thousand?"

"I've got over $300,000 in my bank account."

"*What?*" Alexis leans up on her shoulder. "How?"

"My dad gave me two hundred and fifty thousand, for my future, to buy a house here."

"Uh—" Alexis puts another Newport in her mouth and lights it. "You're killing me. It's just one thing after another now. Where the fuck did you come from? I swear—"

"I came from Connecticut," Dylan says, dryly. "I'm an only child. I grew up in a mansion. My dad sold his shares in his tech company and we got millions. Hundreds of millions. My mom just stays home and reads books. They went to their clubs and I mostly just stayed home when I lived there."

"You had boyfriends?"

"A few. I never really liked them. Then I had one in college. An art guy. For a couple years."

"Didn't go so well, I take it."

"No. Not at all. I just hate most men, they're—"

"Not all of them. Seriously. Guys like Ricky. They're okay, right?"

Dylan looks confused for a moment and then reluctantly nods her head.

"They're a few," she says. "Some of them are okay. As long as you don't sleep with them."

"More than a few are okay. Like my old friends, the ones off in the woods. Those guys were good. I mean, not all of them were men, some of them don't even have a gender. But the ones who are men are *okay*. Trust me, I know better than you. I know *all* about men, and this Chad guy sounds like any of the guys who've paid me for it. Only they think they're special, they don't really like paying for sex, so they do shit like put a roofie in your drink and rape you all night."

Dylan winces and tries to ignore the coldness in her stomach.

"It's sick," she whispers.

"It's fascism. That's what you call it. That's all it is. Corporate fascism. It's how they get people in line. That's why I can't believe you're real. You resist! Don't you get it? You're just some random person. I don't mean that in a bad way, but you've had it, you're done with all this."

"I'm done." Dylan nods her head. "I want to leave. I want to get out of here."

"But you *are* out. Like you said, you're free."

"Alexis, seriously, we should take my money and run." Dylan sits up cross-legged. "Let's get out of here. Look at this, look at all the money in this city. Look at that tower right there, that giant new sky-scraper. That's BoonDoggle! It's a giant company that controls every-body's commercial data, and they just ate OingoBoingo."

"Sounds so *fucking* stupid! Why do they name their shit these kiddy names?"

"I don't know," Dylan says. "I always thought OingoBoingo was the name of a band. Anyway, there's something else. You ready?"

"Oh my god, are you serious? What is it now? You're freaking me out."

"There's a protest tonight at 9:00. They're gathering at the BART station down the block and they're going to march on the building. I read it on an anarchist website. It's real."

"You want to go? Let's go, let's go! What time is it right now?"
Alexis quickly turns to her left.

"Excuse me," she says to an older man. "What time is it?"

With a confused look, the man glances down at his smartphone.

"8:17. You don't have a phone?"

Alexis doesn't respond. She grabs her sweatshirt, pulls Dylan to her feet, and together they start walking down the grassy hill. Once they're through the field of blankets and wine bottles and weed smoke, they bolt across Dolores Street towards Mission. They decide they're hungry so they go to a falafel shop on Valencia and order the same thing. They hum to each other while they eat and their mouths become stained with red chili sauce. They devour their falafel at the same pace and chug down multiple glasses of ice water. The man behind the counter watches them. He smiles as they chew their fried chickpea and vegeta-bles. Dylan likes the way he's looking at her. It makes her feel safe.

"What time is it?" Alexis asks him.

He widens his eyes and points at the clock mounted on the tiled wall.

DARLINGTONIA

"8:35," he says, calmly.

"Should we go?" Alexis asks. "We can take the long way."

They get up from their seats and wave to the man behind the counter. He nods at them warmly and for a moment it seems as if Dylan's known him forever. She throws her trash into the waste bin, smiles at the man one last time, and then leaves the restaurant with Alexis.

Valencia Street is busy when they step outside. The sun is going down, the sky is purple, and the air is still warm from the daylight. They walk down the sidewalk past young people panhandling on the cement with messages scrawled on cardboard and old women muttering to themselves with cigarettes in their hands. They pass well-dressed young people eating dinner at fancy restaurants and see Lamborghinis cruise down the street with growling engines. The wealthy people strut along in large packs, their faces lit up from the glow of smartphones. They smoke American Spirit cigarettes and wear high heels on the hard pavement. Their clothes are nice and their voices loud. They have nothing to be afraid of on Valencia. Their happiness feels obscene.

"Is this gonna be weird for you?" Alexis asks. "Going to a demo outside your building?"

"I don't know. Maybe."

"You didn't secretly plan this all, did you?"

"No! It was on an anarchist website."

"What if people start throwing rocks at your building? Here, wait, let's do this."

Alexis steps into the doorway of an apartment building and takes off the pink jacket. She removes her tank top and puts the leather jacket over her bra and bare skin. She pulls the black sweatshirt over the jacket and wraps the tank top around her face so it serves as a mask. She stuffs it down to her neck, smiles at Dylan, and tells her to do the same thing. With the pink jacket underneath her black sweatshirt, Alexis looks sixty pounds heavier.

"Did you do this with your old friends?" Dylan asks, taking off her blouse. "Put on masks?"

"Sometimes."

"Did you fight the police?"

"Sometimes"

Alexis gets behind Dylan and ties her blouse into a mask. The fabric hangs to her belly and covers her bare chest. Dylan can hardly breathe. Her heart is pounding and she begins to sweat. Her body feels like an apartment radiator as she stands in her bra and pants, exposed to everyone passing by. Although many people look at her, Dylan ignores their expressions of confusion. All she can see is the image of Alexis throwing her fists at the face of a cop.

"Like, did you do it a lot, or—"

"No!" Alexis says. "I mean, we didn't do *this* all the time, but it happens."

"I don't get it."

"It's just—" Alexis finishes tying the mask for Dylan and pulls the black fabric up to her nose. "It's just sometimes you're at home then you get a call so you go and there's a helicopter with its spotlight on, police chasing people, crazy shit happening everywhere. It's all a matter of what you want to do when people are on the street. Do you just want to Netflix and chill or do you want to throw down when the people are angry, when you're angry, when you don't even know how you feel, when all you know is something isn't right? I don't know, here, I'm done now."

Dylan puts her silver jacket over her naked skin, pulls up the metal zipper, and then tucks the face mask inside her collar. It makes her feel confident although its nothing but a black blouse tied around her neck.

"I can't believe this is happening," Dylan tells her. "I've never done anything like this."

"And it's against your own building even. I *never* did anything like that. This is crazy!"

"It's not like it's *my* building. It's just where I live."

"Fuck, *I'd* live there if someone gave it to me, but I'd never pay four grand a month for it."

"Almost five grand."

"Out of control," Alexis says, shaking her head. "Fucking insane."

"But seriously, *this* is insane! How is this happening?" Dylan asks. "How is this real?"

"You're asking *me* that? I don't even know how *you're* real!"

"But that makes no sense," Dylan says. "I'm so normal, so boring."

"Not lately! Maybe before I met you, okay, you were probably boring, fine, you win. But this is some serious shit you just did. Anyway, come on." Alexis takes Dylan by the elbow and walks her from the doorway. "We've been pretty safe, but you should sit and think on this later. You just set in motion some big moves by some big people. And whatever happened to Ricky is part of it. This is all really complicated and neither of us know anything. At least not very much."

"All I did was tell a story to a journalist about Bernadette and Elizabeth. And I posted some pictures of my neighbors. I didn't—"

"Right, that's *all* you did." Alexis rubs the back of Dylan's head. "You just don't get how special you are. Do you? You're a miracle. I couldn't dream you up, not ever."

Dylan's entire body fills with light. No one has ever told her anything like this. Not a single one of her old friends. Not even her parents. It makes her feel like crying but Dylan doesn't want to spoil the moment. She doesn't want to look afraid.

The crowd is thick and loud when they arrive in the red brick plaza. The air smells like cigarettes and marijuana and sage. Hundreds of people are packed together on both sides of Mission Street. Some hold identical signs made by communist organizations while others in black masks hold twenty foot long banners, one of which reads **POLICE = MURDERERS**. Behind the banners are several people dressed in Aztec clothing who dance in a circular pattern around three drums. The rhythm in the air is furious.

Further down 16th Street are a line of cops in white helmets sitting atop their motorcycles. Their helmets glisten like reptile eggs under the bright streetlamps. Behind them are nine white vans with their engines idling, the exhaust lit up by red break lights. Each van is filled with ten riot cops waiting for their orders to charge the crowd. They have transparent visors over their helmets and hold black batons in their hands. The blue and red van lights strobe at a constant rate above their heads.

"You recognize anyone?" Dylan asks.

"Not yet. Maybe I won't even. It's been a while."

"Really? I thought—"

"Come on, let's look around."

They walk through the sea of bodies to the edge of the brick sidewalk and stand behind one of the banners. A few local network trucks are raising their antennas in front of the Vermillion while the news-casters prepare for broadcast. Hundreds of conversations blend in Dylan's ears against the frantic drum beats as the smell of sage blows in with a cloud of smoke. Every particle of the air seems charged with electricity. It creates a haze in her vision that Dylan assumes is coming from the sage but might only be her imagination.

"Are we gonna take the streets or what?" Alexis asks the nearest person.

"That's the plan," the woman says, her face covered in a mask. "Lot of cops tonight."

"More of us than them, though." Alexis winks. "I never seen them this outnumbered."

"I know, right! We're gonna turn it upside...wait, I know you, you're—"

"Lets go!" someone yells from behind.

"I gotta go."

The woman steps out onto the street and the crowd begins to surge.

"Who was that?" Dylan asks.

"No idea. Come on."

Alexis pulls the mask over her face and Dylan does the same. They grab each other by the hand and follow the banners into the streets. The intersection of 16th and Mission is now filled with nearly a thousand people and both entrances to the BART station are crowded with stragglers. The Aztec dancers circle around the drums and enact a final crescendo of rhythm and motion. Someone in the middle of the street blows a conch shell towards the stars. People begin to whoop and yell and cheer as the march heads out from the intersection, propelled by an invisible engine. Dylan sees a line of police lined up in front of the Vermillion. They stretch out across the street with clubs in their hands and white helmets on their heads. The camera crews turn their lights on, the newscasters stand across from the apartment, and the thirty foot antennas begin their live transmissions.

Like a beast with 2000 legs, the crowd moves behind the giant banners. The largest of them has the words *#VENGEANCEFORMARIO* written in black on red fabric. It takes ten people to hold. Everyone marches slowly while a mobile sound system blasts hip-hop from somewhere within the crowd. A woman waves a tie of burning sage above her head and fills the air with its pungent smoke. The conch is blown once again and Dylan thinks it sounds like the ocean assembling her army. It makes her feel as if they're marching to war.

The siren lights strobe from building to building as the police start to back away from the Vermillion. The crowd is too strong, too powerful. It fills both the sidewalk and the street and pushes the police away without a fight. The crowd is cloaked behind a wall of banners and marches in total opacity, unseen by the eyes of the police. For a moment, Dylan smells a hint of gasoline in the air. It seems to be quite close. And then five people suddenly ignite road flares from within the crowd and hold the red flames high above their heads, filling the air with sulfur. The conch is blown one more time. This is when it happens.

With the Vermillion completely surrounded, a dozen dark objects fly towards the luxury apartments and explode in bursts of color against the windows and walls. In reds, pinks, greens, and yellows, the paint drips down as the first rocks crack the large panes of glass. Dylan sees one of the road flares go flying towards the police and watches dark figures swing black flags against white helmets as another group tears at the front door of the Vermillion. Dylan takes out her key fob, waves it in front of Alexis' face, and then nods towards the front entrance.

Without saying a word, Alexis snatches it out of her hand, sprints over to the steel door, and scans the key fob at 9:31 pm. There's soon a blossom of fire in the front lobby, then another. They look like orange roses kissing themselves. By then Alexis is already back with the key fob in hand. The entire lobby burns red and Alexis stares at Dylan in ecstasy, her chest heaving. There's no time to speak after this. Dylan puts the fob in her pocket just before she and Alexis are forced to run.

The police have gathered in one big group and now charge at the demonstration. They chase people down with motorcycles and blare orders through loud speakers. As fire arcs through the sky, Dylan sees a police car burning, she hears the sound of glass breaking, and then suddenly Alexis pulls her into a loud bar filled with voices. They quickly take off their leather jackets and Dylan stuffs them back in her bag. They get their shirts on, wait for the police to disperse, and fail to hear the men heckling them at the bar.

"Seriously, let's go back to my place," Dylan says.

"What?" Alexis breaths heavily, she shakes her head. "Are you crazy?"

"It's better that way. It'll look like I was trying to get back in. It'll look like the mob assaulted me. You scanned it already. They know I was there now."

Alexis starts to say something. She opens her mouth but it stays open. Nothing emerges.

"I didn't think about that," she eventually mutters. "I'm sorry."

"Hey, baby! You wanna lift your shirt again, that was nice!"

Alexis flips off the bar without looking at the men and walks Dylan out onto Mission Street.

"Don't worry," Dylan says. "We'll go in through the side door. Just act scared."

They sprint in a giant circle around the block. They sweat and pant as their hair flies backwards in wild tendrils. The Vermillion parking garage is surrounded by police and blocked off with yellow tape when they arrive. Dylan takes the key fob out of her pocket, waves it in the air, and forces herself to cry. The cops see them and bark orders to stop. This makes Dylan cry even harder.

"Is it safe to go in?" she sobs. "Is it safe?"

"Do you live here, ma'am? Is this—"

"They tried to rob me, to get inside, to...is it safe to go in now?" she yells. "Is it safe?"

"Yes, yes, yes, go, go, go, quickly."

They push Alexis and Dylan by the shoulders toward the parking garage door. One of the cops responds to his radio, informs his superiors of two residents being let in through the side door, and the voice on the speaker quickly approves. Dylan keeps sobbing. She thanks the cop multiple times and scans her key fob into the Vermillion at 9:41 pm. Dylan cries as they walk past the security cameras and up the stairs to the second floor. Alexis tries to cry, her eyes and mouth make her look distraught, but there are no actual tears.

The neighbors in the hallway stare at Dylan and Alexis as they walk past. Many of them are crying but Dylan doesn't look. She doesn't want to see their faces. She just wants them to see her crying. The fire has been extinguished and the entire hallway smells like fresh smoke laced with the faint remnant of burnt petroleum. There are firemen downstairs in the lobby talking on their radios and listening to the metallic babble of their superiors. Dylan opens her steel front door, locks it behind them, and then stares into the peephole. The neighbors are looking at her apartment. All of them.

"This is unreal," Alexis says. "Un-fucking-real."

Dylan wipes the black tears from her cheeks and smiles.

"You really worked yourself up there," Alexis tells her. "You were really crying."

"I'm totally stressed out."

"Come on, let's take a shower together."

They undress in the bedroom, Alexis gets the water hot, and they wash each other under the stream. Dylan relaxes her muscles, her jaw, and her face. She begins to feel pleasure running through her body and all of her tension melts away when Alexis kisses her neck. They eventually get out of this long shower and put on fresh towels. While Alexis shakes out her hair, Dylan goes to her computer desk and grabs the metal locket. She feels its tiny weight in her palm, looks at her picture from Instagram, and then strings it around her neck.

"What's that?" Alexis asks.

"Ricky gave it to me. Come see."

Alexis crosses the bedroom and opens the book-shaped locket. She sees the picture of Dylan in the center where she's wearing black sunglasses and staring up at the sky. A single tear suddenly dribbles out from the corner of Alexis' left eye. She doesn't rub it away. She lets it fall to her chin.

"This is how I found you," Alexis whispers.

She closes the metal locket, wraps her arms around Dylan, and finally lets go of her sadness. Her entire body convulses and trembles. She sinks to the floor, curls over her knees, and opens her mouth in a scream that doesn't come. This silence makes Dylan panic. She pulls Alexis up by the armpits just as her lover's sobs and spasms return. They lay on the bed and Dylan strokes her hair until the painful noises stop quaking from her body. Outside, the red and blue lights strobe against concrete walls and panes of glass. The police chase people down alleyways and streets as helicopter spotlights illuminate the skyline. Alexis and Dylan see none of this. They spend the night between sleep and consciousness, intense pleasure and pure sadness. They hardly speak to each other. There's no need for words.

CHAPTER 7

Dylan tightens her grasp when she realizes Alexis is still there. They've slept with their legs entwined and their bodies curved together. Alexis doesn't stir but occasionally snores into the pillow while Dylan breathes into her back. Dylan thinks she's in a deserted apartment but soon realizes this is a dream. The stairs of her building lead nowhere. The doors don't open. The refrigerator is empty. When she eventually wakes up, Alexis is singing to herself in the shower.

"Why are you up so early?" Dylan asks into the steam.

"I have to work at noon."

"Oh." Dylan looks at her feet. "I didn't know you had to work."

"Aww. Don't worry. Seriously."

"What time is it?"

"A bit after 10:30."

"I'll go with you to work. I mean, to get the—"

"You should come in *here*," Alexis says. "Right now."

Dylan steps into the warm steam and Alexis kisses her on the lips. She whispers into Dylan's ear and touches every part of her body. They're in the shower for fifteen minutes and moan loudly into the steam. It makes both of them pant in pleasure. Their sweat is instantly washed away.

Alexis turns off the water and they both get dressed. Dylan puts on black pants and a blue blouse, something slightly different from what she wore yesterday. In the mirror, Dylan thinks she looks professional, like she's going to the office, but when she sees Alexis in the pink jacket, it suddenly makes her feel afraid.

"You look really beautiful," she tells Alexis, her eyes now filled with tears. "You look—"

"Stop, stop. What's wrong? Why are you crying again?"

"I don't know."

"Look, this is how I make money. You don't need to worry."

"Maybe it's that." Dylan wipes her eyes. "I just feel scared."

"Don't be. Everything's fine. Come on."

With some sustained effort, Alexis convinces Dylan to put on her shoes. They make coffee together while Alexis tells funny stories about interesting people from all over the world. She describes their ear lobes, their nostrils, their eyes, their piercings, and their speech patterns. Dylan eventually laughs as Alexis tells her of tumbling down redwood hills like a brown snowball and fishing for crawdads with old men on a leaking boat. She talks about the desert hell-town she came from, the creepy old men in vans, the violent women who didn't take any shit, and the police who ruled over everyone with fear. While she tells these stories, Dylan drinks her coffee and begins to feel better. The wave of terror vanishes.

"I mean, I come from a rough place, you know. I've been fighting these pigs my whole life."

"When was the last time you went home? Back to Mojave?"

"Uh, never! Hell no! I don't ever want to go back. Ever! Wouldn't be a good idea either."

"Seriously, we should take my money and run," Dylan says. "We should run."

"You keep saying that."

"Yeah!" Dylan sits up on the kitchen stool. "Because I want to!"

"We've got time to make plans. We've got time. But not right now. Right now we gotta go."

At 11:06 am, they leave the Vermillion through the parking garage door. They don't encounter a single neighbor as they walk away from the building, its surveillance cameras, and the yellow police tape blocking off the lobby. It's another sunny day in the Mission District with not a single trace of fog. They head south on Capp Street towards the brown grass of Bernal Hill glowing in the distance. There's little traffic on the street and only a few people are on the sidewalk. A flock of pigeons flutter in the air until they decide to perch on a black power line. Everything's calm today.

"Where's this Airbnb anyway?" Dylan asks.

"It's at the end of Capp down there. Look, I don't want you to come upstairs. It feels—"

Alexis shakes her head and blinks rapidly.

"I don't have to come," Dylan says.

"I'll just toss the thumb drive out the back window. I'll show you, come on."

DARLINGTONIA

They run across 24th into Lilac Alley where the lower walls of every building are covered in jagged graffiti and bright murals. The backyards are visible through chain link fences and wooden slats that reveal glimpses of grass and full laundry lines. The alley is thick with the smells of beer and urine. It's completely deserted except for a small black cat sniffing through a pile of trash.

"There's a lot of buildings like this one," Alexis says. "Its basically an informal brothel."

"Who owns it?" Dylan asks.

"A guy one of my friends knows, an old client of hers, some tech guy. We use it so much he just charges us a really low flat fee and doesn't advertise it on Airbnb like the other apartments."

"Does he own the whole building?"

"Yeah, and a couple others. He said something like that once."

"Why don't you want me to come in?"

"That one," Alexis says, pointing. "The second story."

It's a tall beige Victorian in the middle of the alley. The lower walls are covered with a chain link cage meant to keep away the graffiti and murals. It appears to have succeeded. The windows are old, the exterior has a coat of fresh paint, and not a single spot of foreign brightness marks the surface.

"I'll just throw it down to you from that window, okay?" Alexis says.

"Why don't you want me to come in?"

"Dylan." Alexis grabs her shoulders. "This is a sick place. And you're a miracle. Stay that way, no matter what. Promise me! Don't let it get you. Okay? Stay true, alright. And stay free."

"I'll come up there—"

"No! I don't want you to! Just—"

Alexis pushes back her tears, kisses Dylan on the cheek, and runs away. She points at the window one last time before disappearing around the corner. The small black cat in the alley pauses for a moment before it resumes eating a discarded chicken bone. An oil-stained KFC bag is at its feet and the paper rumples every time it takes a bite. The cat looks at Dylan when it chews, licks its mouth, and then tears another piece of meat.

It takes Alexis longer than Dylan expects so she begins to pace through Lilac Alley. She kicks an empty spray can across the pavement and follows a path of yellow paint to a series of murals spread across the wooden fences. In huge strokes of yellow, orange, and green are the words **KILL ALL COPS** with a masked Virgin of Guadalupe standing above them. On the next fence is the phrase **KEEP HOODS YOURS** with the image of a Molotov cocktail flying in the air. From the paint marks on the ground and the color of the empty spray-cans, Dylan can tell these murals were painted last night, either before or after the riot. She knows all of this is real.

Dylan anxiously looks up at the wood and glass windows of the Victorian apartment building. She feels an emptiness invade her stomach and a black hole pull at her lungs so she tries to concentrate on the small black cat eating off the chicken bone. It has nice yellow eyes that are alert and bright, but those same lovely eyes suddenly grow wide in fear and the cat tears off as frantic stomping emerges from the Victorian.

The window flies open and Alexis leans outside, her black hair exploding in every direction. For a moment, it looks like a dark octopus suspended in honey. She drops the black thumb drive to the ground and it falls perfectly into Dylan's outstretched hands. Dylan isn't aware of what's happening inside the building. It doesn't make sense yet. She puts the drive into her back pocket, looks up at Alexis, and sees nothing but anger burning in her lover's eyes.

"Run that way," Alexis says softly, pointing at 25th Street. "It's the Feds, you need to run."

"I love you."

"Run," she hisses.

The window slams shut and Dylan does what she's told. She sprints to the end of Lilac and peers around the corner. There are no men with badges or guns, no black SUVs, no police cruisers, so she runs away through red stoplights and groups of school children and lines of oncoming traffic. She runs past old women and their shopping carts, teenage boys on skateboards, and young men drinking beer on staircases. Dylan has no consciousness of who might be chasing her. She can hardly see anything but the distance bobbing ahead.

She keeps running until her body is screaming for her to stop, until her calf muscles feel like bursting water pipes, until her clothes are drenched in sweat and she's surrounded by a sea of brown grass. In her fury, Dylan has run to the slopes of Bernal Hill. She can see the entire gray city sprawling around her in every direction, she can feel the coastal wind blowing through her hair, and she can smell the scent of salt traveling in from the ocean. There's no one following but she keeps running until she eventually collapses in the dry grass and disappears from sight. Dylan hyperventilates with her eyes fixed on the blue sky. She tries to wake up from this terrible dream that has invaded her heart. She shuts her eyes tightly. Then she opens them. It doesn't work. She wants to be lying in bed with Alexis, she wants to be in her arms, she wants it to be this morning, she wants it to be forever.

INTERLUDE

His smartphone alarm goes off and he doesn't want to hear it. Not today. Not ever. His wife is still asleep when it happens and starts to moan. She doesn't want to hear it either. He sits up with a grunt, deactivates the alarm, and gets out of his warm bed. He lumbers into the shower but the hot water only makes him more sleepy. There are some mornings where he's even fallen asleep against the tiles, so he doesn't take longer than five minutes to finish bathing. He sets the water to cold, wakes himself up with a burst of shivers, and covers his skin in goosebumps. After this, he puts on his hotel uniform and then leaves the apartment as quietly as possible. His daughter is still asleep.

The sky is dark but tinged with purple as he walks down the concrete staircase and through the housing complex parking lot. He gets into his old Mazda, warms up the engine, and smokes a small bowl of weed. He doesn't roll down the window and holds the smoke deep in his lungs. It makes all the morning lights glitter as he heads towards the Coliseum.

He pulls the Mazda into an illuminated McDonald's drive-thru and orders a large coffee with cream and a sausage muffin. He pays $2.50 at the window to a woman wearing a red hat and a black headset. He drinks his coffee on the freeway and eats his sandwich with one hand on the wheel. He drives the red Mazda through the morning mist and listens to KMEL on 106.1 FM. The CD player in the car stopped working last year and there's no USB port or auxiliary jack on the stereo. He hates driving with headphones in his ears because it makes him feel claustrophobic. So he plays the radio, listens to the traffic report, and moves his torso to the music.

The sky is mostly purple when he parks his car by the train tracks. He keeps the engine running and listens to Beyoncé sing "Formation" while he smokes another bowl of weed. This one is bigger than the last. The Mazda faces south towards the new luxury apartments and he sees the Teslas and BMWs and Porsches stream out of the parking garages on their way to San Francisco. It makes him angry to watch this spectacle every morning but it also keeps him grounded in his reality. The song on the radio ends and is replaced with commercials for cars and diamonds and theme parks. He knocks the ashes out the window, puts his pipe in the glove box, and takes a cigarette from the pack of Kools he keeps under the driver's seat.

He smokes the cigarette as he strolls along the waterfront docks and remembers how the police interviewed him after he found the body. They asked him why he was on the docks that morning and if he knew the man in the water. For a moment, it seemed as if they suspected him. This made him angry so he stopped talking and said he wanted to go. One of the Oakland Police Department officers went over to a man in a dark suit, probably an FBI agent, and asked him a question. The agent shook his head and waved the cop away as if he were annoyed. After that, the cops said he could go. He thinks about this while he smokes, throws the cigarette butt onto the pavement, and then walks inside the air-conditioned lobby of the London Lodge. He'll be behind the front desk until 3:00 pm with one hour for lunch at noon.

He chews gum and stands at the computer, sometimes talking with his coworker but mostly just going through his Twitter feed. He eats the free pastries provided to the guests, drinks the free juice, eats the free fruit, and sips the free coffee. It's his complimentary breakfast, although there's little protein involved and his stomach growls throughout the day.

His coworker turns on the television in the back room and the opening song of the morning news floods the front desk. He checks an elderly white couple out of the hotel and once they're gone he goes back to watch. The television sits beside the copy machine and is plugged into the hotel cable that extends from the wall. After a short segment on the Oakland A's and their upcoming baseball game, the newscasters speak of a recent arrest in the Mission District of San Francisco.

They explain that a woman named Alexis Segura was arrested yesterday inside an Airbnb unit and charged with the murder of Ricardo Florez, an OingoBoingo employee found dead near Jack London Square a few weeks earlier. It was first ruled a suicide by the Oakland Police Department but during a press conference the Federal Bureau of Investigation revealed it had uncovered multiple profiles for online prostitution created by Alexis Segura.

DARLINGTONIA

One of these profiles connected her to Ricardo Florez and surveillance footage taken near an Airbnb brothel revealed that Segura met with Florez on the night of his death. An FBI spokesperson told the press conference that Alexis Segura has maintained her innocence and refused to speak with them. When asked about their involvement in the case, the FBI spokesperson told the press they had reason to believe the murder was possibly a contract killing carried out on behalf of a third party against OingoBoingo, the famous game company now owned by BoonDoggle. The FBI explicitly condemned BoonDoggle for denying them access to activity logs for Ricardo Florez and has not ruled out the possibility that Alexis Segura was working for a foreign government. They also claimed that BoonDoggle's lack of cooperation was a threat to national security. Later that evening, the Central Intelligence Agency issued a tweet stating that Alexis Segura was definitely not working for Russia, China, or any other foreign power. In a follow-up tweet, the CIA reprimanded the FBI for their groundless speculation.

"What the fuck," his coworker says, looking at him. "Can you believe that? And *you* found the damn body. Now look at all this shit. CIA, FBI! And they thought *you* did it?"

"It's messed up, I know," he says. "Dude was mixed up in some heavy business."

"No kidding! Not town business though, this is some international business."

"They're all on some creepy shit at Google and BoonDoggle, they're in all our fucking phones." He takes the black Samsung Galaxy out of his pocket and wiggles it in the air. "Back in the day I was always telling people don't have one of these things, it's a fucking microphone. Hella fools be asking Siri questions or talking their texts out and shit, obviously it's a fucking microphone. Feds got all of it. They got this conversation here, they got me and my girl talking about dinner, and of course you got some street cat posting pictures of his guns and money, his exact location, shit like that."

"Yeah, well speak for yourself. And stop cursing. Anyway, I just got my flip phone, never had no smartphone. I use my daughter's thing when I gotta do something for work or life or whatever. I don't like 'em. They give you cancer, that's what I keep telling people, but they don't listen."

"You know nobody listen. Anyway, you probably read that on the internet."

"It *does* make those kids smarter, though. They can do stuff I can't even think about."

"Yeah, well I got one, too"

"Cuz your girl work at the cell phone store. That's why you got the biggest one. We all know that stuff be fallin' off the back of a truck at the warehouse."

They both laugh just as an elderly white couple approaches the front desk. He coughs once, winks his left eye at his coworker, and leaves the back room to help the guests. They smile meekly at him while he types, they're very polite when they speak, and they check out of the hotel with the least possible hassle. Before leaving, the gray haired couple smiles at him as if they're proud of something.

For the next several hours, he goes between working the desk and swiping on the screen of his smartphone. A whole host of blogs he never reads have unearthed a large amount of information about Alexis Segura including her pictures, her videos, and her social media accounts used for online prostitution. One website calls her the *Cyber-Hooker from Hell*, another refers to her as the *Airbnb Call-Girl Turned Contract Killer*. Many other websites have similar headlines, all of them sensationalizing her profession and featuring semi-nude pictures.

As the 11:00 am check-out deadline approaches, the lobby is flooded with Chinese families all trying to leave together, each with separate bills. He and his coworkers spend the next hour checking them out while a dozen children run around and scream and yell. The Chinese mothers and fathers don't argue over the high bills they've accrued, they pay in cash, and almost all of them leave in private cars with blacked out windows. By the time they're done it's 11:40 am. He and his coworker have each received nearly $800 in tips.

"I know where *I'm* going to lunch," she says.

"I'll go with you."

"Damn they was loaded! You know what they was here for? A convention?"

"No idea."

At their noon lunch break, when another coworker arrives and takes over the desk, they both go across the railroad tracks to The

Home of Chicken and Waffles. He normally doesn't eat here because it's too expensive but now it doesn't matter. They each get big plates with a waffle and three wings. They order multiple side dishes and drink coffee while they wait. They talk about their kids, they laugh about ridiculous stories, and when their food arrives they eat ravenously. Syrup and butter mingle in the squares of the waffle, the golden fried chicken steams when they tear it open, and the greens release tendrils of steam into the air. Neither of them expected to get tips this big. They talk about what they could do with the money, how they could spend it on their families, and how much a hotel on the beach costs per night. They finish their food, drink their coffee, and pay $20 for each of their lunches. It's been a good morning. He never gets this full at work. He's usually starving.

At 3:00 pm, he clocks out and goes back to his Mazda. He smokes a small bowl of weed, listens to the radio, and then starts the engine. There's no point getting on the freeway with all the traffic so he drives along the waterfront past the motels and marinas and industrial equipment. He finally gets on the 880 freeway near Fruitvale Boulevard and heads south with the commute. All the lanes are clogged, it takes him several minutes to merge, and he creeps forward until the traffic picks up at the Coliseum. The radio plays "Formation" as he drives through an exhaust filled cavern of big-rig trucks and oil tankers going thirty miles an hour. He crosses the border out of Oakland and then takes the Davis Street off-ramp into San Leandro.

His wife works at the Verizon store in the Westgate Center mall and every weekday morning she walks their daughter to school. She drops her off at Woodrow Wilson Elementary for her fourth grade classes and then crosses the freeway overpass into the mall. She always wears her black Verizon uniform on the way to work. Every weekday afternoon, around 3:30 pm, her husband comes to pick her up in the Mazda. This has been happening for four years. Today is no different. This is their routine.

He pulls into the parking lot while she's smoking a cigarette and scrolling through her phone. There are strands of purple and gold in her hair, her black uniform is covered in yellow pollen from the tree above, and she throws away the cigarette once he pulls up. When she gets inside, he smells her jasmine perfume waft through the car.

"How you doing, baby?" he asks.

"Alright." She kisses him on the lips with her eyes closed. "Fucking tired."

"You got this yellow shit all over here."

She squints her eyes and looks down, quickly brushing away the tiny yellow threads.

"It's from that weird ass tree," she says.

"It's your dandruff."

She punches his shoulder and laughs.

"Shut up! Hey, you hear that new shit about the dead body?"

"Been looking at it all day. You can't make this stuff up."

He drives her out of the parking lot and they cross the bridge over the 880 freeway. They talk about what they saw on social media, all the articles, all the details. They joke about the movie *Jason Bourne* and the CIA and how the FBI are probably just the dumb little kids of the federal government. He pulls the Mazda up outside the elementary school, kisses his wife on the cheek, and then runs across the street to the after school program where his daughter's playing ball outside with the other children. She sees him standing at the fence, runs to get her pink Disney Princess backpack, and then points her dad out to the supervisor. The two men wave to each other, his daughter sprints to the exit, and in one big explosion she jumps into her father's arms.

"How was school, baby?"

"Good! We learned about volcanoes today!"

"You did?" He puts her down and walks her towards the street. "Tell me about it."

"We poured vinegar onto baking soda and made a volcano. We made the volcano out of clay, we wrapped it around a cup, and then we painted the clay green and brown. Then we made it blow."

"Come on, let's run."

They cross the street to the Mazda and his daughter gets in back. She hugs her mom while her dad puts the key in the ignition and starts the car. He drives them up Williams Street and waits in the median lane to take a left on Pacific. There's too much traffic so he sits there for over a minute and listens to his wife and daughter talk about the miniature volcano. When there's a gap between the cars, he guns the Mazda onto Pacific and drives halfway down the block to their apartment complex.

"We don't need no groceries do we?" he asks.

"We can have hamburgers," she says, clearly tired. "We don't have any vegetables though."

"We got all those oranges from the truck guy."

"I like oranges," his daughter says. "Can I have one?"

"I'll go," he says. "I'll get some salad stuff."

"Get kale. I like kale," his daughter says.

"How'd you learn about kale?" he asks.

"She ate it at school," his wife answers. "Use the rest of my cousin's food stamps then."

"Alright."

His family gets out of the car and he waves goodbye as they climb the cement staircase to the second floor. He turns the radio up and an old Drake song fills the speakers with the words: *started from the bottom now we here.* He takes his pipe out of the glove compartment, packs a small bowl of weed, and smokes it down until there's only black char and a circle of ashes. Now that he's high, now that the music sounds like heaven, he's ready to buy groceries at the FoodMaxx with his cousin-in-law's food stamp card.

When they're done eating, his daughter returns to the television and presses play on *Malificent* with Angelina Jolie. His wife kisses him on the cheek, puts her plate in the sink, and then goes to the bathroom for a shower. Her husband does the dishes while she bathes. He cleans all the pans and wipes the table down with chemical spray and a paper towel. By the time his wife emerges from the bathroom, everything's clean, the dishes are drying in the rack, and her husband's sitting on the couch with their daughter watching Angelina Jolie fly through the air on wings made of black feathers.

"I like this movie and all," his wife says, "but why everybody gotta be all white still?"

"I *love* this movie, momma!"

"At least Angelina dresses in black," he says. "And at least she stands up to her racist ass dad."

"Yeah, *at least*. Whatever, you know you like watching white girls. Like that fucking bitch who keeps liking your posts. Why don't you tell her to stop that shit?"

"Come on." He gets up off the couch before his wife can sit down. "Not now."

"Why don't you tell her to get off your damn Facebook?"

"I can't stop people from liking my shit."

"What're you talking about?" their daughter asks.

"Nothing, baby," his wife says. "Just some dumb bitch on your daddy's Facebook feed."

"Which one's Facebook?"

"It's the blue one I showed you," her dad says. "With the funny pictures on the feed."

"All of them are blue, daddy. All of them have pictures. All of them have feeds."

"Don't go showing her that stuff. I know how your friends be acting on there."

"Come on." He takes his wife around the waist and pulls her away from the television. "Please, baby, you don't got nothing to worry about. I never like any of her shit. I bet you check, too."

"Damn right, I check it," she says, barely cracking a smile. "I got my eye on you."

"Oh yeah, check this out." He hands her the wad of cash from the Chinese guests. "This was a tip I got today. We should go somewhere, get a motel in Santa Cruz for the weekend."

"Alright!" She gently grabs the money and starts counting it. "I guess you did alright today."

While their daughter finishes *Malificent,* her parents go into their bedroom, lie down on the bed with the door open, and start smoking a hash oil vapor pen. They hold each other close and rub their skin together without speaking. When their daughter reaches the credits of the Hollywood film she runs into the bedroom, flies onto the bed, and then slides between their bodies. Her father tickles her belly and asks her about school, her friends, her teachers, and her math. Her mother keeps puffing on the vapor pen silently, happy to just listen. The hash oil calms her nerves and makes her sleepy so she tells her daughter bedtime then pushes her husband up to his feet.

He's in the bathroom with his daughter for the next ten minutes. First they brush their teeth, then he gently combs her hair, then he tells her to put on pajamas and get into bed. He turns off the television, makes sure the front door is locked, switches off all the lights, and when his daughter's in bed he kisses her cheek. He pulls the blankets up to her chin, tells her goodnight, to sleep well, and then flips the light switch. She lies there with the glowing Hello Kitty night-light and listens to her parents talk in their bedroom, although she can't hear what they're saying. She falls asleep to their muffled sounds and dreams about flying above the bay with wings made of black feathers.

As her consciousness ascends into this beautiful vision, her tired parents get under their own covers and open up Netflix on their laptop. They search through the films, bicker over which one to watch, puff on the vape pen, and settle on a movie called *Dead Presidents*. Both of them have seen it before. They know how it ends. They fall asleep to the sounds of squealing tires, gunshots, and police sirens. There's no charge in the laptop when they wake up. The machine is completely dead.

CHAPTER 8

THEY WENT DANCING ONE NIGHT. THE ENTIRE OFFICE MET AT AN expensive club and reserved a large circular couch with bottle service and all-you-can-eat tapas. Everyone was there except Chad. The company had flown him out to Beijing to meet with the heads of the Communist Party. OingoBoingo was then engaged in a furious effort to penetrate the country's market and release a Chinese version of the Dream Game. The advertising department had just finished their samples of marketing material for the Party delegation and decided to celebrate by spending thousands of dollars on themselves.

Dylan danced that night like she was trying to expel a demon from her body. She danced near other people, not with them, always maintaining a healthy distance. When another man approached, Dylan backed away and turned her eyes another direction. When a coworker tried to touch her, she moved to the nearest woman and never looked back. The only person she ever let close was Ricky. When he smiled it was with honest joy and when he touched her it was out of genuine happiness. There was no predator in his body or raptor hidden in his eyes. They danced with their bodies close together, laughed at the neon lasers, and met at the containers of ice water once they were sweaty.

They chugged down glass after glass and noted how silly the men from their department looked. Ricky said they could get away with being dumb on the dance floor simply because they were white. Ricky thought Dylan looked good when she danced and said she knew how to move with rhythm. He told her she was the only one with any style or independence or personality in the department. He said she had a confidence the others lacked. She wasn't afraid to be who she was.

"Anyway, listen," Ricky said, putting down his glass of water. "There's this spot just up the block from your pad. I think you should go there?"

"What is it? A strip club?"

"Get out of here, Connecticut. No, it's a hacklab."

"A hacklab? What's that? You mean like hackers?"

"A place where you learn *not* to be a total idiot on the internet. I'm not trying to talk shit. I'm just saying, it'd be worth you're while to go there. They'll teach you about computer security, how to avoid surveillance, things like that."

"I'm just not a techie! I'm *not*. I actually *don't* want to learn more than I already know."

"Come on. Seriously. This world is too dangerous to be that ignorant."

Dylan didn't know how to respond. Ricky seemed to feel bad so he rubbed her shoulder and then dug a business card out of his wallet with the address of the hacklab. Dylan promised to go there next weekend but by the end of the night she'd lost the card. All of this happened nearly a year before Ricky was killed. She only remembers this now, while she's lying in the grass.

Dylan returns to her apartment once her body's stopped shaking. She has no other choice. There are a few things she needs to get. At 9:31 pm, after taking all night to get home, she scans herself in through the parking garage entrance and climbs the steps to her apartment. The hallway still smells like smoke and yellow police tape blocks the stairwell to the lobby. The building seems deserted. There's no sound, nor is there any movement.

She enters her apartment at 9:33 pm and closes the steel door behind her. She turns on every light, paces from room to room, and then goes to the window. Her brown blood is still smeared across the glass, although now it's overshadowed by two globs of pink and yellow paint hurled from within the demonstration. The altar across the street has grown bigger over the day and contains nearly a hundred flickering candles that illuminate a dozen images of the Virgin Mary. Dylan looks at the paint on her window and notices a large crack left by a stone that resembles a frozen spider web. The refrigerator hums steadily in the background. The red light of her flatscreen television blinks on and off. Everything is where she left it.

At 9:37 pm, she goes into the bedroom, opens her closet, and begins to pack a variety of clothing into a dark duffel bag. Dylan grabs three nice dresses, three pairs of pants, two skirts, a jogging outfit, and several blouses she usually wears to work. She packs socks, underwear, bras, and two dark sweatshirts. She takes her running shoes, running pants, running shorts, some leather sandals, and a pair of flats. She opens up a shoe box, dumps several plastic packages atop her clothing, and then zips up the duffel bag. She puts her toothbrush, toothpaste, makeup, and deodorant in the side pocket then goes to look at herself in the mirror. The golden locket is still tied around her neck. It calms her breathing, but only for a moment.

Dylan grabs the keys to her BMW from the computer desk, turns off the bedroom lights, the living room lights, and the kitchen lights. At 9:42 pm, she leaves her apartment and rides the elevator down into the parking garage. She looks underneath her BMW, inspects every crevice, pops the front hood, and checks the engine for anything suspicious. The pipes and hoses and metal pieces are arranged before her like a metal spider. None of it makes any sense, nor does she know what she's looking for. She closes the hood, starts the car, and drives the BMW out of the Vermillion at 9:50 pm.

Dylan gets on the 101 freeway and heads south with the flow of traffic. She doesn't drive slow, nor does she drive too fast. She passes SFO airport and eventually fixates on a series of lights strung along the western hills of San Bruno. She takes the next exit off 101 and ascends into these hills on a series of winding roads that lead her through neighborhoods where every porch light is on, every brick staircase is illuminated, and every lawn carries the sign for a private security company.

At the top of the hill, Dylan finds a parking spot overlooking the airport and turns off the engine. She stares at the illuminated landing strip, the pulsing red lights, and the immense white glow in the sky that never changes color or hue. Once she's calmed down enough to think, Dylan puts on a dark blue sweatshirt, cracks the windows, and leans her seat all the way back. The planes scream as they take off from the airport and keep her heart racing furiously. The sounds make her feel tense and anxious, as if someone's yelling in her ear, but eventually she notices a rhythm between the take-offs, a hidden tempo under each acceleration. Her mind becomes familiar with this terrible, rhythmic pattern and the harsh noises of the jet engines. At some point before midnight, Dylan falls asleep. She doesn't dream.

The roar of a Delta jet pulls her from blackness. She lies there a moment and stares at the padded gray roof of her BMW. The car smells new even though it's over twenty years old. She raises her seat, takes off her sweatshirt, starts the engine, and drives down the hill towards the freeway. Dylan reaches the commercial area of San Bruno after a few minutes and pulls into a Starbucks parking lot. She walks into the air-conditioned cafe, smiles at the barista, and orders a *grande* coffee. There's no one else in line. All the other customers are seated alone with their smartphones and morning paper. Once her coffee is ready, Dylan leaves a three dollar tip in the transparent container and then fills her cup with cream. On her way out, she sees a copy of *The San Francisco Chronicle* sitting on a newspaper stand.

The headline reads *Airbnb Hooker at Center of Local Murder* with a mugshot of Alexis on one side of the page. She looks angry, fierce, almost evil. On the other side of the page is a picture of Alexis where she's smiling, heavily made-up, and wearing a jade necklace. Dylan pays for the newspaper at the counter and quickly returns to the BMW. She reads the entire article without rolling down the windows or sipping her coffee. By the end, her shirt is soaked through with sweat.

Dylan doesn't believe a single word. The article says Alexis Segura murdered Ricardo Florez, that she may have been a contract killer, and that the FBI suspects her of working with a foreign government. The article explains: *Alexis Segura was with Florez in the Airbnb unit on the night he drowned in the bay. Surveillance footage from a business around the corner shows the two walking together down the sidewalk several hours before the estimated time of death. The FBI has been unable to find any footage of Ricardo Florez leaving the Airbnb on the night of his death.* Dylan crumples the paper, turns the key in the ignition, and drives the BMW south on El Camino Real.

The engine makes the car even more of an inferno and Dylan eventually turns the air conditioning up to the maximum setting. Just as she begins to cool down, Dylan pulls the car into a parking lot and keeps the engine running. All of the cars in the lot have green and orange price numbers on their windshields. The sign above her reads

Mike's Auto Sales. There are several other BMW's for sale, none of them as nice as her own.

She keeps the air conditioning on and gathers the registration, the title, the smog test results, and all of the repair documentation from the glovebox. In the mirror, she puts on black eye-liner and blue eye-shadow. She ties her hair into a simple bun and puts on blue lipstick to match her eye-lids. Once she's done, Dylan turns off the engine and steps outside. She throws on her silver jacket, strings her bag over her shoulder, and walks into the yellow office holding her cup of Starbucks coffee.

A bald man is sitting behind the counter underneath the air-conditioning. His face is red, so are his hands. The radio is tuned to the am morning news. Someone is talking about the need to support the President and the need for greater unity. The man behind the counter doesn't notice Dylan at first. He looks bored, slightly hopeless, as if he's remembering something that's gone forever. But then he sees her as the door swings shut and stands up excitedly with wide blue eyes.

"How can I help you today?" he asks.

"Hi." She sets her keys and coffee on the counter. "Any chance you'd want to buy a BMW 3 Series? Nothing's wrong with it."

"What year?"

"2001."

"Is it in good condition?"

"Perfect condition. I'd also need another car. Maybe to trade? Do you do that?"

"Sure do. Just like it says on the sign out there. Let's take a look."

The bald man steps outside with her, inspects the BMW, looks over the documents, and offers $3,000. She accepts this amount and finds a blue Mazda priced at $1,500. After explaining how reliable this little Mazda will be, how it'll last for decades, and how it gets great gas mileage, he takes her into the office where they fill out the necessary paperwork to complete the transaction.

"I like the name Mazda," Dylan says.

"It does have a nice ring to it, doesn't it?"

"It comes from Ahura Mazda, the Lord of Light."

"Like the god the red lady worships in *Game of Thrones*? You watch that show?"

"Of course, yeah, her religion's based on an old Persian religion, the same Lord of Light."

"Well, go figure. I *do* know Mazda had its HQ in old Hiroshima. *They* survived an atomic bomb. The damn owner was driving in his car when the shock wave sent him spinning like a football. *He* survived, so did the Mazda factory, and everyone else got burnt to shit."

Dylan can't respond to this, nor does she want to, so she continues filling out the last of the paperwork. When they finish, when she has the title for the new vehicle in hand, when all that's left to do is collect her $1,327 balance, Dylan asks the bald man a question.

"So what happens now? You send my BMW slip to the DMV?"

"Yeah, but I won't get it in there till later this week if that's alright."

"Take your time. But the Mazda plates are good until then, right?"

"Yeah, don't worry. Just go to the DMV on Friday. I'll have it in by then, but don't wait too long after that. It won't be officially yours until you do that. Here, let me count this out for you."

He lays out thirteen hundred dollar bills, a twenty, a five, and seven ones on the counter. He slides over the keys and then firmly shakes her hand. He says he likes the way she does business, no haggling or arguing. He says business is all about trust in the end. He says the Mazda will never let her down. He calls it a little tank and swears on his life it'll never fail her. He keeps talking while she moves her belongings to the Mazda and helps her look through the BMW for anything left behind. All they discover is a map of New England and a crumpled edition of *The San Francisco Chronicle*. After hesitating a moment, she decides to keep the paper.

Dylan waves to the man as she pulls the blue Mazda onto El Camino Real and drives south with the traffic. The newspaper resting on the passenger's seat reminds her of Alexis sitting in the county jail. It reminds her there's something important on the flash drive, something Ricky sacrificed himself for. Dylan remembers the necklace on her chest, remembers Alexis touching it, and in this moment she sees a fire burning in her imagination. She follows the signs to the 101 freeway, merges into the northbound traffic, and eventually sees the new Childhood Memory Game billboard hanging over the freeway. It makes her feel sick, although it's probably just the coffee.

Dylan gets off the 101 and drives into the Mission District. She parks on 17th Street between a red SUV and a battered pick-up truck. Both vehicles are empty and box the Mazda in so no one can see her change clothes. She takes off her silver jacket, puts on a black sweatshirt, and pins her hair up in a flat bun. After this, she opens one of the plastic packages from her duffel bag and fluffs out a blonde wig.

Over a year earlier, Dylan bought twenty wigs of every color for a party that never happened, a party where the men in the office would have worn long, feminine hair. Dylan ultimately decided against it, she didn't want to host the party at her apartment, nor did she want the men in her space. She never mentioned the idea to any of her coworkers, not even Bernadette or Elizabeth.

Dylan puts on the blonde wig and smooths the fake hair around her cheeks so it looks natural. The inside of the wig is scratchy and thick and clings to her real hair, making it hard to fall off. She puts on her black sunglasses, wipes the lipstick from her mouth with a clean sock, and stares in the rear-view mirror until the person she sees is no longer herself. Dylan takes the flash drive out of her pocket, pushes the USB connector out of its plastic sheath, and sees the thin metal reflect in the sunlight. Dylan sees another burning flame. She puts the drive back in her pocket, locks the car doors, and walks off to find the hacklab.

Ricky said it was near her apartment so she takes a left down Mission. The people on the street don't pay Dylan much attention, just a few tattooed men on the corner who look her up and down while she passes. One of them flashes a gold tooth. Further down the block, she stops in front of a three-story building with a Mexican market on the ground floor that's packed with fruit and vegetable stands. Next to this business is a gated doorway with a black and red sign hanging above it. Printed on the glossy vinyl banner is a diagram of audio circuitry and the words *noisebridge.net* written in white. Dylan assumes this is the hacklab but before she can do anything a woman with curly red hair and freckles opens the metal security gate. She looks at Dylan and holds the door open with an inviting smile.

"It's pretty dead right now," the woman tells her. "Might bore you to death."

"That's alright."

"Don't fall asleep in there."

Dylan smiles and walks inside Noisebridge without looking back. The first thing she notices is a surveillance camera in the stairwell with a green light blinking on and off. It records her entering the building at 12:14 pm. At the top of the stairs, Dylan finds a vast room with several empty terminals near the back windows. The hum of computers fills her ears, the air smells like burnt coffee, and no one responds when she says hello. There are two additional surveillance cameras mounted on the walls so she sits down at an iMac which is out of sight, wiggles the mouse, and waits for the screen to wake up. Dylan notices the camera atop the iMac has a piece of black electrical tape over its camera. This makes her feel safe for a moment, although she keeps her left hand inside her pocket and does nothing but stare at the computer. And then she remembers Alexis sitting in jail, she clenches her jaw, inserts the thumb drive, and opens up the file.

At 12:16 pm, a series of seemingly normal requests from computer terminal seven begin to leave the Noisebridge firewall at an extremely high frequency, far too high to be normal. A young man in a room just ten feet from Dylan is monitoring the Noisebridge traffic on a laptop when this sudden burst of activity occurs. He's wearing headphones and hasn't heard Dylan come in. He leans back in his swivel chair to find her sitting at computer terminal seven. He sees the thumb drive inserted into the iMac, throws off his headphones, and proceeds to rip every cable from the Noisebridge server.

Just as Dylan realizes the files are encrypted and cannot be opened, a series of frantic noises emerges from the room behind her. She turns around just as a young man with curly black hair runs out of the back room and disconnects the power and internet cables from her iMac. He tries to remove the flash drive but Dylan doesn't let him touch it, she wrestles the device away and puts it in her pocket.

"What the fuck *is* that?" he yells.

The young man can only see a woman wearing a blonde wig and black sunglasses. Dylan can only see disaster reflected in his eyes. She's gone to great lengths to disguise herself, she's clearly in a lot of trouble, and at this point she's said nothing incriminating. Dylan knows this.

"I need help," she whispers. "This is encrypted."

"You just brought a bunch of shit down on us! Someone wants that...fuck! Fuck!"

"Calm down, please."

"What is that thing?" he asks.

"It's encrypted!"

"Fuck!"

"Listen, this is important!"

Suddenly there's another person in the room, a short bearded man with glasses.

"What the fuck's going on?" he asks loudly.

"Someone just got inside, this USB started sending out all sorts of requests! I disconnected the server, everything's offline, but they've gotten something into our system by now—"

Both of the men look at her. She can tell they're furious. They want to call the police. They want to turn her in and exonerate themselves. But something in them hesitates. Neither of these men ever thought this would happen, that someone would test their ideals in this way, that someone would make them choose a side, and that it would be a woman asking for help. Dylan doesn't know what they're thinking as they glare at her, but her instincts tell her she's safe.

"I'm on it!" the bearded man yells, running into the back room. "Deal with her!"

"Please—"

"Listen! *You* listen! You don't know anything! Whatever's on that thing...fuck! Fuck!" He runs into another room and quickly brings back a laptop and battery charger which he stuffs into a paper bag. "This thing won't connect to the internet. If it's encrypted you'll need the key but I can't help you anymore than—"

"What about the surveillance camera—"

"We'll wipe it! We'll wipe everything! Go! Run! Get the fuck out of here!"

"I'm sorry!"

"Get the fuck out! Go!"

Dylan runs out of the room, hurries down the stairs, and slowly opens the security door. There are no police cars outside, no black SUVs, no sirens of any kind, so she runs down 18th and away from Mission Street. Now everyone is looking at her, this blonde woman in a dark sweatshirt and black sunglasses. She slows her pace but they keep looking, the mothers and their children, the gangsters and their friends, the techies and their smartphones, they stare at her as if she were on fire with sparks flying into the air. Some of these people smile as she passes. Dylan doesn't understand.

She sees cameras on every other building and police cruisers on every other street. She clutches the laptop tightly to her chest, lowers her gaze, and walks forward blindly. At some point, Dylan begins to pray without speaking and sees the Virgin of Guadalupe floating like a vision in her mind. She remembers smoking a blunt with Alexis, remembers the men in the low-rider, and begins to feel safe in this neighborhood although she doesn't know why. When she looks up, there's no one paying attention to her and she's made it to Shotwell. The Mazda is just down the street.

Dylan gets inside and puts the laptop on the back seat. She takes off her wig, her glasses, and her sweatshirt. She puts on her silver jacket, lets down her real hair, and drives the car along 17th Street to Potrero. She can't remember how to get on the freeway and accidentally ascends the on-ramp for I-80 near Bryant Street. By the time she realizes what she's done, Dylan is irreversibly headed towards the Bay Bridge and the City of Oakland.

She passes the county jail on her way out of San Francisco. The jail is a long building made of curving glass and from the outside it can be easily mistaken for the offices of a tech company, a fancy condo building, or the local headquarters of a multinational corporation. Dylan has seen this glass building before but still doesn't know what it is. She has no idea that Alexis is locked up behind those wavy glass windows, wearing an orange jumpsuit, sitting alone on a metal bunk, staring out at the passing cars, and waiting for her chance to speak.

CHAPTER 9

IT WAS THE LAST TIME THEY CELEBRATED BEFORE EVERYTHING COLlapsed. The Communist Party of China rejected the proposal to introduce OingoBoingo mind games to their domestic population. It was all a complete failure. The new ad designs were scrapped and the company delegation returned home disappointed and disgraced, especially Chad, who then displaced his anger onto Bernadette and Elizabeth. Their work was disappointing, their work was missing something, and they never saw the big picture. Dylan observed this all silently and was relieved Chad never chose her as the object of criticism. But then he was suddenly called away from the office for two weeks and when he returned his mood had altered. He was now compulsively nice to everyone, extraordinarily positive about everything, and continued to avoid Dylan to the best of his ability.

After the disaster in China, nearly all of the tech blogs and newspapers began to run variations of a story involving CEO Bilton Smyth and several officials from the Communist Party. Everyone agreed that Bilton Smyth had engaged in a heated ideological argument with these officials and began to yell about unrestricted free market capitalism in the middle of a state dinner. An anonymously uploaded video showed ten seconds of Bilton Smyth calling the Chinese officials "savages" and "cretins" while standing atop a large banquet table filled with crab. The collapse of the deal was never elaborated to the media, although the outburst in Beijing was widely known to be the cause of it.

At the time of this incident, the stock price for OingoBoingo was close to $30 a share but dropped below $20 once the Chinese market was lost. This caused widespread sadness and depression in many employees, including Dylan. It was the first time her company had not gotten what it wanted, the first time its internal narrative of changing the world broke down and rang hollow. Until that moment, Dylan had been thrilled with the success of the OingoBoingo Dream Game and felt proud of how smart it made ordinary people, how it sharpened their memory and taught them to face their fears. Like the rest of her coworkers, Dylan felt very attached to OingoBoingo in those days.

Her identity and drive were bound up in the success of each product, each campaign, and each billboard.

And then one afternoon Ricky pulled her aside during the lunch break. They walked past the elevators towards the tall windows that faced the bay. The sunlight was reflecting off the water and seagulls filled the blue sky in swirling patterns. From where they stood, Dylan could see the steel towers of the Bay Bridge looming over the waterfront as ferry boats and cargo ships sailed beneath.

"So check this out," Ricky said. "They got me on something new. I'm supposed to help take the company in a new direction. That's what they keep saying."

"What new direction?"

"I don't know. Just new. But it's got to do with data. I know that much. They want me to take the stuff I was doing for the Chinese deal and apply it here."

"Are you going to be a techie now?"

"Might as well be. Gotta play the game. But it's not what you're thinking. It's visual."

In the days that followed, Dylan began to see Ricky going through page after page of user data on his computer. He studied the ninety-nine answers provided by each Dream Game player and practiced synthesizing the various written elements of their dreams into coherent visual images. He eventually began to write down keywords generated from these user answers and used them to create aggregate dream characters for the next billboards.

Ricky was excited about his new assignment and spoke to Dylan about it often. He told her of the strange user data and how each mind game generated an infinitely complex world of both nightmares and dreams, something he found quite beautiful. But within a month, Ricky seemed to lose this excitement and stopped talking about it with the same enthusiasm. This coincided with his constant disappearance for the entire workday, returning from upstairs only to get his jacket and bag. When he did talk to Dylan, it was mostly about how dumb their coworkers acted, how detached Elizabeth and Bernadette were becoming, and how insufferable Chad's presence was. Aside from these occasional jabs at their boss, Ricky lost his sense of humor for the next few months.

But in the spring he asked Dylan, Bernadette, and Elizabeth to go clubbing with him in the Mission. All of them agreed. Dylan was very surprised that Ricky invited the other two but when she arrived at the club it all made sense. Ricky just wanted to see them out of the office and away from the others. After drinking together for twenty minutes, Ricky told them to get out on the floor. They all danced as a group, kept their bodies close together, and for a moment everyone was happy. Then something broke this connection, perhaps it was just a change in the beat or a shift in the music, but either way the rupture was definitive and made them all drift away. Ricky and Dylan eventually gravitated back to the table, drank some water, and that's when he told her to stay safe.

"What do you mean stay safe?" she asked. "You mean like walking home?"

"No. In general. Just be careful. This world's going down fast."

"That's what everyone always says. But things are fine, everything's—"

"Everything *isn't* fine." He nodded toward the dance floor. "Just look at those two. Look at what happened to them. This world's terrible, and you're my friend. I want you to stay safe."

"Why are you so worried all of a sudden?"

"No reason, really. But you hear me, though, right? Stay safe. No matter what."

Ricky took her by the shoulders and looked into her eyes. He was trying his best to smile but Dylan could tell there was something dark behind his brown eyes. All she managed to do was nod before Ricky leaned over the bar and asked for a glass of soda. Dylan never understood why he said this to her, not until now, not until she remembers it.

It costs nothing to cross the new bridge from San Francisco to Oakland. This is only the fifth time she's driven under its pyramidal support beams since moving to the Bay Area. Dylan saw the eastern portion of the old bridge being dissembled when she first drove across over a year ago. She watched the steel ribs disappear piece by piece over the next months until there was only one orphan section standing above the water. At some point during this process, it was decided to blow up the remnant rather than take it apart and Dylan remembers seeing the collapse on Twitter. She watched the video in a loop until she got bored and forgot about it. Now she drives the speed limit in the slow lane, looks out at the water, and sees no traces of either steel or concrete. The old bridge is gone. There's nothing left.

Dylan is relieved when she finally leaves the new bridge and passes along the palm trees that line the westbound toll plaza. Several of these trees are dead, their fronds brown and withered, and their trunks blackened by exhaust. No one is following behind her but she keeps gazing into the rear-view mirror and is too distracted to realize she's taking the highway north to Sacramento. When she figures this out, it's too late, she's irreversibly headed past an Ikea store, a giant mall, and a strip of high-rise hotels. She drives the Mazda along marshlands lined with cypress trees, behind snarling big-rigs and oil trucks, along a small lake with a water-ski ramp, and then takes the first exit she recognizes, the one for University Avenue.

She remembers her friend Melissa from RISD who's attending UC Berkeley for her PhD in Art History. Dylan has only seen Melissa five times since she moved to San Francisco. They never talked on the phone, only through their Instagram accounts, and Dylan has no other way to reach her. She follows University Street towards the brown hills in the distance, hoping to see something familiar, a place they went together. Between the stoplights, she passes Indian restaurants and gas stations, cheap motels and grocery stores, none of which trigger any recognition.

It's not until Dylan crosses Martin Luther King Jr. Way that she sees a cafe they went to, a place that serves dinner in the back and espresso in the front. The words *Au Coquelet* are written in the center of the green awning and Dylan can see a few empty tables through the front windows. She pulls over outside an abandoned movie theater, turns off the engine, and keeps her windows rolled down so the breeze can cool her skin. On the floor of the passenger side is the paper bag with the laptop and battery charger. She makes sure the thumb drive is still in her pocket before she opens the computer and presses the gray power button. Nothing happens. There's no charge.

Dylan rolls up all the windows, stuffs the laptop and charger into her bag, and then looks into the rear-view mirror. She wipes off all her makeup and fluffs her hair so she looks frazzled and frumpy and no longer recognizes herself. Dylan gets out of the car, carries her bag into the cafe, and waits in line beside several trays of pastries, cakes, and pies. It's all too much for her, the sweet scent of glaze, the glistening syrup atop slices of kiwi and peach, the flaky butter crusts she can already taste.

She orders three pieces of different cakes and a double Americano, pays $20 for everything, and carries it all to a seat beside the window. Before checking the thumb drive, before turning on the laptop, Dylan devours the pieces of fruit cake and tart and cherry pie. She wipes the crumbs off her mouth, burps softly, takes a sip of her Americano, and then realizes it needs cream.

After making it turn brown with half and half, Dylan walks through every corner of the cafe, the dining section, even the bathroom. Her friend Melissa isn't there. Everyone in the cafe is a stranger and she returns to her seat feeling defeated. There's nothing else to do but wait. Dylan plugs the laptop into the socket at her feet and an orange light begins to blink. When she presses the power button, the screen flickers and comes alive. Her heart pounds as she puts down the Americano, wipes her palms on her thighs, and waits for the system to load. Across the cafe, four flatscreen televisions mounted on the wall combine to create a single large display. The channel is set to CNN. The commentators are discussing the new President.

The laptop loads a Linux operating system while Dylan plugs in the thumb drive. A screen soon pops open revealing the hidden content. At the moment everything is in a single compressed file and after she clicks on it another screen appears asking for the decryption key. This is the same message she encountered at Noisebridge, the same impasse. She stares at the screen for a long time and then collapses every window. She right-clicks on the thumb drive icon and discovers that the file contains 17.8 GB of data. Dylan ejects the thumb drive, puts it in her pocket, turns off the laptop, and leaves it plugged in so the battery can charge.

She studies everyone who comes into Au Coquelet and sits at the window table for half an hour watching people stroll by on the sidewalk. She hopes one of them might be Melissa, but none of them look like her, not even slightly. Dylan does this for so long that when she finally looks at CNN it's hard to comprehend at first. The words don't make sense, the images can't possibly be real, and yet there she is displayed on the four screens: a blonde woman with black sunglasses and a dark hooded sweatshirt. Dylan begins to sweat when she reads the closed captioning and sees the images floating above.

Shortly after 2:00 pm, the FBI and the Department of Homeland Security raided a hacker space in the Mission District of San Francisco. Two men were arrested inside, all the electronic equipment was seized, and every member of the Noisebridge collective was served subpoenas to appear at federal court on Monday. A spokesperson for the Department of Homeland Security told the press that a woman with blonde hair and dark sunglasses attempted to open classified government information inside the hacker space earlier that afternoon. The men arrested inside Noisebridge have been charged with aiding and abetting the theft of classified government data, a federal crime.

The CNN broadcast shows images of Mission Street blocked off by a dozen black SUVs. It shows FBI agents removing the servers and computers from Noisebridge and a grainy surveillance image of a woman with blonde hair and dark sunglasses. The DHS spokesperson asked the public for help in locating this woman. He said to consider her extremely dangerous, possibly armed with a weapon, and reminded the public to not approach her. He said there was too little information to know for certain, but it was better to be safe and call 911. The main caption below all of these images reads SAN FRANCISCO IN TURMOIL and the newscasters quickly shift to the riots on Friday night.

Dylan watches CNN display images of police cars burning in the street, grainy footage of fire in the Vermillion lobby, and a smartphone video of cops beating people with clubs outside a fancy restaurant on Valencia Street while the diners watch in mute horror. And then there's a picture of Ricky, stock footage of OingoBoingo headquarters, and the mugshot of Alexis taken from inside the county jail. All of it's woven together fluidly on the screen.

Dylan discretely glances at everyone in the cafe. Very few of them are actually looking at the CNN broadcast, only two old men with newspapers spread out on their tables. Everyone else is on their laptop, typing on their smartphone, reading a book, or writing on paper. No one appears to notice Dylan when she gets up from her seat. They're all distracted by one medium or another. She walks below the four flatscreens with a giant knot tightening inside her stomach. Her skin feels heavy and cold.

Dylan goes into the women's restroom, runs into a stall, and locks the door behind her. In one giant heave, she expels the delicious food she's just eaten. The vomit is green and red and filled with streaks of digested dough. She heaves until all of it's gone and the taste of coffee acid fills her mouth. The toilet bowl is now splattered with vomit and she flushes it down while transparent drool dangles from her lips. Dylan breathes frantically, wipes her mouth with toilet paper, and rubs the rim of the bowl until it's perfectly clean. She stares at the spiral of water as it flushes, breathes until the nausea is gone, wipes the tears from her eyes, and then leaves the stall.

Dylan crosses the cafe without looking at the flatscreens and drinks two glasses of water from the pitcher near the bus tubs. When she returns to her seat, Dylan finds her new laptop charging at the table and her bag exactly where she left it. She lifts the Americano to her lips but the smell makes her queasy so she puts it down and doesn't drink it.

The CNN newscasters are now talking about the new President, the new policies, the new promises, the need for unity, and the need for healing. Dylan doesn't pay much attention. She wants her friend Melissa to appear and help navigate this horrible situation. Dylan knows the odds are very slim and Melissa is probably at home working on her dissertation. In total defeat, she puts the computer in her bag, forces herself to drink the last of the Americano, and throws the cup into the trash. When she glances back at the flatscreens, Dylan sees the grainy image of a blonde woman with dark sunglasses. The woman isn't smiling. No one can see her eyes, nor do they know what she's thinking.

For the next hour, Dylan drives around Berkeley with no clear direction. She passes through downtown and ends up near the

BART station on Ashby Street where hundreds of people are gathered at a flea market. The entire station parking lot is filled with shoppers and food-carts and merchants of every variety and ware. Dylan smells frankincense and burning meat and onions roasting over grills. It makes her feel ravenous. She wants to eat everything but doesn't pull over, no matter how good it smells. Dylan takes a left on Ashby for no particular reason and drives the Mazda east towards the hills. She passes a Whole Foods grocery store, crosses Telegraph Avenue, drives past a big gray hospital, and comes to a red light on College Avenue.

Dylan looks in the rear-view mirror and realizes the golden locket was around her neck inside Noisebridge. She spins the chain around, unfastens the clip, and puts the locket into the cup holder. When the light turns green, Dylan takes a left on College towards the UC Berkeley campus and drives until she's forced to take another left. She ends up back in downtown Berkeley but rather than retrace her path to the flea market, Dylan starts to circle the campus. She drives the Mazda up the steep and winding streets past a sports stadium, a swimming pool, and through a canyon filled with oak trees. The air smells like soil and dry grass. It makes her feel safe.

Dylan pulls over near a hiking trail, turns off the engine, and keeps the windows rolled down. The air is hot and scented by drying oak leaves. She hears a hawk cry out somewhere in the canyon and a few cars pass by on the road. When silence returns, Dylan convinces herself she's on a country road in a small town somewhere else, someplace far in the mountains, a place where she's not afraid. This thought lasts until a troop of young men emerge from the hiking trail speaking in loud voices. A few of them look at her, but none of them say anything. They laugh and punch each other playfully and disappear down the road, their synthetic running shorts swishing like curtains. Once they're gone, Dylan reaches into the cup holder, picks up the gold locket, and opens the metal cover.

She always found this gift very odd. In her mind, a locket was meant to contain the picture of a partner, a child, a parent, or a beloved, but never one's self. Such a thing would be too narcissistic, too self-involved, too vain. Dylan stares at her Instagram picture nestled inside the gold metal where she's wearing dark sunglasses and staring up at the sky. These are the same dark glasses she wore into Noisebridge, the same glasses millions of people have now seen on CNN.

She plays with the cover of the book-shaped locket, tosses it up and down, and feels the weight of the chain against her palm. And then Dylan sees a flame burning in her memory. She looks around at the hiking trails to make sure she's alone and presses her finger against the picture. The image is covered in a small piece of glass but the paper edge is sticking out from beneath. Dylan reaches for her keys, finds her red Swiss Army knife, and then uses its tweezers to pull out the picture. When she looks on the back of the image, there's a long string of small numbers written in blue ink.

She doesn't know what to do at first, nor what to think. She breathes heavily and looks around in every direction. The air is so thick it feels like she's inhaling liquid. Her hands tremble as she puts the picture back in the locket and then starts the Mazda. If there were any food in her stomach, Dylan would have thrown it up already. She's covered in sweat, her face is flushed bright red, and the steering wheel is slippery under her palms. She drives back down the canyon road, passes the sports stadium, and eventually finds herself on College Avenue in front of a cafe called Espresso Roma. It looks like a comfortable place.

Dylan parks the Mazda around the corner and cranks up the windows. She puts the necklace in her pocket along with the thumb drive, slings the bag with the laptop over her shoulder, and then heads to the cafe. It's cool inside the building, the floors are lined with red tiles, the ceilings are high, classical music fills the room, and the air smells like pizza. She waits in line and stares at the food displayed behind the front counter; an array of pies with peppers and sausage and pepperoni. All of it smells delicious and makes her mouth water. She orders two slices, one of them with pesto, and takes them into the back room of the cafe where no one will be able to see her screen. The pizza is hot and the oil burns the roof of her mouth but Dylan's too hungry to notice. She eats both slices within five minutes.

When she's finished, Dylan puts her dish in the bus tub and drinks three plastic cups of ice water from the cooler. She takes the fourth cup back to her seat, plugs the laptop into the electrical socket, and then presses the power button. The other patrons are distracted by their own smartphones and Macbooks and don't even glance at her. Dylan looks too frumpy, too normal to be noticeable. She pulls a strand of black hair in front of her eyes and looks at it for a moment to make sure it's still black.

The Linux operating system loads on the laptop while Dylan digs the locket and thumb drive from her pocket. She removes the picture from behind the glass and lays it down on the key board. The blue digits are written in extremely compact handwriting, the os and Os are differentiated with a slash, and there isn't a single smudge of ink. Dylan takes a pen from her bag and carefully transcribes this encryption key onto the back of her Espresso Roma receipt. Once every digit is copied down, once she's made sure each one matches the other, Dylan slips the Instagram picture back behind the glass and then puts it in her pocket.

She plugs the thumb drive into the laptop, clicks on the file folder, and types the key numbers into the prompt. Dylan looks at the other patrons before pressing *enter*. She makes sure none of them care about her, that she's just another millennial checking her Facebook, her Twitter, her Instagram, and her Gmail. No one notices when she hits *enter*, nor do they have any idea what's about to happen.

CHAPTER 10

THE ENTIRE OFFICE WISHED HER A HAPPY BIRTHDAY. THEY GAVE HER gift cards for Amazon and Blue Bottle Coffee and even a hotel north of Santa Cruz good for a weekend vacation. Dylan was genuinely happy they remembered. Chad was gone that day but even he sent a short email wishing her well. The strangest present of all came from Ricky. At first, Dylan was sad he didn't appear to have any gift. Ricky kissed her on the cheek and hugged her warmly, but there was no present, no physical token of his friendship, and Dylan remained sullen until he asked if she wanted to get dim sum in Chinatown. They caught a Lyft in front of OingoBoingo headquarters and Dylan made fun of Ricky for never using Uber and always insisting it was evil.

"They *are* evil!"

"Come on," Dylan said. "*How* are they evil?"

"They're *so* evil even Google had to cut them loose. Now that's saying something."

"You're still not answering the question. The old bro CEO is gone, so how are they evil?"

"They don't give a shit about their drivers, for one. Fuck, they don't care about anything. You know who's on their board? You know who else wanted that piece of shit Kalanick to step down? The fucking government of Saudi Arabia!"

"Okay, that's pretty big," Dylan admitted.

"And you know what *they* do in Saudi Arabia, right? They cut your head off if you're queer, if you're an angry woman, a nasty woman, they just cut your head clean off. Every week. They don't even try to keep it a secret from the world. And then the State Department calls what Assad had in Syria a totalitarian regime but the Saudi's are just fine cutting off people's heads. No big deal. And let's not forget the Saudi's most likely helped organize the 9/11 attacks."

While he was saying this, the Lyft driver nodded and would occasionally interject to confirm that Ricky was telling the truth and none of it was made up. Ricky kept going, he explained that Uber and Google had once been closer, they'd planned to introduce self-driving cars together, but eventually Uber broke away and was now introducing its own fleet of black self-driving Volvos and semi-trucks.

"And then we're all out of a job," the driver said. "Even Lyft is doing it now, using those Google cars like they got in Arizona. And god-damn, even Ford is making self-driving cars. They have to!"

"That doesn't make any sense," Dylan said. "If there are no more cab drivers, if every cab driver is a robot, if every truck driver is a robot, if every worker is a robot...it doesn't make any sense."

"Sure it does," Ricky told her. "You have to think long-form on this one. They want to get rid of vehicular autonomy. They don't want anyone to have a car of their own. They just want a giant fleet of self-driving vehicles. The Uber CEO even said it out loud."

"Yeah, but why would they want that?" the driver asked.

"So no one can go anywhere without being monitored. That's it."

"Yeah, but this ride is monitored right now," the driver said. "They monitor everything already."

"But all three of us can still get to Los Angeles without them noticing if we really wanted to. That shit's still possible at least. Only they want to stop that. It's like in Cuba where they have travel restrictions. Even in Mexico they got checkpoints. They destroy your ability to move freely. They just want you to stay near work, in your cube, watching your screen, staying out of trouble."

"I don't know," the driver said. "That's kind of conspiracy theory."

"Is it?" Ricky asks.

"Whatever. We're using Lyft," Dylan said. "You win."

"I win, too," the driver said. "Fuck Uber."

She dropped them off in Chinatown and thanked them for the conversation, after which Dylan and Ricky went into the dim sum parlor and began ordering everything that rolled by on the silver carts: shui mai and shrimp dumplings and steamed sticky rice and Chinese broccoli and fried sesame balls filled with meat. They laughed about work and made fun of Chad while they ate. They even had an expensive bowl of shark fin soup while Dylan finished off the pot of tea. In the middle of the meal, Dylan ran to the bathroom and peed for over a minute, her mind awake from all the caffeine. When she returned, Ricky had placed a small box on the table.

"What's that?" she asked, sitting down.

"It's your birthday present."

"What is it?"

"Open it up."

So she did. It was a gold locket shaped like a book. Inside was a picture from her Instagram where she wore dark sunglasses and stared up into the sky. It made Dylan happy at first, but the more she looked at her own image, the more confused she became. Something about it didn't make sense.

"You look like a gangster in that picture," he said. "I always thought so."

"You go on my Instagram a lot?"

"I like what you post."

"It's mostly flower pics."

"No, I see the graff you're posting, all the street murals, I see it."

"I like the simultaneous contrast of opposites."

"Nah, really?" He rubs her back and then picks up his chopsticks. "Happy birthday, though."

"Thank you, Ricky."

"I just hope you remember it," he told her.

Dylan paid no attention to his last remark. She finished the last of her spareribs, drank three more cups of lukewarm tea, and Ricky paid the bill for their lunch. She thanked him as they walked to the street and then pretended to call for an Uber. They wrestled over her iPhone until Dylan admitted defeat and let him call a Lyft. They rode back to OingoBoingo with full bellies and stared out the windows at the crowded city streets. It was a good day for Dylan, a significant day, although she wasn't aware of it then. Only now does it make sense. Now that she remembers it.

Espresso Roma closes at 10:00 pm and Dylan leaves the back room just as the workers start wiping down the tables. Since she's been here, Dylan has eaten a whole pizza, drank an Italian soda, and consumed two cups of coffee along with several glasses of water. She's wide awake when she gets into the Mazda, drives up Ashby towards a giant white hotel, and ascends into the Berkeley Hills.

Dylan eventually reaches a dark crossroads lit by a lone streetlamp. The road to her left leads further into the hills and after turning this direction she drives carefully along the edge of the cliffs. The fog becomes thicker the further she climbs. It gives each street light a dreamy white halo and mists her windshield with droplets of water. When she reaches the top of the Berkeley Hills, her car is completely encased in fog and Dylan can only see the few feet illuminated in front of the hood. She drives through this gray void until street signs and houses begin to appear on the side of the road.

Dylan takes a left and parks her car at the bottom of a dead-end street. None of the windows are lit in any of the nearby houses, just the porch lights, the driveway lights, and the stair lights. All of this makes her feel safe. She cracks the front windows of the Mazda and climbs into the backseat. She piles her jacket and clothing together for a pillow, puts on her black sweatshirt, and lays down with her heart pounding relentlessly. Dylan tries to remember Alexis and their time in the shower but these memories feel distant and coated in plastic. Her mind returns to what she's just read in the files. It forces her eyes open and causes her mind to branch in a thousand directions. She isn't aware of falling asleep, but when she wakes it doesn't feel any different. She's still thinking about the files.

The morning fog in the air is so thick that she can't see the houses, not even in the daylight. Her parched mouth is dry and there's no water in the car, nor can she remember how she got here. Dylan clambers into the front seat, starts the engine, and drives the Mazda up to the main road. She follows a long sloping street to the bottom of the hill, rounds a traffic circle with a water fountain in the middle, and drives in a straight line towards the bay. There's too much fog for the world to have a clear shape. Everything appears as it would in a dream, blurred at the edges, its borders erased.

But the fog eventually thins once she passes the BART tracks in Albany and follows the signs to the I-80 freeway south towards Oakland. The traffic along the Bayshore Freeway is thin and unobstructed but eventually she encounters a sea of red brake lights creeping towards the Bay Bridge. Dylan merges away from this procession and takes the ramp for downtown Oakland. The freeway begins to curve south to San Jose so she gets off at the first available exit before it's too late. Dylan believes she's in West Oakland, although she isn't sure. She knows there's a BART station nearby and follows the tracks until she finds it.

Dylan parks the Mazda on a residential street a block away from the station and looks around to ensure there are no surveillance cameras recording either herself or the car. All she can see is a white Google bus roaring down the street. Satisfied with her anonymity, Dylan hops into the backseat and puts on black pants, a white blouse, and a pair of black shoes. A few passersby see her changing clothes but they keep walking and don't heckle her.

Dylan combs her hair in the mirror, ties it into two pigtails, and then puts on eyeliner. Even with her hair braided she feels something is missing, her disguise isn't sufficient, so she finds her sunglasses, positions her thumbs over the black lenses, and firmly pops each one out of the frame. When she puts the glasses back on, when she sees a new person reflected in the mirror, Dylan begins to feel confident. The cosmetic frames make her look like a young waitress on her way to work.

The thumb drive is in her pocket, the data is now copied onto her laptop, and she knows where to meet Natasha. Dylan tells herself she can do it, that everything will be okay, although her heart refuses to stop pounding. She hides her bag and laptop in the trunk of the Mazda and makes the backseat look messy, worthless, and filled with dirty clothes. From the sidewalk, she's sure no thief will be interested in the car or what's hidden inside.

Dylan walks past a liquor store on her way to the BART station and keeps her head down the whole time. She knows the store is covered in surveillance cameras and that someone could intercept the footage in real time. Once she passes the store, Dylan hurries across the street to the station and begins to dig money out of her pocket. Her heart is pounding even harder now. The station is filled with more cameras than the liquor store.

At the silver ticket machine, an old man asks for spare change and Dylan gives him a $5 bill without looking him in the eyes. She feeds another five into the machine, presses a button next to the digital screen, and receives a white and blue ticket with a black magnetic strip. The ticket machine doesn't appear to have any cameras so she lingers for a moment in safety, staring at nothing.

"Thanks a lot," the man says, still holding the $5s. "You alright?"

"I think so."

"Where you trying to go?"

"Work."

"Fuck that shit."

"Excuse me—"

Someone taps her on the shoulder, they want to buy a ticket, they want her to move, so Dylan walks away before they can see her face. She lines up with the other commuters, keeps her eyes on the floor, slides her ticket through the gate machine, and rides the escalator up to the platform. She notices a surveillance camera on the roof but keeps her head lowered until she's out of its range.

Several dozen commuters stand along the concrete ledge of the platform gazing at their smartphones and listening to music. In front of them is the jagged skyline of San Francisco rising into the fog above the gray waters of the bay. None of these commuters look up as Dylan passes. All of them have headphones in their ears, they're dressed nicely for work, and each of their phones has two cameras. The smaller one points directly at their faces while the other, more powerful lens points towards the train tracks. Both are constantly recording.

Dylan puts her elbows on the rough concrete ledge, stares at the towers of downtown Oakland, and keeps her back to anyone who might be filming. The morning fog hangs over the hills and drapes the eastern city in haze. Dylan doesn't have a jacket, she wears only her white blouse, and yet somehow she isn't cold. Her body is producing too much adrenaline. It keeps her warm and fills her with a desire to run, to sprint, to spend this accursed excess that boils her veins and constricts her heart. And then the sudden screech of the approaching BART train tears into her consciousness.

Dylan waits until the silver cars have come to a stop before she gets in line and boards quickly with her eyes on the floor. She walks to the exact middle of the train, takes her place in the crowded aisle, and holds onto the metal grip. This is the furthest from the four ceiling cameras she can get. It's where she's stuck when the doors hiss shut and the train begins to move. Her heart pounds in her mouth as the train car wobbles from one side to the other. Soon it plunges into darkness. The metallic screech is terrible in the long transbay tunnel and makes Dylan feel like the flu itself were clawing into her ears. No one else can hear it. All of them are wearing headphones.

She puts her hand over her mouth and looks up at the passengers. Many of them have corporate badges clipped to their belt loops. She sees that Twitter, Uber, Google, Firefox, and BoonDoggle employees are all represented. Some of them are dressed like hipsters but many are wearing expensive clothing. None of them look happy. They stare into their smartphones with desperation, afraid to look up and see where they are. The train, the ticket, the commute, the walk, the office, and then back again. All of it leading in a circle with no end. Their headphones mute the screech of the train, their cameras film everything, and their social media feeds distract them as their presence is captured inside a glowing screen. Only now does Dylan understand what this all means.

The train explodes into the Embarcadero BART station and the commuters crush and crowd themselves towards the door. Dylan has never ridden this direction in the morning. Up until now, she had no idea how many San Francisco tech workers lived in West Oakalnd. On the escalator she smells their cologne, leather, mint gum, perfume, deodorant, and sweat. She keeps her head lowered as she approaches the exit, clenches her fists in anticipation, and then notices two policemen standing at the gates. They have their hats on their heads, their hands on their holsters, and they're scanning the crowd for someone. Both of them look serious. Neither of them are talking, nor are they smiling.

At first, Dylan wants to turn around but there are too many people pushing forward so she lines up at the exit and slips her ticket into the machine. The gates hiss open, she takes her ticket back, and then walks forward with the rest of the surge. Dylan keeps her head lowered and waits for a hand on her shoulder, the bark of a command, or the feeling of metal around her wrists. But nothing happens. She keeps walking, climbs the final escalator to Market Street, and feels the foggy air hit her lungs.

The hands of the Ferry Building clock tower read 8:14 am as Dylan walks along the waterfront beneath a row of palm trees. She wanders through parking lots, pauses inside doorways, and hides behind bushes to make sure no one's following, all the while repeating aloud the name of her destination. It's a place called Greenwich Street. She's supposed to climb the stairs towards Coit Tower, stop at the second retaining wall, and wait somewhere in the trees. Natasha will be there at 9:00 am.

Dylan takes a left off the Embarcadero and walks through a small park where she finds the beginning of Greenwich. At the corner, she sees an office for Sotheby's International Realty and lingers at the featured listings displayed in the window. None of these houses or apartments are less than a million dollars, although she's too preoccupied to read the descriptions. Dylan makes sure no one is hovering in the park behind her, checks the nearby buildings for cameras, and stares at the passengers of each passing vehicle. When the sidewalks are clear, when no one's around, Dylan walks toward the tree covered slope and ascends the concrete steps of Telegraph Hill.

She's never been here before, nor has she been to Coit Tower. She climbs above the first retaining wall and finds a flat cement pathway lined with plants of every color. Green birds with strange cries circle overhead, the sound of traffic fades, and her heart begins to calm. There are several houses to the left of the pathway painted in light colors. Some of them look expensive and deserted while others look cozy and old. None of them have security cameras. Across from these houses is a lush garden with freely growing plants and a dirt pathway winding between the trees. No one seems to own this garden. It appears to belong to everyone.

Dylan keeps walking and comes to the second retaining wall. To her left is a long cement staircase while to her right is a steep dirt path that leads into the garden. Dylan climbs this path on her hands and feet. She finds a small grass clearing near the wall and sits down facing the bay. No one is standing at their windows, none of the blinds are open, and no one sees her recline in the grass. She stares at the ferry boats and cargo ships, watches the green birds bolt through the air, and hears the cry of seagulls lost inside the fog. Her body is still warm from the climb when she flips over onto her stomach, puts her head on her hands, and closes her eyes just long enough to fall asleep.

"You're serious?"

Dylan opens her eyes. She can't remember where she is.

"You're seriously asleep? I've been up since dawn losing my tails and you're *asleep*?"

She sees the grass below her hands, smells it in her nostrils, and then it all comes back. She sits up quickly and finds Natasha standing above her in a red Stanford sweatshirt, black running pants, and white running shoes. Her gym bag is strung over her shoulder, her hair is tightly braided down her back, and she isn't smiling, not at all.

"Were you followed?" Natasha asks.

"No. Were *you*?"

"No, of course I wasn't, like I just said. I haven't been back to my apartment since the article came out. It's been crazy. Anyway, you look different."

"I wanted to disguise myself."

"It's definitely professional looking," Natasha says. "Very."

She leads Dylan into a grove of trees inside the garden, a place where no one can see them. They sit down on the dirt slope and Natasha takes out a notebook. Her bag is packed with clothes and she struggles to keep them all inside while fumbling for a pen.

"Who do you work for?" she asks, stuffing a blue shirt back in the bag. "Just tell me."

"I worked for Oingo—"

"Who do you really work for? Come on!"

"No one. I mean, I *did* work for OingoBoingo, but you know that."

Natasha doesn't look away from Dylan. She studies her eyes and waits for a sudden flinch, a slip in the gaze, anything to indicate she's lying. Dylan knows what Natasha's searching for, she can tell what's at stake, so she clutches the grass and stares back with every spark of illumination inside her body. She stares at Natasha with the eyes of Alexis. She stares at her with the eyes of Ricky.

"You're not lying?" Natasha asks.

"No!"

"My boss thought it was all a trick, a bluff to hide the real story, the story no one knew about. You know? That little thing about OingoBoingo getting bought by BoonDoggle. My boss thinks you were sent to lead us astray, so we wouldn't catch wind of what was happening."

"Then why would I be here?"

Natasha cracks a smile for the first time.

"That's what I told him. If she's there, she's real."

"I'm real, Natasha." Dylan takes her hand and holds it tightly. "And I need to give you something. It's really important that you—"

"Are you okay?"

"Yeah." Dylan wipes her eyes. "You know about Ricardo Florez, right?"

"Uh-huh."

"And you've heard about Alexis Segura?"

"The one they've charged with his murder?"

"She didn't kill him. I know her, Natasha. I was with her...*minutes* before they caught her. Ricky was murdered, but not by her. He gave Alexis a thumb drive before he died, he told her to contact me if anything happened to him. And after that she gave me this—"

Dylan reaches into her pocket and Natasha gasps.

"You have it *here*?"

"Alexis tossed it out the window to me, from the Airbnb they caught her in. I took it and ran, I was stupid, I didn't know what I was doing, I went to—"

"Noisebridge. Fuck. Fuck!"

"I went to Noisebridge, I tried to open the thing but it was encrypted—"

"What the fuck? This is all serious federal—"

Dylan holds out the thumb drive and presses it towards Natasha.

"Someone died for this," she says. "And another person's in jail. Take it"

"This is the Department of Homeland Security and the FBI that raided Noisebridge. You realize this, right? If what you're saying is true, this is classified government information."

"It isn't what you think."

"You've *seen* it?" Natasha takes the drive and shakes it in her palm. "How did you decrypt it?"

"I didn't just see it. I *have* it." Dylan takes the Espresso Roma receipt and hands it over. "Here. I copied the decryption key down for you."

"How did *you* get the key?"

"Ricky gave it to me. Months ago. I had no idea until last night. None. I don't know how long he was planning this, but I guess—" Dylan lays down on the soil. "I guess it must have been for a while, ever since the Chinese deal went bad."

DARLINGTONIA

"What'd you find when you opened it?"

Dylan sits up, grabs a stick from the ground, and begins to snap it into little pieces. Natasha puts her notebook down and waits for an answer but Dylan just grabs another stick, snaps that one into five pieces, and cups them all in her palm. She shakes them, lets them fall to the earth, and stares at the pattern they create. It resembles an octopus.

"They're running programs on us," she finally says. "On everyone. Sophisticated ones run by this thing called GSX. It has a director, someone based in Oakland, and he corresponds with someone in the State Department, someone at the NSA, someone in the CIA, someone at the State Department, someone at Facebook, someone at Google. But I don't think GSX is a government entity exactly."

"Sounds like a private company. What are they doing, though? Come on."

"It's hard to explain. I'm sure you'll figure it out—"

"*If* I take it."

Dylan suddenly feels rage boiling in her chest.

"You'll take it!" she says finally. "This is bigger than Snowden. Bigger than anything! It's not just GSX, the CIA, the NSA. It's also OingoBoingo, BoonDoggle, Google, Apple, Facebook, Twitter, Dropbox, Uber, everyone. It's Verizon and T-Mobile and Sprint and Comcast. It's in everything, every device, every cable. And they have hundreds of professors working for them, contracted out from UC Berkeley and Stanford and MIT, helping them build these models of—"

Dylan can only shake her head and rub her eyes.

"I'm listening."

She tries to collect herself and remember what she just read.

"Let's say you take a lot of selfies in your bedroom," she says. "Your camera captures a pretty high quality image of the objects in the room, the art on the walls, the odds and ends. Let's say you've got a piece of art on your wall, the painting of an octopus, alright? A visual algorithm will pick it up and store it away somewhere. And let's say you have your smartphone when you start talking about an octopus one night. An audio algorithm picks up that conversation and stores it in a file with other octopus conversations. It doesn't take these algorithms very long to do this, it's really quick, and so over enough time, with enough data, they can tell if the octopus is linked to some deep rooted aspect of your personality, because maybe you bring it up all the time for consistent reasons, unconscious reasons, something you aren't even aware of."

"Okay, maybe I bring it up all the time. So what?"

"Maybe you bring up fifteen other things in your recorded conversations. Octopus, fish, seagull, whatever. Maybe you've got five seagull paintings in the living room. At some point in your recorded conversations the same things always come up, a list of keywords, access codes."

"Access codes?" Natasha tosses a few pebbles onto the ground. "What do you mean?"

"To a person. Access codes to a person. There's a threshold they keep referencing in these files. It's the amount of data necessary to generate one of their profiles. Once they've passed that threshold, once they've gathered enough data, they can generate a list of keywords from phone conversations, texts, photos, videos, internet activity, and purchase history. And then they send someone out to your location, one of their people sits next to you on a park bench or at a bar, seemingly at random. They act friendly, they bring up a few of the keywords, they record the responses on a hidden microphone."

"They *did* this?"

"Thousands of times. For years. They illegally target random people to see how far these keywords can go. I read the results. They're almost always positive. It took some skill in conversation, but as long as the operatives stuck to the keywords, as long as they hit the right bells, the test subject would ask for their number, their account names, that kind of thing. They'd be happy! Like they'd met someone special. The success rate was in the nineties."

"But what're they gathering this for?" Natasha picks up a few rocks and begins to shake them in her palm. "What's the justification? Anti-terrorism, population control? What is it?"

"They never say, really, not clearly, not yet. Maybe you can find it. But they're running other programs, more sophisticated ones. The most basic are all built around the smartphone. The other programs just expand off it. Take those same kind of profiles on each person. You gather a couple million more. Soon you've got an aggregate of all the keywords. Keywords for a whole city, a whole country even. But if you've got an OingoBoingo mind game asking 400,000,000 people about their dreams and then another one asking about their childhood memories, then...if you've got those memories, if you've got those dreams, then you can really manipulate people. You can program them in massive groups."

"*That's* what this is?"

Natasha tosses the rocks on the ground next to the pebbles and sticks.

"What do you mean?" Dylan asks. "Keywords?"

"The OingoBoingo Dream Game? The Childhood Memory Game? It's *programming* us?"

"It's not that simple. GSX makes these programs to modulate us. That's what they call it. *Modulation.* They want to provide the right stimulus at the right time to keep the subjects happy. Seriously, that's what they call us, they call us *the subjects.* They want everything to lead us back into happiness, or stasis, they call it stasis. If the camera knows we look sad the GSX programs will trigger a memory in another person, that person will call the subject, the subject will be happy because they've been thinking of that person recently, looking at their pictures, and GSX knows that—"

"Because GSX is recording everything."

Natasha looks at the stones and sticks lying atop the soil. She shakes her head in disbelief.

"Exactly," Dylan says. "They're recording *everything.* And their algorithms are so powerful they actually can just let them run now. But there's one catch. If the subject becomes conscious of the modulation, the desired effect drops exponentially, close to zero. They've done tests to prove this. The keywords stop working, the modulation breaks down. But right now people keep feeding this thing, they hand over their entire lives, their stories, their dreams. And it's used against them, they don't even know it. They think its fate or god or good luck or bad luck. They don't wonder *why* this game is so addictive, they don't wonder *why* they want this liquor, *that* perfume, *this* vacation, *that* person."

"Are the tech companies directly involved?"

"All of them. GSX officially contracts with everyone. I don't know what the corporations are getting out of it, but GSX has access to

Google's data, the NSA regularly gifts GSX huge data sets, Facebook contracts with them too. BoonDoggle also, they give them huge amounts of data"

"Maybe the corporations just get better insight into their customers," Natasha says. "It sounds like an exchange, data for profiles."

"Are you gonna take that thing or what?"

"Don't worry." Natasha puts the drive in her pocket. "You've convinced me."

"That's not even the half of it. I hardly slept all night and I only just told you the smallest fraction. They're doing this right now, on everyone. But you need to send it to Wikileaks as soon as possible. They'll publish it, no matter what."

"Wikileaks! What about me?" Natasha asks. "I want to publish it."

"Just don't get caught when you send it to Wikileaks, that's all. I want this to spread. For Ricky. So Alexis can get out of jail. She's in fucking jail and someone's dead because of this, and—"

"I promise. I promise. As soon as we can, I promise I'll get this to Wikileaks, but only if they promise to hold off full publication until I've gotten the story out there. And keep in mind we're both breaking a variety of federal laws as of twenty minutes ago."

"These programs aren't legal."

"Neither were the ones Snowden revealed, but hey, those programs are still going and he's still hiding in Russia. Nothing stopped after the leaks."

"It's even worse now."

"You're right. This is big," Natasha says. "I'm glad I came here. Almost let my boss convince me this was pointless. Sorry about that earlier, I just...I mean I still can't *quite* comprehend you. You come out of nowhere, spill the beans about your rapist boss, the whole company gets liquidated, and now you've handed me a thumb drive that proves OingoBoingo was directly involved in this program."

"You need to be careful, Natasha. They killed Ricky."

"It's alright. I already have a plan. The boss and I have a system. If I call him from a payphone and hang up when he answers it means he has to meet me at our spot. He's an old dog so he knows how to handle himself, he won't get followed. We'll figure something out."

"He'll publish this, right?"

"Of course, but he and I are going to hunker down for a week, two weeks, we have to go through everything and write up a bunch of stories. Once we get our tech guy on it, I'll send it to Wikileaks. I don't know how to do that safely, it'll take our guy a day or two to figure that out, but I'll tell my boss it's a condition of getting first scoop. I'll tell him if we don't send it you'll just publish it without us, because I *know* you've got another copy. But listen, Dylan—"

"Yeah?"

"Who the fuck are you? You don't work for China? Russia? I mean come on."

"Are *you* a Russian agent?" Dylan asks. "*Your* name's Natasha."

"Yeah, ha ha," she groans. "Right."

"Look, you don't have to trust me. Once you see what's in there, when you read a few of the case studies, when you see the visualizations, you can make up your own mind. I don't work for Russia, I don't work for China, neither does Alexis, and neither do you. Right?"

Natasha winks at Dylan and pats the thumb drive in her pocket.

"Yes, I am *not* Russian agent," she says in a thick accent. "I am innocent girl."

"Seriously, you're not—"

"No! Fuck! Are you? Just kidding, no, no, no, just kidding. But seriously, did you hear anything from Bernadette and Elizabeth? Did they even *read* the article I wrote?"

Dylan shakes her head and looks at the ground.

"Yep. They read it. Bernadette said I made it all up and denied everything. Elizabeth said I was cruel and insensitive. They wanted me to call but stopped emailing once the company folded. After that I didn't hear anything. I don't think anyone expected the company to disappear like that."

"They're covering their tracks," Natasha says flatly. "And now we've got this thumb drive, *you're* a fugitive, and I'm about to just, you know, publish a story that's going to make my life a living hell for the next few years."

"What do you mean?"

"Dylan, when this gets published, there's not going to be anything left. If what you're saying is true, if they're really running this on all of us—"

The green birds suddenly return. They scream and cry, circle over the garden, and land in the trees almost in unison. These birds have red feathers around their eyes, their beaks are curved and small, and they talk to each other in a frantic language more complex than the other birds.

"Chad," Natasha says. "Where's Chad?"

"I have no idea. Out of town, he said."

"The article I wrote about what he did to Bernadette and Elizabeth, it puts the spotlight right on him, obviously. And where is he? He's gone. Maybe someone will find him floating in the bay, maybe he's dead. I don't care. The point is, the company folds a few hours after that article is published. It wasn't long after. Anyway, I guarantee you no one's asking about Chad. But he's still gone and he's never going to answer for anything."

"He was involved," Dylan says. "It's in there. He's the one who brought Ricky in."

"Holy Mary!" she yells at the birds. "This is gonna be huge!"

"And there's the facial studies, studies on eye movement. They can even read your pulse by watching your neck, your temple. They watch people become emotionally affected by content, they study it, they modulate it. It's sick what they do."

Natasha sits up for a moment, squats atop the soil, and looks up at the trees.

"You got somewhere to go?" she asks.

"No. But I have something to do."

Natasha suddenly stares at Dylan, her brown eyes wide with alarm.

"What do you have to do?"

"I need to find out who killed Ricky."

"No. That's *not* what you need to do. Actually, what you need to do is something else. Not that. It's called get the fuck out of here and go rent a room with cash out in the middle of nowhere. Don't show anyone your ID, no hotels, find a room for rent. Don't look at the fucking cameras. Stay low."

"No. I'm going to find Ricky's killer. That's all there is to it."

Natasha stands up and wipes the soil from her hands.

"Here, let me help you." She pulls Dylan up and takes her by the shoulders. "I don't care what you say, I don't care what you do, but you're going to meet me right here in one week. This exact same place, the exact same time. You understand?"

"Why here?"

Natasha lets go of her shoulders and starts pacing through the garden. Dylan follows behind, their pace slow, their movements languid. The green birds keep circling over their heads, crying out in a bizarre language, unable to decide where they can relax.

"My dad gave me a book about this hill," Natasha says. "I mean, not about this hill, but they talked about it. Prostitutes from all over the world lived here in little wooden houses. The children were every race, every combination of color. Bad things happened to them but they survived, they survived everything, even the great fire in 1906. I mean, the fire literally started down there."

Natasha stops for a moment and points towards the Ferry Building.

"And then you know what the fire did? It circled around the hill, destroyed everything all the way up to the Mission, then curved around this way." Natasha points to the top of the hill. "It came right up to the backside of Telegraph Hill and then stopped. Only this ground right here survived, where we're standing now. This is the center, the exact center of a circle made of fire. It's a powerful place. I thought it would bring us luck."

A rustle of wings fills the air as the green birds descend into the branches above. Dylan and Natasha remain still, their eyes cast upward towards the branches. The birds have pitch black eyes surrounded by a circle of red. They murmur together in their frantic language, squabble over branch space, and ponder these two humans with endless curiosity. Dylan wants to understand what they're saying to each other with their little gray tongues. She wants them to tell her a beautiful secret, something she doesn't know.

CHAPTER 11

A FEW MONTHS BEFORE HIS DEATH, RICKY INVITED DYLAN, ELIZABETH, and Bernadette to go clubbing. He sent them a link to the show flier and when Dylan opened it her screen was filled with neon images of palm trees, blunts, and bullets. There were several musical acts listed on the flier, all of them with Spanish names. The only thing Dylan could understand was the time and place listed at the bottom. Ricky explained in the email this was a *reggaetón* concert one of his sister's friends was performing at. Dylan had no idea what *reggaetón* was and when she looked it up on Wikipedia the entry explained it was *influenced by hip hop and Latin American and Caribbean music. Vocals include rapping and singing, typically in Spanish.* It was going to be a wild time, Ricky said, not to be missed. Elizabeth and Bernadette responded enthusiastically, so did Dylan, and that Friday they met at a club in the Mission.

Ricky was there when Dylan arrived. He sat with a dark haired woman wearing red lipstick and a fake leopard skin jacket. She puffed on a vapor pen and wore dark makeup that made her look like a cat. She laughed loudly with Ricky and began to yell at him in Spanish as deep bass vibrated throughout the room. Dylan stood in front of their table unnoticed for over a minute. She waited for them to see her but they just kept speaking Spanish. When she finally sat down, both of them were visibly surprised, as if they hadn't expected her to show up.

"Dylan!" Ricky leaned over and hugged her. "You're early."

"I just live down the street, you know," Dylan laughed. "It didn't take me long to walk."

"*Chinga,*" the woman said.

"Sit down. This is Luz."

"*Mucho gusto,*" the woman said to Dylan. "You work with this guy?"

"Yeah. We've been friends over a year now."

"Then stick with him, okay? I know he's obsessed with white girls or whatever, but you better trust him 'cuz he's real, he knows what he's talking about. This guy's real. He's doing real good shit. You don't even know. Here, you wanna hit this?"

"No, thanks. It makes me paranoid."

"You gotta get over that, girl," Luz said. "Come on. You wanna live in fear?"

"We got a lot to be paranoid about these days," Ricky said. "That's what she means. You smoke you get paranoid, for sure, but after a while you get used to it. You get a grip."

"*You* don't smoke weed?" Dylan asked.

"At home, yeah, sure I do."

"Don't lie, you just smoked some of this," Luz said. "He smokes hella weed. Anyway, I hear you live in that place down there. What's it fucking called? The Empenada? What the fuck's up with that? They named a condo the Empenada? That shit's a fucking, like, savory Chilean pastry."

"That shit's hella good, though."

Ricky and Luz started to crack up and laugh hysterically, unable to speak.

"I live in the Vermillion," Dylan said. "It's the one next door, it's cheaper."

"Oh, uh-huh. So you live *there*?"

"Come on, Luz, she's my homie."

"Yeah, whatever. I'm sure you're cool, Anna, but I miss my friends, too."

"My name's Dylan."

"Dylan, right. Anyway, *pinche* Ricardo, you better stay for my set—"

Luz and Ricky began to speak Spanish after that. They kissed each other on the cheek, threw back a shot of tequila, and started laughing about something. While they did this, Dylan gazed out at the neon dance floor filled with women. Hardly anyone in the club was white. Many of the people on the floor had short dresses on. All of their legs were brown. Luz didn't say goodbye to Dylan when she left. She walked over to a more crowded table and disappeared behind its cushions.

"Don't worry about it," Ricky said. "This is her neighborhood. She's pissed."

"It's alright. You don't need to explain."

"I don't?" Ricky smiled at her. "How does it make you feel, her acting like that?"

"I understand. I never thought I'd walk into this situation. I got the lease when I was still in Providence, and now I'm here. And I'm a gentrifier. You know I am."

"It's structural, though. A structural problem. And it's only about race because capitalism is racist, structurally racist. The ruling class is mostly white and they keep most of us locked out. But you could be from New Delhi and still be a gentrifier, so long as you had the money. You could be black from Zimbabwe and still be renting a luxury apartment in the Empenada."

Both of them laughed at this absurdity. Dylan felt her body lighten, her muscles relax, and soon Ricky ordered a bottle of tequila. They squeezed limes into their mouths, licked salt off their hands, threw back the clear liquid, and rubbed their shoulders together. Ricky could always make Dylan feel at ease. She'd never known a man who didn't prey on her when given the chance.

"How many sisters do you have again?" she asked.

"Seven. I got seven sisters."

"That explains a lot."

"Does it?"

"It does. I always feel relaxed around you."

"Maybe it's because I'm not some stuck up white guy with a million bucks."

"It could be that, but I think it's your sisters."

"So I don't get any credit?"

"No, you get a little bit."

"My sister inspired me to go to school," Ricky said. "My sister Gloria moved up here to go to City College when I was a youngster, that's how she knows Luz over there. Gloria was the first sister to get out of Watsonville. She's why I'm here. She taught me a lot. Anyway, she knows Luz from back then. They love each other."

"It's better Luz didn't meet Bernadette and Elizabeth. They're worse than me."

"Yeah, but, you know, remember what happened to them, what Chad did to them. Just stick tight with those two, I know they're kind

157

of weird or whatever, but no one deserves that. And you're the smartest of them, so just keep an eye...shit, they're here."

Elizabeth and Bernadette ran over to the table and hugged Ricky and Dylan. They made a lot of noise, peered around the club with expressions of nascent terror, and when the eyes of the dance floor lingered on them they sat down and started to drink tequila. The concert began shortly after and the four of them laughed about memes, spoke of how ineptly most techies dressed compared to the men at this concert, and eventually began to shake their bodies to the blaring speakers. None of them could help it. The tequila and the beats pulled them to the dance floor and when Luz got on stage the entire floor erupted into applause. There was a burning Molotov cocktail projected on the wall behind her, deep bass vibrations shook every glass in the nightclub, and Ricky laughed when Luz held up one hand in the shape of a gun and sang the word *victoria*. Dylan doesn't know why she remembers this particular detail right now. The image is burned into her memory as if Luz had been made of light.

Dylan walks along the palm trees towards the Embarcadero BART station. There are more people on the waterfront now, more joggers, more mothers with strollers, more men in business suits. She lowers her head and doesn't look up, not for any reason. Sometimes she even covers her eyes. The closer she gets to Market Street, the more terrifying it all becomes. Hundreds of people swarm in every direction and nearly all of them are holding smartphones. Dylan keeps her vision fixed on the ground and follows the red brick sidewalk until the piss smell of the BART station fills her nostrils. She covers her mouth, descends the escalator, and pretends to cough the whole way down.

The silver ticket machine isn't recording her face when it dispenses the magnetic slip of glossy paper. There is no camera above the screen, no black sphere recording her movements, and no cops standing nearby as she walks to the platform entrance and puts her new ticket in the gate machine. The plastic orange doors hiss open, she takes the ticket from the other end, and then quickly walks onto the next escalator. Dylan doesn't look up, not even when she reaches the platform. She knows there are cameras on the ceiling. She assumes everyone has a smartphone.

When the eastbound train arrives, she presses herself into the rush of passengers and takes an empty seat halfway down the aisle. She puts her hand over her mouth and leans back into the cushions so the ceiling cameras can't see her. A terrible screech begins when the train enters the transbay tunnel heading into Oakland. Dylan breathes slowly, methodically, intentionally, trying not to panic. She keeps her eyes closed and doesn't open them until the screech of metal ends and the train car fills with light. Through the scratched and greasy window she sees metal cranes looming over Chinese cargo ships and endless stacks of multicolored shipping containers stretching off into the distance. It looks like a child's scattered playthings. None of it seems real.

The train comes to a stop at the West Oakland BART station after a brief announcement from the conductor. Dylan keeps herself close to the other commuters as the doors hiss open and everyone files towards the escalator. She waits in line at the gate, puts her ticket in the machine, and suddenly there's a loud beep and a red flash. The doors don't open. The machine spits her ticket out.

"Give it here!"

Dylan sees an annoyed looking woman wearing a blue BART uniform step out of a glass booth and extend her open palm. Dylan pushes out of line, hands her ticket over, and watches the attendant slide it into her desk computer. Only then does Dylan realize she purchased two separate tickets for no reason. Now she's captured on camera. She knows she's made a mistake.

"You didn't use this ticket to get on. You got another one on you?"

Dylan quickly searches her pockets and finds the other BART ticket.

"I think this is it," she says.

The attendant swaps tickets with her and puts the correct one in the computer. Dylan keeps her head down throughout all of this. She's afraid to look into the glass booth. She doesn't want to see the camera that's filming her.

"Gotta keep track of your tickets," the attendant says. "Go on through the bike entrance."

Dylan thanks the woman and pushes open the metal gate. She walks out of the station, crosses the street, passes the liquor store, and cautiously looks up from the gray sidewalk. There's no one ahead of her, nor are there any surveillance cameras. Her car is just around the next corner. Nothing happens when she gets inside and closes the door. No one surrounds the Mazda or brandishes a gun or binds her wrists with metal handcuffs. It appears that she's safe. Dylan starts the engine, pulls out of the parking spot, and keeps checking the rear-view mirror. No one is following her.

And then Dylan realizes she didn't check the trunk. By the time this epiphany occurs, she's already on the freeway heading east towards Walnut Creek. She takes the first available exit onto Telegraph Avenue and drives until she sees a cafe with metal tables on the side-walk. She quickly pulls over and turns off the engine. Dylan wants to vomit but knows there's nothing in her stomach. She goes to the trunk, puts the key in the lock, and then opens it. The knot in her stomach suddenly vanishes. The laptop is in the bag. Relief covers her arms in goosebumps. The sweat becomes ice on her skin.

Dylan slings the bag around her shoulder and walks towards the cafe. She goes inside with her hand over her mouth and finds a table near the wall where no one can see her screen. She plugs in the laptop, opens the screen, and presses the power button. Only then does she see the other customers lost in their various screens and devices. Dylan counts the number of smartphone cameras in the cafe, the number of laptop cameras, and tries to figure out which direction each lens is pointing.

Two people near the windows are scrolling busily on their phones. They don't seem to be doing anything important but their cameras pan around in multiple directions. The other laptop cameras are static, they're directed at their owners, and most are facing the ceiling. There are no surveillance cameras in this cafe, and no black eyes filming her from above the espresso machine. None of the customers are paying attention to Dylan. No one looks at her when she walks to the counter and orders a cup of pour-over coffee, a croissant, a muffin, and an apple. She hands over twenty dollars, stuffs a $5 bill into the tip jar, and returns to her table with the food.

Dylan eats the croissant first. She savors the buttery strands of dough and licks her fingers in delight. Then she tears into the blueberry muffin. She breaks it apart on the plate, stuffs the pieces into her mouth, and feels the berries explode under her teeth. The muffin is gone too quickly and she regrets not buying another one, although she still has to eat the apple and put cream in her coffee. After confirming the position of every smartphone camera, Dylan crosses the room with her head down, fills her coffee with whole milk, and decides to go ahead and buy another muffin.

It's just as delicious as the last one. Somehow she manages to eat it faster. Dylan washes it all down with coffee and then devours her apple. When the food is gone there's only the laptop, the screen, the keypad, and the touch-pad cursor. She wiggles it to life, opens the GSX file, and stares at the thousands of files copied over from the thumb drive. Dylan rubs her temples and tries to remember the last thing she read at Espresso Roma.

The files concerned eye motion, bio-metric data, pulse rate, and breathing patterns. They were filled with documents about the Snapchat bio-metric data set, access issues with live Skype communication, evaluations of different camera performances, and other technical aspects of gathering visual data. The last file she read was number 37 out of 795. Dylan isn't sure who numbered them but she assumes it was Ricky. All the information is curated very well, it flows from one file to another, and it's been easy for her to understand.

Before clicking on file number 38, Dylan scrolls to the bottom of the window and clicks on file number 795. The other files contained thousands of documents each. Much to her surprise, file number 795 contains only a single document. She begins to read.

In a brief paragraph, someone apologizes for the reader feeling sick:

I'm impressed you've made it this far. I'm sorry if you feel sick. There's only one thing left for you to do. The entire capitalist system runs on the backs of individuals. Some craft the system while others have to live in it. GSX offered its services to those with the infrastructure, the capital, and the data to make their work possible. The NSA and the CIA have built extensive profiles on the population. Google, Facebook, and Twitter have helped modulate that population. And OingoBoingo is there to soak up the dreams and memories of those forced to live within this nightmare. GSX was built by individuals who knew exactly what they were doing. You will find a document below that is a list of every person directly involved in creating this parasitic structure that has attached itself to the population. You must make the identities of these individuals public. Their fate should be decided by everyone.

Below this text is a long list of professors, engineers, doctors, several California Senators, five CIA employees, two NSA employees, and the top figures of several major tech companies, among many others. It includes their home addresses, their work addresses, their personal numbers, their work numbers, and their emails. There's nothing else at the end of this list, no further message from the author. Dylan scrolls back up to the name of a psychology professor at UC Berkeley. She begins to sweat as a flame takes hold of her mind.

When she read file number 29 at Espresso Roma, Dylan learned that Ricky was analyzing the OingoBoingo data sets with a professor named Pamela Gustafson. Dylan read several documents they wrote together about the Google data-set, including a separate report that Ricky and Chad wrote to the director of GSX regarding Facebook. She learned how the findings from the OingoBoingo dream data could easily be integrated with the Facebook and Google data-sets to create a cohesive psychological profile. Pamela and Ricky had worked on this together. It was their pet project.

In one letter written to the director, Ricky explained: *Visual algorithms can be used to locate the source of a subject's dream images by analyzing their internet searches, their video streams, and their pictures. Correlations between dream images and specific commodities can be used to generate advertisements for Google, Facebook, etc. This same principle can be applied to search engine results with links modulated to reflect a subject's dreams. Everyone chases their dreams. They chase them beyond reason and logic. This behavior is instinctive and can be modulated by selectively revealing the dream to the dreamer. This unlocks an additional malleability factor.*

That's what Ricky called it. A malleability factor. It was a phrase GSX would soon incorporate into its lexicon. The director often praised Ricky for his ability to distill complex visual images from the written user responses given to the Oingo Boingo Dream Game. His dream visualizations generated thousands of positive results when incorporated into the visual algorithms, with the dream object often being located in real life. More work needed to be done, but Ricky had contributed a vital insight into the behavior of the population.

In file number 29, Dylan learned what Pamela Gustafson added to the process. She compared the OingoBoingo dream data of targeted subjects with their Facebook and Google data. In one letter, the director scolded her for spending an entire week on a single subject, going so far as to look for the real life sources of their mediocre poetry. In another, the director cited Pamela's obsession with pop music as a distraction from the fundamentals of the program. Pamela often studied the musical listening habits of targeted individuals, looked for patterns in their browsing habits, read their emails, traced their relationships, listened to their phone conversations, studied their art, monitored them at work, saw what movies they watched on Netflix, and listened to them talk to their children.

Pamela determined that dreams were not enough. In one letter, she explained:

> Dreams are very useful for understanding a subject's behavior. Our dream modulations have been battle-tested and there's no reason to hold back on incorporating these new algorithms into our portfolio. However, there is something missing more important than dreams. As our tests have shown, the life of a dream image can be extraordinarily short. We have found that only dream images with a deep connection to the subject's psyche will last longer than a month. No amount of direct modulation will sustain a dream image beyond this general threshold. To get at the root of these dreams, I propose the creation of a mind game built to study childhood memory.

Pamela was the primary author of the ninety nine questions every user had to answer before their individual Childhood Memory Game world was generated by the engine. Within a week of Pamela finalizing these questions, Chad had delivered the department their next assignment. He announced the creation of the new game and Ricky got busy creating advertisements once the user data came flooding in. Dylan remembers this very well. At the time, Ricky and Chad were the only ones in the department who understood the role GSX played in determining the content of the new game. They were the only ones who knew Pamela Gustafson had written the ninety nine questions. To everyone else, OingoBoingo was simply making the world smarter.

Dylan copies down the name of Pamela Gustafson's department, her building name, her office number, and the floor she works on. She closes the file window, powers down the computer, and shuts the screen over the keyboard. While she nibbles on her apple core, Dylan looks at the faces of everyone in the cafe. About half of them are dressed in a manner Dylan would describe as arty. They have tattered clothes, weird symbols on their shirts, triangle earrings, black rimmed glasses, dirty shoes, military backpacks, and vintage shoulder bags. Most of them are reading books, using pencil and paper, but all of them have a smartphone sitting within easy reach.

The other half of the room are people who look like Dylan. They're on their laptops, engrossed in their work, and dressed professionally. They have fancy watches, expensive clothes, pearl earrings, designer glasses, and leather shoes. Nearly everyone in the cafe is the same age, somewhere between their mid-twenties and mid-thirties. They're being directly monitored by their devices and generating endless streams of data. She knows this for a fact. But as she watches these young people, Dylan becomes transfixed by how thoroughly they do it to themselves. Everything becomes disturbingly silent. There are thirty-seven cameras in the room. No one is speaking.

She parks the Mazda near the UC Berkeley football stadium on a residential street shrouded by bay trees. Dylan has only ever bought bay leaves in a glass jar at Whole Foods and had no idea they grew in the Bay Area on trees this beautiful. She's never seen them in the wild with their slender trunks curving like the ribs of a wooden boat. Dylan leans her head out the window and breathes in the delicious scent of their drying leaves, a sharp smell that cuts into her nostrils and reminds her of warm soup.

She digs through her bag of clothes, puts on black synthetic running pants, white socks, and then slips into her pink and white running shoes. She throws on her blue sweatshirt, pins her hair up into a flat bun, and then fixes a brown wig atop her head. After this she puts on her empty glasses, looks in the mirror, and repeats the building name and room number for Pamela Gustafson. She says it aloud until it sounds like a song. Before she can doubt herself, before she can become afraid, Dylan gets out of the car, locks the door, and starts jogging towards the center of campus.

Dylan runs past a swimming pool built atop a creek bed, then a baseball field, then a soccer field, and then a football stadium. She runs underneath sprawling oak trees, past old brick buildings with pointed roofs, and along a small creek lined with redwoods. She follows the flowing water and reaches a giant brick plaza with a green-iron entrance where hundreds of students are moving in every direction, most of them holding smartphones with headphones plugging up their ears. Dylan weaves through this crowd of bodies, finds a colored map of all the buildings, and realizes the Department of Psychology is on the opposite end of the campus. Dylan checks her brown wig, makes sure it's still in place, and jogs towards the northwest corner of UC Berkeley.

She continues down the babbling creek and passes a field of grass lined with eucalyptus trees. She sprints across a traffic circle and jogs between a row of stone buildings with red tiled roofs, thick stone balconies, and tall Roman columns. One of these buildings has the phrase *TO RESCUE FOR HUMAN SOCIETY THE NATIVE VALUES OF RURAL LIFE* engraved above the capitals of each column. Dylan assumes the building has something to do with agriculture, although she isn't sure.

The Department of Psychology is in Tolman Hall at the edge of campus on Hearst Street. Unlike the others buildings surrounding it, Tolman Hall is a giant box made of cement, metal, and glass. It was built in the 1970s or '80s and meant to look futuristic. Now it's shabby and out of place, a stale precursor to buildings like the Vermillion. Dylan feels depressed when she looks at it, she can feel how worn out it is, how outdated it's become, how sorry it looks.

She stands underneath the shade of an oak tree and gazes at this four-story building. She lets the sweat dry on her back and watches the students stream through the doors in their short skirts, their sandals, and their workout clothes. None of them look up from their smartphones. Dylan's wig is still stuck to her natural hair but she smooths it down just to make sure and then waits for the flow of students to subside before entering Tolman Hall.

Pamela Gustafson works on the third floor in office 332. Dylan climbs the crowded staircase shoulder to shoulder with the crush of students lost in their digital trances. She keeps her eyes on the linoleum even though its pointless to do so. She's surrounded by smartphones on every side. When she reaches the third floor, Dylan knows her image has been captured by dozens of cameras.

She peers into an empty classroom and sees the clock on the wall reading 12:37 pm. Dylan paces through the third floor, finds office 322, and then walks counter-clockwise through the old hallway until she reaches office 332. The door is open and someone is standing near the desk. Dylan begins to hyperventilate. It's as if she were breathing her own blood.

She can hear someone moving around, she can hear typing on a keyboard and the sound of papers being shuffled. Before she can do anything, a woman with blonde hair walks out of the office and smiles at Dylan on her way to the bathroom. The woman isn't holding a smartphone, nor does she have any pockets to hide one. Dylan follows behind, gets control of her breathing, and manages to speak through the knot in her chest.

"I know about Ricky."

The blonde woman stops and turns around.

"Excuse me?"

"Pamela." Dylan steps closer. "I know about Ricky."

"Who are—"

"I know everything, Pamela. And we have all the GSX files. If you don't want your career or your life destroyed I suggest you follow me right now."

"I need to—"

"If you tell anyone it won't matter. If anything happens to me those files get leaked immediately. And you're directly involved in—"

"Okay, okay, but I have class in—"

"I don't care about your class. You need to come outside with me *right now*."

Pamela looks terrified. She widens her eyes and takes a step back. "Alright," she whispers.

Dylan nods for her to keep walking. She follows Pamela down the staircase and stays several steps behind. Pamela's in her early fifties. She's wearing black pants and a purple blouse. She has a silver watch on her wrist and a silver necklace around her neck. Dylan can smell her tasteful lavender perfume wafting up the stairwell. Pamela doesn't turn around once. She walks down the steps and into the warm air where a few leaves spiral down from the branches of an oak tree. Squirrels and crows comb over the ground looking for buried acorns. Students walk by with headphones in their ears and gaze at their screens as a gentle wind blows in from the ocean. None of them look up. Dylan waits for Pamela to meet her eye but this doesn't happen. The professor stares at the tree branches, bites her lower lip, and begins to cry. None of the students see her standing there. Dylan doesn't care. She feels no sympathy. She pushes Pamela away from the building. Together, under the harsh sunlight, they walk toward the distant hills.

CHAPTER 12

Shortly before the meeting with the Communist Party of China was announced, OingoBoingo and Dropbox held a joint party at the Palace of Fine Arts Theater in the Marina District of San Francisco. Dylan had no hesitation about attending. It was a celebrity event for Silicon Valley and all the big names would be there. The companies reserved both the inside and outside of this complex and hired a variety of performers to entertain the guests. The public wasn't allowed to enter and everything was gated off to control access. Each invited guest had to pass through a metal detector. Every bag was searched, every coat was scanned, and every identity confirmed.

Dylan, Bernadette, and Elizabeth arrived in the same Uber and went through security together. All of them wore black dresses. Only their hair, their jackets, and their bags set them apart. Most of the festivities were centered inside the complex where the crowd was thicker and the music louder. The three friends stayed away from this bustle and drank champagne near the entrance so they could watch the celebrities arrive. They stared at the artificial lake, the strobe lights, the ducks, the fountain, and the grand arches of the palace hanging over their heads.

Standing near the theater entrance was a large glass display case filled with plants. It was bathed in green laser light and shrouded in a layer of artificial mist. Inside, red and green lilies stood like rigid cobras, upright and ready to strike. Dylan and her friends gazed at the strange plants with translucent skin that resembled plastic. A placard revealed them to be carnivorous plants native to California. Their name was *Darlingtonia californica* and the green laser mist made them appear ominous. There was no explanation for their presence.

After staring at these plants for a moment longer, the three of them went back to the artificial lake and drank more champagne. This is when Ricky arrived with a glass of liquor in his hand. He kissed them on the cheeks and leaned against the railing alongside Dylan. He seemed tipsy as he stared out at the glowing lake that pulsed through every color of the spectrum.

"Condoleeza Rice is in there," he told them. "Chad just introduced me."

"What?" Elizabeth snapped. "*You* met Condoleeza Rice?"

"She's not *that* great," Bernadette said. "She helped invade Iraq, fucking bitch."

"Yeah, well, now she's with Dropbox," Ricky said. "Chad introduced me to a lot of people in there. He wants my help with something, I can tell, because why else? And fuck Condoleeza Rice. I don't give a shit if she *is* black. Back there I just smiled at her, I shook her hand, I played the game just like I do because fuck it."

Bernadette and Elizabeth were silent while Ricky finished his drink and lit a cigarette.

"I don't know if you can smoke here," Elizabeth said. "What if—"

"Sure we can," Bernadette said. "Give me one."

"I fucking hate Chad," Elizabeth said. "Piece of shit."

"We're techie scum living the high life," Bernadette muttered, lighting her cigarette. "We can do whatever we want. Smoke wherever we want, do whatever we want...motherfucker, gets to get away with whatever he fucking wants!"

"What do you mean even though Condoleeza Rice is black?" Dylan asked.

"I mean you can be a nasty fascist of any color, that's all. You know what I mean? They got to invade Iraq, everything got all fucked up, and then there was ISIS and Syria and the war and the Saudis and Iran and Israel and all that. Just so their friends could become billionaires."

"But you shook her hand," Elizabeth said. "You played the game."

"I played the game. *I did.* So did she. But at least my job isn't dropping bombs on people."

"Right," Dylan said. "You're just an artist like us."

"*Artist?*" Elizabeth scoffs. "If I'd have known art school would lead me here—"

"Better than pure business," Bernadette said. "Better than Wall Street."

"I never had the brains for that anyway," Elizabeth said. "Too many numbers."

"Dylan could have done it," Ricky said. "Right, *güera?*"

"Maybe. But I didn't want to. My dad's a business man. I never wanted it."

"Did your mom read a lot? Was she an artist or something?" Elizabeth asked.

"In her way. But she was more of a sponge. She soaked it all up but it never went anywhere."

"Except into her head," Ricky said. "You can never really tell what's going on in there."

They kept talking, Ricky and Bernadette finished their cigarettes, and Dylan went off to get more champagne. None of them wanted to follow her inside where the famous Silicon Valley figures were mingling and cavorting and networking. From the bar, Dylan saw the OingoBoingo and Dropbox logos digitally projected on a giant red curtain hanging inside the building. There was a vast array of food spread across huge banquet tables. Through the crowd, she could see Chad talking with his peers, holding a champagne glass in the air, putting his arm around different women, laughing at all the jokes, and enjoying his role as the center of attention.

All of the men in the advertising department were positioned around him like gargoyles in the hope of gaining his favor. Chad was their chance for promotion and a conduit to the upper levels. If Dylan cared more about her career she would have been in that circle, she would have been standing her ground, vying for the spotlight and competing for respect. But after what happened to Bernadette and Elizabeth, Dylan decided it was best to stay away, to forgo the entire ascension process and get by on the bare minimum.

So she hung back near the glowing neon water with her friends and drank three glasses of champagne. She even smoked a cigarette. They all talked about fashion, Hollywood, and the Silicon Valley gossip. They managed to feel happy. The sound of water soothed their ears as the ducks' silent ripples spread across the artificial lake. But soon Ricky became restless and started looking over his shoulder at the crowd. Before going back inside, Ricky pulled Dylan away from the others. He put his mouth next to her ear and kept his hand on her shoulder.

"You think Chad really raped them? Like, no question?"

Dylan nodded and then looked down at her feet so she wouldn't cry.

"I drank too quickly," she said. "Don't want to fuck up my mascara."

"I don't like Chad either. And I always believed them. You know that? Do *they* know that?"

"They know that. I know that. But that doesn't change anything."

Ricky brought his hand to his mouth and began to bite his nails.

"I gotta go back in there. I just gotta go for it," he muttered. "I just gotta play the game."

"It's what we're all doing, I guess," she told him. "I don't know what else to say."

"I got your back no matter what, Dylan, no matter what happens. And them, too."

Ricky kissed her on the cheek and Dylan put her arms around his body for longer than normal. When she finally let go, Ricky looked sad and turned his back on her with resignation. As he walked into the building, Dylan saw his shoulders slowly loosen and his movements become fluid. Ricky slid into the crowd with grace and ease and overshadowed Chad for just long enough to assert himself. Dylan watched him melt into this circle of very important people, she watched him flirt with the women, and then she watched him flirt with the men. He didn't stop smiling.

When she returned to the railing, Elizabeth and Bernadette were both on their iPhones. Neither of them looked at her. Neither of them said anything. They just kept typing on their screens and texting messages to someone who wasn't there. Dylan stared out at the glowing neon water, the tall bubbling fountain filled with light, and the ducks drifting back and forth in the luminous water. She remembers how alone she felt that night, how absent Elizabeth and Bernadette were, how distant they all seemed from what was happening to them.

Dylan tells Pamela to walk into the hills above the football stadium and says she'll be right behind her, watching. They climb up Hearst Street, a long sloping road that goes directly towards the tree covered slopes. They pass the northern gate of UC Berkeley and weave their way through a trickle of students. Dylan stays ten feet behind, careful not to get too close.

Halfway up the hill, just before they pass under an elevated crosswalk, Pamela holds up her hand and waves at someone approaching. It's an older woman with curly gray hair. She's wearing a purple scarf, a dark green blouse, and black pants. She has gold earrings, she's carrying a leather bag, and she's smiling at Pamela as if they've known each other forever.

"Where you off to, Pam? Don't you have class?"

"I had to cancel. Something came up."

Dylan walks past them, leans against a nearby pole, and glares at Pamela.

"Is everything alright?" the woman asks.

"I'll tell you about it later," Pamela says, looking away from Dylan. "Could you tell them I won't be there? I've got to go."

Dylan starts walking before the gray haired woman can turn around.

"Sure, call me later, okay?"

"I will, once I get this figured out."

"Don't stress, I'm sure it'll resolve itself. You always—"

"I know, I know. See you, Diana."

"Bye," the woman says.

Dylan waits under the elevated crosswalk until Pamela catches up. She says nothing to the professor and stares at her angrily. Pamela looks down at the ground and keeps walking. She crosses the next intersection and climbs up another curving road with Dylan close behind. Now they're closer to the trees. The scent of dry grass and eucalyptus hangs heavy in the air. The earth smells fresh again. As they walk up this empty stretch of the road, Dylan sees a blue sign hanging on a pole with the words Cyclotron Road printed in yellow.

"What the hell's a cyclotron?" Dylan asks, loudly.

Pamela looks around to make sure they're alone and stops walking until Dylan catches up.

"It's where they figured out how to enrich uranium."

"Oh? You're right at home, then."

"Are you going to kill me?"

Dylan squints her eyes for a moment. And then she smiles like a devil.

"If I was, trust me, I would've gone to your house. Tonight. While you're sleeping."

"I have children," she says, her eyes tearing up. "I have a family."

"Whatever. Keep walking, get us into the woods already."

"We can—" Pamela turns around and points ahead. "It's just through that parking lot."

Dylan follows behind, although this time a bit closer. They pass along a grove of eucalyptus trees, cross Cyclotron Road, and enter a parking lot that curves below the hill. A giant retaining wall made of cement bricks holds the soil above the empty parking spaces and prevents the crumbling slope from burying the absent cars. At the end of this retaining wall is a large pile of wood chips spread out across four parking spots.

It's here that Dylan and Pamela stop. They freeze their bodies. They make no sound. A family of deer is now looking at them in apprehension. They stare at the humans with pitch black eyes, wag their short tails back and forth, and then bolt off into the oak trees. Their muscles flex underneath brown fur, their hooves clatter against the concrete, and the deer vanish deep into the forest. Their steps are no longer audible. Silence returns to the parking lot.

"No one's around," Pamela says. "We can talk—"

"Go into the woods, like I said. Above the stadium."

"If this is about having power over me, getting revenge—"

"For now it's about you going into the woods!" Dylan screams. "You want to start talking about revenge? You want to start talking about power?"

"Okay, okay—".

Pamela shakes her head and leads them out of the parking lot onto a dirt road. They climb a steep slope, kick rocks into the grass, and begin to sweat as a cloud of dust swirls behind them. At the first cutback, Dylan beholds the immensity of the Bay Area stretching beyond her vision. She sees the pyramid of the clock tower in the middle of campus, downtown Berkeley sprawling around it, and the metal and glass skyscrapers of Oakland reflecting the sunlight off in the distance. Beyond all this is the deep blue of the bay, the jagged skyline of San Francisco, and the red curves of the Golden Gate Bridge standing above the Pacific Ocean. She's never seen it from this angle before.

"Beautiful isn't it?" Pamela asks.

"Shut up!"

"Look, what do you want?"

"Go into the fucking woods!"

"We're *in* the fucking woods!" Pamela is crying now. "Above the stadium! Like you said you wanted! What do you want?"

"Fine, just—" Dylan points to the top of the ridge. "Up there, we'll talk up there."

Pamela is correct. They are directly above the sports stadium and from this height it reminds Dylan of Rome. She can see the yellow Cal logo emblazoned on the green grass, the long rows of yellow bleachers, and the little men running back and forth wearing helmets and shoulder pads and white spandex pants. She and Pamela eventually climb out of its view, turn another cutback, and Dylan sees a rope swing hanging from the branches of a eucalyptus tree.

"There, let's go there," she says.

"Fine, great, *we'll go to the swing!*"

Dylan runs ahead of her and sits down on the wooden seat.

"You know there's a tree house on the other side of the canyon," Pamela says. "Maybe you'd like to go there instead, given you're acting like a complete child! My colleague had her smartphone in her bag, you know that? Someone'll know I'm gone."

"No, they won't."

"Oh, yeah? Why not?"

"Because no one knows who I am. And tenured professors cancel classes all the time, especially when they have two jobs. You see anyone coming to rescue you? You think we would've gotten this far if they gave a shit about you?"

Pamela's eyes fill with tears once again. She throws her butt down on the ground, lifts her knees to her face, and begins to weep. Dylan smiles, she can't help it. She pushes her feet off the ground and begins to swing back and forth. The bay has never looked so beautiful, nor has it looked so refreshing. It makes her want to jump off the hill, fly off the swing, and pierce the water in a perfect dive. Her body is overheated, sweat is trapped between the wig and her hair, and she wants nothing more than to swim towards the Pacific.

"Maybe we could go swimming in the pool down there," Dylan

says. "The one they built on top of the creek. Seriously, why build a chlorine pool over a fucking creek?"

"Tell me what you want!" Pamela shrieks. "Why am I here?"

Dylan's face hurts from all the smiling.

"You're going to tell me who killed Ricky."

"That woman did! It was Alexis Seg—"

"No it wasn't, you bitch! No it was *not*!"

"And you know this how? Exactly?"

"Stop your fucking games! Who killed Ricky?"

"I don't know!" Pamela is weeping. "I don't! I really don't! I loved him!"

"What?"

"I loved him!" she cries. "Ricky and I...it's my fault he's dead."

"What the fuck do you mean?" Dylan yells.

"Stop, please!"

"I don't have time for your tears, tell me!"

Pamela catches her breath, wipes her cheeks, and tells Dylan the story. While they were working together on the Dream Game, Pamela and Ricky would sometimes go out for drinks at a bar on Euclid Avenue. It was mostly filled with football players and none of her colleagues ever went to it. From these after-work conversations, Pamela became convinced that Ricky had an obsession with white women that originated from some sublimated childhood experience or trauma. When she told him this theory, Ricky just laughed. He asked her to guess what the traumatic experience was. They spent the whole night playing this game, and it soon became a running joke whenever they got drinks on Euclid. She would go on and on, listing different scenarios about playing doctor, school yard encounters, Caucasian school teachers, and high school crushes.

"And then I realized I was obsessed with him," Pamela says.

Dylan doesn't react, she just swings back and forth.

"That makes sense," she eventually says.

"The only traumatic experience he ever had was a bunch of white women being obsessed with him his whole life. I was so so stupid, so naive."

"Makes even more sense."

"And with all the Black Lives Matter protests, the new President, the way everything's getting exposed now about racism, about white feminism...I've never had an experience like that before. He flipped everything upside down for me. He exposed *me!* We started...we started sleeping together, I had an affair, we had an affair for some months. And then I gave him access, I showed him the full picture, I showed him everything. He had access to all of the GSX data because of me, he knew my codes. And then one day he never returned my calls. A few days later they found him in the water."

"He stole the files from you?"

"The director told me he did. A thumb drive entered my computer and took 17.8 GB of data. The files were numbered the way I numbered my own, so no one noticed at first, it all looked normal. I always put tape over my camera, the director knew that, Ricky did too. I don't like it watching me. No one saw him at my desk while I was asleep, when our phones were in the living room. He planned it all perfectly, it took him whole nights, he used some program to crawl around and grab the documents and put them in files based on keywords. The director figured out it was Ricky, he had all our conversations transcribed, he knew about our affair, he showed me the exact time Ricky took the files. Then he showed me footage, footage of me and Ricky in bed. He said he'd tell my husband, in fact—" Pamela sits up straight. "He acted a lot like you're acting, actually. He said he'd ruin my life, my family, my career. But now I guess you're the big man? You seem to have one-upped him."

"Who is this guy? The *director?*"

"He's...ex-CIA. He founded GSX. He's horrible. Essentially."

"Your boss? Is horrible? Essentially?" Dylan frowns. "So why'd you work for him?"

"It didn't start out this way, you know, it wasn't always like this. In 2008, it was less militarized, more experimental. I mean, they were giving people access to the early database six months after the first smartphone came out. You realize it's just over a decade old, right? It didn't use to exist. People forget that, somehow. Back then it was brand new. People were even sending their kids out to gather data. They gave them a free iPhone and told them to use it everywhere. Imagine a bunch of twenty year old college students going to parties, taking photos of everything, trying to promote this new behavior. It wasn't a sure thing the device would take off. They were supposed to make it look cool, necessary even. Google did it. Apple did it. Everyone was promoting it. Everyone just wanted that data. *We* wanted that data. We never saw so much intimate data. Look, I just want to understand my species, whatever your name is. That's all. I want to understand my species, to help them."

"Oh, I see. That's why you manipulate them? Toy with their emotions, their insecurities—"

"I know what it looks like. But you don't know the other side. I don't know exactly what Ricky stole, but you haven't seen the other data sets, the NSA data sets. You don't know what horrible things people are doing right now, right as we speak. Left to their own devices, people do terrible things, things you—"

"All I know is *you've* done unspeakable things. *You* treat people like rats."

"I know what it looks like—"

"You keep saying that."

"Would you rather someone rape their daughter? Or would you rather I channeled them away from it? Huh? If someone is showing signs of becoming a pedophile, joining ISIS, what would you have me do? Nothing? You don't know what our algorithms have done, how they saved—"

"I know it made Google and Facebook a whole lot of money. I know it killed Ricky. And I know you're lying. Sure, fine, you did some big humanitarian stuff, but they're using this to control everything, to—"

"Keep capitalism functioning, I know."

Dylan is silent. She plants her feet on the ground and stops swinging.

"I've already read it all," Dylan bluffs. "I know how bad it is. So why'd you support it?"

"It was a tradeoff. I got access to the data and another salary. I could test theories that couldn't otherwise be tested. The universities just don't have access to that data. The government and the tech companies keep it from us. They use it as bait. They want to lure us away from the academy."

"They sure lured *you* pretty far."

Pamela tightens her eyes and looks out at the bay.

"They invented part of the internet here," she says. "Now its out of our hands entirely."

"Kind of like enriched uranium."

"You're insufferable! You know that? Who are you?"

"Wrong question." Dylan resumes her swinging. "The real question, the one I first asked."

"I don't know who killed Ricky."

"You don't think it was your director?"

"I don't...I don't—" Patricia looks at the ground.

Dylan doesn't need to know anything else. The answer is evident.

"You should get your family and run," she says. "Do you love your husband?"

"*What*?" Pamela is shocked. "What do you mean?"

"*Do you*? If you wrote him a note on a slip of paper, told him to not speak out loud about it, to just get in the car with your kids, without your smartphones, without—"

"We have computers with GPS in our cars."

"Holy Mary!" Dylan moans. "Is it not *clear* yet how terrible this all is? This is—"

"It's been clear to me for some time. I'm trapped, like a fly, yes, that's clear to me. And yes, *Holy Mary*! Ricky used to say that, too. In Spanish and English. He loved the Virgin of Guadalupe, the indigenous virgin."

"You should run, Pamela."

The professor sits there on the soil, stunned, as if a bird has just flown into her face. She laughs hysterically after this and then falls to the ground. When she finally sits up, Pamela stares at Dylan with red eyes burning from tears.

"You don't know *anything*! Tell me, have you seen the Virgin of Guadalupe recently?"

"I live in the—" Dylan stops talking but can't close her mouth. "Never mi—"

"See? You don't know anything!"

"You're crazy." Dylan squints her eyes. "I see the Virgin everywhere."

"Ricky *programmed* you! I can already tell. He probably wrote it himself. That's what we did together, he helped me write programs to manage people, to divert them into stasis."

"Yeah, and it clearly made you crazy."

"Listen, I don't know who the hell you are, but data isn't everything. This should be proof of that. Somehow, I'm up here with a child like you and they don't know about it! No, I don't have any proof, I don't know how he could have done it, but he ran something on you. *That's* why you're here."

"You're job's made you deranged! You know we live in a place that used to be Mexico, right? Of course the Virgin's everywhere. You're paranoid, you're *really* paranoid."

"You're wrong. You'll see. This is just his way of getting back at me."

"Whatever, you're insane, and I don't—"

There's a slight rustling in the dry grass that gets louder and louder. A face soon emerges, the face of a dog with yellow eyes. The dog doesn't snarl at them but keeps its black nose close to ground and takes a few steps forward. Dylan realizes it isn't a dog. This dog is in fact a coyote. The creature approaches them steadily and doesn't look away. Pamela starts to panic. She pushes herself back towards the tree but Dylan tells her to stay still. The coyote notices all of this. It stops moving and gazes at them with its piercing yellow eyes. The coyote stares for so long everything goes silent: the coastal wind, the insects, even the pounding of their hearts. And then the coyote turns around. It trots down the hillside and disappears into the dry brown grass.

"Was that a coyote?" Pamela asks.

"That *was* a coyote."

"I guess it was thirsty. It's pretty dry out here."

"They probably shouldn't have built that swimming pool over the creek."

"I know. It's stupid." Pamela sighs. "But why'd it get so close to us?"

"I don't know." Dylan starts swinging again. "Maybe Ricky programmed it."

Pamela tightens her eyelids and clenches her jaw.

"I really hate you," she says. "You know that?"

"No you don't."

Pamela doesn't look away from Dylan as she swings back and forth. Neither of them speak for the next few minutes, they just listen to the wind and the sounds of distant cars. A few airplanes fly overhead, hawks spiral in the sky, and the coastal winds begin to subside. Pamela coughs loudly and stares at Dylan with what is clear and unmistakable affection. Her eyes are no longer red.

"Thank you," Pamela says, standing up.

"For what?"

"For telling me to run."

"Are you going to?"

"Not today, but as soon as I can. Are you going to release the files?"

Dylan waits a moment.

"I'll be honest with you," she says. "Because you were honest with me. It's out of my hands. That's the truth. So if you want to run, the sooner the better, because I can't do anything to stop it."

"It's fine." She kicks the ground and smiles. "Even if it comes out, I can answer for myself."

Pamela starts walking down the dirt path with her hands in her pockets and doesn't look back. Dylan just keeps swinging. She clutches the white ropes and looks out at the water tinged with sunlight. It's some time before Pamela disappears from view. The professor doesn't walk very fast. Her steps are languid, calm, and intentional, as if they mean something. Pamela takes her hands out of her pockets, lets them hang freely at her sides, and after reaching the cutback, Dylan can see that the professor's eyes are closed. She can tell that Pamela is smiling.

CHAPTER 13

Ricky asked Dylan if she'd like to get coffee after work. It was a Thursday afternoon, their sample advertisements for the Communist Party of China had just been approved, and no one in the department was very busy. So they took the bus to the Mission District and went to a cafe with orange walls where they ordered mochas and tipped $5 at the counter. Ricky looked healthy, his skin was glowing, his hair neatly combed, and the only thing unusual was his brown eyes. Dylan thought they were more empty than usual.

They sat by the window and watched the people pass by on the sidewalk. They spoke about the Dream Game, they talked about fashion, and remarked on how uniformly most techies dressed. They pointed out examples on the street, the latest trends spilling over from the Marina District. Dylan said they reminded her of Connecticut with their pastel polo shirts and brown deck shoes and khaki shorts and matching reflective sunglasses.

"I went to high school with people like that," she told him.

"That's right, I always forget you're a rich kid."

"What do you mean?" She took a sip of her mocha and looked at him. "Do I act different?"

"No, you're alright, but that's a whole different world."

"Apparently not." She pointed out the window at the men passing by. "There they are."

"Damn East Coast is taking over."

"The company that owns my building is from New York, too."

"There you go. Shit creeps me out. I mean, San Francisco's only been colonized by the white folks a couple hundred years, a bit longer, but still, the East Coast has been colonized since the 1500s. It's old out there, old money, old power, old traditions, shit like that. Creeps me out."

"I know what you mean. My family comes from money, inherited money."

"They're loaded, right?"

Dylan nodded, took a sip from her cup, and then looked out the window.

"Yeah, they're loaded," she said. "So am I. Not quite a Mayflower family, but almost."

"At least you don't act like it, all stuck up and whatever."

"I guess I never talk about how much money I have. No one ever asks."

"That's because most people in the department are just like you. Tell me the truth, you got this job through a family friend or a friend of their friend? Am I right?"

Dylan smirked. There was no need to answer.

"See, I knew it," Ricky said. "Same as the rest of the office. I asked everyone, in different ways, you know, probably because I grew up poor. Y'all got connections, I got a scholarship."

"Now you're climbing way above us!" Dylan patted his shoulder and smiled. "So what's going on with this Chinese project? What's Chad have you doing?"

"Oh—" Ricky started spinning his cup around on the table. "Mostly data analysis. It took a while to generate those concepts for the Chinese deal. We don't know anything about China. We don't know what their consumers want. And I keep saying we *won't* know, not until we get more data. The Chinese keep it all to themselves, obviously."

"I don't know if I understand."

"Never mind. It's just I've been telling Chad we should take the data from the Dream Game and feed it back into the advertisements, use it to generate composite dream characters and make each billboard regional, an aggregate of the surrounding area's data. If someone sees a piece of their dream characters reflected on the billboard they'll want to keep playing."

"So *that's* how you did it."

"Did what?"

"Climbed way above us rich kids."

"We'll see about that. For now they think it's a good idea. They want to see what I can do with the Chinese data. If we get it. That's just it, it's not a sure thing at all. Bilton Smyth is fucking nuts, you know that, right? The guy's a lunatic."

Dylan held her finger to her lips but Ricky just laughed.

"Come on, you know it's true," he said.

"He's a bit eccentric."

"*Eccentric?* No, if anyone's going to mess this up, it's him. Just watch. Sure, the Dream Game is the number one downloaded game on the App Store. The Communist Party likes that, they like big amounts of data on their population, they like popular games millions of people play. But if you put Bilton Smyth in a room with those party officials and...I don't know what's going to happen."

"We shouldn't be talking about this."

Dylan looked around but no one was close enough to hear them. Most of the customers were sitting on a row of cushioned couches facing a flatscreen television. The others were in the back room eating Mexican food. Dylan gazed at their steaming dishes and began to feel hungry. She hadn't eaten since breakfast and her stomach was filled with acid.

"Competitors could use it against us," she told him. "No one heard, fine, but—"

"Everyone knows it's true."

"Still, we work for him."

"Right." Ricky finished his mocha and then leaned back. "Don't worry, seriously. I'm not saying anything I haven't already skimmed from *The Wall Street Journal*."

"Alright, good point. I saw that article, too. The one with the headline—"

"'Angel Investors Fret Over Eccentric Ceo'? Yeah, and I saw they mentioned the deal with China in the article. That was the whole point of them writing it. It's what I'm saying, everyone already knows. I mean, dude never comes out of the seventh floor except to use the elevator, he's always somewhere else. Honestly, all the guy ever did was pay some people to design a game for him. That's it. And since the company hasn't gone public yet, it's pretty much the Bilton Smyth show."

"This is what they tell us not to—"

"I know, insider information." Ricky looked around to see if anyone was close but just shrugged his shoulders. "No one's over there, Dylan. No one can hear us. Except our smartphones. *They* can hear us. You ever go through all that stuff, the Snowden leaks?"

"I watched the documentary on Netflix. Saw the Oliver Stone movie."

"It's basically a surveillance device. And it's not a secret either."

"They can record my boring life all they want. I'm sure it puts them to sleep."

"There is no *them* recording you. Computers never forget, not unless they're destroyed, and algorithms never sleep."

"Neither do you, apparently," Dylan said. "You're on Facebook until three in the morning."

"How do you know?"

"Facebook tells me. It tells everyone. That little green chat dot."

"So you're stalking me?"

"No." Dylan grinned at this. "No more than anyone else is."

"I stay up late working on stuff, yeah. I've told you, I turn into a night owl."

"It doesn't show. You never look tired. Maybe a bit—"

"I don't have time to be tired. Sometimes the nighttime's the right time to be alive."

They laughed at this for a moment and then stared out the window at the horribly dressed techies in their button up shirts, brand new pants, and colorful running shoes. Dylan eventually ordered a big plate of enchiladas and shared the food with Ricky. They leaned close together over the plate, took turns cutting themselves bites, and mostly ate in silence. Anyone who looked at them would have assumed they were on a date, a couple, or married. But all of this was very casual between Dylan and Ricky, there was no affect or presumption. They were both hungry, they were both friends, and so they both ate from the same plate. Dylan remembers the taste of the enchilada sauce, the tortilla, the cheese, and the chicken. Dylan realizes she's starving.

A hawk cries out over the eucalyptus, the coastal winds flair up, and the brown grass begins to whisper. Dylan waits for the dust to settle before she gets off the swing and runs down the hill through a grove of oak trees. The path eventually disappears and Dylan begins to slide as crumbling earth cascades beneath her feet and brown soil fills her shoes like water. She uses her palms to bounce off tree trunks, slows her descent by grabbing onto roots, and then explodes across the canyon road covered in dirt. Her clothing is drenched with sweat as she runs past the swimming pool, the baseball field, the soccer field, and then stops at a water fountain. It's the most delicious water she's ever tasted. She drinks it with her eyes closed and doesn't stop until her stomach begins to cramp.

Dylan burps loudly and heads towards the Mazda. It's cool underneath the canopy of bay trees and the air is rich with the smell of their leaves. Euphoria permeates every cell of her body. The fear should have disabled her by now but instead she's retained calmness and precision in her movements. She's proven herself to the world. It makes her feel high. It makes the car keys feel electric. It charges the air with a soft, burning light.

Dylan gets into the Mazda, pulls off her wig, and starts the engine. She drives out of the tree covered street and rolls down the windows to let in the air. There are more football players on the sidewalks now, more soccer players on the fields, more bare-chested men running in packs behind tan women jogging in sports bras. The long winding road through the canyon is filled with people exercising, keeping fit, losing weight, staying in shape, and determined to succeed.

She pulls onto the main road and glimpses the bay shimmering in the distance. Her body is so hot she wants to catapult directly into the water. She drives along the hilltops until she reaches the now familiar crossroads and descends another windy canyon road towards the flat lands. She passes the large white hotel at the base of the hills and glimpses the umbrellas of a swimming pool. Her memory fills with images of inflatable pink mats, the chemical scent of chlorine, and the glimmer of chemical water underneath the sun.

At the next intersection, Dylan smells burning meat from a burger shop and her stomach begins to convulse. She pulls into the parking lot without hesitation, goes inside, studies the menu, and orders a bacon cheeseburger with onion rings from the man behind the counter. Dylan asks him for a cup of ice and fills it with water at the soda fountain. She spends the next minute hydrating herself and cannot get enough, not even when her brain freezes. In the middle of her third cup, she realizes a middle-aged couple is looking at her in confusion. Without thinking, Dylan reaches for a wig that isn't there.

"Does my hair look weird?" she asks them.

"Sort of," the woman says. "Like an octopus."

Dylan opens her mouth but says nothing. She touches the back of her head and realizes three of the pins have come out. She smiles politely, removes the rest of the pins, and shakes out her crow-black hair. The couple is still looking at her, only now they have childish expressions.

"Thanks," Dylan says. "They must have come out when I was running."

"You look a bit dirty," the man tells her.

"Yeah, I thought it'd be a good idea to slide down a hill instead of take the path."

"Not such a good idea, I guess," the woman says.

"Nope, it wasn't."

The three of them laugh and Dylan is very relieved when her food is placed on the counter. She takes her basket outside and sits at a table underneath an umbrella. She doesn't look at the couple again. Dylan eats her bacon cheeseburger and watches people play tennis beneath the giant white hotel. In the midst of car noise, she can hear the clatter of their rackets, the squeal of shoe rubber, and the cries of exertion from determined players. Dylan feels mayonnaise, ketchup, and mustard sticking to her lips but doesn't wipe it off until the burger's gone. Once her onion rings have cooled she eats them all very quickly, wipes the grease from her face with a napkin, and takes the empty basket back inside the shop. By then the couple have left their seats.

Dylan drinks one more cup of water, puts a $5 bill in the tip jar, and returns to the blue Mazda. She digs through her bag and finds a black sports-bra, black running shorts, and one of her nice dresses. She tosses the clothes onto the passenger seat, drives behind the giant white hotel, parks beneath a tall eucalyptus tree, and then takes off her pants. She puts on black running shorts and a black sports bra and then covers herself in a blue dress. She ties up her hair in a single tail and puts on black eye-liner and blue lipstick. When she's done, Dylan looks rich.

She slips into a pair of sandals, gets her bag from the trunk, and walks through the side entrance of the white hotel. Dylan has never been here before, she doesn't even know its name. The building smells clean and air conditioned and the only people she encounters in the hallways are the maids with their vacuums and carts. When she reaches the lobby, Dylan passes the front desk, smiles at the sharply dressed employees, and follows two older women in workout clothes to an indoor gym where she finally discovers an entrance to the pool.

It's here that she notices a flatscreen television mounted above the bike machines that displays a picture of Ricky with a headline about San Francisco in turmoil. Dylan runs across the gym to the screen and listens to the newscaster explain how the murder suspect, a prostitute named Alexis Segura, had a dramatic court appearance earlier this morning. Dylan sees footage of Alexis being led in front of a judge by two sheriff's deputies. She is bound in shackles and wearing an orange jumpsuit. Her eyes are filled with anger. Her dark hair hangs heavy around her face.

The newscaster explains the circumstances of her arrest before the soundtrack switches to the courtroom audio and Alexis yells: "OingoBoingo killed Ricky! OingoBoingo killed Ricky! Go ask Bilton Smyth who killed him! Go ask the psychologists OingoBoingo hired! Maybe *they* know who killed him! I'm innocent! I'm innocent! I'm innocent! I'm innocent! *I'm innocent!*" And then two sheriffs slam her to the ground, pull her up, and drag her away. The newscaster explains that Alexis is now charged with contempt of court and her next appearance is scheduled for the following Monday. Because of her outburst, Alexis Segura has still not been formally charged with murder.

The topic switches to the profiles and online-dating websites Alexis used to make money. Dylan sees multiple images of Alexis in her underwear, in bathing suits, and posing nude with her bare chest to the ground. The newscaster explains how the FBI is not charging her with any additional federal crimes, although the local murder charges would proceed as announced by the District Attorney. The news segment ends and is replaced with a commercial for laundry detergent. Dylan becomes aware of two sweaty men peddling on exercise bikes who were watching the broadcast with her. Both of them have gray hair and nice watches on their wrists. They begin to speak but Dylan can't understand anything. It's as if they're conversing in another language.

"Yeah, it's pretty strange," she manages to say.

"It's like someone dropped a bomb on San Francisco."

"It's those damn millennials."

The sweaty men both laugh. The television displays a can of dog food. Dylan is not amused.

"You're a millennial, am I right?" one of them asks.

"I suppose I am. Why? Are you a baby boomer?"

The men keep laughing and Dylan leaves before they can say anything else. She grabs a towel from a pile beside the door and walks onto the pool deck where the glare is piercingly bright. She wishes her sunglasses still had lenses. There are a few dozen people outside reclining in the blue lounge chairs or swimming in the water or pacing along the cement deck. There aren't many children but quite a few infants with their mothers, some of them nursing.

Dylan puts her bag on an empty lounge chair, lifts her dress over her head, and then drapes it over the blue cushions. She steps out of her sandals and immediately dives into the glittering water with her arms in the shape of a V. She holds her breath and swims to the other end before surfacing. The water relaxes her muscles, cools her skin, and calms her mind. She decides to pee in her bathing suit and this brings nothing but pleasure. She floats for over twenty minutes, mostly staying on her back. No one reports her to the management, no one suspects her of being an outsider, and she swims until sleep starts tugging at her consciousness.

Dylan pulls herself out of the pool, grabs her towel, and opens an umbrella over her chair. Her eye lids are heavy with exhaustion when she lays down on the blue lounge chair. The air is warm and a slight breeze blows in from the bay. Dylan closes her eyes as she adjusts herself on the cushion and falls asleep in less than a minute. Her dreams are erased when she wakes up. Dylan has no memory of what she saw, not even the blackness. She doesn't remember when she arrived at the hotel but the clock at the end of the pool now reads 3:57 pm.

Dylan lies there on the blue fabric and tries to discern between the absent dream and this strange reality. She wonders how she came to this pool, how she made it to the hotel, and how the afternoon is almost over. She knows all of this is real and remembers it quite abruptly when two teenage girls sit down beside her with iPhones in their hands. Dylan listens to them talk about Taylor Swift, Netflix movies, and a boy from school before one of them takes a selfie. She points her iPhone at Dylan and herself just long enough to capture both of their images.

The girls keep talking about Netflix movies as Dylan sits up, turns her back to them, puts on her blue dress, and steps into her leather sandals. The girls giggle nervously, as if they think she's famous, and Dylan walks out of the pool area before they can take more pictures. She leaves the hotel too quickly to learn its name and descends a sloping driveway that leads her to the burger shop. She finds her blue Mazda beneath the eucalyptus tree where she left it, gets behind the steering wheel, and turns on the engine.

At first she does nothing. She lets it run and stares blankly at the peeling bark of the eucalyptus. Her armpits begins to sweat and she smells the deep scent of stress in her body odor. Dylan pulls the deodorant out of her bag and rubs it over the small black hairs that have been growing since she last saw Alexis. Dylan rolls down the windows, turns off the engine, and then takes the laptop out of her bag. The screen flickers with light, she opens up the GSX folder, scrolls down to the last file, and finds the home address for the program director. He lives on Oak Street in the city of Oakland. His name is Charles Thorpe. He lives in unit number 507 of a building called the Sierra.

Dylan copies all this information down on a scrap of paper and shuts off the laptop. The screen goes black, she returns it to her bag, and then gazes at her hands as she grips the steering wheel. The keys dangle out of the ignition and the mentholated scent of eucalyptus fills the car. She sweats beneath her blue dress and clenches her jaw. She imagines how beautiful Alexis looked in the courtroom, how defiantly her eyes burned, how she kept yelling even after the sheriffs tackled her to the ground. In this moment, she sees a flame burning behind her eyes. Dylan turns the keys in the ignition, backs on to the canyon road, and then drives towards Oakland. All she needs is a map. Then she'll know where to go.

CHAPTER 14

AFTER THE CHINA DEAL COLLAPSED, THE ADVERTISING DEPARTMENT was in a state of depression, their weeks of work had all been for nothing, and their next assignment was the same as the last one: to design another series of advertisements for the Dream Game. Their initial release was still gaining tens of thousands of daily users every week and the instructions handed down from Bilton Smyth were simple. Their job was to keep those user numbers climbing and ensure the Dream Game remained number one downloaded game on the App Store. They set to work over the next few weeks but only Ricky seemed to show any determination. He'd lost his sense of humor by then, his eyes were always focused on his tasks, and his jokes became laced with bitterness.

In those days, Dylan often sat with Ricky at his desk to work on the new designs. His iMac screen was filled with user data and his notebooks were a mess of sketches and phrases from which he generated coherent visualizations that kept getting approved. The other men in the advertising department quickly grew frustrated with this arrangement. None of their designs were meeting with the same success, nor could they compete with Ricky. He seemed to have found the magic formula. Even Bernadette and Elizabeth had time to complain about it, although none of this affected Dylan. Her job was to assemble the department's designs into a unified whole, place them in the approved advertising context, and orient the variety of dream characters so each element in the frame was balanced. Dylan brought visual harmony to the endless cornucopia of images sent her way and ordered the madness of a million people's dreams.

Just before their latest designs were released, Ricky asked Dylan if she wanted to meet him in the cafeteria during their lunch break. They sat in cushioned chairs at the far end of the room where they could see the downtown skyscrapers enveloped in fog. Red lights blinked on and off inside the mist and the traffic was thick down Mission Street. Both of them silently watched this panorama, each from a different angle. Neither had ever sat in this corner of the cafeteria before. All of it was new.

"So you're happy with what I put together?" Dylan asked him.

"Of course. It's always perfect. That's why they make you do all of it."

"You'd think I might even get a raise, huh?"

"Bring it up when the daily users spike again," Ricky said.

"It's pointless. I don't show enough team spirit, that's what Chad will say. Which I don't."

"Don't worry, I'll take care of it. Just bring it up, Chad will say yes. I'll tell him the truth, I'll tell him only *you* can make those harmonies, only *you* can work that fast. I don't get it, I mean I got my own creative frenzies that take over, but yours are pretty intense. That last poster you made—"

"Which one? The city panorama?"

"Yeah, the horizontal one. It's fucking crazy you did it that fast."

"It's *The Last Supper*. That's it. There are a lot more people at the table, they look kind of funny, but that's all the design was. Plagiarism, blatant plagiarism. You can't go wrong if you stick with da Vinci. Our vertical posters make it a bit more complicated, though, so I used Bruegel, *The Tower of Babel*. The first tower he did, the lighter one, before the tower gets too high, too dark."

"Is that some inside joke or something?" Ricky asked her.

"What do you mean?"

"You think the company's going to collapse?"

"Our stock just went up two dollars last week, even after the China deal! We're solid. I just use that Bruegel as a model because its one of the earliest depictions of a skyscraper. He painted it before a sky-scraper ever *existed*. The first depiction has all the positive activity. The tower's swarming with people, the figures are bathed in light, just like the ads I've been putting together."

Ricky squinted his eyes and then smiled at her.

"You have your phone?" he asked.

"Yeah, I...wait. No, I guess I left it."

"I don't have mine either, just wondering what time it is. Maybe I should get an expensive ass Apple Watch. No, but yeah, what were we talking about? Oh, yeah, so did you ever tell anyone else you're using Bruegel?"

"No. I don't think so. Why?"

"It's just funny. I love your vertical posters, the way the characters inhabit the entire building. And of course a tower makes sense given they told us to stick with this whole urban dream city motif. Bilton Smyth says make it a city, so we make it a city. And then we get our paychecks."

"I just do what they say. Bruegel, though."

"Bruegel," Ricky said, grinning. "*The Tower of Babel*. We'll see I guess."

"Yeah, we'll see. This deal with China falling through. That was definitely a setback."

"Maybe, but if you think its stressful dealing with Chad, imagine having to deal with the Communist Party of China. They would've had the final word on everything, it would've been their terms or nothing, just like they had with Google, like they have with Apple, like they have with everyone who operates there. And not a single one of us is Chinese. What do *we* actually know about marketing in China?"

"You were right about Bilton Smyth," Dylan told him. "He messed it all up."

"Didn't we make a bet? Don't you owe me something?"

"I'll buy you lunch."

"I'm alright, I'm just kidding. Smyth really did sink the whole thing, though. None of us ever got an explanation, either. Remember how he was in those long private meetings before the banquet? Then suddenly he's up on the table calling them cretins and degenerates."

"They really wanted you for that China deal, didn't they?"

"Yeah, but I'm just transferring the same idea over to our domestic advertising, and it's working. I mean, we'll see when the ads come out. My whole trip was how we didn't know anything about China, so why not take the first round of data and feed it back through the advertisements, use the aggregate dream characters to keep people using the game. I don't know, they would've had to hire a bunch of people, people who could speak Chinese and English fluently, everything would've changed. At one point they were even talking about setting up a Chinese office."

"It's just weird how no one knows what happened or even why it happened," Dylan said. "Most CEO's don't do things like that."

Ricky shrugged his shoulders and looked out the window.

"They do all sorts of weird shit," he said. "Where's he from again?"

"Switzerland. But he's half British."

"Maybe he's Illuminati," Ricky said, widening his eyes. "Maybe it was all a set up."

Dylan laughed and they went on to talk about art, about the recent exhibition at SFMOMA, and the multiple parties that happened afterwards. Dylan attended these events with her friend Melissa from Berkeley, someone she hadn't seen in many months. There was a lot of free food and alcohol at the after-parties and they mingled together holding glasses of champagne. It reminded her of being in college when she and Melissa would go to art shows and openings in New York City. She told all this to Ricky that afternoon. She told him how removed she felt from her old life and who she used to be. Now all she did was think about work and food and her company. She never went to art shows anymore. She mostly stayed in her apartment.

Ricky told Dylan he'd go to an art show with her, he said they'd find something that didn't sound awful and escape the tech world for an entire night. Dylan agreed to this, even the possibility of it made her excited, but as the weeks went on Ricky never brought it up again. He became more absorbed in his work, his sense of humor didn't return, and he would often be gone for many hours consulting with the techies on software capabilities.

On the following Monday, Chad asked Dylan to step inside his glass office. He pretended to be on his iMac, told her she was getting a raise, and said the change would be reflected in her next paycheck. He hardly looked at her, just enough to know she was listening. Dylan thanked him and left the office without another word. On the way to her desk, Ricky winked at her with his left eye. Dylan was finally being paid the same as Bernadette and Elizabeth. She remembers when her world was as small as that paycheck. She remembers when the raise made her feel happy, when it was something to be proud of, if only for a moment.

Dylan steers the blue Mazda under the roaring freeway along College Avenue and enters the Rockridge neighborhood of Oakland.

She passes the BART station, drives past a strip of storefronts, and pulls the Mazda over in front of a bookstore. She finds some change in her bag and then feeds the parking meter until she's purchased thirty-seven minutes of time.

The blue and red neon sign reads Diesel Books. She walks through the store's loss-prevention detector and emerges into a long room with wood paneled ceilings and cylindrical metal air ducts extending to the back wall. She doesn't see any cameras, not even above the register where a woman sits typing on the computer. Dylan runs her fingers over the books on display and wanders into the fiction section. She forgets why she's there or what she's looking for. Over the next half hour, Dylan looks through two dozen books, inhales the scent of new pages, mouths beautiful sentences, recites poetry in whispers, and visualizes entire passages with her eyes closed. But eventually she remembers what she needs to do and walks away from the shelves with great reluctance.

At 5:03 pm, Dylan goes up to the counter and asks if they carry maps of Oakland. The woman nods and points to a small rack in the corner where Dylan finds what she's looking for. The map of the city is blue and green and feels crisp in her hand. She spins the metal rack, glances at the children's section, and then sees a black ball-camera hidden above the neck of a headless plastic doll. Dylan instantly looks down at her feet and goes to the counter. She keeps her back to the camera and doesn't turn around even though it's too late. Her image has already been captured.

"You from out of town?" the woman asks her.

Dylan just nods, hands over the map, and watches the woman scan it with a laser gun. She's perhaps a decade older than Dylan. She has short black hair with bangs, wears a black dress, and smells like jasmine flowers. Some of her hair is gray.

"Trying to get anywhere in particular?" she asks Dylan.

"Just want to know my way around."

"Well—" She hands the map over and smiles. "Good luck."

Dylan wants to hold this woman tightly. She wants to tell her the truth. But instead she takes the map and silently mouths the words *thank you*. The woman behind the counter doesn't understand. At 5:06 pm, Dylan leaves Diesel Books and gets into her blue Mazda.

She unfolds the map over the steering wheel and finds the name Oak Street listed in the directory beside a grid reference. She runs her finger down to the waterfront near Jack London Square and sees her destination just beside the 880 freeway. All she has to do is take a right up ahead onto Broadway, drive through the center of Oakland, and take a left on 3rd until she reaches Oak Street. This seems very simple so she puts away the map, pulls into the street, and leaves Rockridge with her eyes fixed on the rear-view mirror.

At the next big intersection, Dylan sees two under-construction apartment buildings that are nearly complete. Both resemble the Vermillion. One has a large green banner draped across its windows with the words LEASE NOW printed in white. These buildings are made of concrete, metal, and glass. They're covered in black surveillance cameras.

The traffic light turns green and Dylan drives past a high school, a strip of small businesses, a hospital complex, and beneath the 580 freeway. She passes auto dealerships and luxury apartment buildings, grocery stores and mechanic's garages, taco trucks and construction sites. For a moment, she glimpses a grove of trees but they vanish as the buildings get taller and the city grows denser. Dylan has never been through downtown Oakland before.

She sees young professionals with corporate badges sitting on the patios of new restaurants. The Pandora tower stands over their heads as they eat and drink and scroll through their smartphones. Beyond this is a former tech-hub that once housed an Uber office. It was set ablaze several months ago and her social media feeds had been filled with pictures of flames and devastation. Most of the new construction was destroyed and the opening delayed by over a year. Now there are several armed men in dark uniforms guarding the doors. The windows are boarded up, the stone walls covered in obscene graffiti, and the guards watch over this ruin with expressions of boredom and shame.

Something shifts at the crossroads of Broadway and Telegraph. There are office towers in every direction that mute the light and turn everything gray. Dylan sees people cruising on bikes, huddling around speakers, and smoking blunts in doorways. The clothing styles change. There are more people in work uniforms, more people with baggy clothes, older clothes, mismatched clothes. She smells marijuana smoke in the air, watches teenagers dance on the street corner, and hears multiple people laugh near a bus stop. Dylan drives through this zone of convergence, past the Marriot tower, past the police headquarters, and travels under the 880 freeway. She sees a fifteen-story luxury apartment tower standing over the waterfront that's made of metal and glass with long green vines draped along its sides. She checks the address on this building but it's not the one she's looking for.

Dylan takes a left on 3rd Street and finds herself in an old warehouse district that looks nothing like the luxury tower behind her. The structures are less than two stories tall with large sidewalk overhangs and big metal shutters that open up onto the street. These squat warehouses give way to parking lots and a Blue Bottle Coffee where several young people in nice clothes sit on metal stools and drink expensive coffee. They all have smartphones glimmering in their hands. The further she drives, all Dylan can see is block after block of luxury apartments in every direction.

At the corner of 3rd and Oak, she finds a five-story apartment building made of concrete, metal, and glass. This one carries the correct address and is named the Sierra. At 5:31 pm, she begins to circle the building in her blue Mazda. Dylan discovers two metal gates on either side that lead to internal stairwells with red walls. There's a private parking garage for residents, a parking lot for delivery trucks, and every entrance is monitored by cameras. On the storefront level, Dylan sees an art gallery, a cafe, a gym, a chiropractor's office, and a sandwich shop. A few of the storefronts look empty.

Dylan parks the blue Mazda across from the west entrance at 5:34 pm and watches the red stairwell, waiting for someone to open the gate. The area is busy, people come and go from the storefronts with sandwiches and coffee, but none of them seem to live in the Sierra. Dylan sits for half an hour with the seat reclined and her feet up on the dashboard. Another hour passes. The metal gate remains static and unchanged. No one enters or exits. At 7:06 pm, she pulls the Mazda out of the parking spot and circles the building.

She drives around to the east entrance, parks across from the metal gate, and turns off the engine. Dylan sits here for an hour. She scratches her temples, clenches her jaw, and taps her feet against the brake pedal. The sun goes down while she waits, the streetlights come on, and the brightest stars become visible in the sky. Not a single person uses the metal gate. At 9:13 pm, she finally gives up and drives south on the 880 freeway. She doesn't know why she does this.

The Coliseum complex is illuminated when she approaches the two circular sports arenas near the freeway. One is made mostly of concrete while the other is made of metal and glass. Floodlights drench the vast parking lots with white light that glistens off thousands of empty cars. The bleachers of the concrete Coliseum are packed with spectators, two helicopters circle overhead, and on the side of the freeway Dylan can see an electronic billboard that displays the image of a woman with dark glasses and blonde hair. It's an FBI wanted poster that promises a 50,000 dollar reward leading to her arrest. Dylan doesn't look away from this flickering image, nor does she feel any fear. That woman isn't her. It's someone else.

Dylan leaves the Coliseum behind and takes the exit for the Oakland Airport. Her only destination is the eastern hills. She drives with no other direction and passes through a corporate strip mall, crosses a bridge over the Coliseum parking lots, and descends into a long expanse of residential neighborhoods. She can't see any of the houses at first, they're mostly obscured by fences, but after she crosses International Boulevard it becomes clear this is a working class neighborhood. From stoplight to stoplight, Dylan doesn't see a single white person. Everyone is either black or brown, every gas station is crowded with cars, every liquor store is packed with customers, and every fast-food drive-thru line stretches to the road. Dylan passes a mall, a police station, a burned down building, and finally begins to climb into the dry hills.

She reaches the top of 73rd Avenue, takes a left near an elementary school, and weaves through the residential streets looking for quiet houses or driveways packed with cars. She wants to find a place where she won't surprise anyone, a place where she can sleep until morning. It presents itself in the form of a one way street at the bottom of a hill. She turns off her head lights, puts the car in neutral, and silently parks under a redwood tree. Dylan studies the windows of the nearest house as the engine cools down and the metal creaks. No one appears to be watching. After waiting a few minutes, Dylan gets into the back seat, makes a pillow out of her clothes, pulls the silver jacket over shoulders, and tries to calm her breathing. At some point during the night, Dylan falls asleep.

The sky is covered in fog when she wakes and everything outside is gray. She starts the car and retraces her path down to the flatland. Before she descends the hill, Dylan stops at a small shop perched on the corner called Quality Doughnuts. The air inside is rich with the smell of fried dough and laced with strong incense that burns in a shrine beside three oranges and two red electric candles. Metallic gold Chinese characters hang behind the thin strands of smoke that climb to the ceiling. Dylan approaches the glass counter and orders a large coffee with a dozen doughnut holes. The two women behind the counter are very nice, they smile excitedly, and Dylan realizes she's still wearing her blue dress.

"You look beautiful," one of them says to her.

"Thank you. So do you. Both of you"

The women begin to laugh, genuinely happy with her presence. Dylan hands over a ten dollar bill and puts the change in the tip jar. One of the women gives her the paper bag of doughnuts, another gives her the coffee, and both of them watch Dylan fill the styrofoam cup with cream. She waves goodbye without a word, goes to the Mazda, and drives down the hill towards the Coliseum. She pops the doughnut holes into her mouth, forces herself to swallow, and washes it all down with coffee. When she reaches the freeway, Dylan has begun to sweat, her armpits are dripping, and her back is slick with moisture. She can't finish the last doughnut hole. Her stomach won't let her.

Dylan drives down the crowded 880 freeway, takes the exit for Jack London Square, and finds her way back to the Sierra where she parks in front of the eastern stairwell. She does this at 6:31 am and sits in her car for the next five minutes. Dylan finishes the coffee with her heart pounding inside her throat and waits for someone to appear. It doesn't take very long. She sees a person on the third floor above the metal gate, an older man with gray hair and a black vest.

Dylan gets out of the car while he descends the red stairwell and crosses the street before he can open the gate. She hears his steps ringing down the stairs, hears the click of the lock, sees the gate open, and discovers a gray haired man smiling at her. He has stylish glasses, his skin is tan and leathery, and his eyes are bright blue. He politely holds the gate open for her, Dylan smiles, and suddenly her left arm twists behind her back, she feels cloth cover her mouth and smells something like gasoline burning in her nostrils. The red walls quickly blur into blackness. Dylan can see nothing. She's gone.

CHAPTER 15

Dylan saw her first iPhone in the summer of 2007 after she graduated from high school. She spent those days on the decks of boats, on the patios of beach houses, and at mansion parties that went on into the morning. Her friends brought their new iPhones to these events and would huddle together to monitor the same Facebook threads on their separate devices. They posed together for endless photos, posted them on Facebook, and then monitored the comments that followed. Dylan tried to participate. She looked over their shoulders and laughed when they did. The novelty was enough to carry her along at first, but without a device of her own she couldn't fully engage. Dylan slowly became invisible whenever her friends went on their iPhones. The glowing screen consumed their consciousness and made human interaction seem inconsequential.

She spent that entire summer without an iPhone. At parties, she'd eventually find the others who didn't have one and would joke about the new device, how it made everyone act like zombies, how it made them look cross-eyed, how their wrists and fingers contorted in strange new positions. It made them look possessed and their hand movements seem occult or even ritualistic.

Her friends stopped being themselves when they were on these screens. They lived according to another rhythm, another tempo, and without an iPhone it couldn't be accessed. Dylan stopped receiving invitations to go on outings, to mansion parties, or on boat trips. Everyone else was using their iPhones now and made their plans over Facebook and Twitter, something Dylan had only ever done on her laptop. Without constant connection to social media, she couldn't keep up with her friends. All of them stopped calling her cell phone.

By the end of the summer, Dylan spent most of her time alone. She packed her bags, bought her textbooks, took her BMW to the mechanic, and ate dinner with her parents every night. They were very happy she was going to the Rhode Island School of Design, although her father had hoped she'd go to Harvard if only for the extra sway it might have on her future. Several of her friends were heading to Massachusetts in the fall but Dylan had no desire to be with them. She wanted to go to RISD where fraternities and sororities didn't exist, where she could be around people who valued art, and make new friends who actually cared about her. At the end of summer, Dylan drove her BMW from Greenwich, Connecticut to Providence, Rhode Island. The car was filled with her belongings and she listened to Taylor Swift's debut album *Taylor Swift* on a loop. Before she left, her mother had given her printed Google Maps directions to Providence. She told her to drive safely.

During that first year at RISD, Dylan made her new friends, started her new life, and met people who cared about art, but she still couldn't escape the iPhone. A couple of her new friends had these devices although they didn't use them much, it wasn't the new center of their existences. Dylan went out with these friends to art shows and parties and met a guy she ended up dating, a painter from New Jersey who cared about art just like she did. And then she drove her BMW home alone for Christmas break from Providence to Greenwich on the 95 freeway. She played Taylor Swift's debut on a loop for the entire coastal journey. It was the only music she listened to that fall.

Dylan and her family cooked roast beef, made roasted Brussels sprouts and mashed potatoes, and then made gravy out of the beef drippings. Dylan helped them prepare this meal over several hours and ate with them at their long wooden table beside the Christmas tree. After dinner they sat around the fireplace and took turns unwrapping presents. When it came to be Dylan's turn, her father handed over a slender box wrapped in red paper. He said it was for the future. He said it was there in case she ever needed it. She opened up the wrapping. It was an iPhone.

Dylan thanked them both, put the box aside, and when they were done opening presents she went into the kitchen to finish cleaning the dishes. Her parents said they were going to sleep, kissed her goodnight, and then went upstairs to their rooms. She cleaned until the kitchen was spotless, wiped her hands dry, turned off the lights, and went back over to the fireplace where her iPhone still sat inside the box. She opened it up, followed the instructions, and was soon connected to a cellular network. She signed into Facebook, checked her news feed, saw her old friend's pictures, and started sending them messages. The fire went out as she typed and scrolled and swiped on her new device. The room grew cold and she fell ever deeper into the screen. The light from her iPhone emitted no warmth. Its glow only sharpened the darkness.

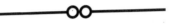

And then light returns. It's blurry at first, but it's definitely light. Then it takes shape. She sees rippling water and green marshland and realizes she's inside a car looking out at the bay. There's a digital screen in the middle of the dashboard and a man wearing black gloves sitting behind the steering wheel with a smartphone in his hand. Dylan blinks and tries to read what it says. She's still too disoriented to discern the small letters, but at the top of the screen she sees a blue and gray hourglass. And then it goes black. The man locks the phone and puts it in his pocket.

Dylan can't make out the details of his face but she knows he's staring at her. The man takes off his gloves, puts them on the center console, and then begins to laugh. It sounds insincere and forced. The humor doesn't penetrate his body but merely inhabits his throat.

"You don't know how close you came to a very unfortunate end," he says.

"Where am I?"

"Near the water. I had to drive you out here. For your safety."

"What happened to me? Who are you?"

"Don't worry." He presses a button and the car begins to hum. "You'll have answers soon."

The electric car is nearly silent. The screen is glowing in the center of the dashboard but Dylan can't read any of it. She rubs her eyes, takes a deep breath, and tries to force her vision back into focus, back into clarity. It doesn't work.

"So who *do* you work for?" he asks her.

"I don't—"

"Never mind," he interrupts. "We can discuss that later."

"Are we getting on the freeway?"

"Correct. Is your vision still blurry?"

"I can't focus on anything."

"That should pass soon. You got hit with something strong. You've been unconscious for about four hours, I'd say. But luckily for you—"

"How did I get here?"

"What's the last thing you remember?"

"My arm was twisted, like someone grabbed me, then this smell—"

"Yes. A lot's changed since then, let me assure you."

Dylan doesn't know what to say. She stares out the window and sees the outline of the Coliseum, its parking lots now empty. Everything blurs together. Dylan can only perceive colors and obscure shapes. She feels the car moving rapidly as the man weaves through traffic at a high speed. She keeps looking at him but can only make out the most abstract contours of his face.

"Aren't you afraid of getting pulled over?" she asks.

"Can't you see yet?" He points at the digital screen. "I know where every cruiser is at this very moment. If you could see the map it would be clear. At our current rate, we won't come near any police vehicles for the next three minutes."

"How do you have that?"

"It's a privilege that comes from my line of work. Alright, we're very close now."

Dylan looks out the window but sees only vague buildings made of shadow and light, ghostly forms pacing the sidewalks, and distortions of space hurtling down the street. And then she's enveloped in shadows as the car comes to a stop. Dylan opens her door but the man is there before she can stand on her own. He takes her arm and gently pulls her upright. The world spins in her vision, she falls into his shoulder, and a sickness invades her stomach as the electric car locks itself. Dylan is pulled into an elevator and everything becomes darkness. They ascend quickly. The ride is smooth and almost silent. When the elevator doors open, he pulls her down a hallway, opens a metal door, and leads her into a room made of light.

"Where are we?"

"This is where I live." She hears him shut the door. "You should relax. It'll help your vision return. Come here, sit by the window. I'm sure it'll help."

He takes her arm and walks over to a glass table. There's something warm and bright next to her that feels like a weak heat lamp. There's also the sound of slowly trickling water coming from within the light. She sits down at the table, searches for the source of the heat, and gazes into the burning illumination hoping it will restore her vision.

"Those are my plants," he says. "When you can see I'll show you."

"They need heat?"

"They need light. The faint heat is a byproduct. Please, relax, concentrate on your vision."

"What happened to me?"

"Well—" The man sits down across from her. "You went to find the director of GSX. And then you were put into a chemically induced sleep, taken to the water, and then you woke up."

Dylan chokes back a surge of bile. She swallows it down and catches her breath.

"You're the director?"

"I am." The man shifts in his chair and crosses his legs. "You see, Miss Kinsey, as I mentioned earlier, you came quite close to a terrible end. Luckily for yourself, someone else is making the moves for you. But please, help me understand, because I must say, I've never seen anything this sophisticated in the past forty years. *Who* do you work for?"

"Are you going to kill me?"

The man is silent for a moment but then she hears him chuckle.

"I *was* going to kill you. But clearly I didn't. You can relax."

Dylan breathes in heavily. Her heart is filled with molten lead.

"Such a surge of emotion," he says. "So *who* is it that you work for? Tell me."

"I worked for OingoBoingo."

"Please." He shakes his head. "Yes, you worked for OingoBoingo, I understand. What I want to know is who you were working for *during* your employment at OingoBoingo. Because when I look at what you did, quite honestly, I'm at a complete loss for explanation."

"I wasn't working for anybody."

"Well, it certainly appears that way, doesn't it?" The man opens a laptop on the table and begins to click. "It appears you come from an extremely wealthy Gold Coast family, Dylan Kinsey. It appears you went to an elite high school and then to the Rhode Island School of Design where you received your bachelor's and master's degrees in graphic design. Your father owned a company that designed the security systems for the most prestigious hospitals in Washington D.C. and New York City. You see—" The man shakes his head and squints his eyes. "This is where it became difficult for me. It turns out your father is very well liked by certain members of the federal government. His company secured their medical data, and you know how politicians love to swipe at each other's infirmities. So when you came up on our lists, we had to discount you at first. We had no choice. But then yesterday we saw the footage from your building, we saw you together with Alexis Segura, and after that I began to personally build a profile on you. And much to my surprise, no less than an hour after I'd collated all that data, there you were waiting in your car."

Her vision starts to return. The director has blue eyes and metal framed glasses. He has gray hair and tan, leathery skin. This is the man from the stairwell. Dylan doesn't want to show any fear so she turns towards the glass tray of red and green plants. They stand upright like plastic cobras with rigid tongues and skin that resembles the scales of a reptile. A constant stream of water is running along their roots while six small UV lights glow above them. The entire ensemble hums together.

"Those are my Darlingtonia. Can you see them clearly?"

"What are they?"

"A carnivorous plant. The Latin name is *Darlingtonia californica*." The man stands up and walks over to the glass tray. "They only grow in northern California and southern Oregon and require a very specialized environment to survive. Soil rich in metal, cold water from the mountains, direct sunlight, and they also need insects to fly inside their chambers."

The director points at the head of a mostly red Darlingtonia lily.

"You can see how the tops of these plants have translucent windows on their roofs. What happens is that insects are attracted to these nectar glands here—" The man points to the long green tongue extending from the head of the plant. "These appendages here, these are the nectar glands. It's a free meal just so long as the insect doesn't investigate any further, because you see these glands lead directly into the head of the plant, into this chamber of windows. Once the insect is inside the chamber, it keeps flying towards the windows of light, it's literally pulled towards the light, and then eventually grows tired from hitting itself against the windows—" The man points to the neck of the plant. "And then the insect begins to sink down this long tube. Small hairs on the inside grab the insect and pull it down to the bottom of the plant where it drowns in a bath of fluid. After that, small organisms break it down and digest it. You see, the plant doesn't digest its own food. It has symbiotic creatures living inside that do all that nasty work. That's how the plant keeps itself alive."

Dylan has never been this scared in her life. She's never felt her body become completely paralyzed. She's never seen something this evil. It's easier to look at the plants than at the man who nurtures them. His blue eyes terrify her, his leathery skin makes her feel repulsed. She cannot stop herself from hyperventilating. It takes command of her lungs. It makes her lose control.

"I know quite a lot about you, Dylan, especially your recent activities. I know that your new friend Pamela has seen fit to leave her husband and their children. Whatever you said to her seems to have sparked a sudden urge to completely vanish last night. Unfortunately for me, she knows precisely how to stay hidden, she knows all of our tactics."

Dylan can barely manage to catch her breath.

"If you're going to kill me, just kill me," she manages to say.

"Dylan, like I already said—"

"Then stop these mind games!" She can't help the tears in her eyes. "What do you want?"

"I want to know who you work for. An agent for Russia or China couldn't have done a better job at destabilizing an entire region. At this point you're going to destabilize the entire country. So I want to know who you work for. Who contracted you?"

"No one. I'm just myself."

"Hardly, Miss Kinsey. You're not *just* yourself." The director sits down at the table and pulls something up on the laptop. "We have footage of you meeting with Alexis Segura outside OingoBoingo headquarters, we have footage of the nights she spent at your apartment—" He spins the laptop around and shows Dylan nude images of her and Alexis. "We have footage of—"

"Fuck you!" she suddenly yells. "Yeah, you have footage of everything, great. Fuck you!"

"My point is, Miss Kinsey—" He turns the computer back around. "We know everything, so you can just assume we have the full picture of what happened over the past ninety-six hours. It appears you had no prior knowledge of what was happening before you met Alexis, before you were given the USB drive with classified government information."

The director clicks on the screen and shows Dylan various images of herself driving the blue Mazda through the Mission and crossing the Bay Bridge. She closes her eyes and refuses to look any further. She continues to breathe heavily. She's never wanted to kill anyone, not until this moment.

"You were certainly used, Miss Kinsey. You were manipulated by other people."

Dylan opens her eyes. She sees an expanse of houses stretching into the horizon, a gray freeway cutting across the landscape, and sunlight burning through the fog. The director stands up, walks over to the window, and deliberately obstructs her view of this landscape. His hands are clasped behind his back while he gazes at East Oakland and the brown hills in the distance.

"You know—" The director looks at her a moment. "When I was younger, closer to your age, there was a lot of manipulation going on in Oakland. You had racist cops terrorizing black people, you had black groups forming to defend themselves, and then you had agents from Moscow manipulating the situation. They didn't care about civil rights, they didn't care about ending racism, they just wanted to destabilize the United States. I'm sure you've heard of the Black Panthers, especially now that Beyoncé went and reminded everyone about those puppets. But you don't know how they were infiltrated by Moscow, how they were manipulated pawns just like you."

"I don't work for Russia!" Dylan yells. "I told you already!"

"Maybe you don't, but you did *someone's* work." He glances at Dylan with cold eyes and scoffs before returning to the window. "This damn city never gives up, I still can't believe it. Oakland is *still* fighting us. What were we supposed to do? Moscow was trying to foment insurrection across the planet. Should we have just sat back and watched them do it here? And now they blame us because *they* bought *our* drugs. What were we supposed to do?"

"I don't know what the fuck you're talking about."

DARLINGTONIA

The director smiles and then walks away from the window.

"Of course you don't." He paces over to the Darlingtonia and begins to stroke one of the cobra heads. "You know these plants are highly specialized. Were it not for this constant flow of cold water their roots would burn up and the plants would die. Were it not for this soil rich in minerals the plants would never grow. I have this system perfectly arranged so the Darlingtonia are always in the ideal climate for their particular growth pattern. But if the water and power were cut, I'm afraid they'll die. Likewise with the planet. If the snowpack keeps decreasing, if the mountains stop gushing water, these specialized plants will soon disappear. That's the problem with specialization, you see? Eventually you're backed into a corner you can't get out of and—"

"I don't care! I don't give a shit! I don't know—"

"It's quite alright. Calm down."

"Fuck you!"

"I'll get to the point since you're so impatient to reach the end." The director angrily sits back down at the table, types something into his laptop, and then spins it around. "Can you explain this?"

It's an image of Dylan in her black sports bra and running shorts. She's lying on the blue lounge chair beside the pool of the big white hotel. Her eyes are closed, her left hand is on her belly, and her mouth is slightly open. The blue dress is draped on the chair beside her. Someone else must have taken it when she was asleep, someone wandering along the deck, most likely a man. Dylan sits back in her chair, looks at the director, and then stares at his tan skin.

"You like looking at me without much clothing on," she says. "You're like a creepy old man."

"The thing is, Dylan, I can't explain it either. I can't explain why in the middle of this you'd sneak into a club you didn't belong to, go swimming in the pool, and then fall asleep for over two hours. If you *did* work for someone, if you *were* a professional, you would have made your escape already, you would be on a flight to Beijing right now."

"It's because I don't fucking work for China, or Russia, or anyone, like I said."

"I agree, we're talking in circles. You don't work for anyone, I agree. When you sold your car, that's when I began to have my doubts. But now look at—"

"I don't want to look at any more of your dumb pictures!"

"You don't know who used you!" The director stands up and slaps Dylan across the cheek, his face bright crimson and his blue eyes burning with malice. "Your new love Alexis, do you know the kind of scum she associates with? They're all criminals, anarchists, prostitutes, arsonists, pornographers, pot dealers! They'd stab each other in the back over a rumor. Most of them are so infiltrated by the FBI they've fled, disappeared, gone to Mexico. It's *these* scum who want to topple the state? And *who* do they send? They send Alexis and Ricky! Neither of them ever told you, but Ricky wrote a program and Alexis carried it out on you *quite* nicely. And now here we are."

"You're lying!" she screams.

"Just take a look."

He pushes the laptop in front of her and begins clicking through a series of images. They show Alexis in bed with Ricky, they show Alexis with people Dylan's never seen before. All of them are dressed in black and brown and green. Many of them have tattoos and piercings. They're smiling in every picture. None of them are posing. These people are clearly friends with Alexis. Dylan sees Alexis in front of an anarchist symbol with a cigarette in her mouth, she sees Alexis in the woods holding a shotgun, she sees Alexis at riots, and she sees Alexis shooting heroin in a bathroom with a well dressed man. And then there are pictures of Ricky holding a black flag with a red star, wearing a brown beret, dissecting a motherboard, shooting an assault rifle in the desert, dancing at Stanford fraternity parties, and posing in a black balaclava.

"Great, that's them. Wow."

"The pattern of your radicalization is quite typical. No one could have predicted the police would shoot someone in front of your building. That certainly seemed to accelerate things, but at root your urges were the same as those experienced by someone joining ISIS or the KKK. They slowly become enraged by a contradiction within our society, their internet searches become more extremist, just like yours did, and usually people reach a breaking point, just like you did. You ended up going to anarchist websites, you began to sympathize with their extremist—"

"Why did the police kill that man? Can you tell me that?"

The director looks away and shakes his head.

"This is all beside the point. You exhibited well-documented symptoms of radicalization. And like every ISIS acolyte you were manipulated, you were used as a pawn. You don't find it strange how easily Alexis fell in love with you?"

"No!"

"You don't find it odd how this all worked out so perfectly?"

"No, I don't! If you're going to arrest me—"

"Arrest you? Arrest? You really *are* ignorant aren't you. Do you have *any* idea what you've just done? Do you know what's about to happen because of this?"

"Maybe you shouldn't have done it."

"I suppose you'd prefer it be like China then? You have no idea what they do to their population. They restrict their intelligence, they censor the internet, and they classify people like animals. Trust me, I've seen it with my own eyes. I know what they do. How do *they* keep everyone in the factories? How do *they* keep capitalism running? *They* treat people like hens in a battery cage. That's how! *They* keep them in utter ignorance, subject to the whims of whatever lunatic is in power. At least we offer *some* choice, *some* breadth of motion, *some* way to get out. Or perhaps we should be more like Russia? Maybe we could—"

"Kill people? Kill innocent people? Fuck you, you piece of shit! Fuck you! You're a murderer!"

"Calm down, you—"

"You killed Ricky, you piece of shit!"

"And I regret it, trust me. I thought I'd contained the leak but I only made it worse. He had two thumb drives. Now everything's over. Just calm down. This morning Wikileaks announced they have 17.8 GB of data, precisely the amount Ricky stole. They're going to release it on Monday, no one can stop them, and that's it, that's why you're still alive. Killing you would only strengthen the argument against us, against our project. No, I wanted to be sure you weren't a foreign agent for myself."

"Just fucking kill me then!" Dylan screams at him. "What else do you want?"

"I want to know why you did this, Dylan."

"You killed Ricky, you had Alexis thrown in jail—"

"Another mistake."

"Everything you've done is a mistake, you dumb fuck!"

"It doesn't change the fact you were manipulated by an indigenous separatist and a known anarchist extremist. They hid themselves very well. I still haven't discovered how they coordinated this, but it's obvious they worked together. We previously believed Ricky had renounced his militant high school beliefs and grown past this infantile separatism at Stanford. We found his continued obsession with the artist Ester Hernández to be a benign remnant of those days, relatively neutral. Turns out we were very wrong. He was involved with some very serious people, most likely throughout his time at Stanford. Only he kept it absolutely hidden. You're too ignorant to have thought this up alone."

"You people are insane! You and Pamela! What the fuck are you even talking about? None of us conspired on this, none of us! You people are paranoid, your brains are damaged, you have too much time on your hands, you have too much data! Look at you! You're just another creepy old man with his computer staring at young people's bodies, making up sick stories, insane stories, and I don't want to hear them anymore!"

The director quickly stands up, still red in the face. His blue eyes burn behind his glasses, his jaw clenches rapidly, and his fingers curl up into fists. None of this matters to Dylan. She can see the weakness invading his eyes.

"You going to slap me again?" Dylan asks him. "Will that make you feel good?"

"Why did you come here?" he asks. "Why did you walk right up to my doorstep?"

"To tell you what a sick fuck you are! To say I hope you die!"

"Is that it? You didn't have a weapon. What do you want, Miss Kinsey?"

"I just told you," she says firmly. "Can I go now?"

"That's it?" The director sits back down and folds his arms over his chest. "You helped destroy the company you worked for, you exposed your neighbors for calling the police, you fomented a riot outside your building, you helped the mob burn the lobby, and you revealed the biggest surveillance program we have in this country. And now you just want to leave?"

DARLINGTONIA

"Yeah! I want to get the fuck out of here right now!"

The director laughs and looks down at the glass table. Dylan can hear the water dripping across the Darlingtonia and the low hum of the electric lamps. She glances towards the front door, looks at the director, and begins to stand until his arm shoots out and pulls her down.

"I'll do you one better," he says, holding onto her wrist. "I'll erase you."

"Let me go!"

She struggles against his grip but he doesn't let go, instead he pushes her into the chair and forces her head towards his laptop screen. The director collapses several files into their central folder, quickly deletes them, and then closes the screen.

"There! There goes your files. Forever! No one will ever learn about you, just like they won't learn anything else besides those 17.8 GB you stole. All of it's gone, all the research, all the profiles, all the algorithms. People are destroying the physical evidence as we speak. Those idiots at the FBI have already told the public these documents are classified government material, but there won't be anything else to find. It destroyed itself while you were asleep in the car, the entire system was deleted, all the automated programs have ceased. The FBI can't be allowed to have *any* access. Those cretins are hopelessly compromised. No. A few people will notice by the end of the day, but they'll only be able to tell the committee, then they'll tell the President, and then—"

Dylan waits, she actually wants to hear what he's going to say, but the director seems to notice this fact. He gets out of his chair, walks over to the tray of Darlingtonia, and leans his head close to the cobra headed Darlingtonia. Dylan finally stands, puts her hand in her dress pocket, and finds the car key nestled inside. It makes her feel a warm rush of safety.

"You're free to go," he says. "But if I were you I'd run."

Dylan paces carefully, waits for him to prevent her exit, and takes the first opportunity to bolt for the door. Her footsteps echo loudly and she's desperate to touch the cold metal of the door handle. The UV lights blind her, the sound of the trickling water makes her want to scream, and the director just stands there passively admiring his plants. He doesn't make a move. He doesn't try to stop her. He lets her pass by.

"You acted very much the insect this morning!" he yells out. "Just like everyone else does. Keep running, don't come up again, because if the FBI figures out who you are they'll have you in prison for life. They could even execute you for high treason. Don't be the insect, don't go inside the chamber, don't be tricked by the lights. Don't fall into the bottom."

Dylan checks to make sure the door is unlocked, props it open with her foot, and then stares at the director one last time to make sure he won't kill her. But the man isn't concerned, he's staring at the red and green cobra heads of the Darlingtonia. They stand perfectly still. There's no wind to move them, no sudden breeze to make them sway.

"People don't *want* to be slaves," she tells him. "You know that? You *trick* them into being slaves, you *put* them in stasis, and you make sure they stay that way, all for some dying system that barely works. People aren't insects, people aren't subjects. Your shit's done! I'm the fucking organism that digested you! You fell into your own flower, old man! Your time's up!"

"My time *is* up," he says to his plants. "And it doesn't matter."

"I hope you get what's coming to you," she says.

"Don't worry. I will."

Dylan can't help it, for a short moment she feels terribly sad for him. He's over seventy years old, his skin looks worn out, and his shiny black vest only makes him look older. The director doesn't look at her, he keeps staring at the carnivorous plants as if they were speaking a secret language only he could understand. But this feeling of sympathy passes and she hates him just as fiercely. She wants to see him dead. She wants the plants to eat him. Dylan grabs the handle, closes the thick door, and leaves him alone with the Darlingtonia.

The next few moments pass in a haze. She descends an illuminated staircase to the red stairwell and follows it down to the front entrance. Dylan opens the metal gate and makes it across the street before she vomits acid and bile and mucus onto the pavement. She keeps her hand on the hood of the Mazda as her chest convulses, her lungs contract into her throat, and her eyes fill with tears. And then she's inside the Mazda, wiping drool from her mouth and driving away from the Sierra.

DARLINGTONIA

Dylan gets on the 880 freeway and heads south in the congested traffic. She pounds on the roof of her car, slams her fists against the steering wheel, and doesn't stop driving until the gas light comes on somewhere in the city of Newark. Her heart won't stop pounding, her short term memory no longer functions, and she has no idea where she's going. But then she notices the red gas light glowing on the console. If she doesn't refill the tank she knows the engine will die so Dylan takes the first off-ramp and finds a Shell station on the corner of a busy intersection.

She parks the blue Mazda beside pump number six, clutches her fingers around the steering wheel, and screams as loudly as possible. She only does this once but it's loud enough for everybody to hear. The other customers hold their pump handles and look at this strange woman in the blue dress. They see her get out of the car and watch her kick the wheel before she sleepwalks into the station with a wad of crumpled bills in her hand. No one pays her much attention. They fill their tanks with regular, watch CNN clips on the gas machine monitors, and wipe their windshields with complimentary squeegees and paper towels provided by the Shell Oil Company. These commuters see women like Dylan every day. It's something they're used to.

CHAPTER 16

THE OINGOBOINGO DREAM GAME REMAINED NUMBER ONE ON THE App Store for the rest of the year. But at the beginning of winter, just after the Christmas holiday, the entire department learned there was a new product to advertise. Dylan flew from JFK to SFO airport, took BART back to the Vermillion, and when she arrived at work the next morning, Chad assembled the entire department in one of the glass conference rooms. It was time to release a new product before the Dream Game lost its number one place in the App Store. They'd come up with a new concept, a new idea that would increase the profitability of the company. It would be called Childhood Memory Game. It was nearly identical to Dream Game, although now the advertising aesthetic would have to change. Rather than the usual medley of psychedelic dream images, their advertisements would now tap into childhood nostalgia and the desire to relive forgotten memories.

The techies had been able to modify and expand the game engine to allow for more complex visualizations and create greater depth, nuance, and flexibility. Chad provided the department with an initial sample of memory characters generated from beta tests of the new game. Everyone looked at them on the main monitor in the glass room and watched silently as Chad scrolled through the images. At the end of the presentation, Dylan asked a question.

"Can you tell us a bit more about the game?"

"Yeah, why didn't we get a beta test?" Elizabeth asked.

"The consultants believed it would interfere with your work. I apologize. Once we're out of the beta test you can download it like normal, for free, with unlimited plays."

"But what about the game?" Dylan asked. "What's the goal?"

"I don't—" Chad picked up his iPhone and began to type into it. "Sorry."

"It's basically the same as the last one," Ricky told his coworkers. "The game asks you about childhood memories that were scary, an animal you were the most afraid of, what parts of the house scared you the most. But they also want to know when you were happy, what brought you joy, and then it generates a world you have to get through."

"Exactly." Chad put down his phone and looked over his workers. "So we need to stretch our imaginations and really think up some new designs. Dig deep into your memories and pull out something you might tell the game. Let's see what we come up with! Alright! Let's go!"

Chad clapped his hands together at the head of the table and waited for them to leave before retreating to his glass office. Dylan looked over the new designs at her desk, copied the files onto her hard drive, and then opened them up on Adobe InDesign. Ricky appeared over her shoulder while she examined these digital snakes, ominous shadows, friendly rabbits, and bedtime monsters hidden in the curtains.

"What do you think?" he asked.

"They have a bit more detail, more body. I like them so far."

"Once we start generating user data I can make them more complex. You'll see."

"Is this what you were going to use the Chinese data for?"

"Basically."

"Then I'm sure it'll be interesting." Dylan looked at Chad's office and then leaned closer to Ricky. "He doesn't do anything, right?"

"Who? Chad?"

"Yeah. Seriously, does he do anything?"

"He keeps things running. He tells us what to do."

"I know *that*. But he's just a business student. He doesn't know anything about design."

Ricky looked around at his coworkers. They all had headphones on.

"I don't know what to say," Ricky said. "He's about two steps removed from Bilton Smyth. He can fire us whenever he wants. What else is there?"

"He's a piece of shit."

"Obviously."

"Glad we agree," Dylan said, glancing around. "I can't speak for everyone."

"No, those guys love him. He's their bro, *man*."

They quietly laughed at this before Ricky returned to his desk.

Dylan watched his monitor fill with InDesign and Photoshop projects and saw him hunch over a notebook filled with sketches, phrases, and ratios. Beside him was the Ester Hernández painting of a woman with the Virgin Mary tattooed on her back. He hardly left this seat once the creative frenzy began. His eyes lit up as if possessed and nothing could stop him until the lunch break interfered and he heard the growl of his own stomach. Ricky worked in this feverish manner for the next two weeks, his designs were always approved, and the department assembled enough dream characters to populate several advertisements.

Dylan was tasked with creating a 30 x 144 inch horizontal poster that would be displayed on the sides of buses throughout every major city in the United States. In addition to this, she had to design two separate 48 x 67 inch vertical advertisements to be displayed behind plexiglass display cases at sidewalk bus shelters and subway stations. This work charged Dylan with as much energy as it did Ricky. It was all she could think about during the day, even at lunch, even in the bathroom.

Just as she had for the Dream Game advertisements, Dylan used *The Last Supper* by da Vinci, *The Tower of Babel* by Breugel, and finished her initial designs by Friday. Everyone was impressed by her work, even Chad agreed, and by the end of the day her designs had been approved. Dylan never told the department what she used as the basis for each design. No one ever asked except Ricky.

Dylan spent the weekend alone. She hiked in the Marin Headlands and went jogging along Ocean Beach. At night, she scrolled through her iPhone, ordered take-out, and watched movies on her flatscreen television. She went to work the next Monday as she always did, rode the bus down Mission Street, listened to Taylor Swift on her ear phones, and when she reached the common room, Dylan learned her latest designs had caught the attention of the board. Chad came over and said they wanted her to design the billboard for the next round of ads. It would be displayed across the entire country.

"There won't be a billboard for the initial release?" she asked.

"No, there will be. It was pre-designed. It's the board's decision."

"So who designed it?"

"Listen—" Chad took out his iPhone and began typing. "I have to go. Good work!"

Dylan watched him leave the common room with his eyes fixed on the glowing screen. He didn't come back for the rest of the day, leaving them to their separate tasks. Ricky and Dylan worked closely for the next five days. She helped him design several posters for subway cars and listened to his theories on dreams and memory. They ate lunch together and discussed concepts like consciousness saturation levels, viral marketing, the Pokémon Go phenomenon, and user's attachments to specific game characters. Both of them were enthralled that week and produced their designs at a speed none of their colleagues could match. Everything was finished by Friday, the new advertisements were approved, and the entire department picked an exclusive club to celebrate their victory.

Dylan wore a black dress and her silver Japanese designer leather moto-jacket. She put on blue eye shadow, black eye liner, and had tall, black leather boots that rode up to her knees. Dylan arrived at the club and found Ricky at the bar talking to a woman with dark hair and a red jacket. Ricky whispered something into the woman's ear, the woman kissed him on the cheek, and then left the bar before Dylan could see her face.

"Who was that?" Dylan asked him.

"Some random person."

"Sure!" Dylan leaned over the bar to order. "Could I get a Long Island iced tea?"

"She had to go real fast," Ricky said. "I was just talking to her about music."

"Then why'd she leave right when I was coming?"

"Get out of here, Connecticut!"

"Hey, let me ask you something? What does the new billboard design look like? Who made it?"

"No one made it! It's just a rectangle that says Childhood Memory Game!"

"That's it?"

"For now. The board wanted to keep it simple. Don't worry, no one's out for your job."

Dylan lightly punched him on the shoulder, the bartender delivered her drink, and together they watched their coworkers group up on the dance floor. The club was packed with people from Dropbox,

LinkedIn, and Twitter. Every table held the glow of multiple smart-phone screens. Even the dance floor was an endless pool of selfies, videos, Tweets, Snapchats, Instagrams, and a few Facebook status updates. There was nowhere to stand without being seen, nowhere to avoid the obligatory club pic. Since moving to the city, Dylan had seen herself tagged in hundreds of Facebook posts, included in countless Instagram pictures, and recorded on dozens of Twitter videos. Several images of her were captured that night at the club but Dylan didn't notice, nor did she care. She remembers leaning her back against the bar and standing shoulder to shoulder with Ricky. She remembers feeling safe.

The traffic is terrible but Dylan has no choice. She creeps towards San Jose past the white, red, and gray Tesla factory in the city of Fremont. She pounds on the roof of the car, hammers down on the steering wheel, and screams when she remembers the shape of the Darlingtonia lily. The Mazda is stuck behind an Amazon Fresh delivery truck for nearly half an hour until the traffic finally picks up and the cars start moving faster. Dylan sees the brown hills towering above San Jose and the housing developments rising up their slopes. She merges off the 880 onto the 101 freeway and heads south through the outskirts of the sprawl. The metropolis of San Jose is far bigger than she imagined and the urban grid seems to extend forever, although most of it's obscured by concrete walls meant to muffle the noise of the freeway.

The housing developments eventually disappear and are replaced with farmland that stretches away towards the hills. Dylan keeps the windows rolled down, lets her hair blow in every direction, and smells the rich, gaseous stench of fertilizer. She drives seventy miles an hour but occasionally allows herself to follow the flow of traffic and gets up to eighty-five. Even this minimal infraction makes her sweat, she constantly looks in the mirror, and these moments of illegal speeding don't last very long. The stress isn't worth it.

She pulls over at a gas station in the agricultural town of Gilroy and buys a map of Central California. Dylan grabs a banana and a blueberry muffin at the counter, eyes the menthol cigarettes, and decides to buy a pack of Newports. Dylan asks the clerk if she can wait a moment and runs to the cooler for a plastic quart of milk. The clerk is a young woman with dark skin who waits patiently for Dylan to find her money and then politely hands back the change. The clerk doesn't offer a bag. The gas station doesn't have any.

Dylan carries her items back to the Mazda, chugs nearly half of the milk, devours the blueberry muffin, and drinks what remains of the carton. Sitting on the passenger seat next to the banana is the pack of Newports. The cardboard box is green and white and wrapped in cellophane. Dylan has never bought a pack of cigarettes before. She finds it odd that she can't eat these cigarettes and yet they'll kill her if she smokes enough of them. The pack sits there beside the banana and makes her think of Alexis. She tears the cellophane off the Newports, puts a cigarette in her mouth, and digs around in her bag for a lighter. All she finds is a pack of matches.

Dylan rips off one of the black and white sticks, strikes it across the sandpaper, and lights her cigarette with the flame. The smoke tastes terrible, worse than she could imagine. She quickly dispels it from her lungs and holds the cigarette out the window. Her second drag tastes slightly better but only because the tingly menthol has numbed the harshness of the smoke. Dylan begins to play with the matchbook before taking another drag. She flips it around and stares at the multicolored floral designs printed on the cover. The matchbook is from the Perla del Pacifico restaurant on Main Street in the town of Watsonville. She's never seen these matches before.

Dylan can't remember if she grabbed them at the banquet after Ricky's funeral, nor can she remember the name of the restaurant, so she takes another drag of the cigarette and opens up her map of Central California. She sees a freeway leading off 101 through the town of Gilroy and over the mountains into Watsonville. Dylan says the name of the freeway aloud, tosses the map next to the banana, and starts the engine of her Mazda.

It takes ten minutes to find the 152 freeway. During her search, Dylan passes churches with red tiled roofs and school yards filled with children playing in their gray uniforms. She passes strip malls packed with Mexican markets, cell phone stores, taquerias, and several fast food chains. She sees mountains standing green and tall above a Dollar Tree and its half-full parking lot. The land soon opens up into long fields filled with every type of crop. There are grapes and orange trees and lettuce and Brussels sprouts all growing in rows and orchards. The road eventually begins to curve and climb away from the vineyards into brown hills dominated by oak trees. The further Dylan drives, the more lush the land becomes. She can smell the scent of water and bay leaves in the air. The brown grass slowly gives way to ferns. The sky becomes obscured by redwoods.

The road flattens out at the summit and the western sun hits her face. For the next twenty minutes, Dylan descends into Santa Cruz County behind a long line of cars. The Pacific Ocean stretches away into the distance, its subtle motion constant and its brilliance almost unbearable. Between the mountains and the coastline is the city of Watsonville, surrounded on all sides by a vast grid of green and brown farmland. It's the biggest town Dylan can see in this coastal river valley and looks tiny compared to the immensity of the glowing water.

The sun is a few hours from setting as she continues her descent to the flatlands. Dylan drives past fields covered in white plastic to protect the crops and arc-shaped greenhouses that refract the sunlight. The first houses appear on the side of the road, the last fields fade in the rear-view mirror, and Dylan drives onward into the commercial area. A digital bank clock tells her it's 6:27 pm and most of the business signs are in Spanish. Further down the road, she sees a clump of red-brick buildings that are taller than everything else. This is the old center of town. This is where Dylan finds Main Street.

She takes a left at the crossroads and looks for the Perla del Pacifico restaurant. She finds it almost immediately. A sandwich-board on the sidewalk announces it's open and Dylan parks across the street in front of an Ace Hardware. This is definitely not the restaurant where she went to the funeral banquet. At this moment, she's certain Ricky put the matchbook in her bag and wanted her to come here. Dylan unbuckles her seat belt, starts to open the door, and then sees something very significant. Beside the restaurant is a florist shop with a green overhang above the entrance. Printed in bright pink are the words *Florez y Florez*. A red and white OPEN sign hangs in the window. The lights are still on. Two women are inside.

225

Dylan digs some paper out of her bag and writes a short message before getting out of the Mazda. She crosses Main Street in her blue dress and sandals, cautiously approaches the shop, and taps on the window pane with her finger. Dylan recognizes two of Ricky's sisters standing in a green room filled with flowers of every color, many of them orchids. One of them is sweeping the floor while the other is going over receipts at the counter. They hear her tapping on the glass and both seem to recognize her. One of them approaches with her broomstick.

Dylan holds the note up to the window, puts her finger to her lips, and points at the Mazda. The sister looks confused for a moment but when she reads the note her eyes suddenly widen as if the world were about to end. She takes the smartphone out of her pocket, leaves it on the counter, motions for her sister to be silent, and walks out of the flower shop. Dylan has the car started and the passenger door open when Ricky's sister crosses Main Street and gets inside.

"You don't got a phone either?" she asks Dylan.

"No, I don't. Sorry to do this—"

"No, no, no. So what—"

"I don't remember your name."

"I never told you is why." She holds out her hand. "Marisol."

"Dylan. Nice to meet you."

"*Mucho gusto.* I thought we scared you off for good!"

"Here I am."

"So what's going on? Is it about Ricky, is it—"

"I know who killed him."

There's no reaction at first. Dylan grips the steering wheel tightly, tightens her jaw, and feels her cheeks become red, although Ricky's sister seems calm. Marisol slowly turns to the windshield, closes the passenger door, and then buckles her seat belt. She has dark skin just like Ricky. She wears a long green dress and has turquoise earrings. Her hair is pitch black, much darker than Dylan's. She smells like the scent of a thousand flowers.

"It's not that person Alexis Segura, is it?" Marisol asks. "I didn't think so."

"No, that was his friend. He never mentioned Alexis to you before?"

"No, never. I've seen her on the TV, though. None of us thought she did it, either. Plus, she's been screaming in court. No one who's guilty does something like that."

"Look—" Dylan grabs the book of matches from her ash tray and hands it over. "I just found this in my bag. The only way it got in there is if Ricky put it there. And look, here—" Dylan lifts the locket from the cupholder. "Ricky gave me this months ago, he hid a code inside of it."

"Wait—" Marisol closes her eyes and mouths a few words. "Who killed him? Come on."

"A sick man, just...a really bad man. Ricky ended up working for him, Ricky stole some—"

"*Santa Maria!*" Marisol bites her lip and shakes her head in disbelief. "That boy. Uh-uh. That *was* him wasn't it? I saw it on Twitter, all that information about to get leaked. I saw that. You know who knew about it first? I'm not even kidding. Our mom! Our mom saw that on the news and she started asking if it was about Ricky. I swear to the Virgin. Anyway, shit, here, let me get Consuelo, I'll tell her to leave her phone, hold on."

Marisol gets out of the Mazda and crosses Main Street back to the flower shop. The road is thick with traffic but between the gaps Dylan can see the lights go off behind the glass. She keeps her foot on the brake and the engine running. She stares through the rear-view mirror at every passing car. She can't help this feeling of vigilance.

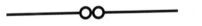

Marisol tells Dylan to drive down Main and take a right on Beach Street. She introduces her sister Consuelo, reminds Dylan to take a right before she forgets, and for the entire journey the sisters ask her question after question. Dylan tries to explain what happened, she talks about the thumb drive, how serious the data theft is, and how close she came to dying. She explains how she went to UC Berkeley and confronted Pamela in the woods. She tells them how she drove to Oakland looking for the director and ended up knocked out unconscious in the marshlands.

"And you're okay?" Consuelo asks. "He didn't do nothing to you?"

"He slapped me. I thought he was going to kill me, but then he let me go."

"Why?" Marisol asks. "That's what I don't get."

"It's because of the leaks," Consuelo says. "Right? He knows nothing can stop it?"

"He said killing me would only prove them right. That's what he said. Something like that."

"But killing our brother's okay?"

The sisters shake their heads and fall into a long silence. In the midst of this pause, Dylan looks at Consuelo through the rear view mirror. She's dressed in black pants and a black blouse. Her hair is in a single long braid that extends halfway down her back. She wears no makeup.

"Our parents live down that farm road," Marisol finally says, pointing out the window. "We can go there later maybe."

"Where are we going now?" Dylan asks.

"To the beach," Consuelo says. "Everyone likes the beach right?"

"Plus the waves make it so no one can hear us," Marisol says.

"You sure this car isn't bugged?" Consuelo asks.

"Yeah, I bought it just the other day. I don't think the paperwork has even gone through yet."

"Gotta get rid of it, then," Consuelo says. "I think we can do that, get you a clean car you can drive. This thing's gotta go, for sure. We'll figure it out. You're right though, this is some serious stuff."

"We shouldn't tell anyone else either," Marisol says.

"You probably shouldn't have told us anything," Consuelo says to Dylan. "We would have helped you anyway. Ricky always liked you. But whatever, now we know classified shit, okay. So when did they say they were gonna leak it? Monday?"

Dylan nods.

"Then *everyone's* gonna know some classified information," Marisol says.

"We just gotta make it through the next five days then," Consuelo says. "Hopefully they don't send Jason Bourne after us."

"That's what this is, though," her sister responds. "No joke. They fucking killed little Ricardo because he was trying to expose their secrets. And they almost got *güera* here. I still can't believe you did that, girl. I mean it was a bad move, bad idea and all that, but still, you walked right up to this guy's apartment in this blue dress—"

"And got knocked out," Dylan interrupts. "I know, it was dumb."

"Hella dumb," Marisol affirms. "But it all worked out for you."

"Obviously, you're rich and white. They don't kill people like you."

Dylan nods, she doesn't want to hear this although she knows it's true. She grabs the pack of Newports, puts a cigarette in her mouth, and tries to strike a match. Marisol holds the wheel as the car hurtles down the farm road, long enough for Dylan to light the cigarette.

"Thanks." She coughs out a cloud of smoke and drives faster. "These make me feel calm."

"That shit's bad for you," Consuelo says. "You shouldn't smoke."

"*She* used to smoke," Marisol says. "She just wants a cigarette."

"Yeah, back in college. Shit, man—" Consuelo rubs her eyes and moans. "*Pinche* little Ricardo. I know he said he was gonna make it to the top, but this—"

"This is our brother's dying wishes here," Marisol says loudly. "He died so this information could get out. We gotta do whatever *güera* thinks is a good idea." She turns to Dylan and gives her a skeptical glance. "Because this shit is out of our depth, it's true."

"I'm *still* out of my depth," Dylan says. "I *still* haven't read all the files."

"Still! You mean you *still* got them?" Marisol asks.

"They're in the laptop, in the bag at your feet."

"Damn, girl. I didn't—"

"You scared, sis?" Consuelo asks, leaning forward. "This is our brothers dying wishes here."

"Yeah, but do we *need* to have evidence on us?"

"I understand, if it's—"

"No, it's not a problem," Consuelo insists. "It's gonna be public on Monday."

"Look, no one's after me, no one *should* be after me," Dylan says. "The director said he erased my file but he told me to run anyway. If the FBI ever figures out who I am, I'll be in trouble, but for right now I'm fine. I think. I just need to be careful not to leave any traces, I need—"

"You *need* to get rid of this car," Consuelo says. "Yeah, just pull up in that park there."

Dylan drives the Mazda into a small parking lot surrounded by caverns of dark green cypress trees. She parks near a public bathroom, throws her cigarette butt in the trash, and walks with the sisters towards the sound of the ocean. There's no fog in the sky, the sun is still warming the air, and soft gusts of wind push at them as they emerge from a tree cavern and trudge through the sand. Dylan sees the white bursts of crashing waves and tastes their salty moisture on her tongue. Her ears fill with the constant roar of the Pacific. She and the sisters walk to the edge of the shoreline where the spent waves explode towards the dunes. Marisol runs from an expanding tongue of water that threatens to overwhelm her feet and becomes lost in the sound of her own laughter.

"She loves the Pacific," Conseulo says. "You like it?"

"I do," Dylan says. "Different than the Atlantic, more intense."

"More powerful, huh? I mean, I don't know, I've never seen the Atlantic."

"The waves are bigger here, there's more cliffs."

"What're you talking about?" Marisol asks, returning from the water. "Making fun of me?"

"We're just talking about the ocean," Dylan says.

"Alright, so—" Marisol takes a deep breath and looks towards the orange sun. "I don't know. I think we should take *güera* back home. We can drive her car into town, drop it off at—"

"I live with my parents still," Consuelo says. "It's what happens when you don't have kids."

"You have kids?" Dylan asks Marisol.

"I do, two boys and a girl. And a husband. We live on the other side of town."

"You look so young," Dylan says.

"Girl, I'm over forty. But yeah, Consuelo can set you up, we'll get rid of that Mazda for you. We can probably get you a new car, but you gotta sell it before the registration expires. It won't have insurance or nothing, so you have to drive safe, you can't get pulled over."

"Yeah, like, check the lights every time you stop," Consuelo says. "Make sure nothing's busted. Don't give them no reason to pull you over. Whatever, we'll get you a good car. If your Mazda's got a decent engine we can sell it then scrap everything else for parts and metal."

"Where do you think you'll go?" Marisol asks. "What's your plan?"

"I don't know, but I have to stay nearby until they let her go."

"Who?"

"Alexis. The person they framed."

"You knew her, too?" Consuelo asks. "I thought she was Ricky's friend."

"Yeah, what the fuck?" Marisol says. "You didn't say that."

"Ricky told her to find me if anything happened, he gave her the files, she gave them to me before she got arrested. But in between all that, we—"

"Aw shit, girl!" Consuelo says. "You're in love with her, huh? Alright, alright, well—" She looks at her sister and smiles. "Let's figure something out real quick. You got any proof in your files that she *didn't* kill Ricky? The guy admitted it to you, right, but can you prove it?"

"No. There's no record I was ever there, he erased everything. Like I said, I haven't gone over all the files. I know Ricky's name's in there for sure, the director's name's in there, the two of them corresponded together, so when this comes out on Monday—"

"They'll link Ricky to the director," Consuelo says. "Makes sense. That would explain a lot, you know? It makes it seem like Ricky leaked the secrets then got killed for it. No real need for questions after that. But what's in the files? That's what really matters. If it's bad enough, everyone will know that's why Ricky got killed. So what's in it?"

"Yeah, tell us," Marisol says.

For the next half an hour, Dylan attempts to summarize everything she learned from the first thirty-seven files. She explains how the federal government and the tech companies are constantly recording video and audio from every smartphone and computer they can access. She explains how they're using powerful algorithms to find patterns in people's behavior and actions. Dylan tells them how the population is classified and sorted, how their behavior is modulated, how their eye motions are studied, and how their heart rates are monitored.

The sisters make Dylan describe what an algorithm is, what behavioral psychology is, and what modulation means. They listen patiently to her answers, they slowly begin to understand, and they stop asking so many questions. Dylan explains how she confronted Pamela, tells them about the professor's love affair with Ricky, and how he stole the data from Pamela's computer while she was asleep. This makes Consuelo rapidly shake her left hand in the air as if it's on fire. She lets out a small hoot and wraps her arm around Marisol. Both of them cry, but they also can't help laughing in joy at the memory of their brother.

"I don't even know," Consuelo says. "Maybe he loved this Pamela. He probably did. Who knows? And that boy was always full of mischief. He'd hide our stuff all over the house when we were kids but we'd always find it somewhere. Like...he'd take my car keys and leave them in the fridge next to my lunch or in the coffee pot or some shit like that, someplace he knew I'd eventually look."

"Always doing something like that," Marisol affirms. "He was a little devil, but never mean and nasty like some boys get. You know what I'm saying? It was always funny, he was always laughing, we were always laughing. I don't know."

Dylan can't listen to them without crying. Every word hammers a crack into the sadness she's repressed and the tears pour out beyond control. The sisters rub her hair and massage her back while Dylan trembles in pain. Consuelo laughs to keep them all from sinking into sadness and pulls them down the shoreline where they stop to watch the sunset. It's burning a deep red now, buried halfway beneath the watery horizon. They watch its last crescent sink away in a long blur of orange and yellow that lights up the sky. They feel the air start to cool. They feel the winds begin to rise.

Marisol gets in the driver's seat and speeds back up the farm road towards Watsonville. She takes a left down a dusty side road and pulls into the driveway of a small blue house. Behind it are two more apartments and beyond that are long fields of green lettuce. Everything is draped in dusk light when they arrive. The sky is purple, the air moist and cool.

The sisters walk her inside the blue house where their parents are watching television. They're short and skinny with skin like polished wood. The mother wears a red floral dress and the father wears blue jeans with a collared shirt. Both of them wear sandals and their faces are illuminated by the glow of the flickering screen. The sisters speak to them in Spanish and motion at Dylan multiple times, after which the parents stand up and walk towards her. The mother kisses Dylan's cheeks, says something in a language that isn't Spanish, and kisses her forehead with warm lips. The father approaches next, thanks her in Spanish, kisses each of her cheeks, and then everyone sits down in front of the luminous television.

They begin speaking in Spanish, everyone but Dylan. She remains silent and looks at the screen. It's over twenty years old and doesn't have a camera on its body. There are no digital devices in the living room and even the clocks are mechanical with gears and time-hands and ticking noises. She counts five clocks in the room, all of them active and in motion. There's a painting on the wall of a large breasted woman with dark skin and brilliant eyes. She holds a rifle in the air and stands in the jungle with a baby girl strapped to her back. Mounted on the wall next to this painting is an old beige telephone with a spiraling rubber cord that drapes down to the floor. A small paper notepad is next to the phone with a yellow pencil tied to a string. The notepad is filled with markings and numbers.

"You can stay in my place," Consuelo says suddenly. "Everyone goes to work in the mornings but my mom says you should come for dinner tomorrow night."

"*Gracias*," Dylan says to the mother. "Thank you."

The old woman leans forward and holds Dylan's hands with her strong and bony fingers. Her hair is mostly silver although still streaked with darkness. Her eyes are so brown they're almost black and she stares at Dylan with total alertness, not once letting go of her hand. The mother looks into Dylan's eyes for over a minute. In that amount of time, Dylan comes to understand what's happening to her and what will happen in the future. She sees it spread out like an ocean where the sun never sets and the sky is always blue. At the horizon is an endless mirror and in its reflection she can see the hidden matrices of the world colliding together like water fountains. But this only lasts so long, the mother lets go of her hand, and Dylan struggles to remember what just happened. The memory doesn't return.

"Come on," Consuelo says. "You look tired."

"I'll take your car into town," Marisol says. "Don't even think about it anymore, okay. I'll take care of it. Maybe not tomorrow, but we'll get you a new car soon enough."

"I have plenty of money—"

"No, no, just don't worry about it right now. Here, say goodnight."

Dylan kisses the father, kisses the mother, and then walks with the sisters down the driveway towards the Mazda. They help carry her belongings to Consuelo's apartment, pile them atop a red fold-out couch, and Dylan returns with Marisol to the little blue car where they kiss each other on the cheek. Marisol still smells like a thousand flowers.

"Thank you for helping my brother."

"I loved Ricky," Dylan says, wiping her eye. "He was my best friend."

"I know he was, girl." Marisol is crying again. "Here, let me get the keys."

Dylan takes the ring out of her dress pocket and removes the two car keys. Neither of them can look at each other from the sadness. Marisol grabs the keys without another word, wipes the tears from her face, and then drives the Mazda away from the ocean. Dylan watches the red tail lights fade along the farm road and disappear into blackness. Soon her vision is drawn upwards to the sky. Night has solidified itself on the horizon and tiny pinpricks of pulsing light hang in a dome around her head. For the first time in many months, Dylan realizes she's seeing the stars.

CHAPTER 17

Two weeks before Ricky was murdered, Dylan happened to meet him in the elevator during lunch. Ricky said he'd just been upstairs with Chad and the Chief Technology Officer. Dylan gave him an excited hug in response and couldn't help but smile at the news. It wasn't everyday one of them met with the CTO, the man who originally designed the OingoBoingo game engine. She and Ricky talked about the new billboard designs, laughed about the absurd childhood memory characters, and then decided to get lunch at a taqueria in the Mission.

Ricky had already ordered a Lyft and they rode down Howard Street in the back of a green Prius. The driver was a young man with acne and red hair. He didn't speak, nor did he look at them, not even in the mirror. He seemed tired and unhappy and drained of life. His dark aura inhabited the entire car and created a silence that lasted until he dropped them off at El Farolito on 24th Street.

"Damn, that guy was really sad looking," Ricky said. "What's up with him?"

"I don't know, but he smelled like chemicals. It creeped me out."

"Looked like he'd been up for a few days. His mouth was open the whole time, too."

"It's depressing. Let's stop talking about it."

Dylan and Ricky walked under the yellow overhang and got in line behind the counter. There were several customers ahead and most of the tables were packed. Ricky ordered four carne asada tacos while Dylan got a wet super burrito with chicken. Both of them ordered Bohemia beers and took them to a corner table where they could watch everyone who entered the taqueria.

"So what's Jim Flanders like?" Dylan asked. "I've never met him."

"Who?"

"What? *Who*? The CTO! The guy you *just* met with! The guy who designed the games."

Ricky chuckled to himself and took a swig of beer.

"He's kind of a freak, and not in a good way. I mean we just sat there and listened to him go on and on about fusing consciousness and synergy and simulated telepathic communication. Dude was wearing sandals and cargo shorts and a polo shirt but his eyes, man—" Ricky took another sip from his beer. "Like he fried himself at Burning Man last summer. I know he designed the game engine and all but I just wanted to know about VR."

"Virtual Reality?" Dylan whispered. "Is that what they're doing?"

"No, they're not interested in VR. Not at all. He said people don't spend enough time seeing advertisements when they're using VR. But we've got our advertisements between each game level, so I was wondering if they wanted to build a VR platform for the Dream Game."

"They didn't want to?"

"Hell no! The fucking CTO got all insulted and went on about how VR was a niche market, a stupid helmet, a dumb trinket. He said we might as well make a sex toy or model trains. I mean, he's got a point there. Most people don't use the damn things, and the people who have VR headsets use them for porn or games or whatever else they're into. I don't see it growing, but I figured why not ask?"

"I've never tried those goggles. Don't think I want to."

Their number was called at the counter and Ricky went to gather their food. Before he could finish one of his tacos, Dylan had already eaten a quarter of her burrito and was so hungry she failed to notice Ricky watching her in amazement. Dylan didn't stop until she was full. At that point, she had a glob of red sauce on her cheeks and only a small fraction of the burrito was left.

"Damn, girl, use a napkin."

"*You* use a napkin!"

"I don't got shit all over my face like you do. I still haven't even finished my tacos and you're almost done. That thing was huge! How can you eat so fast?"

"I've always been this way, I don't know why. My body just burns it up. Everyone used to make fun of me about it, so thanks a lot, Ricky. You've really brought up some childhood trauma!"

"Get out of here, Connecticut."

Both of them laughed and Dylan realized something was different.

"You're a lot happier," she said to him. "You're less gloomy."

"Me? Was I gloomy before?"

"Sort of. I mean we're always laughing about something, but when you weren't laughing...yeah, you looked sad. Like there was less light in your eyes."

He looked at her for a long time after that, so long Dylan thought she could see a flame.

"Well...if I seem happier it's because I don't care about being sad anymore, being overwhelmed, being stressed. I've seen how companies like OingoBoingo work, how the decisions get made, how the economy reacts, how social media influences the economy, how social media *is* the economy. I just don't let any of it affect me anymore"

"I think I know what you mean."

"I don't know. You don't—" Ricky shook his head and drank more beer. "At least *you* refuse to interact with these management dudes and be their bro and laugh at their stupid shit. All day, a bunch of white guys yapping like poodles to each other. It used to bother me, obviously, but what could I care, otherwise why work here? You know? But it was stressing me out, that's probably what you noticed, that's where my sense of humor went. Only now I just don't care. That shit doesn't bother me anymore. And it's not like I don't see it, I still see it. I see *all* of it. It just doesn't bother me."

"So you've reached a Zen state?" Dylan asked. "Is that what you're saying?"

"Definitely not Zen. I'd say it's closer to nihilism."

"But nihilism means you don't care about anything, Zen means—"

"That you don't care about anything. Right. It's just a matter of how you approach it."

"Then stay on the Zen end of the spectrum," Dylan said. "Don't turn into a nihilist."

"Don't worry," he told her. "I try and stay in the middle."

They finished their food, sipped down the last of their beers, and kept talking as they waited for their Lyft to arrive. Dylan remembers they spoke about the ocean. Ricky said he grew up next to the beach and used to ride the waves with his body. Ricky told her in a hundred years his childhood house would be surrounded by saltwater. All the farmland would flood, the town of Watsonville would become beachfront property, and his great grandchildren would probably be sailors. Ricky spun the empty beer bottle as he said this to Dylan.

She remembers how the gold foil on the brown bottle bore the image of an indigenous person wearing a headdress made of feathers. She remembers this was the last time she went out to lunch with Ricky. She remembers feeling happy.

Dylan spends the night on the foldout couch in a pair of borrowed sweat pants and a white t-shirt. Consuelo takes a shower in the early morning, gets dressed with the bedroom door open, makes herself coffee in the machine, and leaves the apartment to catch a ride into town with her mother. Dylan sleeps through all this commotion and late into the morning. Nothing rouses her, not even the sound of children playing next door. When she finally wakes up, all her dreams are forgotten, her eyes don't want to open, and her entire body feels like limp rubber. She gets off the foldout and walks over to the kitchen counter. A coffee pot is half filled in the machine next to a tray of pastries. Beside the coffee is a note written by Consuelo.

Dylan reads the words: *Make yourself at home when you wake up. Eat whatever you want, it's all up for grabs. If you need anything, my sister Favi is next door with her kids. Don't worry about cameras or smartphones, we don't have any here. The computer in my bedroom doesn't have a microphone or a camera so go ahead and use the internet, just be smart. There's also a TV on my dresser if you want to watch that. I'll be home around 7:30 tonight. Everything's going to be fine. Don't worry.* Consuelo signed her name at the bottom next to a big heart.

Dylan heats up the coffee in the microwave and eats two pink pastries covered with white strands of coconut. She makes her bed, folds it back into the couch, and replaces the soft red cushions. She takes her coffee to Consuelo's room and sits at a computer desk in the corner between the bed and the wall. The computer is over ten years old, its black tower hums steadily, and the monitor clicks to life when Dylan moves the mouse. On the desk beside the keyboard are a stack of documents, the topmost of which is a water bill made out to *Florez y Florez Floristas LLC.* Next to these documents is a framed picture of Ricky and his seven sisters standing on the beach.

Dylan sits down on a cushioned swivel chair and opens up the

Firefox browser. She types the letter C into the address bar and is relieved to find multiple entries for old CNN news stories that Consuelo has already looked at. Dylan goes to the CNN home page where the title story reads: *World Awaits Mysterious Wikileaks Release*. For the next half hour, Dylan reads every story CNN has to offer on the subject. She learns that several politicians have publicly blamed Russia for masterminding the leak and the Department of Homeland Security has no leads in the ongoing data-theft investigation. One of these stories includes a hyperlink to an article about Alexis Segura and the murder of Ricardo Florez. Dylan clicks on it and reads the article through to the end. The author doubts the guilt of Alexis Segura and is critical of the way sex-work has been used to demonize her in public court. Dylan is not surprised when she learns this article was written by a woman.

She types the words *alexis segura* into the Google search engine and the first results are no longer about online prostitution or contract killings. Instead, they concern Alexis' outburst in court and her allegations against OingoBoingo. For the next twenty minutes, Dylan opens all of these links. One tech blog explores the possibility that OingoBoingo hired psychologists to design the mind game questions. The article provides numerous screen shots from the Childhood Memory Game and postulates on what elements of behavioral psychology could be involved. One blog has a graphic that depicts the OingoBoingo dream characters holding knives stained with blood.

Several other articles feature a recent photo of Bilton Smyth talking on the phone while standing on the balcony of an expensive hotel in Geneva, Switzerland. His white shirt is unbuttoned, he hasn't shaved in several days, and his eyes are red from exhaustion. After this picture was taken, the former CEO disappeared and has not been located since. The picture is from two days ago.

Dylan switches on the television with the remote control and finds the channel for CNN. She turns up the volume and goes to the living room for her laptop. She opens it on the desk and soon her consciousness is effectively split into three screens. She goes from the desktop to the television and then back to the laptop. She reads through the GSX files and listens to the television as an FBI agent tells the press that BoonDoggle still refuses to hand over information on Ricardo Florez and is flagrantly endangering national security. The company hasn't responded to any of the FBI's repeated requests and their continued refusal has generated dozens of articles speculating on the tech-giant's wall of silence.

For the next three hours, Dylan is enmeshed in these three mediums. When the television informs her of something she didn't know, Dylan researches it on the desktop while making it appear to be an organic flight of curiosity. In between this, she hovers over the laptop and reads through endless case studies of Facebook users, their psychological profiles, their instant message histories, and their malleability factors. Over the speakers, she learns the FBI has issued an arrest warrant for Bilton Smyth and Jim Flanders, the former CTO of OingoBoingo. Before she can comprehend this last fact, Dylan hears the name of her former boss spoken on the television. She hears the name Chad Williams.

The newscaster explains that his body was found yesterday in the marshlands of San Leandro Bay, just across from the Oakland Coliseum. A pair of kayakers discovered it while exploring the wildlife refuge in search of water birds to photograph. Rope was still tied around the leg when they found the body floating face down in the reeds. The police believed it had been sunk into the bay several days earlier. Dylan searches on the desktop for articles about the body and discovers numerous journalists who no longer believe Alexis Segura is responsible for the murder of Ricardo Florez.

One journalist asserts that if Chad Williams was found in the same general location as Florez, it would point towards the same killer, not Alexis Segura. Another journalist went so far as to cite tidal charts in order to prove the body of Ricardo Florez could have conceivably floated from San Leandro Bay all the way to Jack London Square. Even a writer for *The New York Times* ponders this new fact and condemns the journalists who used Alexis' profession as a way to generate clicks and sensationalize a tragic story. Dylan scrolls back to the top of this article and discovers the author is a woman. In the midst of all this reading, the front door suddenly opens.

"You here?" someone asks.

"I'm here."

Dylan closes the laptop, turns off the television, and hops into the living room. She glimpses a few children playing outside but the person quickly closes the front door. Dylan sees a woman younger than Consuelo, although not by many years. She wears a black blouse and blue jeans, she has a digital calculator watch on her wrist, and her hair is tied back with a pink band. She wears no makeup. Her body is youthful but her eyes look ancient.

"I just wanted to see if you were hungry, I got you food when I took the kids to town." She places a white bag by the coffee pot and then kisses Dylan's cheeks. "My name's Favi. I know you're name, don't know if I should say it though."

"Probably not."

"Good practice, right?" She laughs and then goes back to the door. "I'll leave you alone."

"You don't have to go—"

"I know, but I have to." Favi laughs and crinkles her eyes. "I'll see you later tonight, maybe when these kids go to sleep."

Without another word, Favi closes the door and leaves the apartment. There's something warm in the paper bag wrapped in white paper and foil. When she opens it, Dylan discovers a torta filled with chicken, peppers, lettuce, and tomatoes. The insides of the bread are covered with white cream and refried beans and when Dylan bites into the sandwich she closes her eyelids in pleasure. She tastes the spicy flesh of the pickled jalapenos and feels her eyes begin to water. When her vision returns, Dylan is staring at a picture of the Virgin Mary mounted above the kitchen sink. The Virgin looks down at her with hands pressed together in devotion. Dylan can hardly move. It reminds her she isn't dreaming.

Consuelo walks inside the apartment while Dylan is reading file number 56. She closes the laptop screen and goes to the living room as the front door slams shut. Consuelo tosses her bag on the fold-out couch and gives Dylan a warm hug around the shoulders. She smells like flowers and burnt marijuana, her eyes are red and smoky, and her skin carries the scent of sunlight.

"Doing some research in there?" Consuelo asks, nodding towards the bedroom.

"I haven't checked the news in a few days. No safe internet."

"Don't worry, I left my phone in the car. You learn anything new?"

"So much! I don't even know where to begin."

"You heard about Ricky's boss, right?"

"That's what I mean, there's so much information, so many people involved," Dylan says. "I read a lot of articles today that make it seem like Ricky and Chad were killed by the same person."

"I saw those. Anyway, come on. Let's go to dinner."

Dylan slips into her sandals and follows Consuelo onto the driveway. The air is thick with water vapor rising up from the farmland and the sky above is a deep purple fading into black. Dylan can already see stars hanging above the eastern mountains.

"Is Favi eating with us?" she asks.

"Probably not. She cooks for her kids inside."

"Is she married?"

"Not anymore. He was a bad guy. My parents warned her about him. But, you know—"

They go up the back stairs and enter the house through the noisy laundry room. They step through the warmth of a spinning clothes dryer and enter a kitchen thick with the smell of cooking. The mother stands over two pots. She wears a black dress with red flowers, looks up from the steam, and holds her hands out to Dylan. As they embrace, she feels a tremendous heat burning inside the mother's body.

She follows Consuelo to the dining room where the father is sitting at the table underneath a dim green lamp. Beside him is a pitcher of water and four brown glasses. He's looking out the window when they enter, his eyes fixed on the darkening fields of lettuce. He stands to greet Dylan and kisses her on the cheek, his skin rich with the sweet smell of sunlight. He mutters something in Spanish and motions for her to sit down at the table. Consuelo and her mother bring the pots out from the kitchen and set them down on brightly painted ceramic serving tiles. The mother returns to the kitchen while her husband serves Dylan a plate of black beans and two big pieces of meat covered in a dark sauce that smells like chocolate. Consuelo sits beside Dylan and waits to be served by her father.

The mother comes back with a bowl of fresh salsa, a bowl of white cheese, and a red towel filled with steaming tortillas. She puts everything on the table and then sits across from Dylan. The father serves his wife and daughter a plate, they sprinkle crumbled cheese onto their beans, and heap spoonfuls of salsa on all of it. The family talks in a language that isn't Spanish and the father begins to eat with a strip of tortilla. He presses it around the chicken and soaks up the thick black sauce. Dylan can see the tortillas are homemade, thick and yellow with the texture of fine cornmeal. She uses one to scoop up a piece of steaming chicken and moans in pleasure at the taste of it.

"You don't know how lucky you are she made this," Consuelo says.

"What is it?" Dylan says, putting her hand over her mouth. "It's delicious."

"If I told you I'd have to kill you."

Everyone smiles at Dylan and meets her eyes with respect. They don't ignore her even though they keep speaking their own language. There's no pause for translation, nor does Dylan ask for one. She keeps eating her food with pieces of tortilla as their ancient tongue fades into the back of her consciousness and she loses herself in the tastes of the salsa, the beans, the dark sauce, and the fresh ground corn. The mother and father smile at her, their faces filled with pleasure and contentment. Dylan has no idea what they're saying to each other, but it seems to bring them joy.

When everyone's finished, when all the plates have been wiped clean by the last tortillas, Consuelo's mother takes the ceramic dishes back into the kitchen. She ignores their protests, mutters something in Spanish, and waves their words away with her free hand. Consuelo hides a burp, takes a sip of water, and speaks to her father for a few moments. He nods in affirmation and then smiles at Dylan. There's a moment of silence between them, they hear the clatter of dishes from the kitchen, and soon the mother begins to sing. It's a powerful song filled with emotions. Her voice rises from note to note and oscillates between the melancholy and sublime. Dylan closes her eyes as her veins fill with fire and the room disappears. She doesn't remember what she sees in this void of her senses. The song never seems to end.

Dylan and Consuelo stand at the edge of a lettuce field and stare off into the darkness. Consuelo lights a long joint, puffs the smoke towards the stars, and then passes it over to Dylan. They stand in silence and smoke slowly, listening to the sound of the distant ocean. The weed eventually makes Dylan think of Alexis. She sees her face hiding within the stars and smells her musky scent scattered in the wind. She imagines sleeping beside her in a field of green grass with the sunlight warming their bare skin.

"This is good shit, huh?" Consuelo asks.

In the darkness, Dylan can see the glow of her teeth.

"Really good."

"Should we go get her?"

"Who?"

"Your friend. The girl you were just talking about."

"I wasn't talking about—"

"Yeah, okay, but what if they release her? They're going to release her, right?"

"I mean, it seems that way—"

"Want some more?"

"No, I'm—"

"Girl, you hella high!" Consuelo laughs. "You need it though, you need to relax a little bit, and then you need to sleep. No, but seriously, what should we do when they release your girl? Because you can't just go get her, she'll be walking out of jail surrounded by a million cameras."

"I know. I need to stay hidden."

"We could do it, though, me and my sisters."

Consuelo takes a long drag and holds the smoke deep in her lungs before blowing it out. The gray tendrils disperse out into the darkness and Dylan eagerly takes the joint back once its offered. She wants to return to the moment she saw Alexis in the stars and smelled her musk.

"You really love her, don't you?"

"I do. I used to think, here—" She hands the joint back. "I used to think it was impossible to feel love, I thought love was all just a big ploy to make us go along with everything. Whatever I thought love was when I was young just wasn't real. I never found it, it never appeared, but I didn't chase it for very long, I gave up. And then I met Alexis."

"It's real, girl. I can feel it coming out of you. You *love* her!"

"I never met anyone like her before. Her spirit's...unbroken."

"They don't like people like that. That's why they're in cages. No, I'll talk to my sisters, we'll go get her. Maybe she'll recognize my face. Here, I *promise* you I'll go get her myself, no matter if the others come with me or not. There'll be hella people but I'll get to her, I'll get her out of there. But doesn't she have friends, though? Isn't someone gonna be there for her?"

"She had some friends but they left, that's what she said. They're gone."

"You know where she lives? She got an apartment?"

"I don't—" Dylan sputters. "I don't know."

"She never told you?"

"I never asked. I mean, she might have just lived wherever she worked."

"She have a car?"

Dylan shakes her head.

"I don't know. I guess she never told me."

"Damn, this girl's a ghost. We definitely need to get her out of there, she's definitely not safe. Maybe she's got a car stashed away somewhere, but damn...she was really working it. She's not like any of us. You know what I'm saying? Here, you want this last bit?"

Dylan takes the joint and smokes it down to the cardboard filter. She can still sniff out the musk of her lover blowing across the lettuce fields. It mixes in with the coastal air and becomes indiscernible from the salt of the ocean. The scent floats unseen in this field of starlight and travels along invisible currents that seem to uphold the sky. Everything grows still. There's only the sound of distant waves tearing against the shore.

"You smoked already?" someone suddenly asks.

"Course we did, sis."

"Good thing I brought this."

Favi appears beside Dylan. She flicks a lighter and brings the flame to the joint between her lips. Dylan watches the ember flare in the darkness, takes the joint when it's passed to her, and then draws the smoke deep into her lungs.

"The kids asleep?" Consuelo asks.

"Yeah, finally! I gotta creep outta there like a cat. What you all been talking about?"

"What were we talking about?" Consuelo asks.

"How none of you are like Alexis," Dylan says.

"Alexis Segura?" Favi asks. "Hell no, none of us are like her. Maybe I'm the closest, right, sis? I ran off with some gangster and lived that life until I got pregnant. Then I had to stay home. But none of us ever went off on our own and lived like she did. I wouldn't want to."

"Maybe that's why Ricky went for her," Consuelo says. "She wasn't like us."

"Maybe. And she's *ladino, blanquita.*"

"What's that mean?" Dylan asks.

"Light skin like a Spanish person," Favi says. "Latino, *ladino,* it's the same word. And *blanquita,* that just means, like, Latin white girl, like this Alexis, not *indigina* like his sisters."

"What's the other language you speak? I'm sorry, I don't—"

"Tzotzil," Consuelo says. "It's called Tzotzil."

"My dad speaks Tehuano, too," Favi says. "That's what they speak in his part of Oaxaca."

"I don't really know anything about Mexico."

So the sisters tell Dylan about the endless jungles of Chiapas and the mountain villages of Oaxaca shrouded in perpetual mist. They explain how their parents left southern Mexico on a boat headed to San Francisco, how they fled the soldiers and eventually reached the farmlands of Watsonville where they worked in fields of strawberries and lettuce. They camped in the woods at night, worked during the day, and saved their money month after month. In 1971, their mother gave birth to Diana, the eldest of the sisters. Every two years another sister was born until Ricky arrived. Dylan listens to these stories, smokes the joint when it's passed, and feels her eyelids grow heavy. She imagines herself in a sweaty jungle filled with parrots and lizards that cling to the dripping branches. Light breaks through the canopy of leaves and warms her face amid the sound of a million insects.

Dylan sleeps until 11:00 in the morning. She stares at the living room ceiling, pulls the covers off her sweaty body, and goes to the kitchen in her underwear and t-shirt. There's a new paper note sitting on the counter that reads: *Hey, Dylan. Hope you have a good day. Don't forget you can always walk to the ocean. It's only a few miles away.* Consuelo drew a big heart and signed her name at the bottom of the paper. Dylan holds it to her chest as she heats up the last remnants of the morning coffee.

She puts on a pair of jeans and goes into Consuelo's bedroom with her mug. She sits on the bed and powers up the television, her laptop, and the desktop. She uses the remote control to find CNN on the television, opens up the GSX files on her laptop, and starts the Firefox web browser on the black desktop. There's nothing on CNN so she keeps reading through the files, starting where she left off.

She learns how GSX created multiple Facebook accounts to manipulate the behavior of those they targeted. After a profile was built on a subject, GSX would use these fake accounts to send them friend requests. Once these requests were accepted, the subject would see pictures, images, and posts carefully modulated to induce a desired behavioral pattern. If a subject wanted a family or had a predilection for young men, they would quickly find the object of their desire in the pictures and status updates of their new Facebook friends. There are many files that explain the technical details of modulating Facebook feeds in real time, altering the algorithms, and hacking into the company servers. As Dylan reads further, she discovers that GSX built thousands of fake Facebook profiles for different federal agencies to help them insert operatives into the lives of targeted individuals. And then the front door opens, someone says hello, and Dylan shuts the laptop.

"Hi!" she says, walking outside. "Here I come."

Marisol is there holding a white paper bag. Her keys are in her hand and an idling car is parked outside. Bass-heavy music vibrates behind the tinted windows emblazoned with the word OAXACA. The air blowing in through the door is warm and tinged with the scent of flowers.

"Good morning, sleepy." She kisses Dylan and puts the bag on the kitchen counter. "I got you some lunch. But listen, I gotta go, I just wanted to see if you're okay. Favi's next door if you need anything. Alright? Everything's gonna be okay."

"Thank you." She hugs Marisol tightly. "For everything."

"Bye, *güera*."

Marisol runs back to her idling car and speeds off down the farm road, a trail of dust following behind her. Inside the white paper bag are four tamales wrapped in corn husks. They're still hot and filled with shreds of chicken covered in red sauce. Dylan eats all of them without sitting down. She chews up the meat and cornmeal and burps loudly when she's finished. She drinks a glass of water, throws away the husks, and goes back to reading the files.

GSX had algorithms running on millions of Facebook users without distinction. Using the color spectrum, the populace was divided into those opposed to the current order and those who upheld it. Those who wished to destroy the government or capitalism were placed on the side of pure red. Those who helped maintain government and capitalism were on the side of pure violet. There were over 300 gradients, each containing dozens of behavioral subsets. Algorithms were constantly running to push people away from the red and towards the violet. Dylan learns how Facebook helped them achieve this end by categorizing and modulating the behavior of anyone who used its platform. GSX found Facebook to be an effective tool in combating domestic extremism because it automatically grouped together those with shared interests and helped map the extent of subversive discourse in mainstream society. Once it was mapped, this discourse was easy to modulate, manipulate, and contain.

When Dylan opens file number 63, she discovers something else, something far more disturbing than Facebook. She discovers the first of many programs dedicated to the modulation of online porn consumption among targeted individuals and the population at large. Her stomach convulses as she reads through these files. She sees horrible images of men and women in painful sexual positions. She sees them being degraded in a variety of violent acts. There are captions beside each of their bodies that state the age of the actors, the genre of pornography, and the primary consumers of these images. Some of the people are younger than eighteen. Some of them are children.

If an older porn user gravitates towards teenage men or women, an algorithm automatically classifies them as having latent pedophilic desires. This classification then triggers a series of programs that attempt to lure the user back towards an acceptable age range. In one file, Dylan learns how these algorithms manipulated porn search results to reflect other fetishes, fixations, or complexes that could potentially divert the user away from pedophilia. With enough data on an individual, these fetishes were often quite easy to locate and this method was a largely successful deterrent to child pornography. If a user persisted in their attempts to find child pornography on the internet, they were given a new classification that focused on containment rather than prevention.

Because these GSX programs were illegal, this information on child pornography couldn't be shared with local or federal law enforcement, nor could any arrests be made. This rule was strictly adhered to except in cases of national security. Instead, the GSX programs would invade a user's computer and prevent them from manifesting their fetish for children in real life by keeping them locked to the screen. According to the data cited at the end of the file, Dylan learns that only a very small minority of the US population ever went into the dark web to purchase children for sex. It was easy enough to monitor this activity, but impossible to act on it. Under no circumstances could GSX reveal this data to law enforcement. No one could know these programs existed.

Dylan keeps reading. She can't help it, no matter how sick she feels inside. The frenzy to know consumes her. In study after study, Dylan discovers how the GSX algorithms used other forms of sexual desire to keep people locked in stasis. If the right combination of factors were introduced into a monogamous relationship through their devices and media, a couple wouldn't seek sexual satisfaction elsewhere but would replicate observed sexual behavior and find stasis in a stable family unit. This family unit would then create more workers to replicate the capitalist system and ensure the health of the economy. It's exactly as Pamela Gustafson described it. The entire program existed to keep capitalism from breaking down and disintegrating.

For those who directly managed the economic system, a state of polyamorous fluctuation was found to be more desirable than monogamous couples. Couples tended to seal themselves off, no matter what their economic situation, and this paralyzed their social relations inside and outside the workplace. In a specific case study, Dylan reads over the sexual behaviors of fifteen polyamorous Dropbox employees between the ages of 25 and 30. Each of them were far more productive and outgoing than couples of the same age group. They maintained larger networks, made more connections, and rose faster in the company hierarchy. Nothing could tie them down.

In file number 97, she finds a case study of the OingoBoingo advertising department. All of the employees were engaged in polyamorous relationships, everyone besides Dylan. In the case study on her department, Dylan is described as being mildly autistic, at once introverted and social, stern and flamboyant, utterly indifferent to stimulus and impossible to qualify using their metrics. She only listened to Taylor Swift albums, usually in the order of their release. She spent money on clothes, food, and the occasional trip or vacation made alone. Although she maintained many different online accounts, Dylan Kinsey primarily used her Facebook, her Twitter, her Instagram, and her Gmail. She never looked at pornography, her movie choices on Netflix seemed to be made at random, she had no coherent political beliefs, and her emails, instant messages, texts, and phone conversations revealed nothing about her personality. For this reason, she was largely ignored in the case study.

As she reads further, Dylan learns that most of the men in her department paid to sleep with sex workers, maintained multiple relationships with women at other companies, and responded well to the standard modulations. Through their devices and media, GSX encouraged these men to pay for sex, to maintain multiple relationships with women at other tech companies, and to spend their money as often as possible. This basic programming increased the quality of their work, allowed them to feel content with their place in the world, and kept them in motion throughout the city. Similar programs were run on Elizabeth and Bernadette, but after they were raped their social lives began to contract and they lost interest in having sexual relationships with either men or women. Dylan finds no mention of Ricky or Chad in the case study on her department. It's as if they never existed.

There are several more of these studies on every major tech company in the Bay Area. No matter how banal the details might seem, Dylan scans through every line of every page and looks for patterns in the algorithms and modulations. She wants to find proof these programs don't work. She wants to locate other anomalies who defy the classifications and metrics meant to contain them. But the more she reads, the more she understands these programs have been largely effective among her peers. The modulations have kept them fixated on work, sex, food, fitness, and money. Of all the case studies she reads, Dylan finds less than a dozen other anomalies, these people who reveal almost nothing about themselves through any of their mediums. She learns that GSX considers a subject an anomaly when their actions cannot be predicted more than 10% of the time. The only option with an anomaly was containment and observation. Modulation simply didn't work.

When Dylan opens up file number 107, she immediately notices a shift in focus. The case studies are no longer concerned with employees of large tech companies. They now focus on the general population and the lower levels of the economic order. This is where Dylan learns about jealousy. She learns how it's the most potent tool for keeping working class populations paired in monogamous couples. It's extremely easy for GSX to modulate jealousy through various mediums and create emotional ruptures and internal crisis within targeted couples. A powerful algorithm was designed to locate the source of a subject's jealousy and use their devices to display content that might trigger it: pictures of an ex-lover, emotional keywords, ambiguous memes, or even flirtatious comments from fictitious Facebook accounts.

A different algorithm was then used to resolve these artificial crises and bolster the strength of the monogamous relationship. In the words of one analyst: *The time and place of a traumatic episode and its resolution can be modulated to unlock different malleability factors. If a traumatic experience takes place at a certain location, the subject will generally associate that location with the trauma until that location is itself physically revisited. This is also the case with traumatic resolution. In these moments of crisis, a subject is malleable to a variety of external, physical stimuli which themselves can be subject to modulation.* Trauma and resolution invariably glued people and places together. The greater the emotional crisis, the greater the bond between the couple. Social media was extremely effective at not only creating and healing these emotional ruptures but also encouraging single individuals to find a domestic partner. The whole ensemble worked together to create strong family units within the working class.

Dylan reads through multiple case studies of targeted couples and feels rage burning through her blood. She wants to murder the director and everyone else who built these programs. Dylan loves all the people she reads about, she empathizes with their pointless suffering, and she knows the director is an old man who lives alone. All she can see is his leathery face and tan skin, his smug mouth and his metal glasses. She imagines him staring at his Darlingtonia plants and wants nothing more than for him to be destroyed, pulverized, rendered into nothing. In the middle of this enraged fantasy, Dylan hears the television for the first time in hours, she hears the name Alexis Segura, and just at that moment the front door opens.

"You here?" Favi asks.

"Yeah, I'm back here."

Favi runs into the bedroom and looks at the television.

"This, this, she's on TV!" she says. "It's her!"

The newscaster is speaking to the camera with the mug shot of Alexis displayed beside her. She explains how earlier in the day, the San Francisco District Attorney and the FBI held a joint press conference where they announced that the charges against Alexis Segura would be dropped. The screen then cuts to footage of the press conference where an FBI spokesperson stands at a podium and says the arrest of Alexis Segura was based on false information provided by a compromised source.

The spokesperson admits the agency made a mistake but insists BoonDoggle still needs to release its internal information on Ricardo Florez. The District Attorney then takes the podium and informs the press that Alexis Segura will be released from the county jail tomorrow morning. He reiterates that charging Alexis Segura was a mistake and asks the press to leave her in peace and outside of the spotlight. He says enough damage has been done because of the reckless behavior of a few rogue government employees. The moment he says this, the FBI spokesperson suddenly whispers into his ear and holds him by the shoulder. The two of them walk away from the podium amid a chorus of questions. The district attorney looks furious.

"What's happening?" Favi asks. "Why'd they just do that?"

"I don't know, I don't know!" Dylan walks closer to the television. "The District Attorney looked pissed off, right? That wasn't just me?"

"No, he looked pissed off. But what the fuck, what rogue government employees?"

"Maybe the—"

Favi closes an imaginary zipper over her lips and keeps her eyes locked on the screen. The CNN newscaster recaps the press conference while the screen shows images of Alexis silently yelling in the middle of the courtroom. Favi nods her heads towards the front door and they leave the apartment together without a word. Her son and two daughters are outside in the driveway kicking a ball back and forth. They stop playing and look at Dylan with curiosity as the ball drifts down the driveway. Dylan tries her best to smile but the children seem perplexed at her sudden presence. Favi tells them something in Tzotzil which makes them scream in joy, run inside their apartment, and leave the door open behind them.

"Want to walk to the beach with us?" Favi asks.

"Sure, yeah," Dylan looks up at the sky. "What time is it?"

"Almost 6:00. I just told them to get their jackets. It's gonna be cold when we get back. Anyway, I got you some food, but go put on something warm real quick, huh?"

Favi runs into her apartment while Dylan grabs her sweatshirt from behind Consuelo's couch. It's still warm outside but Dylan can already imagine the nightly winds covering her arms with goosebumps. She sees the waves breaking under the night sky, tastes the salt on her tongue, and only then does she realize her eyes are closed.

"You alright?" Favi holds out a burrito wrapped in foil. "Güera's like burritos, right?"

"I love them. They're perfect."

Favi shakes her head and chuckles to herself.

"What?" Dylan asks.

"It's just funny. White girls love burritos. They don't make these in Mexico, you know. In Tijuana they do, near the border, but you go any further south you don't see any burritos. But they're good, sometimes I get one when I want to be full all day."

Dylan has unwrapped the foil by the time Favi finishes speaking and takes a huge bite from the top. The chicken is marinated and slightly charred and Dylan can't stop herself from devouring it. Favi shakes her head and chuckles as her kids bolt outside with sweatshirts in hand. The five of them walk down the driveway and cross the dusty street into the long fields of strawberry and lettuce. Dylan eats the whole time. She listens to the children speak in Tzotzil and watches them run down the pathway between the crops. It helps her forget the files she's just read.

"I'm gonna ask my mom to watch the kids tomorrow and then I'm going with Consuelo to get your girl. Me and Consuelo already talked about it this morning. Best not to tell anyone else, right? And Marisol's busy getting you a car so she's got enough going on, plus she needs to open the...damn, girl! You ate that shit quick."

"Uh-huh," Dylan manages to say. "Thank you so much."

"Seems like you needed it. What've you been into all day?"

"I don't—" Dylan shakes her heads. "I don't know where to start. It's fucked. It's all just a way to control millions of people, brainwash them into these patterns, these—"

"It's best not to even say. I already know."

"How do you already know?" Dylan asks.

"I just never trusted any of that shit."

"But you don't know what they're—"

"Listen, girl, if you talk about it too much you just give it power. Don't worry about it right now, we need to think about your girlfriend. So what the fuck happened at the press conference, anyway? You think that DA was talking about this director guy?"

"I hope so," Dylan says. "I hope the director dies."

"He will. Don't worry."

"How do you know?"

"Because Ricky already killed him," Favi says, definitively.

Dylan swallows the last bit of burrito and then crumples the foil. She waits for a response but Favi doesn't say anything else. The children spread dust in the evening air as they chase swallows toward the ocean. There are dozens of these little birds flying low above the ground. They swoop over the crops and catch insects out of the air in their tiny pyramidal beaks. A few of them spin circles around the children out of curiosity. They don't seem threatened, not at all.

"What do you mean he killed him?" Dylan finally asks. "How did Ricky kill him?"

"Some things you just have to trust, *güera*. There's things bigger than us."

Favi keeps walking, yells something in Tzotzil, and hurries forward to her children. Dylan doesn't know what to say, nor what to think. The five of them keep on towards the ocean and navigate through a winding maze of crops. Had she tried to do this by herself earlier in the day, Dylan would certainly have become lost. Now she follows Faviola Florez and her three children to the Pacific. They've known this place their entire lives and will never forget the way to the shore.

Dylan watches them run from the crash and spread of the waves, hears them laugh at the fleets of sandpipers darting across the sand, and breathes in the salty mist that drifts like smoke ejected from the ocean. Within half an hour, the sun begins to set. The sky turns the deep color of blood. Dylan is certain the director is dead. There's no doubt in her mind this is true.

CHAPTER 18

THE LAST TIME DYLAN SAW RICKY WAS IN FRONT OF OINGOBOINGO headquarters. Dylan would have walked past if he hadn't stopped her at the giant glass doors. They hugged each other under the red neon, stepped aside for the stream of workers, and Ricky smiled as if he'd just gotten a promotion.

"You excited about the billboard?" he asked.

"Of course I'm excited! Were you just looking at it with Chad?"

"Unfortunately. Dumb motherfucker. He's obsessed with that one character, the lizard made of metal, the one you put on the left. He keeps telling me it's important, the fucking dipshit."

"I hope he falls down an elevator shaft."

Dylan said this last sentence with complete detachment.

"He'll probably do that on his own," Ricky said. "The guy doesn't have a clue about anything, he's just a frat boy. But listen, I wanted to ask you something serious. When you used *The Last Supper*, you really never had any hidden meaning?"

"What? No! What? Do I think some cartoons are Jesus and the apostles? No!"

"You ever wonder what da Vinci would have thought of Silicon Valley?"

"He probably would have loved it. At first."

"Right, *at first*."

"Then he'd get bored *very* quickly."

"Like all of us do," Ricky said. "Eventually."

"He'd be disappointed, I think. He'd wonder what it was all for."

"Fucking ice caps melting, Elon Musk telling everyone reality is a simulation, that all of us need to go to Mars and download our minds into machines and support capitalism."

"At least we're doing some good here, we're improving people's memories."

Ricky sighed when she said this last part. He looked down at the ground, nodded his head, and then started walking away. Dylan followed even though she was late for work. They drifted along the plate glass walls in silence and paused beside a metal trash can.

"What's it all for?" he suddenly asked her.

"What's *what* all for?"

"You realize some heavy shit's coming, right? We're doing this here, we're saving our dollars, we're trying to get ahead, but meanwhile everything's falling apart. No one can deny it, not anymore. I mean... there are some *serious* problems, systemic problems, and they've reached a...I don't know, I mean everyone's always talking about the end of the world, right?"

"I don't know, you kind of lost me, I think."

"*You* got money. Most people don't."

"I know that," Dylan said meekly. "I know."

"*You* can buy a future. Most everyone else, they can't do sh—"

"I know, Ricky. It's bad, I know it's bad, I'm sorry, it's—"

"Don't worry, *güera*."

Dylan still didn't understand what this word meant, nor did she have time to ask before Ricky wrapped his arms around her so their foreheads brushed together. She listened to him breathe, felt his warmth, and smelled his skin. For a moment, Dylan saw a fire so bright it made her want to cry. But then Ricky let go and put his hands on her shoulders. He looked into her eyes and smiled at something she couldn't see. Dylan didn't know what to think, nor did she know what to feel, nor did she realize Ricky had slipped a book of matches into her bag.

"I'm spending the rest of the day out of the office," he told her. "You want to get dinner on Friday after work? Maybe go to a bar in the Mission?"

"Sure, yeah, if you have time."

"I'll have time. I'll make time."

"Don't work too hard, Ricky."

He let go of Dylan and began walking away.

"You know *me*," he told her. "I just can't stop."

Dylan remembers these were the last words Ricky ever spoke to her. She can hear them in the crash of waves and in the evening wind. She remembers his brown eyes illuminated in these final moments. She realizes she's never forgotten them. Everything was already there. She simply hadn't seen it. Not until now.

Dylan doesn't sleep. She stays up past midnight discussing the plan until Favi gets tired and goes back to her apartment. Consuelo falls asleep soon after, while she and Dylan are watching CNN on her bed. The plan they've made is very simple. Consuelo and Favi will wake up at 4:00 am and drive north to San Francisco. They'll beat the morning traffic and park near the jail, close enough to get away but far enough not to be suspicious. They'll wait outside the jail doors like everyone else and when Alexis sees them she'll know what to do. Dylan didn't understand how this last part would work but Consuelo insisted it would just happen, simple as that. Dylan eventually let the point go and accepted it as the truth, supernatural or otherwise. After that Consuelo fell asleep.

Dylan tries to read the GSX files but once the sickness fills her stomach she turns off the laptop and hides it under the foldout bed. She returns to the humming desktop and reads an article about the high carbon levels fixed in the atmosphere. She reads another article about a bankrupt shipping terminal now empty of cargo, its metal cranes motionless, its workers idle. And then she discovers that an anonymous sex-workers collective has called for a demonstration outside the county jail to welcome Alexis Segura back to freedom. Dylan wants to wake Consuelo and tell her the news but thinks better of it and decides to wait until 4:00 am. The clock says it's now 1:47 am. Dylan decides not to sleep.

She changes the television station to the local news and makes coffee in the kitchen. While the pot fills with black liquid, Dylan glances under the fold-out bed and contemplates opening the GSX files. In the end, she decides against it. Coffee is more important. When it's ready, she pours in some milk and takes it to the desktop. She learns everything there is to know about the sex-workers demonstration, reads every article she finds on Google, and sees that over 500 people say they're going on Facebook. There's no information about the sex-workers who called for the demonstration and the anonymous authors encourage everyone to wear a mask to protect themselves. The people who say they're attending are mostly women.

Dylan spends the next hour bouncing from link to link, article to article, following no specific thread and revealing nothing about her identity. She makes a second pot of coffee and opens the back door so she can stare into the hazy starlight, smell the salt of the ocean, and hear the insects speaking to each other in a language she can't understand.

In the middle of this refreshing darkness, the front door suddenly opens and Favi walks inside. She's dressed in a dark blue sweatshirt and black jeans. Her eyes are tight from lack of sleep. She walks into the kitchen with her hands stretched ahead of her like a blind person.

"Oh my god, thank you," she mumbles, pouring herself a cup of coffee. "Consuelo!"

"Yeah!"

"You ready?"

"No!"

Faviola takes a sip and looks at Dylan.

"You stay up reading more of your secrets?" she asks her.

"No, I can't anymore, it makes me sick. But listen, there's going to be a few hundred people outside the jail wearing masks. A bunch of sex-workers and strippers announced it on Facebook. They said to wear masks and keep your identity secret."

Favi grins behind the steam of her coffee but says nothing, nor does she seem surprised. Dylan hears Consuelo groaning as she gets up from bed and goes to the bathroom. Favi drinks her coffee black while her sister gets ready. She savors each sip and stares intently at the kitchen wall, the mug cupped between her hands.

"Consuelo!" she suddenly yells.

"Yeah!" Her sister steps out in her underwear. "What?"

"Güera says a bunch of hookers are gonna show up in masks."

"No shit?" Consuelo looks at Dylan and smiles. "That makes our job a bit easier. Hold on."

Consuelo goes to the bedroom and puts on a black sweatshirt and blue jeans. She returns with two brightly colored handkerchiefs covered in lapis lazuli floral designs and orange swirls and green spirals. They remind Dylan of Buddhist mandalas or Mayan pyramids made of color. Consuelo and Faviola tie these fabrics around their necks, lift them over their noses, pull the dark hoods over their heads, and become something else. The sisters look like soldiers in an army of light. Dylan can only see their eyes, the same brown eyes as Ricky, the same eyes Alexis will soon recognize from within a sea of masks.

She can't help it. Once the sisters leave, Dylan reaches under the fold-out bed and grabs the laptop. She puts it on Consuelo's desk, turns it on, then powers up the desktop. While both screens flicker to life, she turns on the television and watches an early morning special about restoring wetland environments in the Bay Area. It's 4:41 am and the news doesn't come on until 6:00 am. The television shows an older man walking through an expanse of reeds in rubber boots, his fingers parting the slender green stalks. He wears plastic pants held up by suspenders. His voice is gentle and kind.

When the laptop finishes loading, Dylan opens file number 112. She reads through case studies of targeted couples and learns how their natural jealousy and desires were modulated through smartphones and computer screens. One analyst seemed to be getting pleasure out of watching a couple fight over a picture inserted on the girlfriend's Twitter feed at a precise moment in an instant message argument. The GSX analysts did these type of things multiple times in order to teach the algorithm what to look for in a target. Soon enough, there stopped being reports from human analysts about specific interventions against targeted couples. The algorithms had proven they could perform these operations over 97% of the time, slightly higher than their human counterparts.

Dylan becomes impatient. She opens up the first document of every file and skims the summaries so she understands each subject. The reports shift from case studies on targeted couples to anti-terrorism programs, anti-subversion programs, meshware, real-time 3D imaging, satellite feeds, smartcars, self-driving cars, Tesla, the Internet of Things, Google, Facebook, Twitter, Apple, Verizon, AT&T, Uber, BoonDoggle, Airbnb, the NSA, the CIA, the DIA, the Pentagon, and the State Department, among many others. Dylan reads just enough to understand that GSX incorporated resources from each agency and corporation, forcibly if necessary. She keeps opening the files at a rapid pace until she eventually reaches file number 200. There are still 595 files left.

The file subjects suddenly change to material infrastructure, data centers, undersea fiber-optic lines, the electrical system of the United

States, the water supply, the collapse of the petroleum economy, minerals, mining, the rise of ocean levels, the certainty of mass unrest, the precariousness of the food supply, global shipping lines, and the long-term viability of capitalism. In file number 488, the subject headings start to concern China, its internet, its censorship, its firewall, its economy, its population, its electrical system, its water supply, its food supply, WeChat, Alibaba, and the data-set collected by Google while it was allowed to operate inside the Communist state.

In file number 632, Dylan discovers the initial plans for introducing the OingoBoingo Dream Game to the Chinese market. The next thirty files contain hundreds of documents about what GSX, the CIA, the State Department, and OingoBoingo planned to do if the game had been successfully introduced. In file number 664, she learns the CIA and the NSA kept close watch over Bilton Smyth. They tracked his movements, read his communications, and monitored all of his associations. In file number 665, she learns of a business transaction Smyth made with a Russian tycoon in 2002 that involved selling large amounts of fiber-optic cable at a huge discount to various shell companies.

File number 665 is filled with analysis of the collapsed OingoBoingo deal and Dylan finds surveillance footage confirming that Smyth never met or communicated with this Russian tycoon after the 2002 transaction. His motivations appeared to be solely for profit. In file number 666, the first document contains just a single page with the bold sentence **NO ONE KNOWS WHO HE IS** floating in a field of white. The second document is an analysis of the incident in Beijing where Smyth insulted the Chinese delegation while standing on a table. Some believed Smyth had unconsciously sabotaged the deal because of deeply rooted psychological problems. A few believed he may be a deep-cover asset employed by Russia. The majority believed he was simply a racist anomaly, an ego-maniac who couldn't be predicted. In the end, the result was the same. There was no deal with the Chinese. Everything was scrapped.

And then the 6:00 morning news invades the television screen, its theme music blaring through the bedroom. The first story is about the imminent release of Alexis Segura from the San Francisco County Jail. The screen is split between the station newscaster and a helicopter shot of a large crowd massed outside the jail. The broadcast then cuts to street level at the edge of the crowd where a hassled looking reporter attempts to narrate the story. There are masked women visible in every direction, some with children. One of them holds a sign in front of the newscaster that reads **CASTRATE BILTON SMYTH** while another woman flips off the camera with both hands covered in purple gloves. The reporter tells the station she doesn't know when Alexis Segura will be released, nor has she learned anything about the organizers. She says the large crowd is energized and appears to consist mostly of women. She tells the station that armored riot police are blocking the doors to the jail because they're afraid the crowd will storm inside. She explains that her cameraman was physically prevented from filming within this large group of people, one woman even threatening to smash his equipment. This was the closest their crew could get to the jail doors.

Dylan has stopped looking at the laptop and now concentrates on the television. She studies every masked face on the screen in the hope of seeing someone familiar. The reporter explains the details of the Alexis Segura case to the viewer as the transmission switches back and forth between the helicopter and the street shot. The crowd is far larger than 500 people, probably closer to a thousand. The station switches over to a morning traffic update and then the broadcast abruptly cuts to a commercial for cat food. By that point, Dylan is already on the desktop looking for live updates on local websites. She soon discovers that Alexis has chosen to walk out the front door and refuses to be driven away in a car. Now the jail is threatening to not release her if the crowd doesn't move away from the police line and back up from the main door.

When the 6:00 news returns, the first image is from the helicopter circling the county jail and Dylan can see the crowd has already backed off. Between them and the police line is a half-circle of empty concrete. The broadcast cuts to street level and the newscaster complains about the aggressive crowd not letting any media or cameras approach the door. Dylan cannot conceive of how the sisters will get Alexis out of this situation until there's a sudden burst of verbal panic in the broadcast, the screen switches to the helicopter shot, the metal doors open, and Alexis bolts past the riot police towards the arms of the crowd. She's wearing black pants and a pink leather jacket.

The helicopter camera zooms in as three giant black sheets spread into the air and stretch out across the pavement. Two women in brightly colored masks run ahead of these sheets, take Alexis by the arms, and then disappear underneath the billowing black fabric as the crowd surges to protect them. The helicopter camera tries to locate Alexis underneath the sheets but everything is opaque, everyone is in masks, and the newscasters speculate on whether her friends organized this demonstration or if it was simply a spontaneous Facebook event. Dylan stops listening to the newscasters. She lays back on Consuelo's soft bed, pushes her body up towards the pillows, and eventually closes her eyes. Dylan sees the black sheets blooming like giant roses. It isn't very long before she's asleep.

When she wakes up it's 10:21 am. The apartment is empty, the bedroom door is still open, and the television is broadcasting a show about cooking. A woman on the screen cuts a piece of pink chicken meat and drops it into a glass bowl filled with brown liquid. Dylan grabs the remote control from off the bed and changes the channel to CNN. The screen reveals another helicopter shot, this one circling around a luxury apartment building in Oakland. Dylan leans closer and realizes it's the director's building. One of the windows is shattered and a body lies in the middle of the street. Dylan can see blood and shards of glass all over the pavement. The caption at the bottom of the screen reads "Director At Heart of Leaks Commits Suicide."

The newscaster explains that shortly after Alexis Segura was released, the website Chumby began publishing excerpts from a classified surveillance program run by a private company called Global Security Experts, or GSX. The first article was written by a journalist named Natasha Malevich and explained how every single US citizen was classified, monitored, and manipulated by powerful algorithms controlled by this company. GSX sold its services to several federal agencies and every major tech giant, all of whom shared their data. The newscaster explains that Natasha Malevich provided the full name of the GSX director at the end of this long and comprehensive article. She instructed her readers to ask Charles Thorpe to explain himself. Less than an hour later, the director shot out his apartment window with a handgun and threw himself to the street.

Dylan watches an interview with a hotel worker who found the body after it burst on the pavement. He tells the camera that he was driving to work at the Jack London Lodge when a rain of glass and a spray of blood filled the air. He slammed on the brakes and ran to the body but the person was clearly dead. Clutched in one hand was a note. The screen cuts to a picture this hotel worker took with his smartphone and displays a slip of paper partially covered with streaks of dark blood. In black handwriting is the sentence *I'M NOT THE ONLY ONE*.

The newscasters inform the viewer that the hotel worker who discovered the director's body is the same person who found the body of Ricardo Florez floating in the bay. The two newscasters marvel at this fact for a moment and have nothing to say. They stare blankly at the camera, shake their heads in disbelief, and then move on to the next topic.

Chumby has continued to release a new article every hour, all written by Natasha Malevich with help from select Chumby staff. Malevich has disappeared along with Richard Fenton, the CEO of Chumby, and several other of his employees. Thus far, the articles have not endangered the lives of any federal employees or revealed the identities of any US citizens. The only name mentioned has been that of the GSX director, a previously well known figure in the intelligence community. The White House Press Secretary just issued a short statement to the press where he stated "the matter will be looked into and it's possible the GSX director hid his true activities from federal oversight." The Press Secretary refused to confirm the validity of the leaks and quickly left the podium without taking any further questions. It's obvious to Dylan that the Press Secretary felt sick when he delivered his statement. His cheeks were puffed out. He kept touching his stomach.

When the commercials come on, Dylan goes to the laptop and speeds through the remaining files. The document titles begin to reflect a concern with the outside influences of Hollywood, the dark web, and non-state actors of all varieties. Dylan sees massive troves of information on the structures of every major tech company, the social webs of Silicon Valley, the flows of money, and the true, hidden influencers. She finds documents implicating San Francisco City Hall and the Mayor in a plan to restructure the city and fill it with people on the violet end of their algorithmic spectrum. They wanted a city cleansed of red. They wanted a city of pure capitalism.

The CNN broadcast repeats itself after the commercial break so Dylan keeps reading on her laptop. In file number 764, she discovers a program named Darlingtonia. It was approved for use five months earlier by the new President and represented the consolidation of every tool GSX had ever created. This new program not only cataloged the entire US population, it automatically modulated the behavior of individuals without any direct human supervision. GSX had succeeded in creating an integrated surveillance platform that combined every device of this new digital era from the orbital satellite down to the smartphone. The Darlingtonia program absorbed billions of hours of real time video feeds through every available medium and could discriminate between what was useful and what wasn't. Dylan finds documents detailing how quickly this program could process what it ingested and delete what was superfluous: silence in conversations, blurry camera footage, spam emails, and robot texts. Once keywords had been generated, conversations analyzed, and profiles updated, nearly all of this data was deleted, freeing up precious storage space in the federal data centers. As of two months ago, the Darlingtonia program was still running.

In file number 793, Dylan finds the preface and analysis to a long list of US citizens who will be arrested in the case of mass civil unrest. She opens this massive document and discovers there are over 15,000,000 citizens on this list. When she opens number 794, there's only a single document. It's the scanned image of a heart drawn in red colored pencil with two black lines in the corner to make it look shiny. There's no explanation for it. The heart simply exists.

Dylan has already read file number 795 but looks it over once again. There's nothing to indicate it was written by Ricky. It doesn't even sound like him. But when the public finally reads the case study of the OingoBoingo advertising department, they'll notice that Ricky and Chad are suspiciously omitted from modulation and surveillance. Dylan thinks about Noisebridge being raided and imagines her fingerprints all over the mouse, the keyboard, and the iMac. She knows it's possible for the FBI to find her because of these mistakes. Dylan needs to run but all she can do is wait. It's 12:26 pm. The sisters still haven't returned.

Dylan falls asleep on the fold-out bed. She can't watch any more television. There's simply too much information to absorb so she hides under the covers and lets her body take over. When she's finally unconscious, Dylan dreams of her mother standing in a field of blooming roses. The red petals drip up toward the sky as if pulled by an inverted gravity. Her mother is covered in colorless honey with a million bees swarming around her. Small bubbles of air escape from her mouth but remain trapped within this coat of honey. An endless army of red ants swirls around her feet. Dylan is afraid to hold her mother.

But then the sun falls down and Dylan is lying on her side next to a fire. There's a blanket over her shoulder and an arm around her stomach. The fire begins to whisper, it speaks in a forgotten language that sounds like the hissing of a snake. Dylan giggles without knowing why, she holds the arm tighter and feels warmth on the back of her neck. She floats through this glorious fire as if it were the ocean. It holds her lovingly and comforts her against the darkness. It never stops speaking to her. It's always there.

"You hear me?"

"Yeah," Dylan says. "I hear you."

"What did I just say?"

"That you love me."

"You believe me?"

"I do." She kisses her fingers. "I love you."

Dylan is no longer in the dream but it doesn't matter. There's no difference anymore. She lets Alexis hold her. She feels her lips and the tip of her tongue and the moisture of her breath. Dylan falls asleep, so does Alexis. Neither of them can remember when it ends and when it begins. In one moment they're naked, pressed together, legs entwined under the damp sheets. Dylan runs her fingers through Alexis' long black hair, stares into her piercing green eyes, and feels the ribs beneath her skin. Daylight illuminates her lover's body and drenches it with brilliance. Suddenly it's dark and moonlight shines through the curtains. Dylan can hear the sound of crickets chirping in the lettuce fields. She lays there for some time listening to these insects until Alexis begins to snore. She holds her lover from behind and smells the scent of her neck. It's exactly as she remembered but even stronger now, more potent, more intoxicating.

"I love you," she whispers. "I love you."

Dylan says this over and over until she begins to cry. She tries not to wake Alexis but can't help herself. The sobbing is too violent. Alexis spins around and holds her silently until the tears stop and Dylan falls back asleep. An hour or more passes but there's no way to know exactly how long. The invisible dreams blur into reality and now Dylan is awake with no memory of nightfall. She stands with Alexis in front of the refrigerator and stares at the glowing racks of food. Alexis removes a white paper bag and hands it over. Inside are four burritos wrapped in shiny aluminum foil. The sight of them makes Dylan laugh.

"We got those on the way home," Alexis tells her. "We thought you'd be hungry."

"So you got *four* burritos!"

"Yeah. We kept joking about how much you eat."

Alexis rubs Dylan's stomach, sets the oven to 450 degrees, then opens up the metal door. Both of them stand naked in front of the warming coils and let the red heat touch their skin. Alexis drops two of the burritos on the rack but keeps the oven door propped open. She holds her hands over the warmth and edges her hips closer to Dylan's.

"How did you all get away from the jail?" Dylan asks. "What happened?"

"I don't know!" Alexis laughs. "One minute I'm running out the door, next thing I know those two sisters had me by the arms and there was a black sheet over my head. Then someone gave me a mask, I put on a rain jacket, a scarf, glasses, then another jacket, a hat, and then we started to run, and then everyone started running with us. We all just ran, we ran and ran until we were under the freeway, then they got me in the car."

"I never asked if you had an apartment. I never knew. Isn't that crazy?"

Alexis squints her eyes for a moment. Dylan feels a tremor in her heart.

DARLINGTONIA

"No, I just never told you about it," Alexis says. "I wanted to be safe. Anyway, it's in Daly City. Or was. I don't know, I'm never going back, I'm gone now. When I went there my roommates weren't even home, I just left them a note and grabbed all my shit. That's why it took us so long. I'm sorry." She puts her arm around Dylan's waist and holds her. "I didn't mean to worry you. I'm just not going back there so I wanted my stuff."

"I was too tired to worry anymore, I fell asleep, I—"

"I know, you were so sweet." She kisses Dylan neck. "You didn't wake up at all."

"It felt like my head was going to explode."

Alexis strokes her hair and kisses her cheek.

"Maybe your head exploded, but now it's back together."

They press their heads together so their dark hair intermingles.

"Maybe," Dylan says. "But can I ask you something?"

"Yeah, anything."

"Before you found me that day outside work—"

Dylan doesn't finish, she just stares at the glowing red coils.

"Yeah?" Alexis says. "What?"

"Had you ever seen me before?"

Alexis is silent and holds Dylan even tighter.

"I'm so sorry. It's...he didn't...Ricky didn't...he kept talking about you and then one night we were in the same area and he was like, come on down to this club. So I did. He said you looked like Uma Thurman in *Pulp Fiction*, he kept saying it, he was so committed to proving you looked like her. I thought it was funny, he was always doing something like that, so I went and had a drink with him, you came into the club, I saw you, then I left."

Dylan looks for some trace of lying in her eyes. She doesn't know what she sees.

"I never saw your face," she says.

"I know." Alexis smiles at her. "He just wanted *me* to see *you*, to know what *you* looked like with my own eyes. He knew what he was doing even if we didn't see it yet. But anyway, I was embarrassed, you know, I just wanted to leave and didn't want to make chit chat with a strange—"

"The two of you didn't use me?"

Dylan asks this last question so meekly that a tear falls out of Alexis' eye.

"Who said that?" she snaps. "Who said I used you?"

"No one, no one!" Dylan buries her head in Alexis' neck. "Forget it."

"I didn't use you, Dylan. Come on!" She caresses her lover's back and then sighs. "I know its been confusing, I know that everything—"

"You're an anarchist?"

"Uh?" Alexis pulls back. "Yeah! Isn't it obvious?"

"Why didn't you tell me? About all those people, all that—"

"Seriously! Where the fuck is this coming from?" She grabs Dylan's shoulders and shakes her. "Why are you asking me this now? Did someone—"

"No!" Dylan returns to Alexis' neck and takes a deep breath. "I'm just starving. I feel crazy."

"It's almost ready. Don't worry."

Dylan stays with Alexis by the oven as the heat rises from the red coils and the smell of meat and onions fills the air. Eventually the burritos begin to emit a sizzling sound from beneath their aluminum wrapping and little red bubbles boil up from between the cracks. Alexis uses a dish towel to pick them up and tosses them onto a wooden cutting board. She slowly unwraps the steaming foil and puts the burritos on ceramic plates. Alexis holds one in each hand and raises them to the ceiling so she resembles an ancient fertility goddess. Directly above her is the framed image of the Virgin Mary. When Alexis asks her if she's still hungry, Dylan doesn't know how to respond.

It takes them many hours to fall asleep that night. Alexis tells Dylan they'll have the apartment to themselves until Sunday when Consuelo gets back with a new car. They don't need to worry about someone walking in on them. Both of them lay on their backs atop the fold-out bed and talk about the demonstration outside the jail, the sea of multi-colored masks, and the long black sheets blocking out the cameras. Dylan laughs when Alexis tells the story of their escape with more detail and humor, describing the smells and the curses and the heavy panting on their long zig-zag through the city. She explains that Ricky's friend Luz organized the entire demonstration, that she wore a pink balaclava with a black star, and that she helped them all escape San Francisco together.

"I love those sisters! I was sweating like crazy, but them...nope! Them and Luz made sure everything got all mixed around like a magic trick so no one could tell who was who or what was what. Did you ever meet Luz?"

"Once, with Ricky. He introduced me at one of her concerts."

"She's cool, I like her a lot. But yeah, I swear, those sisters took me by the arms and then, I'm not even joking, perfectly synchronized, they said they were Ricky's sisters. Just like that, one sister on each arm, speaking into both of my ears. *We're Ricky's sisters. We'll take you to Dylan.*"

Dylan feels a shiver of goosebumps rise atop her skin.

"See!" Alexis yells. "That's how it is! That's how crazy this all is!"

"Spooky."

"Beyond spooky. But seriously—" Alexis flips onto her stomach and looks at Dylan. "We fucked up so bad. So bad. If I'd just gotten it to you immediately instead of hiding it—"

Dylan puts her finger to Alexis' lips.

"We can't talk about it," she whispers. "Ever. It's safe here, but—"

"Okay, I know, but come on. We fucked up, right?"

"We did. But even if you'd gotten it to me sooner, we would have just fucked up together, got caught together. So it worked out perfectly, somehow, even though we were—"

"So fucking dumb! It's a fucking miracle we're even here right now."

"Are you mad?" Dylan asks.

"Huh? At what?"

"At Ricky?"

"At *Ricky?*" Alexis asks. "No! Why would I be mad at Ricky?"

"Because he didn't tell us anything. Nothing."

Alexis is silent. She lowers her head into her arms and starts breathing heavily, as if she's angry. Dylan is too petrified to move. She lays on her back, looks at the ceiling, and clutches the sheets to her chest. Her eyes are wide open. She can't close her mouth.

"We were listening to the radio," Alexis mumbles. "On the way here. Whatever Ricky did, everything he did...I'm okay with it. Obviously he wouldn't tell us anything, right? How could he? And yeah, I got locked up for a minute, my picture is everywhere now, yeah, okay, he kind of...no, he didn't, though. *They* locked *me* up. *They* killed *him*! I don't fucking care what he did. It was right. It's going to bring those fucks down. You know it was right! *Don't you*?"

Dylan hesitates and Alexis shakes her by the shoulders.

"Where the fuck is this coming from?" Alexis asks. "What happened?"

"Nothing."

"Tell me! They said you saw him, the dead guy, the director. It was *him*, wasn't it?"

"Yes!" Dylan sobs. "I was so scared! I can't—"

Alexis tries to quiet her down but there's no point. All Dylan can imagine is the paralysis invading her heart, the stillness of the Darlingtonia plants, the trickle of the water, and the buzz of the ultra-violet lights. It reminds her of when she was going to die. All of it returns, every minute of it, every impression, every emotion. It bursts out of her eyes and escapes in the long, terrible moans of hyperventilation. Alexis takes it all in, she clutches her lover tightly and doesn't let go until the tears have stopped and the bed is no longer shaking.

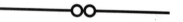

When the sun comes out, Dylan tries to open her eyes, although not for very long. She quickly falls back to sleep. When she opens them again, Dylan is on top of Alexis like a seal. She kisses her ears, her neck, and the middle of her chest. They spend most of the morning like this. They explore each other in the new daylight and speak only in the midst of laughter. They sweat, moan, and stare at each other for so long the world dissolves and the past vanishes. There's only this moment and there are only these eyes. Nothing else exists.

Towards the afternoon, Dylan feels the familiar pangs of hunger in her stomach so she puts on a shirt and starts warming up the last two burritos. Alexis pees in the bathroom, puts on some clothes, and then chugs down a glass of water at the sink. She smacks her lips when she's done and burps loudly in the middle of the kitchen while Dylan hovers in front of the glowing red coils.

"My burrito's in your oven," Alexis tells her.

"I'm fucking starving."

"What else is new?"

Dylan grabs an orange from a basket on the counter and begins to peel it.

"Want some?" she asks.

"Sure." Alexis waits for her to finish and pops a piece in her mouth. "Thanks."

"So what should we do?" Dylan asks.

"Today? Uh...do what we've been doing. Stay here. Eat burritos."

"Should we turn on the TV?"

Alexis chews silently. She eventually shakes her head.

"Not yet," she says. "I want to hear it from you first. We'll find out what the media says later, we got enough time for that. Tell me in your own words, though." Alexis refills her water glass in the sink and turns back around. "I don't want to hear it from the enemy. I want to hear it from you."

Dylan doesn't know what to say. She looks at the linoleum floor in silence and waits for the burritos to sizzle inside the foil. Once they're heated up, both of them eat ravenously at the counter, their fingers becoming thick with oil and sour cream. Alexis moans while she chews and nods her head in affirmation of how good it all tastes. Dylan can hardly think through the pleasure. She eats as if possessed by a fire demon needing fuel for its survival. Her vision goes blank until the food is gone.

"You ate that thing twice as fast as me," Alexis says.

Dylan burps, nods her head, and takes a long drink of water.

"I could eat another one," she says, wiping her mouth.

"You're not getting the rest of mine. I just got out of jail."

"I'm so sorry—"

"Stop." Alexis shakes her head. "None of that. It's done. Okay? I'm here. Right now I'm here, and I'll be here, with *you*, for a long time. Like, a *long* time. It wouldn't have worked out any other way. I knew there was a risk, I knew it and I did it anyway. I love you, Dylan. That's the only reason any of this worked. You know that? *Love*. It was because we fucking *loved* each other. We gotta keep it alive. We gotta stay together."

"I love *you*," Dylan moans, wrapping her arms around Alexis. "I love you."

"So tell me what happened. What should we do?"

Dylan closes her eyes. She tells the story but doesn't start at the beginning. Alexis finishes eating while her lover explains buying doughnuts from two Chinese women that morning. Dylan describes the director's apartment in detail and how the Darlingtonia plants exuded nectar from their tongues in order to catch insects. She describes how it felt to know she would die with the sound of trickling water in her ears. She felt small and trapped and unable to use her body. It took all her will-power just to breathe uncontrollably. Dylan explains how the director drugged her in the stairwell and then drove her to the marshland where he dumped Ricky and Chad. This time she doesn't cry, nor does she tremble, nor does she feel afraid.

"How'd you find out where he lived?"

"It was in the files. At the end. That's how I found out about Pamela."

"Who's that?"

Dylan tells Alexis how she dressed in jogging clothes, wore a brown wig, and found Pamela Gustafson at her office in the UC Berkeley campus. She explains how they walked into the hills and saw a thirsty coyote with yellow eyes. She tells Alexis what Pamela did for GSX, about her love affair with Ricky, and how Pamela gave him access to the entire database. Dylan says if it weren't for Pamela, none of this would have happened.

"He probably loved her then," Alexis says. "And she probably loved him. Right?"

"She did," Dylan says. "I know she did. But...she also said he ran a program on me."

"Ran a program? I don't get it."

"The director said the same thing, he said you helped Ricky run it on me."

Alexis clenches both her fists and is instantly enraged.

"Ricky didn't tell me anything! Why would he? He would have put me at risk."

"I know, I know. Trust me, I yelled at both of them, I called them crazy—"

"They're worse than crazy, they're evil!"

"No, no." Dylan firmly shakes her head. "Pamela wasn't evil. Not all the way."

"Oh yeah? Then why was she working with those fuckers? Fucking rich bitch!"

"I'm not—"

"Not you! Her! Why was she working with them?"

"I don't know, she said a lot of different things. She said she wanted to stop child prostitution, she wanted to stop people raping their children, that she just wanted to understand her species?"

"Her *species*? By what, manipulating us?"

"I let her have it. Trust me, I made her cry."

"I bet you *did*! But you also let her get to you, clearly, *and* you let the director get to you! You have to forget all that shit, no matter what they showed you about me—"

Alexis looks down at the linoleum, kicks something that isn't there, and then throws her butt down on the fold-out bed. She lifts her knees to her nose, wraps her arms around her legs, and keeps her eyes fixated on the ground. It looks like she's shivering.

"He only showed me pictures of—"

"I don't want to know!" Alexis yells at the floor. "I'll tell you everything one day, Dylan. I promise I will, but please, just—"

"It wasn't—"

"I don't want to know! Seriously!" Alexis looks up pleadingly. "Don't tell me! Everything he showed you was just to manipulate you one last time, to fuck you over because he knew we'd beaten him. I want you to get to know me, but I want to be the one who tells you about my past, not some old creep like him. We beat that piece of shit good and he wanted some revenge so he planted these seeds in you. And now we gotta get them out."

"They're gone." Dylan sits beside Alexis. "I promise. I won't mention it again."

"I hope you don't. They even made you doubt Ricky, too. I mean—" Alexis wraps her arm around Dylan. "I know Ricky didn't tell us anything and...yeah, we had a lot of help we didn't know about. So let's say he did use some program. It still doesn't matter. All of this needed to happen. The truth has to come out, no matter what."

"I know." She puts her cheek on Alexis' shoulder and closes her eyes. "We have time, lot's of time. We're safe and you can take as long as you need. I want you to tell me everything, whatever you want, anything, everything. There's no rush."

"I've had a hard life, you know. I'm not like you. Not at all."

"But you love me, right? You promise it's real?"

Alexis pulls Dylan down to the fold-out. She whispers that she loves her and promises it's real. Dylan looks into her green eyes and searches for any sign that Alexis is lying. But after a few moments, it's clear that she isn't. The smile on her face is genuine and the longing in her eyes is real. Dylan has no doubt at this moment. She hopes it will last forever.

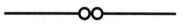

They eventually turn on the television and sit down on Consuelo's bed. The channel is set to CNN and they learn the CEO of Chumby has just issued a statement to the press. After numerous calls for him to emerge from hiding, Richard Fenton appeared outside the San Francisco Federal Building shortly after being questioned by the Department of Homeland Security. He told the press that he doesn't approve of Wikileaks and their promise to release the full 17.8 GB on Monday morning. He believes it will harm the lives of innocent people.

He tells the press that Chumby will continue to release articles on the leaks and will not disclose the identities or confidential information of any government employees, undercover operatives, or private citizens, nor will it disclose the source of the leaks. After reiterating his general condemnation of Wikileaks and their stated refusal to redact this sensitive information, Richard Fenton goes on to strongly condemn the media personalities, politicians, and corporate officials who have publicly called for the suppression of his company and the arrest of his writers. Fenton firmly states that every secret program Chumby has revealed is completely illegal. There is no denying that GSX operated outside of federal law and was highly autonomous from government oversight. After clearing his throat, Fenton informs the press that tomorrow morning, Chumby will release a series of articles detailing the extent to which every major tech company collaborated with GSX. And then Fenton quickly leaves, he gets into a black car with tinted windows and the newscasters return to the screen.

"How many articles have come out?" Alexis asks.

"I don't know, several. Hold on."

Alexis keeps watching CNN while Dylan turns on the desktop and waits for it to load. She listens to a news commentator say the credibility of the federal government has been irrevocably damaged. The President has yet to issue a statement on the matter and the White House Press Secretary told the media there would be no official response until the information was released on Monday.

"Holy fucking Mary!" Alexis gasps. "What the fuck?"

"That's not even the half of it." The computer finishes loading and Dylan opens the browser. "Just hold on a second."

"How do they *not* know? Why are they waiting until Monday? It means they don't know, right?"

"Right. They don't know anything. He destroyed the system, that's what the director said. He destroyed everything. There's nothing left."

"No, no, someone knows. The fucking President knows!"

Dylan can't take this last bit in. She focuses on the Chumby website and clicks on the main story. The latest article details the case studies that focused on the micro-targeting of individuals rather than the greater population. It explains how operatives would meet subjects in real life and conduct psychological experiments using verbal keywords generated by the GSX algorithms. The article explains the nuances of what Dylan already knows so she skims the rest and goes back to the main page. The bulk of the stories concern the basic nature of the programs, how they use the cameras and microphones of every device, and how they generate profiles and keywords from conversations, texts, and internet searches. But there's one article that stands out with its strange title. Dylan clicks on the words *Tangled in the Web of A Dead Man* and is directed to an article written by Natasha Malevich.

"How much more is there?" Alexis asks. "These newscasters are just saying the same thing over and over now. Smartphones, cameras, algorithms. But it's more than that, right?"

"I can't even begin to explain."

"Holy Mary." Alexis walks behind Dylan and holds her around the chest. "You've been deep in this shit for a while, I don't even know how you're handling it. I mean, I used to think about this stuff when I was high, I'd freak myself out a lot of the time. It was always too big to even try and think about so I just stopped using digital stuff except for work. But now it's like...*confirmed* that they're streaming from everyone's cameras at every moment."

"And digesting it. The data just flows through these servers. It's all automated."

"*Was* automated. You said he destroyed everything, right?"

"He did, that's true."

"Watch your present tense, girl. Don't freak yourself out even more. And don't freak me out! My brain would be fried from whatever you've seen."

"I couldn't finish all the files, though. I had to skim. I barely got halfway through—"

Both of them suddenly turn towards the television as the newscaster announces Wikileaks has just tweeted the full legal name of the GSX director along with links to previously leaked material that details the relationship between the CIA and Charles Thorpe. The newscaster briefly explains that after Thorpe retired from the CIA in 1992, he moved to Silicon Valley and founded a company that designed and built servers for tech companies. In addition to this, Thorpe worked closely with Stanford and UC Berkeley, often giving lectures on data analysis and electrical engineering. The newscaster explains that Thorpe was a vocal critic of the invasion of Iraq in 2003 and after the bombing of Baghdad he retired from the media spotlight. In his last public speech, Thorpe explained that the stability of the United States had been permanently endangered and new methods were needed to ensure its safety. There is no official public record of GSX, nor is it a publicly traded company. None of the tech giants or government agencies named in the Chumby articles have officially responded.

"No one is responding!" Alexis yells. "How long did it take them to respond to Snowden?"

"No idea. I was still in undergrad."

"And the President's not denying it either. This is *huge!*"

"But wait, come here, read this with me. This is her, the journalist who published it."

Alexis sits on Dylan's lap and reads Natasha's article *Tangled in the Web of A Dead Man*. It begins with a simple question: *Can you imagine why Charles Thorpe killed himself? When he jumped from his fifth story window, the director of GSX hoped to be taking the truth with him. He left only one cryptic message. He told the public he wasn't "the only one." There will never be an answer to this last mystery unless people look for it. The truth is buried somewhere in these leaked documents, covered in the webs of a dead man.*

"You gave all of it to *her?*" Alexis whispers in her ear.

Dylan nods her head and keeps reading.

"How did you know you could trust her?"

"I read one of her—"

Dylan stops talking and takes a sharp, sudden breath.

"No! Not again!" Alexis cries. "What is it?"

"Nothing."

"No, not nothing," Alexis says. "You have to tell me."

"I read an article she wrote and—"

"And you think Ricky put it on your feed through one of these programs? Is that it? So what? What if he did? Whatever. He *didn't!* You just went to the right person. That's all."

Dylan knows this is true so she keeps reading the article. Natasha describes the near total scope of the surveillance programs and how GSX had clearly crossed over from anti-terrorism into the outright manipulation of the population for the purposes of maintaining capitalism within the United States. At the end of her article, Natasha writes:

> *Everything I have just written is an understatement. If anyone doubts that GSX helped operate a totalitarian control network, they need only wait for the release promised by Wikileaks. I strongly disagree with divulging the full 17.8 GB of data, as its intimate nature will surely compromise the lives, identities, and privacy of several thousand innocent people. Nevertheless,*

I understand why the anonymous source opted for the full release. Had they not, the entire editorial staff of Chumby might be in federal prison at this very moment. The urge to tell the truth often outweighs the risk to others. Even to oneself.

"I like her," Alexis says, finishing the article before Dylan does. "This is good. You see how she mentions Ricky at the end?"

"Without saying his name."

"Nobody knows about him, right?"

"Yeah, but listen. When we leave here—" Dylan grabs Alexis' wrist and holds it tightly. "When we leave we can never talk about him, about what *he* did, about what *we* did, not unless we're deep in the woods and no one's following us. I went to a hacklab to try and open the files and it got raided later that day. That was another one of my endless mistakes. Those hacker guys helped me out, though, they gave me the lap—"

"Wait, you went to Noisebridge?"

"You know it?"

"Yeah, I know it. It got raided?"

Dylan nods and lowers her head.

"Come on, you promised," Alexis says. "No more of that. Keep going, what were you saying?"

"The Noisebridge guys wiped the security cameras, I hope they wiped down the keyboard and desk like they said and...you see what I'm saying? That was *me*, I left prints everywhere. I had a wig and sunglasses on, those black sunglasses from the picture. My face was all over the television but—"

"Alright, now I'm freaking out. Stop!"

"I'm just saying we need to go. I promised Natasha I'd meet in our secret spot on Monday, in the morning. We need to drive up to San Francisco, I need to meet her, and then we need to disappear. Everything's fine for now, but seriously, I don't want to take any chances. We need to disappear."

"No, you know what we need to do?"

Dylan waits in anticipation but Alexis just laughs.

"We need to eat. I'm fucking starving."

Alexis pulls Dylan into the kitchen and begins rifling through the cabinets. She opens a large can of black beans and pours them into a pot over the stove. She slices up a jalapeno and a red onion and sweeps them from the cutting board into the bubbling pot. Then she takes a bag of rice and measures out two coffee cup's worth into a metal pot. Dylan leans her hip against the counter and admires the smooth movements of her lover's hands.

"I just want to cook something we can keep eating."

"What are you doing to the rice?" Dylan asks her. "Frying it? Sauteing it?"

"Browning it, so it doesn't clump. You want to cut some garlic real quick?"

Dylan grabs a few cloves from a wicker basket and starts peeling them on the cutting board. She slices away the rigid bottoms and then dices them into little white pieces. Alexis sweeps them up with the knife and drops them into the brown, sizzling rice. The aroma of cooking garlic fills the room.

"It's just hard to know that my whole life—" Alexis shakes her head. "I've lived through some crazy fucking shit, I've met some bad people, people you don't want to know. And I've done shit...I've done shit I wish I could forget. And they have it all. They won't forget any of it."

"*You* don't start now. Okay? Not after what you told me."

"But you don't understand—"

"It doesn't matter. You know good people too, those friends you—"

"Yeah, I don't know where they are. They're gone. They just left. I can't find them."

"You will. One day, I prom—"

"Here, fill this with water and dump it in four times."

Alexis hands over the coffee cup and keeps stirring the rice. Dylan pours the first cup of water and a plume of white steam erupts from the pot. She cools the frenzied water down with the next three cups and when she's done there's only the slightest beginnings of a boil. Alexis turns the heat down, stirs in tomato paste and salt, then puts the lid on the pot.

"I just want to forget it all," Alexis says.

"You can tell me anything, I won't be afraid."

Alexis tries to maintain eye contact but the tears make it impossible. She clutches Dylan's shoulders as if everything depended on it. The pots boil under their lids, the kitchen fills with steam, and the afternoon sun continues its descent into the ocean. Alexis begins to speak. She tells Dylan about the horrible men, the gangs, the drugs, and the meth labs in the desert. She tells her about fleeing Mojave, finding anarchists in East Los Angeles, and going to punk shows in sweaty bars. They move from the kitchen to the fold-out bed and Alexis begins speaking of anarchist collectives in San Francisco that shared everything they had, organized actions against the police, and dispersed into the world once the FBI came looking for them.

"But it wasn't just the Feds," Alexis tells her. "There were people I never knew who did things I'll never find out about. Who knows who they worked for, but they fucked a lot of things up for us. One minute people are together, the next they're torn apart by some infighting over nothing. The stakes were so fucking high and people threw it all away over some rumor."

Dylan coughs and has trouble taking her next breath.

"What?" Alexis asks. "Did he say something about that too?"

"The government probably provoked all of it. To tear you apart."

"Yeah, and we're all just dumb shit humans, that's the simple truth. We can't help our feelings, we *shouldn't* help our feelings, but this whole culture is designed to repress everything natural we feel, every good instinct we have. Or exploit it. Our instincts and feelings make us weak in this shit world."

"And they prey on all of it," Dylan says. "We have proof now."

"The food's ready. Come on, get a bowl, it's time to settle down."

Alexis grabs a small tupperware of Consuelo's salsa from the fridge and stands with Dylan at the counter eating rice and beans. Their forks clatter against the ceramic bowls as they rapidly consume the starch and proteins. They keep pouring the green salsa over their food, the spice never hot enough, their taste buds always craving more heat. They finish their bowls and go to the stove for seconds, both of them laughing at their endless appetites. The steaming food calms their nerves and makes their minds grow sleepy. When they're done eating, Dylan does all the dishes, puts the leftovers in empty plastic containers, and stacks them together in the fridge.

Alexis doesn't help Dylan. She puts on a pair of jeans, grabs a pack of Newports from her bag, and goes out the back door without saying anything. Through the steam of the sink, Dylan watches her lover smoke along the edge of the lettuce field. Alexis stands barefoot in the dusty soil and faces the setting sun with a stern expression. She puffs on her menthol cigarette as the sky turns orange and then becomes red. Dylan can't stop looking at her. The water keeps running in the sink, the insects begin to sing, and the last glimmers of sunset start to fade. Alexis lights a second cigarette. She doesn't turn away from the approaching darkness. Not once.

CHAPTER 19

She got on OkCupid. It just happened. Prior to that moment, Dylan had never used a dating website. After creating her account, she searched through dozens of supposedly compatible men, scrolled through their pictures, read their descriptions, and lingered over just a few. In the end, the one person she felt matched with was named Ricardo Florez. He was the only man who seemed to actually enjoy art. Dylan knew him from work and had spoken with him several times. She liked his sense of humor, although she'd never talked to him for very long. After reading his OkCupid profile, Dylan suddenly knew his interests, his birthday, and his hobbies. His two favorite artists were Georges Seurat and Ester Hernández. He was fascinated by organic harmonies of color and the simultaneous contrast of opposites. All this agreed with her tastes so she sent Ricardo Florez a message, received a response, and scheduled a date for the coming Sunday. They decided to go out for brunch.

Once she committed, Dylan immediately began to regret her decision. She had been lonely, bored, restless, eager for any variety of real human contact. For the past month, she was either at work or inside her apartment and felt as if she were growing lazy. She watched Netflix all day, took forty minute showers, and had food delivered for every meal. Something was wrong with her. Going on a date seemed like a way to break this malaise, only now it felt like a mistake. She thought about canceling but then remembered her boredom. It was enough to make her keep the date.

Ricky chose the restaurant, a place in North Beach called Acquolina. Dylan had never heard of it and looked it up on Yelp. The restaurant opened at noon on weekends and didn't appear to serve brunch, just a variety of salads, meats, pastas, and pizzas. Dylan thought about sending a message to Ricky alerting him to his fact but then decided against it. Dylan wasn't very picky when it came to food. She was happy to eat most anything. It was one of the few pleasures she considered her own.

Dylan took an Uber across town and up the hill to North Beach. When she got out, Ricky was seated at an outside table overlooking the green cypress trees of Washington Square Park. He stood up when she arrived, opened his arms, and gave her a quick hug. The physical contact made her feel uncomfortable, mostly because she didn't expect it, although Ricky didn't hold her for very long, nor did he press himself against her. This seemed like a good start. They both sat down at the table and Dylan looked around at the restaurant. Every table was packed and a few tourist families were waiting in line for a big table. Most of the customers were young, either in couples or large packs. All of them had mimosas on their tables. Most of them seemed hungover.

"I thought we were getting brunch," she said.

"Pizza's the hottest new brunch trend in North Beach. Soaks the booze right up. Plus, all the techies who moved here want some authentic Italian food. This *is* an Italian neighborhood, after all, or at least it was. It's okay if you don't like it. You want to go somewhere else?"

"No, I like it. I just though you meant, like, a real brunch."

"This *is* a real brunch. It's afternoon, it's Sunday morning, and we're out in public."

"Is that all brunch is in San Francisco?"

"Brunch is just displaying yourself after your wild Saturday night. That's all it is."

"I didn't have one of those. Must have missed it."

"What? A wild Saturday night? Don't worry, me neither. But *they* don't know that." Ricky cast his brown eyes across the crowded restaurant, scanning each table. "Look at them. They're just like us, moved here two months ago. Far as they know, we're the hottest couple around, we're millionaires, we're famous, we've designed the latest whatever the fuck."

"If only, right? We're just two underlings in the advertising department."

"Not me. I'm on my way to the top. Don't worry, though, I got your back."

"How feminist of you."

Ricky just chuckled and looked away. When the waiter arrived, they ordered mimosas and Dylan felt relieved when the drinks were placed on the table. She took a large gulp of champagne and orange juice, swallowed it down, and began to feel more relaxed, more comfortable. She and Ricky soon told each other the abridged versions of their lives: where they grew up, what their university was like, and how they came to work at OingoBoingo. Dylan talked about going to RISD for her graphic design MFA, about the stereotype of the Connecticut blonde, and how she stood out at school with her crow-black hair.

"Are you Black Irish or something?" he asked her.

"No. I'm not Irish at all."

"That shit's so funny. The blackest that white people get are some dark haired Spanish Moors who crash landed on the coast of Ireland. You've heard those stories, right?"

"I think so. No, my dad's family comes from England. Cheshire originally."

"Like the Cheshire Cat?"

"*Exactly* like the Cheshire Cat. Only they didn't stay in the tree. They left in the 1600s during the English Civil War."

"Damn. That's an old ass civil war. And they came over here on a boat, right?"

Dylan nodded, already anticipating where the conversation would go. She waited for Ricky to say something about modern-day refugees but instead he remained silent. There was a clear warmth in his eyes that made her feel safe, as if she could tell him anything. So she stuck to the subject and talked about her family in Connecticut, about her childhood mansion on the Gold Coast, and about how absolutely rich they were. Ricky didn't ask many questions, he just sipped on his mimosa and let her speak until she was finished. Then he began to relate his own past. Dylan learned that Ricky received a Stanford scholarship out of high school, joined a well-known fraternity, and received his MFA in design the previous summer.

"What do you mean *design?*" Dylan asked him. "Just design? Not graphic design?"

"They never offered that at Stanford. It was just the Design Program. More interdisciplinary, I guess you'd say, sponsored by two departments. I got to focus on what I wanted. Data visualization, graphic design. Acquired all the skills I needed for a job, got my MFA, and here I am. Anyway, they got rid of that program I was in. That was the last class."

"Got rid of it?" Dylan asked. "Why?"

"They didn't think art had anything to do with technology. They wanted them separate."

"They're the same thing. Art *is* technology."

"Not anymore, apparently. They're trying to purge art from everything. And the humanities in general, they don't want that either. Art and art history have nothing to do with engineering, they say. Not profitable enough, too specialized. Different fields. One more profitable than the other, obviously."

"What the fuck?" Dylan asked. "It's not like art *sells* or anything. If Steve Jobs hadn't embedded *some* artistry in the iPhone, it wouldn't have taken off the way it did."

"For sure, but now it's fucking hopeless. You heard about that stupid VR tech Google built? They named it after Seurat! Man, at this point, art and technology are so divorced you got these techies naming VR technology after artists they don't understand at all. I mean, right before he died, even, Seurat was trying to warn people about screens and spectators, let alone these VR helmets."

"Seurat *did* predict pixels, though."

"Maybe. But he also hung out with anarchists and would have hated Google."

"I know. I studied him at school. For him art was the harmony of opposites. Art is *everything!*"

"Totally, but Google doesn't care anymore, not when there's a billion Androids out there that all look the same. Anyway, students want a fast track to a good job, and if a company wants a plain old mechanical engineer, having an MFA in design just muddies the water. An employer sees that Master of Fine Arts degree instead of that Master of Science—"

"Then you don't get the job." Dylan said.

"That's right, you're out."

"So you know about computers then? Circuit boards, microchips, processors, all that?"

"Not really. I know graphics systems, engines. Computers—" Ricky took a big gulp of his mimosa. "Nah, I don't really fuck with computers. They're too much trouble. Once they're built they're built, but that's just the way I see it."

"I don't mess with them either. I kind of hate them."

"Well, good thing we spend our whole fucking lives on computers, then. But listen, can I ask you something?"

Dylan looked at Ricky's mimosa glass and saw it was nearly empty.

"Sure," she said, draining her own. "Go for it."

"Why'd you use OkCupid? I mean, we work together."

At first Dylan could only laugh. The more she thought about it, the less it made any sense. Instead of talking to him at lunch, instead of speaking to him after work, Dylan had used a computer and hidden behind a screen. After realizing this, she became nervous, her face flushed, and she began to spin her champagne glass on the white table cloth.

"I don't know," she managed to say. "Lonely. Bored."

"Me, too. When you sent that message, I was like, why not? Beats being lonely and bored."

"I was on there, I don't know...I didn't even think about it that much. I just sent it and then—"

"Don't worry. I'm not offended or anything. I mean, to be honest, if we were attracted to each other we would've already been talking at work, right?"

"I guess so. Sure."

"It's cool to just be friends. Forget this whole date thing. I never go on dates anyway."

"Me, neither," Dylan said. "I just stay home."

"To be honest, I use OkCupid the same way I use Facebook, to see what people are up to, what they're thinking about, that's it. I never even respond, except to you, mostly because we work together. I swear to the Virgin, there's so much pressure to just fuck non-stop, fuck everyone you can. And then work out at the gym in between. And then post pics of it online. It's the Silicon Valley sexual economy. Display yourself at the office, at Burning Man, on Instagram—"

"At brunch."

"Right! At brunch! Exactly!" Ricky laughed and clinked his empty glass against her own. "Like it has to be *all* sexual *all* the time. A never ending meat market, endless competition. And all for what?"

"Nothing. I mean, I never have male friends for this exact reason."

"That's because most men are shit," Ricky said. "Except me, of course."

When he said this, Dylan could only grin and shake her head in annoyance. She happened to glance at the other tables and saw several curious eyes fixed on them. Dylan and Ricky were loud, the champagne had gone to their heads, and soon the waiter returned to quiet them down and take their order. After some exaggerated deliberation, they decided on a sausage and arugula pizza. They asked for bread and olive oil, a vase of water, and another round of mimosas. Dylan liked being with Ricky that morning. Not because they were mistaken for a couple, but because no one in the restaurant could imagine them being anything else. This was the first time Dylan felt truly comfortable with a man. It wasn't just the champagne or the grins of admiring customers. It was something that existed between them, something real. Dylan remembers all of this now. She remembers the fog burning off and the sun bathing them in light. Ricky looked like someone from the future that afternoon. He looked like someone from tomorrow.

Consuelo returns just before noon. They see her pull up in a green Audi station wagon and walk up to the front door. The blinds are drawn, the windows are open, and Alexis and Dylan have spent the entire morning cleaning the apartment. The fold-out bed is tucked back into the sofa, the pots and pans are in the drying rack, and the bed sheets are folded neatly in the laundry basket. When she opens the front door, Consuelo carries a bag of Chinese food in one hand and car keys in the other. She puts these items on the kitchen table and grabs three plates from the cupboard. The smell of Chinese food has already invaded the room.

"Those are your keys now," she says to both of them. "You gotta sell the Audi before the registration runs out, but that's a good car. It'll get you somewhere."

They sit down at the table and Consuelo serves them something from each carton; steaming heaps of noodles, oily red chicken, and green beans mixed with pork. Consuelo tells them how she went to Salinas and stayed with her *compa* who's ex-boyfriend was a mechanic. It took Consuelo a few days of pestering the guy, but eventually he found them a clean car with the registration slip. Her sister Marisol had tried to get it delivered over the phone but the guy was being difficult and Consuelo had to go straighten it out personally.

"Normal bullshit" she says. "He just wanted an excuse to talk with one of us sisters."

"Why?" Alexis asks. "What's his deal?"

"He loves us. *He* says. Anyway, I've been listening to a lot of radio, watching a lot of TV when I was with my girl, and this shit's popping. Everyone's talking about it. It's on all the Spanish channels and in all the papers. And I swear, I've seen less smartphones outside. I didn't see anyone using them in Salinas, except a few people. I mean, they probably still have them, just no one was taking them out. Even my girl was talking about how she couldn't trust her mic was disabled even if the screen said so."

"Good!" Alexis says, her mouth full. "You'd think people would stop."

"People are freaked out. For sure. No doubt."

"We just saw on the news that all the cell-phone stores are empty," Dylan says. "There was a morning special about it. They showed an Apple store completely vacant."

"Too bad everyone already bought one," Alexis says.

"Anyway—" Consuelo finishes chewing her food and nods at the front door. "My mom's cooking tonight, all my sisters are gonna be there. We want to see you both off, because—"

"What?" Dylan asks.

"We probably won't see each other ever again. We shouldn't. At some point, they'll figure out little Ricardo did this, then they'll come here. I don't know when, but probably Monday after they release the rest of it. You both gotta be gone by then."

"We're going to the city tomorrow," Dylan says, nodding her head. "I need to be there at 9:00."

"But yeah—" Consuelo hides a burp. "We'll have a little send-off tonight, to wish you well."

After they're done eating, after all the dishes are put away and the paper cartons thrown in the recycling bin, the three women go outside to smoke a joint. They watch over the lettuce fields and listen to Consuelo tell stories of the mischief Ricky got into as a child. He liked to hide in tree branches or within big tufts of sea grass so he could scare his sisters when they approached. He never took credit for his grander pranks and would smile to himself as Marisol struggled to explain how a stray poodle ended up in her Nissan. And then there's the sound of a car pulling up, someone honks the horn, and Consuelo hands the joint to Alexis.

"Alright, be back tonight. Gotta get to the shop."

Consuelo smiles and runs towards the driveway. They listen to the car speed off, finish the joint, and then go back inside. Their bags are packed next to the fold-out sofa and the laptop sits atop the duffle bag. Dylan doesn't want to open it again but can't decide what to do with the files. While she stands there gazing at it, Alexis goes into the bedroom and turns on the television.

They spend the afternoon absorbing all of the information flowing through the various screens. Dylan pulls up articles on the desktop while Alexis reclines on the bed and watches the unfolding spectacle. Dylan occasionally reads Alexis a quote from a Chumby article or explains the mechanics of the OingoBoingo mind games, but they mostly listen in silence as the newscasters and journalists fill the speakers with their analysis and commentary.

The White House Press Secretary announced that the President would issue a statement tomorrow once the leak had occurred. Peter Thiel, the CEO of Palantir, released another tweet demanding the federal government force Chumby to shut down, that Richard Fenton be arrested, and that the authorities stop the leaks before it was too late. In response, Wikileaks tweeted it was already too late for Peter Thiel and his comrades in Silicon Valley. The truth would come out and their ship would be sunk. In response to this, a prominent California Senator accused Julian Assange and Wikileaks of exhibiting more of their blatant misogyny by endangering the lives of federal employees with the impending release. She asked the public to remember Assange's behavior prior to the election and that Wikileaks is still under the sway of Russia.

The television informs Dylan that Bilton Smyth has requested permanent asylum in Switzerland and soon the broadcast is filled with details of how the ex-CEO refuses to leave his hotel in Zurich. In a series of frantic tweets, Smyth claimed that he was entrapped by the federal government, that the new President fully militarized the secret program, and that he would gladly tell Geneva and Brussels every-thing he knew about the surveillance network and how it operated. Bilton Smyth later tweeted that he only went along with GSX because the committee forced him. He did not specify what committee he was referring to.

The newscasters briefly narrate the long and chaotic path of this "serial entrepreneur" before switching to a panel discussion with an ex-CIA agent and two liberal Senators from San Francisco. When asked what he thought of Bilton Smyth, the ex-CIA agent tells the newscaster that the ex-CEO is an agent of Russia and should have been charged with high treason after he sabotaged the deal with China. This makes the Senators begin to yell over him before the panel descends into chaos and CNN switches to a pre-recorded seg-ment on how OingoBoingo gathered intimate personal data for the surveillance network.

"They're losing their minds," Alexis says. "On CNN! They can't even keep it together on fucking CNN. That's how bad this is. What the fuck? I mean, this is bringing everything down. Fast! It's like Ricky just silently arranged all this—"

"You never met Luz? The lady who organized your escape demo?"

"No, never. I been to her shows. I'd seen her once before on my own. And then Ricky took me to this big show but she was already on stage and I never met her, Ricky just got me up close so I could see her. You know what I mean? Anyway, what's up with this CEO? Is he crazy? What the fuck's he talking about?"

"I don't know. I read the files where the government's paranoid about him. No one knows who he is, they think he's an anomaly, some-one who can't be predicted. Some of them even thought he was a spy. Me and Ricky used to joke he was part of the Illuminati or something."

"Maybe he is."

"There *is* no Illuminati. That's just what they call people they don't understand."

"Then who is he?"

Neither of them have an answer to this question, although by then the broadcast has shifted to a new disturbance in San Francisco. Dylan instantly stands up and Alexis begins to laugh as the screen displays a live helicopter shot of the Mission District. A giant plume of black smoke rises into the air from a luxury apartment building bathed in flames. Two police lines keep a massive crowd away from the inferno and block all traffic along Mission Street. Most of the crowd is clapping and cheering and several people hold large banners in the air. One of them reads **WE ARE WITH YOU** and is clearly directed at the helicopter camera.

It takes a moment for Dylan to realize this is where she used to live. The large glass windows of the Vermillion blacken and shatter to the ground as the metal is engulfed in tendrils of flame. Fire creeps along every angle of the structure and thick smoke rises higher than any skyscraper. The newscaster explains how the blaze was intentionally set but stops talking when the helicopter camera reveals people in masks throwing rocks at the SFPD. Dylan starts to laugh once she understands what's happening. The crowd is preventing fire trucks from reaching the Vermillion. They want to see it burn.

Later in the afternoon, while the two of them are on Consuelo's bed watching television, Alexis tells Dylan the story of almost getting thrown into a white van when she was smoking weed under a bridge. The van rolled up below the overpass and a bearded guy in a trucker hat jumped out with black leather gloves on his hands. She threw a rock at him and started running so fast she couldn't see straight. She finally stopped at a corner store where the woman behind the register gave her free water and watermelon slushees and let her wait in the store until her mom came. This was around the time she dropped out of high school and never went back.

Alexis tells Dylan how she drank three Red Bull energy drinks every morning, how she wore baggy clothing to hide her body, and how she watched beautiful women disintegrate into toothless zombies or start hooking out of a motel just to get their daily dose of smack. She tells Dylan about all the bad guys with money who wanted to get inside her pants. Guys like that chased after her, some of them protected her, some of them stalked her. Alexis says she fucked them to keep a few from killing her, to get money for her mom, and because sometimes it was just too dangerous to resist. It could have been worse, she tells Dylan, she could be buried some-where in the desert.

"Why did those guys want to kill you?"

"Because I was me," Alexis says. "And I didn't want to belong to any of *them*."

"But you slept with them?"

"Sure. And I stole hella money, too! And I stayed alive, more important."

Eventually, she saved enough for her mother to get along comfort-ably, paid for a Craigslist ride to her cousin's house in Pasadena, and started her new life on the fringes of Hollywood. Alexis explains how empty porn made her feel after a few months, how horrible some of the men were, how it made her distant from herself and her body. Alexis explains how she used artificial lubricants between scenes and describes the contrived sounds she emoted according to script. She stopped doing those types of movies after a while and started making money through her multiple webcam accounts. It earned her much less but at least it was consistent and she got to work from home.

Every few months, she would take some guy home and try to feel something but it never worked and the guys just kept calling back. When she got bored, she found a gangster from East Los Angeles to ride around with for a few months but never told him her real name or where she lived. While she was with him, Alexis saw shootings and stabbings. She learned how the urban underworld operated, she learned how to break into a house, and she learned how the gangs fought with each other over flows of capital and territories of distri-bution. It got too dangerous in the end so she disappeared back to Pasadena. That's when she started to date women.

"It happened real easily," she tells Dylan. "One of my cousin's friends came over, my cousin went to sleep, then we got together in my bedroom. She was cool but she couldn't be open about it, not with her family. They were real Catholic, conservative."

"So she was a naughty Catholic schoolgirl? Like, a real one?"

Alexis starts smirking at this question and Dylan feels her face flush red with blood. She gets off the bed and opens up the window to let in the breeze. Outside, a group of swallows circle the lettuce fields and occasionally chirp to each other as they shift direction in unison.

When Dylan finally turns around, Alexis is patting the bed with her hand.

"Don't worry, you can come back. I won't bite."

She lays back down and let's Alexis hold her close.

"I guess Catholic girls get me excited," Dylan says. "Must be a WASP thing."

"There are so many bad ass ex-Catholic girls in LA, I can't even tell you. But yeah, I started going to punk shows and dyke bars and met a lot of girls like that, started learning about all this new stuff, anarchism, feminism, how to survive in the woods. I stopped sleeping with men down there, for a while. So, yeah, LA was cool, I liked it, but then I found out how much money I could make dating johns up in Silicon Valley. I mean, yeah, I could have stayed with my cousin forever, her family was chill, but I wanted something else, I needed to get away from the desert finally, a place where nobody knew me."

"Did one of those guys ever—"

Alexis pushes back, looks Dylan in the eye, and then shakes her head.

"There just aren't words for it," she says, slowly. "I had to get far away. Even the gangster guy in LA found out I was at the dyke bars, he started sniffing around by the time I left. I went in a car with a couple of my anarchist friends, they drove me up to San Francisco and introduced me to a whole house of crazy people. They were brilliant, I never met anyone like them before, they didn't give two shits about the law or what people thought. And they were smart, they had books everywhere, they smoked weed, they did martial arts and shit, they shot guns out in the mountains and built little cabins in the woods, places they could live for free. They helped me get my GED, helped me get into City College, introduced me to all these people. We loved each other. You know? They saw me, they really did. They got to know who I really was, who I've always been."

"Are these your friends? The ones who left?"

"Some of them. And before they left, you know, we fucked some shit up. We really did. I mean, I know how to put on a disguise, I know how to act, I know what's up, and so did they, all of them knew how to do everything. I mean, it was *together* that we knew how to do every-thing. I threw down money for all sorts of shit because it made work less of a burden for me, it made it all have a purpose."

"I know what you mean now," Dylan says. "Everything I just did, buying the car— "

Alexis nods frantically and suppresses her own laughter. She shifts on the bed and props herself up by the palms, never once taking her eyes off Dylan. Her bright green pupils burn with light. The excitement is infectious.

"I know!" she cries. "Right? You threw your blood money at what you hated. You just went and did it, you spent what you needed to sink those fuckers. For my friends and I, you know, it only lasted so long as we were together, as long as we had something in common. At first, it was like we were unstoppable, you know, rolling along with everything, making headlines, organizing demos. We all said we were building the commune, but not like the old hippies. That shit just turned into the internet. We were starting over. That's what we all thought, but then the infighting kicked off. I was working this whole time, but once people were swinging on each other and acting like cops I was done, I just stayed to myself, started working more. I saw my friend knock out our buddy for no fucking reason, for some rumor spread by the pigs. Then it got worse, then people took sides, and I swear, some of those people were Feds the whole time. Or secret police. Who knows who they worked for?"

"GSX," Dylan says, flatly. "I'm sure of it. They have these operatives in the case studies, people who go into the real world and make things happen."

"Does it have their names?"

Dylan nods, grimly. She looks towards the living room and the laptop sitting atop her duffel bag. They lay there another moment, the babble of television fills the apartment, and neither of them get up from the bed. Alexis lowers her head to her arms and closes her eyes while Dylan watches footage of riot police being chased down Mission street by a mob of angry rioters. The Vermillion burns behind them, its structure partially collapsed.

"There were files towards the end about that," Dylan says. "They were files about anti-subversion programs, a lot of reports written by operatives. I mean, like, there were a ton, it looked pretty extensive, but I skimmed them, I didn't—"

"Don't worry," Alexis hums. "We'll all find out tomorrow. When people learn how these secret police operate, when they find out who they're dealing with, how this is a regime—"

Alexis doesn't finish, she only shakes her head.

"Pamela mentioned something about people's children," Dylan says. "She told me they were like free workers for GSX."

"Yeah, I met some weird ass rich kids, for sure, up to all sorts of shit."

"We could look in the files. They're right over there. Those files are big, too, I'm sure—"

"No. We need to destroy that shit. Once you talk to Natasha, we need to smash the hard drive, drill a hole through it, throw the pieces into a big bonfire so they melt, then bury it. I don't want to know the details because trust me, I already know what they did to us, I just didn't know *how* they did it. This is why I got on smack, thinking how pointless it all was, how easy it was to destroy. I got so depressed all I could think about was money, started dating a heroin dealer, got to know more rich techie fucks, guys from Google, BoonDoggle, Palantir, Twitter, Facebook. Sometimes I tricked myself into thinking I was gathering info on them but I didn't do anything with it, I just took their money and rode around in fancy cars and stayed in mansions and got smacked out all day."

"Alexis—"

Dylan holds her tightly, wanting to keep her close, where she's safe.

"And then I met Ricky on Seeking Arrangement," Alexis says, closing her eyes in comfort. "I went on a date with him, then I got clean. I liked him, you know, we met off the books, we talked about cool shit. My dad was from Mexico so we got close over that, too. It's not like Ricky *got* me clean, I got *myself* clean, but he gave me something, some hope I guess. My dad died when I was little so I never had those connections, I just know his family was from Mexico City but I never met them. Ricky helped me with that, the world made a bit more sense when he talked about it like he did, as an outsider. You know how he called you *güera*?"

"Yeah?"

"He called me *blanquita*, somtimes. Little white Latin girl, but nice, you know?"

"Do you remember something from back then? Do you remember him talking about China?"

Alexis opens her eyes and stares at the flickering screen.

"That's *all* he was talking about back then. About how the deal collapsed, you mean?"

"So he met you *after* that?"

Dylan hears Alexis gulp. Both of their hearts are pounding.

"Yeah," she finally mutters. "Why? Tell me."

Dylan begins to cry. She waits to catch her breath and then puts her mouth above Alexis' ear.

"He *found* you," she whispers. "Do you understand? He *found* you—"

Alexis suddenly takes Dylan's arm and starts to laugh.

"Did he? Or am I a witch? Maybe I found *him*."

"*Are* you a witch?"

"Don't you get it yet?" Alexis bolts upright and gets off the bed. "So are you!"

"How am I a witch?"

"How are you *not*?" Alexis laughs loudly. "Look at what you've done!"

Dylan can't respond to this, nor can she laugh. She doesn't know how. The light of the television screen bleeds into the room and Dylan is blinded by a thought so bright it paralyzes her entire body. When it passes, the laughter still echoes through the room and Dylan can only hold Alexis tighter for fear of losing it. Both of them know the truth at this moment, a secret of recognition that will never be deciphered. Alexis grins at Dylan until she finally smiles back. There's no fear of what just occurred, no anger in her green eyes. Nothing is wrong at this moment. Everything is good.

Consuelo walks them through the darkness to the backstairs of the main house. The kitchen is filled with laughter and the rich smells of spiced soup boiling on the stove. All the sisters hover around their mother and her boiling pot while their father sits alone in his sandals at the kitchen table, spinning a glass of water on the polished wood. The sisters embrace Dylan and Alexis and pass them along like royalty. None of the family speaks English or Spanish, they carry on in Tzotzil while their visitors stand silently atop the linoleum.

What comes next is something neither of them will remember. It passes in flashes, like sleep interrupted over a long night of thunder. Dylan eats the rich soup and listens to the ancient language flood the dining room. She holds Alexis' hand underneath the table and smiles at everyone uncontrollably. She feels no need to speak. They'll both remember a strong flame burning in the fire place. They'll remember it being the only light. All of the sisters were bathed in the glow of these flames as their mother squatted before the coals. She slowly became the only figure in an endless room. No longer young or old, no longer anyone in particular, this woman told them something they cannot remember, no matter how hard they try.

And then events become clearer. Dylan stands with Alexis and Consuelo at the edge of the lettuce field. She hears the sound of crickets and smells the piercing salt of the ocean. This is the last time she'll ever see this particular darkness, under these specific stars. This land is now utterly familiar. It feels like yesterday and the day before that. It feels as if they have been standing at the edge of this lettuce field forever, waiting for something that has only just arrived.

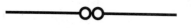

Dylan hears Consuelo making coffee for them at 5:00 in the morning. Consuelo's already dressed, her hair is combed, and she's wide awake. Dylan and Alexis groggily get out of bed and start folding up the sheets and blankets. Consuelo pours them coffee and leaves the cream carton on the counter. They fold the bed into the couch and then fumble into their clothes. Alexis puts on jeans and a sweatshirt. Dylan puts on a black dress and black leggings. They go into the kitchen with messy hair and bleary eyes and stand alongside Consuelo with their steaming coffees. Each of them stare blankly at different objects in the room. Through the kitchen window, Dylan can hear the chirp of birds as they fly invisibly through the darkness. The caffeine begins to wake her up.

"Maybe one day," Consuelo says. "We'll see each other again."

"How?" Dylan asks. "When?"

"After all this shit's over, when the world's started to heal. I don't know."

"Everything just changed, though," Alexis says. "We might see each other sooner than not."

"Not until this system dies," Consuelo says. "Not until we don't have to live like this anymore, running around like little starving foxes in the woods. It's not a way to live."

"We'll be fine," Alexis says. "I'll take care of Dylan."

"Shit, girl, she'll be taking care of *you*," Consuelo laughs. "Unless *you* got all your millions stashed away somewhere."

"Just the $7000 I took out of the bank." Alexis looks at Dylan nervously. "We haven't talked about money, I hate talking about money, I just—"

"I *will* take care of you," Dylan says firmly. "That's not even a question. Consuelo, was it even a question you'd help us out?"

"Nope," she responds flatly, staring at Alexis. "Not a question at all."

"You've got nothing to worry about," Dylan says.

"But how are you gonna get your money out?"

"I'll just go to my downtown Chase. I'll be wearing this dress, I'll have make up on, and I'll wear my silver jacket. Just like I always look. They'll give it to me, trust me. I've been in there a couple times about getting a house loan. They never quite talked me into it, even though I qualified. They'll recognize me, don't worry. I'll get it."

"What, in cash?" Alexis looks confused. "You're gonna walk out of there with a bag of cash?"

"That's right, and then into a taxi. Then we'll get the fuck out of there."

"Are you crazy?"

Even Consuelo is looking at Dylan quizzically, unsure of what she's hearing.

"No, I'm not crazy. We *need* this money. We'll never get it again. And I have every reason to want to flee San Francisco. I'll just tell them the truth, that my building burnt down."

Alexis and Consuelo look at each other and begin to laugh. The tension leaves the kitchen and they finish their coffee with smiles on their faces. They discuss the plan further, fill in the missing details, and grow comfortable with this last moment of vulnerability. When they're done with their coffee, Alexis and Dylan start loading their bags into the back of the Audi wagon. The first shades of violet have already entered the eastern edge of the horizon and the morning air is cold and misty. It makes Dylan feel alive.

She opens up the compartment for the spare tire, places the laptop at the bottom, and then piles the bags on top of it. When everything is arranged perfectly, she closes the trunk and turns around to see Consuelo. Dylan is already crying when the sister takes her by the waist and whispers something in Tzotzil that fills her with a happiness she doesn't understand.

"Stay free," she says. "Stay safe."

Consuelo lets go of Dylan, kisses Alexis on the cheek, and then walks inside her apartment without looking back. She closes the front door, turns off the porch light, and leaves them shrouded in the last darkness of the morning.

Alexis climbs into the passenger seat of the Audi while Dylan glances at the keys in her hand. The old laser-clicker from 1993 no longer opens the door locks. She clicks it again and again to make sure it doesn't work. When she's satisfied that it's truly broken, Dylan gets inside the car and adjusts the rear-view mirror. Alexis caresses the back of her head, watches Dylan put the key in the ignition, and laughs when the engine starts. Up above them is an expanse of purple clouds tinged red at the horizon. Dylan drives towards these colors with her headlights on until she reaches the highway. She doesn't get lost. Not once.

Alexis says they should drive up the coast. She's very insistent. Dylan's worried about being late and doesn't want anything to interfere with meeting Natasha so she does her best to discourage this plan. Dylan wants to take the direct route over the Santa Cruz Mountains but when Alexis remembers the meeting is at 9:00 am she points at the dashboard clock and insists there's time to see the ocean. She hates the sight of Silicon Valley and could go her entire life without seeing that worthless section of the 101 ever again. So they drive north through Santa Cruz into the strawberry farms and cypress trees perched above the ocean. The sun rises over the coastal hills, the morning fog burns off under the heat, and when they reach the small town of Davenport the entire car is bathed in sunlight.

Dylan keeps looking at the digital clock but Alexis tries to distract her by monologuing on the beauty and majesty of the ocean. It took her nineteen years to finally make it to Venice Beach and see the Pacific for the first time. Alexis fell in love with the ocean after that. All she'd ever known was desert. She points at the beautiful blues and greens and silvers of the coastline and describes the different coastal plants. She marvels at the power of the crashing waves and tries her best to distract Dylan from the digital clock. Dylan appreciates the effort but can only think in mathematical equations. If she travels the maximum speed limit, she'll reach San Francisco just after 8:00 am. There will be enough time to find parking, put on makeup, and make her way to Greenwich Alley on Telegraph Hill. She knows these facts to be true, she could enjoy the grandness of the ocean and still make it on time, but in the end she resigns herself to the fact that only Alexis is meant to enjoy this coastline right now. No matter how hard she tries, Dylan cannot calm down.

Her stress begins to decrease when they descend a winding stretch of highway into the coastal town of Pacifica. The mileage signs inform Dylan that San Francisco is close, the speed limit increases, and she merges onto the 280 freeway just before entering Daly City. Alexis points in the direction of her old apartment and tells Dylan about her roommates. It was their names on the lease. One of them was a bartender, the other worked for a catering company. Neither of them dated men. They'd met at a dyke bar called the Lexington before it closed. It was the last lesbian bar in the city. Neither of her roommates were anarchists, nor did they know anything about that side of her life. They knew what Alexis did for work, they knew she would defend them in a bar fight, and they knew she would pay her rent. Dylan asks if she'll miss them and Alexis just shrugs. She says maybe.

They get off the 280 freeway near the baseball stadium and when Dylan checks the digital clock it reads 8:14 am. She drives the Audi along the Embarcadero as the road curves underneath the steel ribs of the old

Bay Bridge. The Embarcadero roadway parallels the waterfront and takes them around the towering blocks of the Financial District while the shifting waters of the bay appear in glimpses of vision between the piers and wharves that line the shore. They pass the Mozilla headquarters, they pass the downtown Google office, and they pass beneath the clock tower of the Ferry Building with its metal hands reading 8:21 am.

"Where you going to park the car?" Alexis asks.

"Somewhere with no cameras."

"Yeah, duh, but where?"

"Somewhere close."

"What about there?

Alexis points left and Dylan pulls the car off the Embarcadero and onto Green Street. The road dead-ends at a giant outcropping of tan rock surrounded by a fence and lined with trees. Standing above this rock is the southern slope of Telegraph Hill. There are no cameras on any of the buildings. Dylan turns the car around at the dead end and parks in the first open space. Both of them get out, stretch their limbs, and hug each other in the street. Dylan doesn't waste much time after this. She opens the trunk, gets out her makeup, and pulls an unopened wig from the duffel bag.

"Where'd you get all those?" Alexis asks.

"I was going to have a party once. But I never did."

"Let me see the blonde one you used."

"No!" Dylan zips up the bag. "Come on, I need to hurry."

Alexis sits in the passenger seat while Dylan use the rear-view mirror to put on thick black eye liner. She opens up a new brown wig and Alexis helps her adjust it. When she puts on the lens-less sunglasses, Dylan appears to be someone much younger. Alexis takes off her black sweatshirt and insists Dylan put it on, saying it'll complete the look. She gets out on the street where Alexis judges her new appearance and nods in approval.

"It's perfect," she says. "You look like a high school goth chick. Like a sad little baby."

"You sure?"

"I'm sure. Trust me, I wouldn't recognize you."

Dylan smiles and looks at the dashboard clock. The small numbers read 8:43 am but Alexis lights a cigarette and tosses the pack in front of the glowing digits. She blows the smoke high into the air and wraps her arms around the baggy sweatshirt.

"I need to go," Dylan whispers.

"I know." Alexis kisses her cheek. "Go to it."

Dylan puts the keys in her lover's hand and runs around the corner without looking back. She stays to the left of Sansome Street and walks underneath the cypress trees lining the slim gap between the slope and the parked cars. On this block, Telegraph Hill is lined by metal nets and cement retaining walls erected to obstruct landslides and stop boulders from hitting the vehicles. Above these impediments are dozens of wild Pride of Madeira flowers growing vigorously from the earth. Dylan can hear hummingbirds buzzing around these green and purple flowers as loose soil crunches beneath her shoes. The fences and walls can't stop these gentle flows of dirt and sandstone from reaching the concrete. Some of the hill always slips through.

She passes a long block of buildings with her head cast downward and doesn't look up until she reaches Greenwich Alley. There are no police waiting for her and no cameras on any of the buildings. She walks towards the long cement staircase and passes the entrance to an underground parking garage. From the corner of her eye, Dylan sees two closed-circuit cameras facing the garage door that she didn't notice before. Neither of them can see her. There's no reason to worry.

She holds onto the metal handrail and climbs the steps through the tunnel of trees that surround Greenwich Alley. Her body begins to heat up, sweat gathers on her back, and she breathes heavily without realizing it. At the top of the steps is the flat stretch of concrete that extends to the second retaining wall. Dylan searches for Natasha between the trees and cactus and creeping ivy. She expects to see her hiding behind a bush or atop a boulder or sitting on a rickety bench but finds only an empty garden stretching up the slope.

Dylan pauses for a moment to listen but all she hears is wind. She climbs the dirt path to the retaining wall and sits down on the grass where she slept the week before. She glimpses Yerba Buena Island through the trees and sees the towers of the Bay Bridge standing over the water. She watches the ferry boats sail past and the seagulls chase each other across the blue sky. There's a chance she's arrived early so Dylan doesn't panic, not at first. Her breathing calms, her heart slows, and she begins to imagine Alexis smoking a cigarette in the Audi or listening to the radio with the windows rolled down. She wants to be in bed with her lover. She wants them both to be safe, somewhere far away from this city. But soon it occurs to her that Natasha has either been arrested or forgotten about their meeting. Her heart pounds, the sweat returns to her back, and Dylan begins to panic. There's no way for her to know how much time passes in this state. She tries to breath through the fear, to calm it into submission and listen only to the wind.

But then she hears the clatter of aluminum cans. It draws closer and closer until eventually Dylan sees an old Chinese woman coming down the steps with two plastic bags strung at the ends of a smooth wooden pole. Each bag is filled with dozens of crushed aluminum cans. She carries the middle of the pole atop her shoulder with the cans balanced in the air. Her head is covered in a red hood, her back is hunched, and she can't lift her eyes easily. Dylan admires all the weight this woman's shoulders have carried over the years, all the steps her legs have climbed, and all the cans she's redeemed throughout her journeys.

The woman pauses at the bottom of the steps and coughs loudly. Now she's ten feet from Dylan and the crushed aluminum cans scrape against the cement retaining wall. The old woman's face slowly comes into view. Beneath the hood is someone with black hair and green eyes who looks just like Natasha Malevich.

"It's me," she mutters. "Is anyone here?"

"No. No one."

Natasha glances around the hillside, climbs the dirt path to the grass, and sets her cans down by the retaining wall. They hide out of sight and squat low over the ground. Natasha is almost panting. She opens her mouth but is unable to convey anything other than the excitement burning behind her eyes. Dylan hugs Natasha until her breathing slows and she's able to speak.

"We did it," Natasha whispers. "We fucking did it."

"This disguise is amazing." Dylan tugs on her red hood and the tattered clothing. "You had me convinced you were an old Chinese woman."

"Yeah, well, my boss didn't want me to come, he said I was being set up to take the fall."

DARLINGTONIA

"No! He did?"

"Can you blame him? He had me ten percent convinced, but I trust you. He still thought it was a risk until I showed him this disguise. Here, feel, I got an airplane pillow on my back."

Dylan presses the soft hunch on her back and starts to laugh.

"It's genius!" she says.

"No, you're a genius! Russia's really lucky."

Dylan's face suddenly sinks and the air begins to feel cold.

"I don't work for Russia, I—"

"Okay, okay, sorry, that's all I needed. Come on, please, this is *the* heaviest shit to ever be released. *The* heaviest. Can you blame me? You heard what happened this morning, right?"

Dylan realizes she didn't listen to the radio during the drive north. The thought never occurred to her. She listened to Alexis talk, counted the miles to San Francisco, and read the digital clock, but not once did she have the desire to know what was happening. This sudden realization makes Dylan feel proud of herself.

"No, I haven't checked anything."

"You know this person Pamela, this UC Berkeley professor who worked for GSX? She seems to have gotten up this morning, walked into a restaurant in the Marina around 7:00, and shot a CIA agent in the head. And then she just ran, she's gone, they still can't find her. I don't know how you got here but the Marina is filled with police and Feds, all the big tech guys already split, Peter Thiel caught a plane, Andreesen's gone, Eric Schmidt left, no one can find Tim Cook."

For a moment, Dylan wants to vomit until she suddenly feels happy.

"Wait, Pamela just killed a—"

"Someone connected to the program. *The Washington Post* says he was one of the Silicon Valley recruiters for GSX. I don't know, but that's who she killed. She went out to this breakfast spot, knew exactly where he was going to be, and just shot him in the head with no disguise, blew his brains out on camera so people would know it was her."

"No!"

"Yes! She did! I saw it on my burner phone during the drive over to Chinatown. Don't worry, its in the car with the battery out. I just had to see, I had to make sure it all got leaked. And it did. Last I checked, everything was going wild. Anyway, when Pamela was done, after she shot the guy, I swear on my life, she takes out a piece of paper and holds it up to the surveillance camera. You know what it said? It said *I WILL KILL ALL OF YOU*. Just like that, and then she left."

Dylan brings her knees to her chest and lowers her head. She remembers the jogging outfit she wore to confront Pamela and the long walk they took into the dry hills. She remembers the piercing scent of eucalyptus leaves and the warmth of the sun beating down on her back. She sees the thirsty coyote approaching them through the grass. She remembers its piercing yellow eyes.

"What's wrong?"

"Nothing, it's just—"

"What—"

"Nothing. I shouldn't say, it's best you—"

"You need to run. You need to get the fuck out of here, quickly. You *told* me you were going to find out who killed Ricky. And it looks like you did! You see what I mean? It's not like I think you're a Russian spy for *no* reason. You went out there and...I don't want to know anything, nothing, don't tell me, but I know you got up to something when you left here last time, and you probably weren't careful. Hold on!" She grabs Dylan's arm before she can panic. "Don't freak out. You're fine! Trust me. I found something, the team found something. It's Chad. All of it leads to Chad, we found a whole folder of his emails and he sounds pissed, he resents not being promoted, he thinks Ricky is taking all the credit. And then he starts saying things like if people only knew. He even says Ricky is going to pay for being so cocky. Pay! Chad says this! Ricky put it all in a file, like a surveillance file, as if the director was monitoring Chad directly. I mean, maybe he was."

"This is fucking crazy, Natasha..."

"Your friend is amazing, rest in peace. This is all so—"

Natasha doesn't finish her words. She fluffs her dark hair from beneath the hood while Dylan leans back against the retaining wall and watches the wind move through the branches. A flock of green birds darts across the blue sky and the soil starts to feel warm as the sun bathes the garden in light. The day promises to be clear and beautiful.

"But you still need to run," Natasha says. "Because of Noisebridge."

"I know."

"It's the weak link. Those guys still don't have a court date, it was supposed to be today but they moved it because of the leaks. Last I heard, they still haven't said anything. The story kind of got buried, but after today it'll come back up. The President's gonna try and find the source of the leak, just watch. It's the only way they can distract from what's coming."

"Have you read all the files?" Dylan asks.

Natasha just nods, her eyes glowing with knowledge.

"Yep. This is going to destroy the government, it's going to force everyone to act."

"I hope Pamela gets away."

"Fuck! I know!" Natasha digs a pack of cigarettes out of her shirt pocket. "Want one?"

Dylan takes a cigarette and both of them puff silently for a few moments in silence. Dylan crosses her legs and pretends to enjoy it. The cigarette makes her heart beat faster and her nerves feel numb. She doesn't find it very relaxing but keeps smoking anyway. Dylan wants to celebrate.

"I've been smoking a lot," Natasha says. "We're all up in San Bruno, writing emails, sending the tech guy out on runs to post articles. Real *clandestino*. Just like that book you bought when we first met. We're living all cramped up like they were."

"Stressful?"

"Sure, but it's also the most exciting moment of my life. And listen...it's *all* going to be released, you know? People are going to know GSX thinks you're autistic, they'll know the details about all sorts of random people, their porn habits, their emotional problems, their mental disabilities, their psychological disorders, their political beliefs, their arguments with their partners. It's not that many people, less than 10,000, but I would have taken that stuff out."

"I didn't have time."

"Well, it's what you wanted, I agreed to it, and believe me, I *fought* for it. They still think it's a bad idea, but I just told them you'd release it in full if we didn't agree and our scoop would be blown."

"And that worked?"

"Perfectly. And now we get to scold Wikileaks. We get to look responsible."

They puff away and watch the smoke get ripped apart by the wind. The sun keeps rising and bathes new parts of the hill in light. The flock of green birds reappears and settles on the branches of a cypress tree. Dylan starts to feel the nicotine in her blood. It makes the world seem to glow.

"I love this hill," Natasha says. "My dad used to tell me about it. He read about this city, all these old letters from Russian sailors. The wildest women used to live up here above the port. Right down there, actually, to the left. There used to be this house, it's gone now, right where that tree is. It was a little blue house that three women lived in. You could call them royalty almost, rebel women, the kind that aren't in the history books, the ones hidden between the lines. I only know about them through my dad and his folk tales about San Francisco. They were real life witches. That's what he says. This was their hill. I swear they're still here. Can you feel them?"

"Maybe. But I can't tell anymore. Not after what we did."

"Exactly. Maybe it's the same thing. Like we got possessed last time we were here. I'm serious." Natasha laughs and grabs Dylan's hand. "Those women are still here. Their ghosts are inside us. But whatever, I'm all loopy from no sleep, I'm sure. You either believe or you don't."

"No, I do. Trust me, I do. What happened after I left here, it was—"

Natasha waits for Dylan to finish but nothing else comes out.

"It was big, right?" she asks. "You fucking ended this, didn't you? That's what you did."

Dylan nods her head when she realizes this is true.

"You're right, I ended it" she tells Natasha. "Maybe something took me over."

"Of course it did. I don't know how we pulled this off, but we did. And now you need to run. Now. Right now. Here, take this." Natasha takes a piece of paper out of her pocket and hands it to her. "In one year send me a postcard at this address. Just let me know you're okay. Please?"

"I will. I promise."

"We won, Dylan. The whole world is going to change. Thanks to you."

"And to Ricky. But no one will ever know about him, will they?"

Natasha frowns, stubs out her cigarette, and puts the dirty filter in her pocket.

DARLINGTONIA

"No," she says. "They can't. It *has* to be Chad. And it definitely can't be us."

"When are you going to come out of hiding?" Dylan asks.

"Let's see how today goes. Maybe soon. But you need to run. Get to where you're going, make sure it's a good place, but *run* there. Get there soon, before they come looking. Stay hidden. You're a miracle, Dylan, a fucking miracle. I don't know what you are, I thought maybe you were a dream, but you're real, somehow you're real."

Natasha reaches out and holds Dylan tight. She rocks her back and forth and begins to cry in happiness. She mutters something about joy, something about feeling whole again. Dylan knows almost nothing about this woman in her arms. There was never any reason for them to trust each other but it happened anyway. They discovered a perfection neither could have imagined. It isn't sadness or regret that makes Dylan cry along with Natasha, nor is it happiness. She cries because the beauty and grace of this moment will never come again.

The black taxi pulls up in front of the Chase Bank on California Street. Dylan opens the door and steps out onto the curb. She's still in her black dress but has taken off her leggings and baggy sweatshirt. Now her hair is up in a small bun, she wears her silver jacket with black boots, and her eyelids are painted a light blue. Alexis waves to Dylan, blows her a kiss as the door closes, and keeps listening to the radio along with the taxi driver.

Dylan opens the glass doors and walks directly to the bank manager's private desk. He's a middle-aged man dressed in a nice blue suit. He recognizes her immediately and begins to smile but then notices Dylan's watery eyes. He asks her to sit down and she explains that her apartment building burned down yesterday, she needs to close her account, and she wants to withdraw her balance in cash.

"It's over $300,000, Miss Kinsey."

"Don't you have it?" she asks, wiping her eyes. "I need to go—"

"Miss Kinsey—"

"Please, my building has been attacked twice, I'm done—"

"Of course, Miss Kinsey, but we don't have that much cash. I can authorize maybe a third of that amount, the rest will have to be in—"

"I don't care." She sucks the snot back into her nose as the tears flow down her cheeks. "I just need to go. Close my account, let me get the hell out of this—"

"I'm sorry, Miss Kinsey, we'll get you out of here as soon as possible. I know it's a stressful moment but we're all trying to keep it together. You heard about what happened in the Marina just—"

"Please, I want to leave! Can we get this done quickly?"

The manager looks at his lap just as the cashiers and customers turn their heads away from Dylan's yelling. After this pause, the manager opens multiple screens on his computer, unbuttons his suit jacket, and starts typing on the keyboard. Dylan uses the tissues on his desk to wipe her cheeks. He makes a motion to offer them but she looks away until he starts typing again.

"Have you heard anything else about the shooting?" she asks.

"They still haven't caught her. A *professor*?"

"Nothing surprises me, not anymore."

She says this last sentence flatly and with no emotion. The manager keeps typing into the blank fields and Dylan gazes up at the high ceilings of the bank. Soft fluorescent light spills onto the carpets, several customers wait in line, and one of them begins to argue with the teller. She's in a similar situation. She wants to leave San Francisco immediately.

"Hell of a day." The desk printer spits out a few forms and the manager starts to fill them out. "I understand why you want to leave. Those leaks are probably out by now. I don't know, I haven't looked at the madness yet."

"You still have your smartphone?"

The manager stops writing, checks to see if anyone's watching, then he shakes his head.

"No. I leave it at home now. I hardly use it. You?"

"Same. It freaked me out."

The manager shakes his head again and continues filling out the forms. When he's done, Dylan signs her name in the last boxes, the manager takes the forms behind the counter, and when he returns there's a printed receipt affirming that her account is officially closed, the balance paid out in full.

DARLINGTONIA

"I thought you said—"

"I lied." The manager says. "I had to try. We've got that much money, of course we do. And given the way things are going today, there might be a run on the banks. I'm serious," he says, glancing behind her. "Anyway, I already took my own money out and feel like a hypocrite telling you no, you can't have your money. Corporate hasn't told me not to do this yet, so I might as well give it to you while we have the chance."

As he says this, a male bank employee approaches the desk with a large blue satchel emblazoned with the Chase logo. The manager counts it out for her on the desk and then stuffs it all back inside the bag. Dylan runs her fingers across the $10,000 bundles, tightens up the satchel, and then gets up from her chair.

"Is that it?" she asks

"That's it," he says, suppressing a smirk. "First time I've ever handed over $300,000 in a bag. You want the guard to follow you out?"

"Please, I know it's only a few feet, but—"

The manager beckons over the black-clad security guard. While they wait, he shakes Dylan's hand and tells her to stay safe. She looks at his suit, notices the lines around his eyes, and sees his belt buckle shine in the fluorescent light. She says goodbye to him and follows the guard across the bank towards the large glass doors. He walks her to the black taxi with his hand on his pistol, the holster unfastened. He tells her to have a good day when he opens the car door. He also tells her to stay safe.

Alexis is smoking a menthol cigarette out the other window. She smiles at the bag of money, waits until the door closes, and then covers Dylan with kisses. The driver looks away from the mirror and tries to ignore what he's seeing. He listens to the radio explain how multiple news organizations have begun analyzing the 17.8 GB of data just posted online by Wikileaks. In a tweet published at 9:11 am, Wikileaks stated it was experiencing a cyber-attack and would publish the material as soon as possible. In a tweet published at 9:27 am, a link to the full 17.8 GB was provided along with a statement declaring that the full GSX files had also been successfully downloaded by *Der Spiegel* and Russia Today. At 9:37 am, *The Washington Post* reported that Pamela Gustafson had been employed by both UC Berkeley and

GSX. The man Pamela murdered was one of her colleagues, someone she'd known quite well.

While Alexis waits in the Audi, Dylan crosses the street and walks over to a payphone. They're parked in the Richmond District just south of the Golden Gate Bridge. Dylan has one final task to accomplish before she can leave the city. She drops four quarters into the old machine, dials the secure land-line in Greenwich, Connecticut, and waits for the connection. The phone rings twice before her father picks up.

"Dylan? Ruth! It's Dylan! Ruth?"

She hears her father leave his office, after which there's a loud cough and a soft click.

"Dylan?" her mom asks. "We were so worried!"

"Hi, mom. How are you two?"

"How are *we*?" her father asks. "Dylan, I heard about your trouble. It's all fixed."

"Were you inside the building when the fire started?" her mother asks.

"No, I'm fine. I haven't been there since the riot."

"I cleared that trouble up for you," her father says. "I was personally offended they suspected you of anything. It won't come up again. I fixed everything. But, listen, Dylan—"

"Dad! I'm fine. Trust me. I'm just glad I made it out of that building, out of this life."

"We saw you withdrew all your money," her mother says. "Is *that* what this is? You're starting your new life somewhere else?"

"I can't be here. Just look at what's going on."

"I understand," her father says. "I've never seen anything like it. You know they were in our system. I just read it online, that's what I'm doing now. GSX compromised our—"

"You sold it, dear. It's not *your*—"

"*The* system, they got inside *the* system! They accessed thousands of medical records."

"It's unbelievable," Dylan says. "The scope of it makes my head hurt."

"Are you getting a new phone?" her mother asks. "Or is it just email now?"

"Probably just email. I'll try to get out there and see you, but I'm—"

"It's your life, sweetheart," her father says. "Do what you need to do. We love you. We're not asking questions."

"I might not come back east for a while."

"Don't worry. We'll come to you," her mother says. "Whenever is a good time, wherever you are. It's your life and we don't want to hold you back in anything. I don't know what it's like to be your age right now, in this world."

"Just stay out of trouble," her father says.

"Okay, I will. I love you. Thanks for fixing this."

"I love you, sweetheart. It wasn't anything, no big deal."

"We love you," her mother says. "We're always here."

After they say goodbye, her father hangs up the phone and goes back to reading the leaked files on his computer. His office window overlooks the vast green lawn and sprawling woods that surround their Greenwich mansion. A green desk lamp glows beside a small French-press and a half-filled cup of lukewarm coffee that he's forgotten to keep drinking. The sky is cloudy and gray but his wood-paneled office is warm, just as Dylan always remembered it being.

While he reads on the computer, Ruth remains on the phone in her vast library at the end of the hall. She sits on a red chair with a book in her lap, the same red chair Dylan loved to climb on as a child. Behind the chair is a strong fire burning in the brick fire place. Ruth waits until her husband has hung up, keeps the phone to her ear, and waits for her daughter to speak.

"Are you there?" she finally asks Dylan.

"I'm here."

Ruth takes a deep breath, lets it out slowly, and then waits a moment longer.

"Do I need to worry about you?" she asks Dylan. "This might have been beyond your—"

"No, I've got everything under control."

"This didn't work out very well for you. Should you continue?"

"It's fine. I'm fine."

"I hope so."

Without any warning, without any further words, her mother hangs up the phone. All around her towers a world of books with over 10,000 volumes stretched along every wall. She stares into the roaring fire and listens to the dry wood crackle and snap under the flames. She's nearly 3000 miles away from her daughter. There's no way to know what Dylan's going to do, no way to tell which direction she'll go. Her mother stares into the fire for a moment longer, allows herself the faintest of smiles, and then picks up *The Red and the Black* and reads until the end of the morning.

Dylan drives the Audi across the Golden Gate Bridge and stares out at the glittering Pacific. All the windows are rolled down, the radio is switched off, and the blue bag of money is wrapped in plastic bags and hidden beside the laptop underneath the spare tire. Unlike the drive this morning, Dylan sees every grove of trees, every curve in the hillside, every swirl in the water, and every hawk spiraling in the air. Alexis is silent. She keeps her arm around Dylan's shoulders as they speed away from the bridge and blast through a tunnel with an entrance painted like a rainbow. Darkness envelopes the car, the air begins to roar, and when she emerges from the tunnel Dylan screams in joy. Alexis screams with her. They've finally escaped the city.

There are very few cars on the 101 as they pass through the city of Sausalito and reach the junction to Highway 1. Alexis lights a cigarette at the first stoplight and releases big puffs of smoke bigger than the car. The signal turns green and Dylan drives the Audi up the long winding road towards the southern foot of Mount Tamalpais. Once the cigarette is gone, the air becomes rich with the scent of eucalyptus. It makes Dylan's body melt in pleasure.

They start their descent down the hills but Dylan pulls the car over into the first turnout and turns off the engine. They get out of the Audi and follow a nearby hiking trail up a gentle brown hill covered in chaparral. A few lone cypress and oak trees stand above the brush land, a hawk cries out in some unseen canyon, and the wind moves gently through the grass. Their path winds along a flat plain that stretches westward towards the ocean. Dylan can't see the water yet but she knows it's close.

"Of course today is gorgeous!" Alexis yells. "Like summer never ended."

"Maybe it didn't. I'm already sweating."

"Good! We need to get this shit out of our systems. Come on!"

Alexis begins to sprint across the plain and Dylan follows behind. Small birds explode out of the brush and fly away in every direction. The path leads them to a crossroads but Alexis keeps running westward to where the horizon becomes lighter. Dylan imagines she's at the end of the world when she sees the endless blue of the Pacific stretching away past the horizon. From this height, the vast ocean is completely silent. She can only hear the wind, the breaths of her lover, and the beating of her own heart. There's no sound of waves.

"Look at that!" Alexis cries. "Holy Mary! I just want to jump in."

"Let's go!" Dylan pants. "Right now! Let's drive down there right now!"

"Hold on. Where are we going?"

"What do you mean?"

"Where are we going? We should know where we're going! We're both excited, but seriously, we need to know where we're going?"

"North," Dylan says. "Just north. Until we find someplace."

"Where? Like Canada? We can't cross the border without being noticed, you know?"

"No, not Canada then. We'll go to Washington and find some small town, somewhere isolated."

"But where? Do you have any idea?"

"No clue. I just know we need to get there."

"But *where*?" Alexis pleads. "Where are we going to go?"

"We need to get to the forest," Dylan says. "We need to get into the woods."

EPILOGUE

It happened on his way to work. He thinks about it now underneath the hot faucet. He remembers how a shadow fell to earth and exploded in a spray of blood and glass. He'd never seen a human body destroyed like this, pulverized by the force of gravity. The blood exploded in every direction and he slammed on the brakes before hitting it. His heart had never pounded so hard. The tiny shards of glass glittering on the road almost convinced him it was a dream.

A pool of blood was already spreading across the asphalt by the time he reached the body. He grabbed a note from the lifeless hand before the paper became thick with red. He tried to look at the destroyed body but only saw a crumpled face and protruding bones. It made him feel sick so he turned away and read the words *I'M NOT THE ONLY ONE*. He read it twice, looked at the body, and then realized something was clutched in the other hand. Before any cops could arrive, before anyone else could notice, he grabbed a thumb drive from the limp fingers and slipped it into his pocket. A few moments later, he was on his smartphone calling 911. When the call was over, he took a picture of the note and posted it on his Facebook. He provided no context for the image, not at first.

When the ambulance arrived, a small crowd had formed around the body. The police showed up soon afterwards, pushed everyone away, taped off the street, and began asking for witnesses. He volunteered immediately, told them about the note, and explained exactly what had happened. When the police were done asking questions he tried to leave but was encircled by the media and their microphones and cameras. He told them how the body fell to the pavement, how it exploded in a mist of blood, and how he found a note in the dead man's hand. He told them about finding the body of Ricardo Florez in the water, how he thought the whole region was about to erupt, and how the entire world had a fever. The media aired none of these last statements. They only wanted to hear about Ricardo Florez. They wanted to hear about the bodies. They wanted to hear about the note.

He arrived at work two hours late to discover a crowd of guests huddled around the lobby television and his coworkers off in the back room watching the morning news. He thought it was about the suicide but swiftly realized it was something else. The government had been paying a private company called GSX to monitor and manipulate the population through digital devices and social media. It also used the population in experiments designed to test theories regarding human behavior and how to modulate it. None of his coworkers looked at him when he arrived, none of them spoke to each other, and none of them knew what he'd seen until the station picked up the suicide from CNN. Only then did he tell them the story.

The first guests began to check out and immediately recognized him from the television. They asked him questions about the suicide and shook their heads in disbelief at what he said. By mid-afternoon, he'd grown tired of telling the story and couldn't wait to leave. Getting into his Mazda never felt better, nor had the anonymity of the freeway. He listened to KPFA while he drove to pick up his wife at the Verizon store and learned how the modulation programs automatically targeted the entire population of the United states. No one was exempt. Everyone was categorized in their proper place. This is when everything clicked together and the puzzle started to make sense. This is when he decided to turn off his smartphone and never power it up again.

His wife was waiting outside the Verizon store in her uniform. The store was closed early and the parking lot empty. She ran to the car and he immediately told her what happened that morning. They watched his interview on her smartphone, looked over the latest Chumby articles, and immersed themselves in the endless cascade of news and information. The main surveillance program, active as of four months ago, was named Darlingtonia. It was able to sort and monitor the population through their devices and social media. It ran multiple operations on groups and individuals, monitored every smartphone camera, recorded every conversation, and generated complex psychological profiles on every individual connected to the internet. It was run by Charles Thorpe, the man who exploded on the pavement that morning. Once they finished reading this latest article, both of them decided to get rid of their smartphones. His wife told him that not a single person had come into the store. She spent her whole day standing in an empty room.

DARLINGTONIA

As he drives to work, he remembers how they picked up their daughter that afternoon, left their smartphones in the refrigerator, loaded their bags in the car, and drove south to Santa Cruz. With the tips he'd gotten from the Chinese guests, they were able to book two nights at a waterfront hotel on a cliff overlooking the ocean. They listened to NPR while stuck in traffic and their daughter asked if the government used her tablet at school to spy on her. Her parents could only be honest. They told her yes, the government was in everything except their hearts and their minds. That was the only place it couldn't go.

After checking into the hotel and bringing their luggage to the room, the family went down to the beach and walked towards the Boardwalk. Their daughter couldn't wait to go on the roller coaster. She was finally tall enough to ride the Giant Dipper, a 90 year old wooden beast that stood above the ocean. While she chased the waves in bare feet, her parents smoked their weed vapor pen and held their hands together in peace. There were only a few people on the beach with their smartphones out. Everyone else was talking to each other, playing with their children, or just lounging on the sand in those last moments of sunlight. All of them looked happy.

While they were walking through the surf, he whispered into his wife's ear and told her about the thumbdrive. He took it out of his pocket and showed it to her. Then he put it back. He said he'd need to find a computer without a wireless card, something that wouldn't connect to the internet. She asked him what he wanted to do with it. He told her he didn't know. So they kept walking until they reached the lights of the Santa Cruz Beach Boardwalk. The sun was beginning to set and the sky above the Giant Dipper was turning red. They rode the rickety roller coaster once, twice, three times in a row. Their daughter couldn't get enough, she kept pulling them back to the entrance when the ride was over. At the end of their tenth circuit, her father bought the pictures of their faces captured by the flash of the roller coaster camera. All three of them looked joyous, their mouths open, their eyes wide.

They had dinner that night at a taqueria in downtown Santa Cruz and ate five baskets of chips along with their meals. They walked back to their hotel afterwards and lay on their beds to watch the evening news. Their daughter listened silently and intently as her parents smoked their weed vapor pen. The newscaster explained more details of the Darlingtonia program and the intricacies of how it functioned. The television displayed images of government offices and server farms, iPhone factories and Apple Stores. Every fifteen minutes, the suicide of the GSX director was mentioned, reminding the viewer that all of this had been run by a man who lived in Oakland.

While he drives along the dark highway, he remembers waking up on Saturday with his wife and daughter. The first thing they did was turn on the television and check the news. He peeked out the curtains, saw a foggy beach, and then went out to get breakfast while his family watched television. On his wayward drive through this unfamiliar town, he listened to NPR on the radio and learned about the operatives GSX sent out in real life to influence and modulate the behavior of innocent civilians.

Eventually, he found a crowded bakery called The Buttery but stayed in his car until the news segment was over. No one was on their smartphone when he walked inside. The same local NPR broadcast was being played over the bakery speakers and the people waiting in line seemed dazed, as if they couldn't believe what they were hearing. At the counter, he ordered six ham and cheese croissants and two blueberry torts and two coffees and one hot chocolate and got them all to go in a cardboard box and tray. He ate one of the croissants and drank his coffee on the drive back through town, all the while listening to the radio. He couldn't stop shaking his head at what he heard.

The family spent their Saturday going on rides at the Boardwalk and when the sun came out of the fog they went to the beach and stood in the water. He splashed his daughter and chased her around the shoreline, pretending to be a monster. He threw his wife into the ocean and got kicked in the balls in return. His daughter laughed when he collapsed into the saltwater and splashed her parents when they started kissing afterwards. Other families were all around them lying in the sun, smoking weed, drinking beer, or watching their children spin in circles. Despite how intently he looked, there were no smart-phones in anyone's hands. All of them seemed to have vanished.

His daughter wanted to eat at the same taqueria as yesterday so in the middle of the day they walked down the river towards downtown Santa Cruz. It took them nearly an hour to get there. They explored every curve and bend of the riverbank and stopped to look at every duck, crane, and frog. When they could no longer follow the river, the family wandered through hundred year old neighborhoods and eventually crossed a bridge into downtown. They ate multiple baskets of free chips and salsa, watched the television as their food was prepared, and soon enough they were full, happy, and unconcerned with the chaos on the screen.

They lingered for a while on the main downtown strip, ate ice-cream on the green benches, and watched countless people stroll by on that warm coastal evening. Only a few had their smartphones out, everyone else walked with their hands free. He and his wife sat there for a few hours while their daughter talked with other kids and played with them on the cement boxes built around the sidewalk trees. Everyone who walked by seemed to be talking about the leaks. None of the passing cars played music from their speakers, only news.

They passed an anarchist social center on the walk back to the hotel but didn't have a chance to read any of the posters before their daughter pointed across the street to a restaurant called Saturn Cafe. She immediately demanded to eat there. Her parents explained it was a vegetarian restaurant but this only increased her desire. Just as the sun was going down, they ate a variety of meat-less hamburgers and fries. They shared their food, compared the qualities of each burger aloud, and agreed they could live without meat, but only if it were necessary.

For the first time in over two years, his daughter fell asleep after demanding to be picked up. They walked the rest of the way to their hotel, went up to their room, and put their daughter to sleep with the television on. They smoked their vapor pen in the dark and flicked back and forth through all the networks. They learned about the immensity of the programs, the scope of their reach, and the totality of their project. Eventually they turned it off, held each other under the blankets, and made love silently so their daughter wouldn't hear.

It was foggy that Sunday morning. He went out to get doughnuts and coffee and came back to find his daughter watching cartoons on the television. They lounged around on the beds, her parents smoked their vapor pen, and the scent of the ocean blew in through the open window. They went down to the beach after the fog burned off and swam until lunchtime. They ate at a different taqueria for lunch, a smaller one closer to the beach, and when they were done they returned to the hotel and packed their belongings. Their daughter was sad and didn't want to leave Santa Cruz. She began to cry as she stared through the window at the vast blue ocean stretching away into the distance.

The tears continued even when they got in the car. Her father didn't want to see their vacation spoiled by this final sadness so he suggested they drive up the coast along Highway 1. They had more than enough money for gas, he showed his wife the wad of bills, and their daughter suddenly began to laugh again. She told her father to drive along the ocean forever. She'd never seen this stretch of coastline before. They hadn't had the time, nor did they have the money.

He followed the main road out of town and entered a long expanse of fields and farms. They saw the ocean hanging below the western cliffs and beheld a coastline covered in brown hills and speckled with dark green cypress trees. The highway stretched northward between the hills and the shore, it curved and straightened and followed a set of old train tracks to a small town called Davenport. It was here their daughter demanded they pull over and let her play.

The family ran across the highway, crossed the old train tracks to the edge of the bluff, and looked out at the blue expanse of the Pacific. Their daughter had stopped crying, all the tears were wiped away, and she jumped and danced happily along the grassy plain. Her parents smoked their vapor pen while she sang a schoolyard song. She didn't stop jumping and skipping until it was time to get going. When they were back on the road, she remained silent and didn't look away from the soft colors of the passing seaside. As this alien landscape mesmerized their vision, the broadcast from the radio filled their ears. The newscasters spoke of Facebook and Google's involvement in the GSX

DARLINGTONIA

surveillance network, how they traded their data in exchange for profiles on millions of people, and how they helped modulate the population into stasis and away from rebellion.

Their daughter wasn't paying much attention to the radio and didn't ask any questions. At this moment, she cared only for the ocean and the approaching sunset. They drove north for two hours and saw pelicans gliding in formation in the red dusk light. They heard seals barking in the air, smelled the fragrance of coastal plants, and listened to the chirp of crickets so loud they overpowered the engine. The stars were out when they reached Half Moon Bay and by then their daughter was asleep. He took a right off Highway 1 and drove towards the bay through the redwood covered mountains. For mile after mile, their Mazda remained the only car on the road.

Nothing woke their daughter, not even the relentless curves of the highway. They descended into the fringes of San Mateo and drove through the center of the penninsula. To the north was SFO International airport and the city of San Francisco. To the south was Facebook, Google, and Apple. He told his wife it felt like driving through a dead empire. He told her there was no way the tech companies would survive this. She told him the Verizon store could run out of customers, that she might need to find a new job. As they crossed the San Mateo Bridge, the radio told them of Twitter's involvement with the GSX surveillance program, explained the manipulation of hashtag search results, and revealed there were tens of thousands of fake Twitter accounts controlled by the GSX algorithms. This last detail made them both become silent. The very idea terrified them.

They returned to San Leandro just before their daughter's bedtime. She slept while her father carried her up the stairs and it was with great reluctance that she finally woke up and let go. His daughter brushed her teeth in the bathroom while he brought their luggage up from the car. They tucked her under the covers, kissed her goodnight, and went into the bathroom to shower. When they were done, they made love on their bed, smoked their weed pen, and went to sleep in each others arms. It was a weekend the family would remember for the rest of their lives.

———————OO———————

He drives along the 880 freeway just before dawn and heads north with the morning traffic. Unlike the days before this one, he doesn't take his usual route through the new luxury apartments of Jack London Square. Even the thought makes him want to vomit. He takes the off-ramp for Chinatown, keeps going past the police station, drives under the freeway, crosses the train tracks, and parks near the Jack London ferry stop. He smokes a bowl of weed in the car, listens to the radio, and learns more about the GSX director, the man who exploded in front of his eyes.

He smokes his morning cigarette afterwards and paces along the waterfront. He watches the small wavelets hit the gray rocks and hears the call of seagulls and crows flying through the lightening sky. From here, he can see the Chinese-owned cargo ships being unloaded at the Port of Oakland. The shipping containers are lifted off the boats by hulking cranes and swiftly lowered to the ground. Every day, he sees them hauled off by semi-trucks onto the crowded lanes of the 880 freeway. From there, these containers are taken to places he'll never see.

He finishes his menthol cigarette, walks away from the water, and keeps his hands in his pockets. There are no guests in the lobby when he begins his shift. He and his coworker linger in the back room by the television and watch the morning news broadcast. Between traffic updates, the newscaster recaps the GSX leaks and reminds the viewer that at 9:00 am the full 17.8 GB of data will be released to the public. In the corner of the screen is a small digital clock counting down. There are three hours to go and the newscasters implore the viewer to stay tuned.

"Here's what I don't get," he says. "The dude jumps right in front my car. *My* car."

"Yeah?" his coworker says, leaning back in her chair. "So what?"

"Dude might have looked me up. I'm sure he did. I found the body of the guy he killed. He probably knew all my habits, my route to work, all my conversations. I mean, I was giving it to him with my smartphone every second, real time tracking and full audio."

She *tsks* at him and shakes her head.

"That's why I never got one of those things. Like I been saying."

"You was right. I got rid of mine. Too late, though. They have one of those profiles on me now."

DARLINGTONIA

"Uh-uh, not me! I'm fine!"

"But you hear what I'm saying, though? He wanted to die in front of me. So I'd find the note."

"That shit's creepy. *I'm not the only one*. All drenched in blood like that. Creepy!"

"I'm never driving that way to work again."

Once they're done with their breakfasts, the older guests begin to check out around 7:00 am. One group are all Chinese. They leave a hundred dollar tip and drive away in a black Uber. The other guests are all white. They speak animatedly about the leaks and claim to have thrown away their smartphones. When the different white guests relate this fact, when they describe getting rid of their devices, all of them have light in their eyes. None of them leave a tip. They all check out before the assassination takes place.

First the newscasters go silent. They listen to their ear pieces, nod to the camera, and begin to speak of a man murdered in the Marina District of San Francisco, possibly in connection with the GSX leaks. After a few minutes, confirmation comes in from the FBI that the killer is a woman named Pamela Gustafson, a professor at UC Berkeley. At 7:04 am, she walked into a Marina District restaurant and shot a man who has not been identified. The television displays black and white footage of Pamela Gustafson walking into a Marina District restaurant and firing at a pixelated blur. The wall is suddenly stained with a black splotch and one of the windows shatters. She watches the body fall to the floor and become still. Then she looks up. After staring at the surveillance camera with a smile on her face, Pamela holds up a piece of paper with the words **I WILL KILL ALL OF YOU** written in black marker. And then she leaves the restaurant. The FBI and the Department of Homeland Security ask for the public's help in locating Pamela Gustafson while the television displays two images. One is an enlargement of her face taken from the surveillance camera, the other is her faculty picture from the UC Berkeley Department of Psychology website. By the time this airs, it's 8:52 am.

As the moment of release approaches, all of the guests congregate around the television in the lobby. None of them approach the front desk as the clock runs out of time and begins to count forward. Nothing happens. The newscasters talk in recursive monologues and televise images of the suicide in Jack London Square. At 9:11 am, a tweet from Wikileaks is displayed on the screen that states they are experiencing a large-scale cyber attack. After this, there is no update for several minutes and a few of the guests ask to check out. All of them are scared, silent, and eager to leave. When the last of them exit the hotel, his coworker yells for him to come watch.

The television displays the image of Pamela Gustafson while the newscaster explains how this UC Berkeley professor was also employed as an analyst by GSX. The man she killed in the Marina District was a CIA agent named Henry Abrams. In a story just released by *The Washington Post*, the new leaks have revealed that Henry Abrams and Pamela Gustafson worked together on several occasions. *The Washington Post* claimed to have successfully downloaded the full 17.8 GB of data. All of this information is now publicly available.

For the rest of the morning, the guests stand in a crescent around the lobby television. Most of them have their bags beside them. No one checks out, no one checks in, there are no cars out front, and eventually the valet attendant comes behind the front desk to watch television. Chumby begins to release article after article, the newscasters are constantly interrupted by updates, and it's extremely difficult to follow what's happening. There is contradictory information from different media sources but eventually the blame begins to circle around something called the Permanent Select Committee on Intelligence of the Republican-controlled US House of Representatives.

Soon, there is confirmation from Chumby that the Committee knew the general outline of what GSX was doing, if not the exact details. The Committee approved the Darlingtonia program and after that it was directly approved by the President. In a letter discovered in the leaks, the President wrote a short message to the director of GSX. He said it all sounded great. He told the director to just make it work. It's not clear how this message ended up in the leaks given its highly confidential nature. The newscasters remind the viewer that all of this information is now available in a searchable format on several different websites.

"This shit's unreal, yo!" the valet attendant says. "The fucking President knew about it!"

"Of course he did!" his coworker says.

"That motherfucker's gonna go down," he says. "Finally!"

"Shit's unreal!" the valet says again.

"Ya'll better stop cursing."

After this everyone is silent. They wait patiently as the newscaster speaks, but learn nothing new, nothing they haven't heard. Just before their lunch break, *The New York Times* reveals that select employees of GSX were contracted by the NSA, the CIA, Facebook, Google, and BoonDoggle to make interventions in the real world based on data gathered on their servers. These people are identified in the leaks as "operatives" and there were at least 2000 of them employed by GSX. It is likely that there were more, given the incompleteness of the leaks.

GSX had grown exponentially after the advent of the smartphone and was now believed to have employed nearly 9000 people worldwide. Over a third of them maintained the physical infrastructure alone. Another third was comprised of a wide variety of analysts working from remote locations across the globe, pouring over the same data sets, coming up with models, and making the algorithms run more smoothly. The rest of the employees were operatives and contractors. There was no board of directors. GSX had been under the control of one man.

"You all want to get lunch?" their afternoon coworker asks, suddenly standing in the doorway with his hair wet from a shower. "Or you want to watch TV? Because I can go take your break while you do the whole front desk—"

"No, I've got the picture pretty clear," Anton says. "You want to go get chicken and waffles?"

"You're too much," his coworker says. "Yeah, let's go! You want lunch, kid, I'm buying."

"Hell yeah!" the valet says. "Thanks, Nancy."

"Just no more cursing. I've had enough of that."

The three of them walk out of the London Lodge smiling and clapping their hands. The valet claims a revolution is about to happen. He says this with total certainty. When they get to the restaurant, his coworker asks for a table away from the television. The hostess doesn't say anything in response. She grabs three menus and sullenly escorts them to a corner table. She shakes her head in disbelief and then returns to the screen. She doesn't look away from the news for the next half an hour. No one else is in the restaurant. The waitress quickly takes their order and joins the hostess at the television. Their food takes longer than usual. When it finally arrives, they all receive double portions and a dozen extra sides. The three of them eat alone.

His brother walks into the hotel just before quitting time. He's dressed in blue jeans and a black t-shirt. He wears a black Oakland Raiders jacket over his shoulders, a black hat over his head, and there's a new tattoo crawling up his neck. It says the word *Victoria* in curly black letters.

"That your new girlfriend?" he asks from behind the front desk.

"What? This tattoo? It mean's victory in Spanish, bruh."

"What you doing down here? Bored?"

"I came to see you, bruh."

"Need a lift?"

"Hell yeah! Thanks for offering. I'm heading to the border. Don't really feel like no bus."

"What happened to your car?"

"It's just best I don't drive right now. I still got the car though, don't trip."

"Man—"

His brother flashes a gold tooth, leans to the side, and looks into the back room.

"Wassup, Nancy!"

"That you, Deven?" She walks out and gives him a hug. "You staying out of trouble?"

"I been out of trouble. It's Anton here who's in trouble with his smartphone."

They both laugh at him so hard their eyes close. All Anton can do is shake his head. He knows they're right. So he asks Nancy if he can leave early, hugs her when she says yes, and then walks with his brother along the train tracks. They immediately start smoking a blunt and when they get inside the car with it, neither of them turn on the radio.

DARLINGTONIA

"You got rid of your smartphone?" Deven asks.

"I got rid of it. I was hella dumb. Not even trying to deny it, so don't even go there."

"I told you, bruh. Didn't I tell you? Just get a burner flip-phone from 7-11 and a new SIM card from my dude in Chinatown. Only put the battery in when you know they'll be tracking you. That's all you gotta do if you want a phone. And you *know* I learned that the hard way, bruh. Talk about hella dumb, right. But it don't fucking matter if you done anything, they was still watching you, no matter how clean you was. See?"

"You still into the same shit?"

"No." He takes a long drag from the blunt and exhales out the window. "Not the *same* shit. A lot's changed since your day, bruh. Cat's is on they shit, like for real. Why you think I got this inked on my neck. We won, bruh. We still here."

"You haven't had enough time in Rita yet?"

"Bruh, I was only in there two years longer than you. Don't get on that high horse shit again."

"I'm sorry, man." He holds his brother and knocks their heads together. "You're right."

They finish the blunt and Anton drives away from Jack London Square along the Oakland waterfront. He drives under the freeway and up to Foothill Boulevard where he takes a right towards East Oakland. From here, there are over ninety blocks stretching south to the San Leandro border. Both of them smoke cigarettes as they cruise past San Antonio Park into the Fruitvale neighborhood. The air becomes thick with the scent of grilled meat and fresh produce left out all day. They pass Aztec murals and paintings of tall indigenous warriors and powerful brown women holding rifles. They pass the Hell's Angels headquarters and the last of the taquerias and cross over into the beginnings of the black neighborhoods. They drive in front of their old elementary school, pass by their childhood street, and keep cruising until they're deep into East Oakland.

"Where we going anyway?" Anton asks his brother.

"My girl's house."

"Who? Victoria?"

"It just means victory, bruh."

"But what's your girl's name, though?"

"Victoria."

They pull up outside a small house on East 102nd Avenue. All of the windows are covered in iron bars and the yard is surrounded by a tall sheet-metal fence wrapped in morning glory vines. These purple flowers are the only color on this part of the block. The two brothers hug each other, tell each other to stay safe, and then Deven gets out of the Mazda. He knocks on the metal gate, waits a few moments, and soon there's a brown-skinned woman standing at the head of the pathway. She's dressed in black and her neck is covered in tattoos. She looks at Anton knowingly. And then she closes the gate.

His wife is outside the Verizon store when he arrives fifteen minutes late. He expects her to be angry but when she gets in the Mazda all she does is talk about the news. She tells him the President hasn't issued a statement and that he's obviously guilty. She tells him there might be a revolution in this country, a real one, finally. He doesn't disagree with her.

They pull up outside the elementary school and Anton runs across the street to get his daughter from the after-school program. As they cross the street back to the car, she narrates to him how fun school was and what games she played. The principle told the students they could either watch the news or have recess all day. She'd chosen to play soccer and basketball and climb on the structures with her friends. Lunch was their only interruption.

"What'd they feed you today?" her mother asks once they're in the car. "More kale?"

"No! The teachers bought us all pizza."

"That's cool! They just watched TV all day?"

"Uh-huh."

"That's all I did, too" Anton tells her.

"Momma?"

"Yeah?"

"What's your name?"

"*What?*" She turns around and squints at her daughter. "You don't know my name?"

She shakes her head nervously.

"Could you not remember or something? Did someone ask and you didn't know?"

"Uh-huh. I forgot when my friend asked me."

"Its Angelica, baby. How you gonna—"

"Okay, okay, I remember now."

When they get home, Angelica prepares to bake some chicken while Anton helps his daughter with math. When she finishes, her father lets her watch *Malificent* again but by then it's time to eat so she pauses it. They have baked chicken and salad and rice for dinner. They all eat silently but Angelica makes her daughter finish the plate before returning to the movie. Angelica and Anton stare blankly at the flapping wings and special effects and loud action sequences. They hover over their empty plates. They don't know what to say.

When it's time for bed, Anton goes with his daughter to the bathroom and they brush their teeth together. Angelica takes a shower but when she's finished her daughter is asleep. She creeps into the room, kisses her gently on the cheek, and then gets into bed with Anton. He's already smoking the electric weed pen. They lean their shoulders together, stare at the outlines of their feet under the blankets, and watch the vapor disperse throughout the room.

"I got one of those computers," she whispers into his ear. "That won't connect."

"Where?"

"In my bag."

"You sure it won't connect?"

"I talked with the tech guy at work. I covered for him while he went to get it. Told him I was scared about surveillance or whatever. He don't know nothing. He turned it on and showed me, pointed to the slot where the wireless card used to be. It's hella old but he says its fast, does everything. So you wanna look at it?"

"You got rid of your phone, right?"

"Shit's in a dumpster outside Target."

"Alright. Let's do it."

Anton gets out of bed and makes sure the battery is still removed from their normal laptop. He goes into the living room, unplugs the wireless transmitter, and comes back to find Angelica in front of a glowing screen. He puts the thumb drive into the port of the new computer, gets under the covers, and leans against her warm shoulder. A small window pops up asking them if they'd like to open the files. Anton looks at the mother of his child, the person he's loved more than any other, the woman he wants to grow old with. There's no fear in her eyes, no hesitation, no doubt. Angelica waits for him to say something but that doesn't happen. She waits so long it makes her smile in amusement. Eventually she begins to laugh. He tries to speak but can't find the words. He's far too nervous. In the end, he only manages to nod before there are two clicks, the computer begins to purr, and their vision is bathed in light. Anton doesn't believe what shows up on the screen. He looks at Angelica in confusion for a moment, unsure if this could possibly be real. All he can see is her endless smile. She doesn't stop reading.

Originally composed March–October 2016

The authors would like to thank Micheline Aharonian Marcom, Elena Georgiou, Mills College, Goddard College, the BENT Writing Institute, the Institute for Anarchist Studies, and the Anti-Eviction Mapping Project.

albaroja.noblogs.org
albadawnroja@riseup.net

Letters of Insurgents

Sophia Nachalo & Yarostan Vochek

as told by Fredy Perlman

Originally printed by Black and Red Books in 1976, Fredy Perlman's classic epistolary novel *Letters of Insurgents* has been unfortunately out of print for several years. However, Left Bank Books is very proud to bring this book back.

"Two individuals living on distant continents resume contact through correspondence. They describe meaningful events and relationships in their lives during the twenty years since their youthful liaison, comparing the choices each took. Yarostan lives in a "workers' republic"; Sophia in a "Western democracy." They both make efforts to lead meaningful lives. Along the way, they encounter bureaucrats, idealists, racists, flaunters of social convention, labor militants, professors, jailors, hucksters and more. In important respects, Sophia's biography parallels that of Fredy Perlman."

Fredy Perlman was co-founder of Black and Red Books, and author of the books *The Continuing Appeal of Nationalism*, *Against His-story, Against Leviathan!*, *Worker-Student Action Committees: France May '68*, *The Strait*, as well as numerous essays, pamphlets and contributions to *Fifth Estate* magazine.

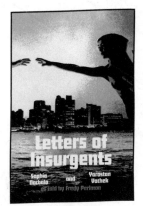

$20.00
728 pages; 6"x9"

ISBN 978-0939306053
Available from Left Bank Books
www.leftbankbooks.com

Love is Not Enough
Frances Gregory

Love is Not Enough was written over the course of the year after the suicide of Frances Gregory's mother. The poems are an investigation into the circumstantial and relational dynamics of grief as well as the bloody spectres of patriarchy and generational trauma.

I still want to hang every ex-husband
boyfriend, father, doctor, lawyer, and stranger at the beach
that made you feel crazy and unsafe
from the moon, by their entrails
as a warning
I want to smear their blood across my face
as a beacon that bakes and stinks in the sun
I want to crush their bones for tea to get strong

"This is one of the most haunting, brilliant travels into grief I have ever read." –CAConrad

"When my mother died I could not find a path. What to evoke? Would the earth open up a swallow? The eyes blurred. The throat closing. Frances Gregory's Love Is Not Enough *is the path needed. Now raw and open, now sorting history, reclaiming the body, the burning, the rupture, the ritual of survival."* –Cindy Crabb

$13.00
77 pages; 7"x4.5"

ISBN 978-0939306121
Available from Left Bank Books
www.leftbankbooks.com

The Failure *of* Nonviolence

PETER GELDERLOOS

In the years since the end of the Cold War many new social movements have started peacefully, only to adopt a diversity of tactics as they grew in strength and collective experiences. The last ten years have revealed more clearly than ever the role of nonviolence. Propped up by the media, funded by the government, and managed by NGOs, nonviolent campaigns around the world have helped oppressive regimes change their masks, and have helped police to limit the growth of rebellious social movements. Repeatedly losing the debate within the movements themselves, proponents of nonviolence have increasingly turned to the mainstream media and to government and institutional funding to drown out critical voices.

The Failure of Nonviolence examines most of the major social upheavals following the Cold War to reveal the limits of nonviolence and uncover what a diverse, unruly, non-pacified movement can accomplish. Critical of how a diversity of tactics has functioned so far, this book discusses how movements for social change can win ground and open the spaces necessary to plant the seeds of a new world.

Peter Gelderloos is the author of *How Nonviolence Protects the State, Consensus, & Anarchy Works*.

$16.00
333 pages

ISBN 978-0939306046
Available from Left Bank Books
www.leftbankbooks.com